ISBN: 978-0-9559909-4-6

I0681491

JEIKLEE

By Makala V. P. Thomas

For:

Nathan Walcott

Brenda Campbell

Sherene Williams

Joseph Smith

Shannon Thompson

Jeiklee

"Jeiklee!"

Jeiklee stopped pedalling, turning to look at whoever called his name.

"Oh- hi Spirit." He rubbed his nose awkwardly. "How are you?"

"You're still finding this hard to believe, aren't you?" she said, pouting.

Jeiklee scowled at her. "What, you think I should be overjoyed?"

Spirit glared at him through pearly grey eyes, startling against her brown skin. "Actually, I do. You have a gift- you're the same as me."

"I'm nothing like you!" Jeiklee's temper snapped. "You're a witch!"

Spirit kissed her teeth and folded her arms. "And you are?"

"Normal!" spat Jeiklee. "A normal eighteen year old guy-"

"You know, when I met you, I didn't think you was the type of guy to stay in denial for longer than a week."

Jeiklee glared at her, getting back on his bike. "Did you call me just to get under my skin, Spirit? 'Cause if you did-"

"Jeiklee, I only called you because I want to help you."

"Help?!"

"I've been around magic all my life, and you- well…"

"I was adopted," Jeiklee said angrily. "For the greater good!"

"Yeah, that's what your fake parents told you."

"It's true!"

"They blackmailed your real parents!" Spirit said angrily. "They said they'd expose them if they didn't let them keep you! And they didn't even stop to think what you *were!* They was just desperate for a baby-"

"Stop! Stop it right now!" Jeiklee said angrily, but she ignored him.

"But at least your parents made sure the fake ones named you Jeiklee-"

"Spirit, stop!"

"They want to meet you so badly, and you're being so horrid!"

Jeiklee lifted his chin defiantly at that. "I didn't say a word."

"Exactly!"

"Spirit, leave me alone!" he said frustratedly. "I can't believe you turned my world upside down- tricked me!"

"I didn't trick you." Spirit was now calm again. "I just didn't tell you what I was- you would never have spoken to me."

"Well, that's *your* time. Because I'm not speaking to you again, ever!"

"Jeiklee!"

He ignored her, scrambling on his bike. As he pedalled away Spirit stared after him, then she called "Nice wheels!"

Jeiklee glanced down- his wheels were glowing!

"Aaargh!!"

CRASH!!

Spirit burst out laughing as she jogged towards him, sprawled on the concrete pavement.

"Need a hand?"

"Get away from me!"

Spirit stepped back, startled. "Jeiklee, it's ok!"

"No it's not- please, just leave me alone. Stop doing magic on me!"

"But Jeiklee, I didn't- that was *you!"*

"Leave me alone!"

* * *

Jeiklee let himself in slowly, angry at himself and Spirit. Exactly a week and one day ago, his life had been turned upside down. Spirit, who he'd known for four months, had refused to hold the secret any longer and dropped the poisonous fact that she could do magic, and so could he.
"Jeiklee?"
"Yes Mum," he said heavily, as his mother peered round a corner. "I'm home."
"How was work?" Evelyn Peterson asked. "Are your colleagues giving you hassle again?"
"Yeah. It's nothing I can't handle, Mum."
"What are they saying, though?"
That there's something about me they don't like. That I'm different.
Jeiklee smiled, saying "Nothing, Mum. They just don't like me because I'm new to the team, that's all."
"Hmm. Well, dinner's in the oven if you-"
"Mum, we need to talk. About my real parents."
Jeiklee always knew he wasn't their real son, the big difference being their skin colour. Jeiklee was tall, dark and handsome, with green eyes. Like Spirit's, they were startling against his chocolate skin.
Evelyn and Richard Peterson were multiracial, and very attractive with an olive skin tone complimenting their features. Jeiklee always joked around and called them "The Sunshine in his life," which made them beam like the sun, making him laugh even more.
Evelyn's smile faded as Jeiklee looked at his feet. "What about them?"
"Did they… you know. Choose a name for me before *you* and Dad named me Jeiklee?"
Evelyn stared at him. Jeiklee gave nothing away.
"I… I think we'd better wait until Richard comes home to talk about this, Jeiklee."
"Come on Mum, I'm not fifteen anymore. It's not like then, when you first told me you really weren't my parents, even though I knew. I just-"
"You're curious about them." Evelyn didn't try masking her hurt. "After eighteen years of our being your parents, you want to know-"
"About my name, Mum. My name," Jeiklee repeated. "It's just… Spirit-"
"Oh yes. Spirit." You didn't need to look at Evelyn's face to tell what she thought about Spirit. "She's been putting things into your head?"
"Well, I just remembered one time- about a week ago-" Jeiklee swallowed, remembering. "Spirit was telling me that nobody else has my name- it's different. We researched it online. There was no results-"
"I think it's best you stay away from that girl, Jeiklee." Evelyn patted his arm comfortingly, though she looked worried. "Your thoughts about your

parents have changed since you met her. Why is that?"

"She- she just asks questions about them," lied Jeiklee. "And- and I don't know the answers, do I?"

Evelyn nodded, Jeiklee probing "So... did they name me Jeiklee?"

Evelyn sighed, then she said "Ask your father."

"Mum!"

Before Evelyn could say something the front door opened.

"Guess who's home!"

"Dad!"

Like he was still ten years old, Jeiklee ran and threw his arms around him.

* * *

Leticia's eyes filled, Spirit touching her arm gently.

"Leticia, I've been trying to get him to- he won't listen to me-" Spirit bit her lip. She felt like crying herself. "Leticia?"

The sorceress stared into the crystal ball at her only son, watching him embrace the mortal lovingly.

"Dad, I need to ask you something."

"Ask away."

Westley moved closer, watching the blackmailer hold his son.

"My name. Did you guys give it to me or did my real parents name me?"

"Your real parents did," Richard said, frowning a little. "Why, son?"

"Well..."

"Spirit," Evelyn said, as Jeiklee fidgeted, still holding his Dad.

"Who? Ah, Spirit," said Richard, scratching his beard as Jeiklee let go of him. "She's a little weird, isn't she?"

"More than a little," Evelyn said, and Jeiklee nodded, Richard saying "Has she been filling your head with nonsense again?"

"Spirit, you must convince my son we're not evil- that magic isn't bad at all," Leticia said desperately, as Spirit raged at Richard Peterson. "Jeiklee needs to know what power he holds within him- let him know we don't want to ruin his life in any way."

"He already thinks his life is ruined," Westley said. "We were almost there when he befriended Spirit. Now we must start over."

"I won't fail you," Spirit said determinedly. "I promise."

* * *

"Wonder where they got the name from?" Jeiklee said at dinner, making Evelyn and Richard splutter on their food.

"What?"

"Jeiklee. I wonder which one made it up- my mother or my father?"

"Son," said Richard uneasily, "You're thinking about them a little too much. I don't want you getting crazy ideas like meeting them."

Evelyn nodded, saying "It will confuse you, Jeiklee."

Jeiklee nodded, but inside he disagreed.

"I guess."

* * *

He'd held in questions about his real parents for too long, Leticia realised. Now, they were shooting out of his mouth without him realising it.

"I'm going to his house right now," Spirit told them. "Maybe he'll warm up and stop being so nervous- who knows."

Westley said nothing, both the girls looking at him. They knew he was angry with himself- he'd been angry the moment Jeiklee hit one.

The Petersons had lost their child a week before Jeiklee was born. Still being treated for shock, Evelyn stayed in the mother-baby's unit a while longer. Leticia had been ready to teleport with Jeiklee and Westley after one last check with the doctor when Evelyn stopped at their door, crying.

Westley hated to see a woman cry. He knew Evelyn was a strong woman- only losing a child could bring her so much pain. So he'd allowed Evelyn to look at Jeiklee, only she'd become smitten with him.

When they left the hospital, Leticia remained in contact with her, telling Westley Jeiklee could have an aunt.

Westley could never forget the day they agreed for Evelyn and Richard to baby-sit Jeiklee for a few hours. When he and Leticia returned home everyone, including their baby boy and his belongings, was gone.

Westley had tracked them down easily, but Richard had snarled he knew what they were. Westley shrugged it off until he held up Leticia's Book of Shadows, threatening to have it burned along with Leticia, at stake.

Then Richard melted down a little.

It had been agreed that Jeiklee would return to them on his first birthday, but it was a lie. The whole deal had been a lie. Westley would never forgive the Petersons for stealing their son.

"It's too late to think back," Leticia said softly, looking at him. "We must be grateful that they never ill-treated Jeiklee, Westley. Glad that he is now of age, and can make his own decisions."

* * *

"Spirit's here," Jeiklee said, and they stared at him.

The doorbell rang.

Richard's heart began pounding as he stood, walking to the front door.

"Who is it?"

"It's Spirit, Mr Peterson. Is Jeiklee home please?"

Richard opened his mouth to say no, then he saw Jeiklee watching him from the living room door. He closed it and took a deep breath before opening the door, quickly forming a smile.

"Hello, Spirit. Come on in."

"Thanks. How are you?"

"I'm fine."

Spirit's smile was just as fake as Richard's. Then it became really real as she saw Jeiklee, her eyes lighting up.

"Hi Jeiklee."

"Hey Spirit," he said awkwardly. "What are you doing here?"

"I just wanted to ask if you wanted to go for a walk? It's only eight."

"Sure, why not."

Richard couldn't stop him from going. He was of age now, with a job and everything. Next thing he knew, Jeiklee would move out.

"Back soon, Dad. Tell Mum I'll see her tomorrow."

Evelyn was going to church. Richard nodded, watching them go. Sighing, he closed the door.

* * *

"So how *did* they make my name up?" asked Jeiklee. "I mean, I guess you know what's bugging me right now."

Spirit kissed her teeth at him. "Now you want to know about them?"

"Yeah," Jeiklee said casually, and she glared at him.

"And you don't see that you was out of order for the past eight days."

"Nope."

Spirit wanted to smile, but she didn't. "Leticia named you."

"Who's Leticia?"

Spirit's temper snapped. "Your mother, Jeiklee!"

"Well excuse me for not knowing jack!"

Spirit wanted to slap him, but she thought against it. Instead she glanced at his trainers: the laces came undone. Jeiklee buckled, Spirit saying "Good! You could've known a few things eight days ago, but *no-"*

"What would y*o*u do if you found out you was a wizard and your real parents were the same?" said Jeiklee angrily. "Accept it on that same day? Your birthday? And don't you think you'd need at least a month to get over it instead of eight days? What's wrong with you?"

Sprit melted down a little. She didn't see it like that for one minute. They walked in silence, Spirit now seeing things from his point of view.

As soon as they entered the park Jeiklee flopped on the grass.

"Don't stain your jeans. Evelyn might go berserk," Spirit said, forcing the sarcasm away before Jeiklee heard it.

Jeiklee just nodded. Then he asked "What about you, Spirit?"

"What about me?"

"Your parents. Where are they?"

"They were killed eight years ago, in a war against dragons. Why?"

"Wait- *dragons?"* Spirit nodded. "I guess I got off lightly."

"You got off *worse,"* Spirit said coldly. "I'd rather know everything about myself and what power I hold than sit like a duck for eighteen years, not knowing jack about my family, world and history."

"Ok, ok. Jeez," Jeiklee said, looking at her. "I didn't mean to offend you. I just… were you alone after that, then?"

"No. Leticia and Westley took me in. Your parents."

Jeiklee sat right up at that. "They raised you?"

"Got that right. And before you think any more rubbish, I'll tell you that they're the most wonderful people in the world. I love them both so much- I couldn't bear it when Leticia was crying today."

"My mother was crying?"

"Yes."

"Why?"

"Because she thought you were lost- that you would never be interested in your real parents."

"I wasn't before my eighteenth. Well, I was- but I pushed that down."

"And now questions are shooting out of your mouth like bullets from a gun," Spirit said calmly. "Because you held them in for too long."

"What's my father like?" Jeiklee asked, ignoring what she said. "What does he look like? And my mother. What about her?"

Spirit hesitated, then she reached into her pocket. Squeezing the key ring hard, saying a private goodbye, she slowly pulled it out and gave it to Jeiklee.

"That's both of them there."

Jeiklee stared at the photograph sealed in plastic, sitting in his palm. Leticia looked like the female Jeiklee- dark and beautiful, but her eyes were grey. Westley's eyes were green, like his son's. He had the same dimple in his left cheek like his son when he smiled, and Leticia had the same lush lips and nose. The Jeiklees before Jeiklee.

"See?" said Spirit, when he gaped at the key ring. "Spitting images."

Jeiklee was speechless. Spirit took a deep breath, then she said "You can keep that, Jeiklee. I mean, I can get another one anytime."

Jeiklee nodded, still staring at the picture. "Where… where are they?"

"Far away."

Jeiklee's eyes flashed as he looked at her, pocketing the key ring. "Don't take me for a clown, Spirit."

"You *are* a clown," she retorted with a smile, and he smiled back. Spirit twiddled her thumbs, then she said "So are we friends again?"

"We haven't known each other long enough to be friends," Jeiklee said, looking at her. "But I'll go with being good acquaintances for now."

Spirit pouted, but let it go. Maybe tonight was the night…?

"Do uh… do you think you're… you know. Ready to meet them?"

Jeiklee scrambled to his feet. "No. Hell no!"

"Jeiklee-"

"I just wanted to know about my name and what they looked like. That's all- I didn't even ask for their names or a picture." Jeiklee tossed the key ring on the grass. "I don't want to know them!"

"Jeiklee, you're not six anymore. Do you know how weird it looks, a guy your age throwing a tantrum?" Jeiklee stopped raging at that, Spirit saying "I think growing up pampered by the Petersons turned you into a big, spoilt baby. You wouldn't last a day in our world."

"Well I don't want to know about your world." Embarrassed, Jeiklee bent and picked up the key ring, dusting it off. He spent almost five minutes rubbing vigorously, as if frightened the picture would change.

"It's not dirty anymore, Jeiklee." Spirit bit her lip to stop herself from laughing. "The picture won't be ruined, anyway."

Jeiklee nodded, rubbing an extra few times before he pocketed the key ring.

He squeezed it hard, suddenly craving a connection with his parents.
"Leticia and Westley…"
Spirit nodded, watching him. Maybe tonight *was* the night.
"I want to meet them. But not tonight. Two weeks, maybe."
"Stalling won't get you anywhere, but have it your way."
Jeiklee felt annoyed with her brash tongue. "Spirit, if we're going to get along, you need to stop being so sarcastic."
"And you need to stop being so babyish. Deal?"
Jeiklee stared at her outstretched hand, then he smiled and shook it.
"Deal."

* * *

As soon as Spirit reappeared Leticia gave her a hug, then a kiss on the cheek as Westley said "Thank you, Spirit."

"You're welcome," said Spirit, voice muffled against Leticia's chest. "It wasn't hard, really. You just need to be firm with Jeiklee, that's all."

"He needs whipping into good shape," Westley said, though he was smiling as Leticia added "Especially in the magic department."

"When will we take him home?" asked Spirit. "Soon?"

"When he's ready," Leticia said. "And he may never be ready, Spirit."

"But Leticia, he's starting to stand out more and more- abnormal things happen without Jeiklee realising it. Wouldn't it be wise to take him before something big happens?"

"No, darling. We can't force Jeiklee into anything, it isn't right."

Spirit pouted, then she nodded. "You're right."

"I always am," smiled Leticia. "Come, let's have our supper."

* * *

Two weeks later Jeiklee ran into his ex, Cara Smith. Both of them didn't know what to say to each other, Cara biting her lip as she stared at him.

She'd witnessed him lose his temper at another guy, who was once his friend. Luke Benjamin had flirted with Cara carelessly, and she back, just a joke. Jeiklee had turned a corner to find them hugging, and though they protested it was just messing around, he hadn't found it funny at all.

As soon as his fist made contact with Luke's face, Luke had shot into the road- the motorway, when everyone was coming home from work- rush hour. Luke was hit by a Land Rover.

Being Jeiklee's best friend, he refused to give the police a name.

Jeiklee swallowed as he remembered that day. He knew there was no way the force of his punch, no matter how hard, would have sent Luke flying across the park, over the playground, and into the motorway.

Cara knew it too. "Um… did you find out how you… you know."

"Yeah," Jeiklee said, sticking his thumbs in his pockets. "Yeah, I did."

"You're some sort of magical thing, aren't you?"

"You always did joke and call me your Magic Man," Jeiklee answered as a yes. "And… there's something else. I met this girl called Spirit-"

"Spirit? What kind of name is that?"

"What kind of name is Jeiklee, but there you go."

Cara closed her mouth. "Is she like you too? I mean, a witch."

"Yes. And… and so are my real parents."

Her jaw dropped. "Your real- you finally found out about them?"

Cara had been urging him since high school to find out about his real family, but Jeiklee had always refused.

Jeiklee showed her his first photograph, Cara taking it.

"I don't even know why I'm telling you this- it's not like-"

"They're beautiful," Cara said quietly, looking at him. "And obviously they have some sort of power- you can tell."

Jeiklee smiled, taking back the photo. "Thanks, Cara. How's Luke?"

"Luke misses you," Cara said, shrugging a shoulder. "He was telling me he didn't think you meant to send him into the motorway."

"Obviously I didn't-"

"So go and visit him. He isn't mad at you- he's fascinated."

"Trust Luke to be the weird one."

"Luke's the weird one?" Cara raised an eyebrow. "You're not serious."

Jeiklee glared at her, saying "I take that back. Trust him to be fascinated with getting hurled miles, is that better?"

"Much. I need to go," Cara said, looking at her watch.

"Still got that watch?" Jeiklee said as he looked at his last gift to her.

"How could I throw it?" Cara answered, and he scowled.

"You don't have a reason to, Cara. I should have split with *you,* not the other way round."

"How did you expect me react? Leap up and down in excitement?"

"A bit of support from my girl would have been nice. Not slapping the hell out of me, screaming it's over and you never want to see me again, changing your number and moving away to your sister's house to get away from me-"

"I was scared, ok?"

"Scared of what?"

Cara stared at him, then she said "Stop acting like you're ok with this. You can do magic- the Jeiklee I remember would have freaked out totally."

"The Jeiklee you remember is dead," Jeiklee said coldly. "The minute I saw my parent's picture, I felt I could handle anything."

"So you haven't met them yet?"

"I'm meeting them in-"

No, Jeiklee. Don't tell her.

Jeiklee whipped round, staring behind him, though he knew that beautiful voice was in his head. Was that his mother?

Cara waited, but Jeiklee shook his head. "Never mind."

"Jeiklee, you can tell me-"

"No, I can't. We broke up, Cara. And we're not starting over."

Jeiklee turned and walked away, breathing deeply. Then he smiled. Where did this tough Jeiklee Peterson come from?

He anticipated his next visit from Spirit. He couldn't wait.

* * *

Jeiklee scanned the photo of Westley and Leticia onto his laptop- what were their last names? If the same, it would have been his too.

Jeiklee blew up the photo, then set it as his desktop background.

"Jeiklee? Breakfast is ready."

"Coming Mum," he called, but he didn't move, gazing at the picture.

"Son, do you-" Richard's words caught in his throat as he stopped dead, staring at the faces he thought he'd never see again, in real life or just a picture.

Jeiklee looked from Richard to the picture and back. "Dad, I-"

"Jeiklee," called Evelyn again. "The eggs are getting cold."

Jeiklee left quickly, squeezing the key ring hard as he went down the stairs and into the dining room, to the safety of his mother.

Richard went and sat on Jeiklee's chair, staring at those faces. How? Jeiklee couldn't have contacted them- he knew nothing about them! Did they confront him? Did they scare his son?

Richard pounded the desk agitatedly, thinking hard.

Then it hit him- *Spirit.*

* * *

The next morning, Richard confronted Jeiklee at the table.

"Son, I know you may not like what I'm about to say. But…" Richard took a deep breath before he said "I don't want you having anything to do with Spirit. Not anymore."

"And you think I'll say 'Ok Dad, fine by me?'" Jeiklee asked coolly. "Dad, I'm eighteen. I can choose who to hang out with myself."

"Jeiklee, what's gotten into you?" Evelyn said sharply, looking at him. "Have you met your real parents?" He said no. "Since you saw Spirit on your birthday, you've been very awkward- with her and us. Why?"

Jeiklee didn't want to cheek his mother as well. He gambled with the idea of agreeing to stay away from Spirit and his life turning back to normal with her gone, or staying in contact with her and meeting his real parents, learning about them, catching up with them. Learn about this world he belonged to, learn to control the powers he had.

Hell, he was staying in contact with her.

"Mum, Dad. I promise nothing's going to change," he said as he looked at their worried faces. "I haven't even met my parents, ok? Spirit- well…"

Jeiklee.

He closed his mouth, but Richard already figured it out.

"She knows your parents, doesn't she Jeiklee? Is she your sister?"

"Wha- yeah," Jeiklee said quickly. "She's my sister. Um… my real parents didn't want to confuse things and left it, but she couldn't take it any longer, and she told me on my birthday."

"Well, it all fits," Evelyn said as she looked at her husband. "Why else would she constantly visit Jeiklee almost every other day? I feel for her, Richard. That's her brother she's been deprived of."

"She must be curious," Richard said grudgingly, and Evelyn nodded. "We should allow her to visit now and again."

"Fine. But she's coming to the house; they're not going out alone."

Annoyed, Jeiklee opened his mouth to remind them of his age-

No, Jeiklee. Stay in their good books.

"Do you have Spirit's number?" asked Evelyn. "Maybe we can talk."

Actually, he didn't have Spirit's number. Jeiklee didn't even know if she had a phone.

"Spirit just pops up out of nowhere, Mum. But I'll ask when I see her next."

"So we don't know when we'll see her again?" Richard scowled at his wife. "How original, Evelyn. Spirit *appears out of nowhere* when she feels like it- ring a bell?"

Jeiklee's temper snapped: "Are you gunning my parents?"

"We're your parents!" shouted Richard, making him jump as he slammed his fist on the dining table. The empty plates clattered as he said "Not them!

We raised you! Where were they all these years, Jeiklee? They only want you now because you're of age-"

"That's not true, Dad!" Jeiklee was just as angry. "They did want me!"

"They abandoned you, Jeiklee! Because you're not one of them!"

"That's a lie."

Everyone turned and saw Spirit standing in the doorway, two tall figures behind her.

"That's a lie, Mr Peterson, and you know it."

"They're back," Evelyn said as she stared behind Spirit, then she cried "No! You're not taking my son!"

"Mum, calm down! Dad!" said Jeiklee, as Richard picked up an empty plate and hurled it furiously. Spirit ducked, Westley blasting the plate to smithereens moments before it hit his face.

"If it's a duel you want, you won't win," he said calmly, stepping into the light with Leticia. Jeiklee gasped: he really *did* look like his parents.

"Evelyn," Leticia said, eyes filling as she looked at her. "How could you lie to him about how he came to be with you? You know we didn't abandon Jeiklee."

"And so do you," Westley snarled at Richard, who glared at him.

"Get away from my son, you magic filth."

"Don't talk to him like that!" cried Spirit, but Westley said *"You're* the filth, Peterson. Only a dirty man could steal a new-born child days after being born, threaten expose us and have his mother burnt at stake unless they let them keep the child-"

"What?" Jeiklee's jaw dropped as he stared at Westley, then Richard. "Dad, what... is that really happened? I don't... Mum, is it true?"

Evelyn didn't reply, and Jeiklee stepped back in shock.

"It *is* true!"

"Their own child died at birth," Leticia said sadly. Her eyes bore no resentment for Evelyn or Richard. "I can understand why they were desperate for one, but taking Jeiklee-"

"Stop," Westley said as he looked at his right hand woman. "I don't want you upset, Leticia. Like you said, it's too late to think back."

Leticia nodded, eyes on Jeiklee. Jeiklee stared back at her.

Sensing the bond between mother and son, Evelyn said "Jeiklee."

He didn't respond.

"Jeiklee!"

"Yes Mum?" Jeiklee said, though his gaze didn't falter.

"Stop looking at her. She may hypnotise you."

"How dare you," Leticia said, looking at Evelyn. "After blessing you with a child of my own for eighteen years, that is how you talk of me?"

Evelyn closed her mouth, Jeiklee saying "It's true, Mum. How can you?"

"Jeiklee, go to your room," Richard said, but Jeiklee couldn't obey.

"I... I can't, Dad. My parents- this is my first time seeing them-"

"Just for half an hour, son. I promise," Richard said, eyes on Westley. "Take Spirit with you."

"I'm not going anywhere," Spirit said, but Westley said "Spirit."

He didn't need to say anything else. Leticia nodded too, so Spirit left with Jeiklee, cursing under her breath.

Once they were in his room, she exploded "I can't believe they lied to you all this time! Why didn't you tell me? Was that why you wouldn't listen when I said you was stolen?" she demanded before Jeiklee could answer. "I can't believe you love such wicked people!"

"They weren't wicked to me, ok?"

"But they *were* wicked to your parents! They robbed you of your knowledge-"

Downstairs, Richard and Evelyn's voices grew louder and louder. Jeiklee was sure Evelyn was crying her apologies. Even though her voice couldn't be distinguished, he knew she was apologising to his parents.

"I didn't even get to say one word to them," he grumbled. "Now what?"

"They said half an hour," Spirit said, looking at Jeiklee's clock. "I'm going back down at exactly eight o clock, and so are you."

Jeiklee didn't argue.

* * *

You could sense Westley's fury at the Petersons a mile away. Now everything had calmed a little, everyone had rationalised. But Jeiklee still hadn't spoken to his real parents. He'd hovered in his bedroom after Spirit went back down; the hovering turned to lying on his bed.

Leticia walked about the first floor, looking at all the photographs of Jeiklee and his family. Westley stood in the corner of the living room, glaring at Richard, who began to feel uneasy.

"Look, what's done is done. Can't we forget the past and look to the future? Jeiklee's future?"

Westley didn't respond, Spirit scowling at Richard's nerve.

"Please," Richard said, begging Westley now. "Please."

Westley turned his head, looking out the window. "No."

Leticia paused at the staircase, looking up. Her son was up there… Upstairs, Jeiklee opened his eyes. He could sense his mother.

Leticia could sense him too: before she knew what she was doing, she was walking up the stairs towards Jeiklee's room.

Evelyn and Richard leapt up at once, Evelyn crying "No!"

Leticia ignored her.

"Leticia, please!" shouted Richard, but she didn't respond, walking almost trance-like, feeling how close she was to Jeiklee, smelling him… Westley blocked the doorway angrily at the Petersons tried running after her, snarling "She has a right!"

Jeiklee sat up, spine tingling. Any minute now…

Leticia placed her hand on the doorknob- Jeiklee stared as it turned… then spun anti-clockwise again. What the-?!

Leticia released a breath, looking down at her lover for confirmation. Westley nodded, still blocking the doorway.

Before his mother could open the door Jeiklee ripped it open, breathing hard. They stared at each other, then Jeiklee said "Um… normally I wouldn't have done that, but- you know, I've waited this long- I couldn't bear it if you changed your mind and went back downstairs-"

"Jeiklee," Leticia said softly, eyes scanning his face ardently. "Look at you."

Jeiklee looked down at himself, nervous. "Are my clothes dirty?"

"You're so beautiful," Leticia said, opening her arms, and Jeiklee fell into them, hugging his mother hard as his eyes filled over.

"You are too."

"I'm so sorry I didn't come sooner," she whispered in his ear. "I was afraid your- Richard would carry out his threat-"

"It's ok," Jeiklee mumbled in her shirt. "You're here now- that's all I want. That's all I ever wanted, deep down."

"And I'll be here, Jeiklee. I promise," she whispered.

Downstairs, Evelyn let out a cry of anguish before dropping to her knees. "Why?!"

"Get up," snapped Westley, Richard kneeling next to his wife, at Westley's feet. "This is no ordinary bond. Jeiklee would have found us on his own if you continued to lie to him about how he came to be with you. He would have sensed the lie. He would have found us. Get up."

Jeiklee released his mother the same time he exhaled, smiling at her.

"I... I feel like I lifted a big weight off my shoulders."

"A weight you carried all your life?" he nodded. "I feel the same."

They walked down the stairs, Jeiklee astounded by his mother's beauty. He couldn't help staring at her as they returned to the living room, then at Westley, his father.

"Um... I... I don't know what to call you," he said meekly, looking at them both. "I mean, I already have a Mum and Dad, so-"

Richard nodded triumphantly, Spirit's scowl looking like it would be permanent.

"You may call us by our names," Westley said, and Jeiklee nodded.

"Yes sir."

Westley smiled, and he cautiously smiled back. There was something fierce about his father; Jeiklee already had a high level of respect for the man. He already knew Westley wasn't a man to cross. And to have his only son stolen right under his nose and unable to do a thing about it- Jeiklee understood the fury a man as powerful as Westley held for the Petersons, how helpless he must have felt. He knew the pain would never go away, and if it did, not anytime soon.

Richard cleared his throat, saying "Well, then. Jeiklee has college, and work afterwards, so maybe we can continue this little meeting another time."

"If you don't mind," Evelyn added meekly, looking at Leticia.

"I'll call in sick," Jeiklee said quickly. "Or tell them an emergency came up- a family emergency-"

"No," Richard said firmly, along with Leticia, Evelyn and Westley. Spirit nodded behind their backs, mouthing *call in for work, we'll talk later.*

Leticia glanced at her, Spirit smiling guiltily as she apologised.

Jeiklee hung his head, everyone looking at him.

"Jeiklee?" asked Leticia, but he didn't answer. "Honey, what is it?"

"I've just met you, and you're going already," he mumbled. "And I didn't even get to talk to my father yet- it's not fair. Please don't go?"

Leticia looked at Westley, but he didn't know what to do.

Richard placed a hand on Jeiklee's shoulder. "Son, you need to go to college. And you need to go to work." Angry, Jeiklee pushed his hand off him. "Jeiklee!"

"I've just met my parents, and you- you're talking like I'm taking Cara to the movies or something!"

Cara? Thought Spirit disgustedly. *Where is she?*

"Son, calm down-"

"No! They mightn't come back-"

"We'll definitely come back," Westley assured coldly, looking at Richard. "Whether they like it or not."

"Good."

Evelyn cleared her throat nervously, saying "Maybe there wouldn't be any harm in Jeiklee… spending the day with them? Just today."

Everyone stared at her, then talk broke out.

"Mrs Peterson, that's a great idea," smiled Spirit, Leticia saying "Why the change of heart, Evelyn?"

"Evelyn, have you gone mad?" demanded Richard, and silence fell.

"It's not a change of heart, and I haven't gone mad," Evelyn said defensively. "I just don't want my son in any more pain. I know he's been pining after you- for years. He could fool Richard, but not me. He may spend the day with you- as long as he's back by midnight latest."

"Evelyn, no!"

"Silence," spat Westley, and Richard closed his mouth. "Thank you, Evelyn. Finally I see you are the brains of this marriage."

"Mum, are you sure?" asked Jeiklee, but she didn't give him a yes or no.

"Are *you* sure, Jeiklee?" He nodded quickly. "Then have a nice day."

Jeiklee's heart pounded with excitement as he left, not daring to look at Richard as he followed Leticia and Westley out the front door, Spirit by his side.

Evelyn and Richard watched Jeiklee and Spirit whisper excitedly, Westley taking Jeiklee's arm as Leticia took Spirit's hand.

When they vanished, Richard looked at his wife.

"I pray you realise what you've just done."

"I… I think I have," Evelyn said, scared now. "Richard?"

"They'd better bring him back," Richard said angrily. "We can't report him missing, because they'll never find him. Come inside."

Evelyn obeyed, the front door closing.

Element Two: Severna

Jeiklee
Makala Thomas

* * *

Far across a deserted landscape, Jeiklee appeared clinging to his father for dear life, heart banging against his ribs. Leticia materialised with Spirit, smiling at her lover.

Westley smiled back, enjoying the feel of his son holding him, as if he needed him. Reluctantly he gently prised Jeiklee off him, making him look around at… nothing.

"Welcome to Severna, Jeiklee."

At his words, the ground began to tremble- Jeiklee yelped, grabbing Westley again as buildings rose out of nowhere, hills, trees- the grass was blue and purple! How could grass be blue and purple?? And the trees! They were anything but their real colour; orange, pink, yellow-

Jeiklee shielded his eyes, a smile forming as he stared around at the people walking in strange coloured clothing, matching the people they were within fact, all the people in the same coloured clothes looked similar to each other.

"Here in Severna, the families go according to colour," Spirit whispered to Jeiklee. "Mine was light blue- but there isn't anymore of us except me."

"And mine?" asked Jeiklee, before Westley and Leticia linked hands. Their ordinary clothing, Leticia's black jeans that hugged her body superbly, and a white blouse with matching white shoes, Westley's white jeans and black shirt with black Oxford shoes- turned into a stunning black and silver gown for Leticia, and a crisp black suit for Westley, with a silver shirt inside.

They wore diamond accessories- diamond cufflinks and a diamond stud in the ear for Westley, diamonds sparkling practically all over Leticia, a necklace, bracelet, earrings, the full works.

Jeiklee's mouth hung open. He hardly heard Spirit when she explained "When two families give permission for their offspring to come together and start their own family, the family colours merge together."

"Which was which?" Jeiklee asked dazedly, and Leticia said "My family wore silver. Westley's wore black- his parents were the Count and Countess of Severna."

"Bet you looked like a Princess in silver, Leticia," Jeiklee said admiringly, and Westley smiled as he said "She still does, no?"

"No," Jeiklee said, gazing at his mother. "She looks like a Queen."

"Awww," people said from across the road, touched. "Is he a friend of yours, Countess Inferno?"

"No," Leticia said as she smiled at Jeiklee, Westley saying "This is Jeiklee, our only son."

Gasps went up, Jeiklee standing behind his father as everyone stared at him. Then cheers went up, startling him.

"You finally brought him home!"

"Welcome to Severna, Jeiklee!"

"Would you like a tour of Severna?"

"Count Inferno, may we show your son around?"

"Another time, perhaps," Westley replied, hand on Jeiklee's shoulder. "We haven't had time to catch up properly."

"Yes sir."

"Spirit!" yelled a group of guys and girls, all around Jeiklee and Spirit's age or a few years older. Multiple coloured lights swirled around them. "Ready to duel again?"

"Another time," Spirit called back, and they pouted.

"Did you upset them?" asked Jeiklee. "Is that why you're duelling?"

"Huh?" said Spirit, confused. "Up- oh, it's not a real one."

Jeiklee raised an eyebrow. "You're duelling, but it's not real."

"Nope."

"I don't get it," Jeiklee said as he looked at his mother, the group whispering as they stared at him.

"I didn't know the Count and Countess had a son!"

"Everyone knows they did- mortals stole him!"

"We should hex them for taking him!"

"Yo Jeiklee, come chill with us anytime!" a guy called, and Jeiklee waved back, saying "Ok, but I don't know how to duel-"

"Nah, it's cool, we'll teach you all the good spells!"

"Come," Leticia said softly, and Jeiklee and Spirit followed her as she walked away, her raven hair glistening in the sun.

"Fake duelling is the same as play fighting where you were raised," Westley told his son as they walked. "But I forbid you from play duelling until you have learnt at least five spells, Jeiklee. You could get hurt."

"Yes sir."

Jeiklee glanced back and the crowd waved happily, him waving back.

"They must think you're staying," Spirit said sadly. "That's why they're so excited- the Count's son has come home to Severna."

"Do they all know about me?"

"Yes," Westley said, looking down at him. "They all know the story. The Petersons are loathed here in Severna."

"Oh."

"We must keep an eye on the time," Leticia said over her shoulder. "Jeiklee must be back by midnight."

Spirit scowled at that, but she said nothing. Jeiklee checked the time: it was only ten fifteen in the morning here. Yay! He smiled as he glanced skywards- his eyes nearly left his head.

"What's that?!"

Spirit glanced up, then she smiled. "You get scared easy, don't you? That's our chariot."

* * *

"Wow," sighed Jeiklee, staring up at the mansion, covered in vines and other colourful plants. "You live here?"

"We are the Count and Countess of Severna," smiled Leticia, and Westley nodded as he walked forwards, his deep baritone rumbling.

"Open Sesame!"

Jeiklee clutched Spirit's hand as the ground trembled like before, the vines snaking away to reveal the twenty foot double doors-

"Cover your ears," Spirit said, as they creaked open. The sound sounded like someone using chalk on a blackboard, only magnified. Jeiklee covered his ears, his head feeling like it would burst. Spirit, Westley and Leticia stood facing the giant doorway, obviously unaffected by the noise.

Once the doors were open, his parents looked back at him.

"Are you all right, Jeiklee?"

"I'm fine," he said quickly. "It didn't do a thing."

Everyone laughed, going inside.

"My Lord and Lady, you're back," a voice said, full of respect for Leticia and Westley. They turned and saw a middle aged man in a suit, beaming. "And Miss McKenzie, of course, and- *aaargh!"*

"Jeiklee, meet our vizier, Antonio," Westley said, amused as the man's eyes rounded to the size of two pound coins. "Antonio, this is-"

"Master Inferno!" Westley and Leticia's right hand man clasped Jeiklee's hand, then pulled him into a bone-breaking hug. "Good to have you home at last, sir! My Lord, shall I plump his room up for when he retires to bed? Or shall I let the maids do the honours?"

Jeiklee felt his stomach twist and knot itself, looking at his parents.

"Leticia? Westley?"

They looked at him; Leticia's heart almost tore in two as she stared at her baby's hopeful face, eyes twinkling like stars. Westley couldn't bear to look at his expression, averting his gaze to Spirit.

"Please can he stay?" said Spirit, looking downhearted. "Just for tonight?"

"We promised Evelyn we'd return him by midnight-"

"Who promised?" demanded Spirit, as Jeiklee looked at his feet. "I didn't hear anybody say 'I promise to return Jeiklee', let alone at midnight!"

"We couldn't keep him," Leticia said, amazed at her. "It would be wrong of us. Evelyn was kind when she offered to let us take Jeiklee out- Spirit?"

Spirit was glowing red- all that hard work she put into getting Jeiklee to meet his parents, and now he had a time limit?!

"An eye for an eye, I say. They stole him, we steal him back-"

"Jeiklee isn't a toy," Westley said sharply, looking at her. "Two wrongs don't make a right, Spirit."

"But when he goes home, he'll be forbidden to see us again! All of us!"

Westley's jaw dropped; immediately he looked at his wife.

"Leticia?"

Being psychic, Leticia knew Spirit told no lie. She'd foreseen it too.

"Leticia!"

Leticia looked at Westley's angry face before she nodded. "It's true."

"I have a choice," Jeiklee said angrily, when furious talk broke out. "I can't just stop seeing you- I mean, I know we only met today, but I feel like I've known you two all my life! Leticia, Westley- stop Mum and Dad- don't let them take me away from you. Please!"

"Jeiklee, don't," Leticia almost begged her son, eyes filling. "I can't bear to see you so distressed- if I had my way, I would have summoned all of your belongings here the moment I saw you-"

"And I would have teleported with you and Spirit," Westley added. "Jeiklee, be strong. You're of age now- in that world. Here you come of age at twenty five. But there, you're of age- which means you have a choice. Nobody can stop you from seeing us if you really want to."

"Nobody," Spirit said angrily, and Jeiklee nodded. "I feel like you're my little brother or something, even though you're a month older. I've got your back, Jeiklee."

"See?" smiled Leticia. "You have a sister."

Jeiklee smiled back, thinking *they didn't say they would stop Mum and Dad. They didn't say to pack and come home at last- should I ask?*

Spirit shook her head, reading his mind. As they walked to the comfort area, she whispered "They know what they're doing, trust me."

* * *

Jeiklee sat on the leather sofa, looking around in awe. His jaw kept dropping every time he noticed more expensive things, exclaiming "This must have cost more than my house!"

"It probably did," agreed Spirit (Westley and Leticia were talking with a lot of excited people outside). "Every three months, people pay to have a tour through the mansion, to take pictures and stuff."

"Are Leticia and Westley like… King and Queen or something?"

"No," a voice said, and they turned and saw Westley with his wife. "We are the Count and Countess of Severna."

"More respected and richer than the King," Spirit added. "He always comes to them for help, like the Dragon War-"

"Dragon War?" Then Jeiklee remembered. "The one your parents died in?" Spirit nodded, looking away. "Did Leticia and Westley take part?"

"Oh, yes we did," said Westley furiously, Spirit scowling as well. "My wife was kidnapped by Dracula himself in the commotion."

Jeiklee's jaw dropped. "Dracula's real?"

"Dracula is very real," murmured Leticia, and he looked at her.

"And so is his wretched daughter," said Westley, scowling. "She attacks Spirit at every chance she gets."

"Are you serious?" said Jeiklee as he looked at Spirit, and she nodded.

"It's nothing. She's just jealous I mastered the Hovering Charm at Thrill." Jeiklee frowned. "What's Thrill?"

"Thrill, the School of Magic," Leticia replied. "You attend when you are eighteen."

"So I'm of age?"

"You're of age," Westley said, nodding as Jeiklee thought about this.

"So what about when you're growing up? Where do you go?"

"Schools similar to the mortals," Leticia said as she sat on her divine sofa. "Where you learn to read, write, speak etcetera."

"Maths, English, Science and whatnot," Westley said with a grin. "Then, when you leave high school, you go to Thrill."

"Cool."

"If you start now you'll only be a couple of weeks late," Spirit said quickly. "I mean, it's nearly the end of September."

"I want to come home," Jeiklee said, startling them. "Back home."

They stared at him, even Spirit. Then Westley said "Jeiklee, we know you're excited about Severna, but-"

"I'm excited about *you!*" Jeiklee couldn't mask his frustration anymore, looking at the clock. It was almost six p.m. "I've waited all my life to meet you, and this- this… I don't want to leave, Westley!"

"Then we'll take you home now," Westley said, then he laughed at his son's

stricken face. "To discuss that with Evelyn and Richard."
"Phew!"

* * *

Broken ornaments, a smashed television and a sound system littered the Peterson's living room with damaged cushions. Cutlery and broken dinner plates was splayed all over the kitchen floor.
Richard and his wife were tied up with firm rope so they couldn't throw anything else, tape over their mouths so they wouldn't scream anymore.
Jeiklee traipsed down the stairs with his suitcases, Spirit looking at him.
"What are they?"
"My clothes," he said uncertainly, and Westley said "We'll give those to Antonio to upgrade when we get home."
"Upgrade?"
"For example, your blue t-shirt with the red writing. It would turn into a black t-shirt with silver writing."
"What, like... I can dress like I'm part of your family?" Jeiklee said amazedly.
"You're not a lodger, Jeiklee." Leticia spoke quietly. "You're our son. Of course you're part of our family- you're an Inferno."
"Jeiklee Inferno," Westley added, pride in his voice as he looked at him.
"Jeiklee Inferno," Jeiklee repeated dazedly, and they nodded.
Tears trickled down Evelyn's face as she stared at him. How did this come to be? Richard's eyes locked on Spirit's, full of loathing.
Spirit glared back at him, sticking her thumbs in her pockets as she said "Ready to go, Jeiklee?"
"Huh? Oh- yeah. Let me say goodbye?"
"We'll be outside," Leticia said gently, Westley making his cases slide through the open front door as they left.
Cara Smith just happened to be walking past; her jaw dropped as she saw Jeiklee's parents- *his real parents*. And a girl who looked furious.
"I always knew the Petersons were crazy. You didn't want to listen!"
"Calm yourself, Spirit." A woman of stunning beauty looked at her. "We were almost the same when the Petersons stole Jeiklee from us."
"You had every right to go crazy," the girl retorted. "They stole your baby. But you're not kidnapping him- Jeiklee *wants* to come home!"
"We know, darling."
"So why are they-"
"The same reason we did," a handsome man said as he looked at the girl. "Jeiklee is, biologically or not, their only son."
The girl closed her mouth. They heard Richard pleading, Evelyn sobbing.
"Well... I only feel sorry for Mrs Peterson," the girl said, folding her arms.

"She's the reasonable one. Richard's the madcap!"

"Mr Peterson to you," the stunning woman said firmly, and the girl apologised, then she saw Cara watching them in awe.

"Can I help you?"

"Spirit," said Leticia, frowning at her. "Do you know this girl to speak to her in that unfriendly way?"

"She's Jeiklee's ex-girlfriend," Spirit said, glaring at Cara. "As soon as she found out what Jeiklee was she dumped him-"

"Cara?"

Cara looked and saw Jeiklee at the door. His eyes were red.

"What are you doing here?"

"I... I was coming to see you," Cara said, looking at Spirit nervously. "Um... are you leaving town or something?"

Spirit nodded curtly, Westley taking her arm and leading her away.

"I'm going back with my real family," Jeiklee said, pulling his front door closed. "It's not like I have much here anyway, I mean- my only proper friend was Luke- and tell him I'll definitely see him."

Cara bit her lip, eyes filling. "Luke was your only proper friend?"

"Well, you was too- but you turned on me. Luke didn't care about it."

"Jeiklee, I was scared- I go to church, for God's sake-"

"It doesn't matter," Jeiklee cut across, not wanting to hear any more on the subject. "I'm going, and I'm only looking back because of my Mum and Dad, and Luke."

"So you'll stay in contact?"

"I'll stay in contact," Jeiklee said, nodding. "You've got my number."

Cara nodded, then she threw her arms around him in a hug.

"I'm sorry, Jeiklee," she whispered in his ear, making his heart tear.

"It's ok, I forgive you. I'm sorry too- you should've seen my reaction when my friend Spirit confirmed it."

Cara looked at Spirit. "She's real mad at me."

"Yeah, she's like a sister. She said I'm like a brother."

"Well, you'd better get going," Cara said, in an obvious attempt to remain cheerful. "You'll probably be fighting dragons soon and stuff."

Jeiklee laughed. "Hopefully."

"You always said you were bored. Now you're off on an adventure."

"Kind off. Maybe you can visit."

"Maybe. See you?"

Jeiklee nodded, turning away, then Cara suddenly pulled him close and kissed him. Surprised but pleased, Jeiklee kissed her back before he broke away. Taking a deep breath, he said "Goodbye, Cara."

* * *

Jeiklee handed his cases of clothes to Antonio, who took them happily.
"I'll spruce these up for you, sir."
"Thanks, Antonio." Jeiklee tightened his black robe self consciously as he walked down the corridor and into the living area, room, where Spirit was wearing a baby blue robe.
"Hi Jeiklee." He said hi, sitting down in an armchair. "How do you feel?"
"All right," he said with a shrug, then he stopped. "Spirit, why am I suddenly… you know. All tough and that?"
"It's Leticia and Westley's aura," Spirit answered. "Leticia has the spirit of a mermaid, and Westley has the spirit of a dragon. Dragons are dangerous, not afraid of anything. They can be lethal when it comes to protecting those they love- just like Westley. Mermaids have sympathy, and are kind. Still, they aren't afraid of anything, because they know they can use their beauty for whatever purpose- even murder. Leticia could have talked the Petersons into jumping off a cliff if she wanted, and Westley- he could have killed them on the spot."
"Why didn't they when I was stolen?"
"It was the good in them, along with their psychic powers. They were only keeping you in that world until you were three months, you know. Then they were coming back to Severna to start their family."
"Cool, but why didn't they just kill my Mum and Dad?"
"The King talked them out of it. He passed some dumb law about rescuing you. He said you'll come back when the time is right," Spirit said. "Plus they would have gone to prison for SMH, or Double M."
Jeiklee raised an eyebrow, Spirit rolling her eyes.
"I forgot you don't have a clue about anything. Severe Mortal Harm or Mortal Murder, then. The King said they'd go to prison for a long time- and they saw that the next adoptive parents would be abusive. King Harlot said it was best to try reasoning with them- but it didn't work."
"Oh."
Leticia and Westley walked in with their normal breath taking air- both Spirit and Jeiklee inhaled sharply as they sat down.
"Jeiklee, we've spoken to the Headmaster of Thrill," Leticia said, looking at her son with eyes full of love. "He said to take as much time as you need to settle down here in Severna before you even consider attending-"
"And you must practice the Hovering Charm while at home," Westley said, looking at him. "We shall teach you when you settle properly-"
"I have already," Jeiklee said quickly, and they laughed.
"When you have stayed three nights, then. Leticia, Spirit and I will teach you a few things before you start Thrill."
Jeiklee *was* thrilled, and he hadn't even started!

* * *

"Master Inferno, Miss McKenzie!"
Jeiklee and Spirit turned and saw Antonio hurrying towards them.
"Yes Antonio?"
"The chef has run out of self-raising flour for dessert," Antonio explained hurriedly. "And the Count and Countess will be returning for supper shortly- is there any chance you can run to the Wal-Mart?"
"You have Wal-Marts?" Jeiklee said amusedly. "Where's Tescos?"
Spirit hit him on the arm as Antonio frowned curiously.
"What is Tescos?"
"The same as Biggs," said Spirit, scowling at Jeiklee. "But it has a different name."
"Of course," said Antonio, already uninterested. "May the pair of you run to the Wal-Mart?"
"Sure," said Jeiklee, Spirit nodding. "Where's the money for it?"
Antonio laughed, Spirit smirking as she said "Well, as your parents are the Count and Countess of the entire land-"
"Get out," said Jeiklee amazedly. "We don't have to pay?"
"We always try to, so take the money just in case," Antonio said, handing them some gold and blue notes. "Oh, and bring some marshmallows for Lord Inferno- he has a weakness for them."
"He does?" asked Jeiklee, Spirit pulling him away before Antonio could reply eagerly about his father.
"They'll be back soon, he said. Come on, it's only twenty minutes away."
"What- we're not going in the chariot?"
Jeiklee had practically been glued to Leticia and Westley for the past five days- wherever they went, he went. He'd gotten used to his life of luxury so quickly he thought walking to the local store was weird.
"No, idiot- we're not going in the chariot. We don't need it."
Jeiklee thought about that. "That's kind of true."
"It's very true."
Jeiklee shielded his eyes against the bright glare of the sun, looking instead at the shaded trees beyond the gates of his home.
A girl stood there, staring at him. Jeiklee stopped walking, feeling like he'd been punched in the stomach. He stared at her pale face, her blood red lips, her green eyes, and red hair. She stared right back at him.
"Who's that, Spirit?"
Spirit looked: nobody was there. "Who's who?"
"I swear I saw a girl standing there- a pale girl."
"Standing in the shade?" He nodded. "I would have sensed that, Jeiklee."
"Oh, ok. It was probably a mirage or something."

* * *

"Yo, Spirit and Jeiklee! Come to duel?"

"Yeah," said Jeiklee quickly, but Spirit said "Not today, Julius."

"Aw, come on! I want to see what the Count's son learnt so far."

"I said not today, ok?" Spirit pulled Jeiklee away by the arm, a group of girls glaring at her, one saying "You won't always be able to keep him to yourself, Spirit McKenzie!"

"What? I'm not!" said Spirit, face growing hot. "I'm just looking out for him until his parents get back, ok? And they'll be back real soon, so-"

"One round won't kill the guy," Julius said, grinning at Jeiklee. "Right?"

"Well... I've only learnt three hexes, two spells and the Hovering Charm."

"Great, he's good to go," smirked a guy, everyone turning. "Bruce!"

Bruce Finnegan smirked, loving the reaction he got just from joining a crowd. Jeiklee's smile faded as he looked at him. He was tall, muscular, handsome- and a real jerk, Jeiklee decided. He didn't like the way the girls squealed and whispered as they looked at him excitedly.

"Hey Spirit," Bruce said casually, and Spirit said hi. "You duelling?"

"No," she said coldly. "We've got things to do, ok?"

"You still cold 'cause I told you to stop calling me?" smirked Bruce. "You know I don't want a girlfriend anymore. Plus I just needed a date for the-"

"Yeah, I know," Spirit said, heat rising. "Get out of my way, ok?"

"Come on, cute face. Let your boyfriend give it a go- I won't kill him."

"I'm not her boyfriend," Jeiklee said irritably, and Bruce grinned at him.

"Great, so Spirit's free to mess about with. How about it, Spirit? You, me, you with love hearts in your eyes and me with cash in mine-"

Everyone burst out laughing, Julius angrily saying "Shut up, Bruce!"

"Why? Everyone knows Spirit loved me for about three years now, but she can't get that she's not wanted or needed anymore, ok? She was good, but she still has the IQ of a raisin."

"Don't about her like that," said Jeiklee quietly, as Spirit looked away in shame, everyone laughing. Silence fell as Bruce's smile faded.

"Or what?"

Everyone looked at Jeiklee.

"Just don't, ok? She's a friend of mine- leave her alone."

Bruce's smile returned. "You're not a fighter, are you Count Junior? Normally, a guy would battle it out- but you're different. I respect people like that."

"I wasn't around then, so it's not my business," shrugged Jeiklee. "We was on our way to the Wal-Mart- we didn't tell you to stop us. Now, you've gone and upset Spirit when she didn't even want to talk to you."

Silence again, Bruce looking uncomfortable. Spirit was staring at her feet, avoiding the eyes of people watching her.

"Well?" said Jeiklee, looking at Bruce. "Are you going to apologise?"

"Yeah. Sorry, Jeiklee."

"Not to me," snapped Jeiklee, everyone flinching. "To Spirit!"

"What? Nah man, you don't know Spirit as well as we do. You only got here five or six days ago- we've been here for time. We know Spirit. She was a little sales girl, wasn't you?" he jeered at Spirit, who glared at him.

"That was a rumour, and you know it."

"Sales girl?" asked Jeiklee, not getting it. "Selling what?"

"Hmm, I don't know. Maybe her body?"

Jeiklee's stomach churned as everyone nodded. "That's a lie."

"You haven't even known Spirit six months," Bruce answered, Spirit saying "Why are you trying to poison his mind about me? It's a lie!"

"Not what I heard from the guys at Thrill," Bruce smirked. "Trust me Jeiklee, you'd better watch out. I feel for you, living with her."

"Leave her alone Bruce!" said Julius angrily. "You're just sore she got over you just like that-" he snapped his fingers. "The minute you told her to get out of your life."

"You stay out of this," Bruce said, rounding on him. "I'm actually preparing Jeiklee for what lives in his own home."

"Come on," muttered Spirit as she pulled Jeiklee away, Bruce calling "Next time I'll pay you, Spirit!"

* * *

"So… is it true?"

Sprit didn't answer, checking out the flour. Jeiklee sighed, asking "Which one does Chef like?"

"I'm not sure. Self-raising if she's making dessert. But which kind of self-raising?"

Jeiklee stared at the glowing packets, unsure. "Uh… how much did Antonio give you?"

"About fifty Vernons," she said as she counted the notes. "In fives and tens."

"Ok then, we'll just grab all of them. I can practice my Hovering Charm on the way back, otherwise we'll have to carry them."

Spirit smiled, glad he didn't press the subject of the rumour.

"That sounds like a good idea."

* * *

Leticia and Westley sat at the dining table, looking at the clock.

"Spirit and Jeiklee aren't normally late for dinner."

"Spirit isn't," Westley said, then he smiled as he said "I can't be sure about Jeiklee yet."

"Sorry we're late," said Spirit meekly, Jeiklee as well as they came in. "We would've got here sooner, but Jeiklee was making the shopping hover."

Leticia and Westley smiled, Leticia asking "Did it stay hovering?"

"All the way," beamed Jeiklee. "I didn't know how to get it down, though-Chef was laughing her head off."

His parents laughed, indicating to sit down. "How was your day?"

"Good until we went to the Wal-Mart," muttered Spirit, Westley's smile fading as he asked "What happened?"

"Julius wanted us to play duel-"

"As always." Leticia shook her head as Spirit continued "Then Bruce Finnegan came. He told Jeiklee a lot of horrible things about me-"

"Those horrid rumours about being a sales girl?" said Leticia disgustedly, and Spirit nodded as the maids set down hot plates in front of them.

"He tried to poison Jeiklee's mind, and when Julius told him to stop, Bruce said he was preparing Jeiklee for what lived in his own home."

Clive the butler clapped his hands enthusiastically, saying "Presenting a new dish from the chef, My Lord and Lady- Seafood Delight."

"What on earth…?" murmured Leticia as she stared at the colourful dishes being placed on the table. "Clive, has the chef gone mad?"

"No My Lady." Clive laughed as he said "You've repeatedly asked for four days straight!"

"Because each day she has made a new recipe for breakfast, lunch and dinner," Leticia replied as the maids placed small signs in front of each dish, with a description of each. "And unless the woman has a valid reason as to why she has decided yet again to go on an experimental cooking spree-"

"Perhaps it is the arrival of Jeiklee," Westley said, and Clive nodded. "Cookie always does that when we have a new arrival- remember how she was when Spirit came, Leticia."

"Her name is not Cookie," Leticia said coldly, picking up her fork. "She is referred to as 'Cook', 'Chef' or 'The Chef,' do you understand me?"

"Yes my darling," grinned Westley, and Spirit and Jeiklee smiled.

Noticing Spirit's downhearted expression, Leticia said "Never mind Bruce, Spirit. Dracula's daughter manipulated him as she did many others, turning him away from you."

"Will she keep doing it, though? It's like she's-"

"Incredibly dark hearted," Westley said as he picked up a sign, reading it curiously. "That we know. She'll do anything to keep you hurting."

"I don't really care anymore, but Bruce went and told Jeiklee a load of-"

"Don't you believe a word, son." Westley looked at Jeiklee. "Your mother would know the truth definitely, being psychic."

Jeiklee nodded. "Yes Westley."

"If Simon and Rachel were alive they would curse that boy magnificently along with Virginia," Leticia said as she picked a dish at random, holding the sign. "As for Dracula- *HAS THE CHEF GONE MAD?!!*"

"That's the twenty fifth time, My Lady!" laughed Clive, then his smile faded at the murderous look on Leticia's face as she rose to her feet, throwing the sign down. "My Lady?"

Leticia turned and stormed down the corridor, Westley summoning the sign and reading before he swore, dropping it as he shouted "Leticia!"

She ignored him.

"Leticia, wait! Cookie probably forgot-"

"Her name! Is not! *COOKIE!!*"

BANG!!

The basement doors flew open, Leticia vanishing through them angrily.

Spirit cautiously reached for the sign, reading it.

"Uh-oh."

"What?" said Jeiklee curiously, Spirit looking at the dish.

"It's dolphin."

* * *

"Never before have I been so insulted," fumed Leticia as she picked at her own meal of choice, which the cook hurriedly made. "How on earth did she get the dolphin in the first place?"

"She must have gone down to the boat harbour," Westley replied. "Come on Leticia, don't get upset. The Chef said it was an accident."

"She must enjoy giving me a heart attack," Leticia said with a grudging smile, and Westley smiled back as he leant back, full.

"She is full of surprises, Tish."

"Mmm. Is everyone finished but I?" she said amusedly, as Spirit and Jeiklee played Punch-You-Punch-Me at the table, Westley making the cutlery hover, a sign of boredom Leticia recognised.

Everyone nodded.

"Well you aren't excused," Leticia said amusedly. "It doesn't look good, leaving the Countess to eat alone at the table."

"We'd never leave you," Spirit said, Jeiklee nodding as he hit her arm. "Ouch!"

"Ha, you voiced pain. My turn."

Spirit turned and hit his arm, Jeiklee struggling not to make a sound. Innocent as ever, Leticia asked "Have you practised the Lowering Charm, Jeiklee? You must practise that as well as the Hovering Charm."

"Yes Ma'am, I have. Well, it takes me a while to lower it, but- ow!"

"Ha, got ya. My turn," smirked Spirit. "Thanks, Leticia."

"Anytime," smiled Leticia, Jeiklee pouting at her.

"Leticia, that's not fair!"

* * *

Jeiklee walked and looked down at the garden below from his balcony, smiling as Spirit lay by the glowing pond, gazing down at it thoughtfully. The magical light illuminated her face as she brooded, highlighting her beautiful eyes.

Jeiklee's stomach did a somersault as he watched her. Then he rubbed it, shaking his head. Spirit? No way...

As if sensing his gaze, Spirit looked up, right into his eyes. Jeiklee stepped back, then he waved. Spirit smiled and waved back.

Jeiklee turned and walked to his bed, getting in slowly.

Within minutes he fell fast asleep.

* * *

Jeiklee snapped awake, breathing hard. He'd had a disturbing dream about what, he couldn't remember.

Only it had woken him up, and his body had no intention of going back to sleep. Jeiklee sighed, sitting up.

"Great."

He got out of bed, stretching as he stood. Then he listened.

The manor was quiet.

Jeiklee hesitated, then he pulled open his door and looked out, listening sharply.

The corridor was quiet. Jeiklee jogged down the massive staircase and turned a corner, crashing into Spirit, who happened to be holding a mug of steaming hot chocolate-

"Ouch," gasped Jeiklee, his front sopping wet. "Watch where you're going, Spirit!"

"Me!" she said, affronted. "It's you who's not looking!"

"What are you doing up at this time?" asked Jeiklee, as he acknowledged once again how quiet it was. Leticia and Westley must be fast asleep.

"I woke up. I couldn't get back to sleep." Spirit shrugged a shoulder. "It happens sometimes. I normally wake up and get some hot chocolate, then go back to bed. But seeing as you made me spill my hot chocolate, I guess I can do with being awake a few more hours."

"Be quiet, Spirit. Come, let's go and make some more. I fancy a hot chocolate, do you want to make me some?"

"We'll make some," Spirit said, amused. "Come on."

* * *

Spirit smiled at Jeiklee over her mug. "So how are you finding it here in Severna?"

They were sitting in the living area of the mansion. Jeiklee smiled back.

"I love it. I feel like I finally fit in."

"Don't you miss the Petersons?" she asked, and Jeiklee shook his head.

"I know I should, but… I don't know, I just feel like… never mind."

Spirit nodded. Then she said "Maybe you don't miss them because you found out the truth about your adoption? How cruel they were to your real parents, I mean. The Petersons lied to you- your whole life with them was a lie."

"I know," sighed Jeiklee. "I don't hate them, but… I feel like I don't want anything to do with them. I'm not going back, I'm looking forwards. Or is that a little harsh?" Spirit shrugged as he said "Maybe I'll forgive them, over time. I'm not sure."

"Ok." Spirit sipped her tea, then she said "You know you've got a lot to learn, right? You're basically a mortal here."

"Well, why don't you teach me?" asked Jeiklee. "It'll be fun. Uh, that is… if you'd like to."

Spirit didn't answer that. It wasn't a question of her liking it.

"Spirit?" said Jeiklee, looking at her, and she sighed.

"You saw how those girls were today." Spirit scowled as she mimicked *"'You won't always be able to keep him to yourself, Spirit McKenzie!'* You saw how they were."

"I saw," said Jeiklee, smiling a little. "What are you saying, that I should ask one of them instead?"

"It's up to you," shrugged Spirit, though her insides screamed *Hell no!!* "Maybe Alicia Garfield, she's good at most things at Thrill."

"What about hunting?" asked Jeiklee. "I know you're skilled with the bow and arrow, I heard Westley praising you last night. So… maybe you could teach me to hunt?"

"You'd need to be up at the crack of dawn," Spirit answered. "And you'd need to be bright awake. It's in the early hours of Saturday morning I go hunting. I leave at five. You think you'd be up to your first hunting lesson then?"

"Well yeah," shrugged Jeiklee. "I'd better go and get another three hours sleep… like you should."

Spirit nodded, both of them rising to their feet.

"Goodnight, Jeiklee."

"Night."

* * *

"Master Inferno?" said a voice, making Jeiklee stir and yawn.
"Yeah Spirit, I'm up…"
"No sir, its Antonio. It's almost five a.m.-"
"What!" Jeiklee tumbled out of bed as Antonio stood there, saying "And Miss McKenzie says she will leave with or without you, so be quick? She is giving you half an hour to meet in the Entrance Hall, and she says she is leaving afterwards with or without you."

* * *

Spirit walked then stopped, eyebrow raised at the shadow almost in tune with hers in the field. She'd left Jeiklee behind, even though Antonio had asked her to wait an extra ten minutes: Jeiklee had hopped in the shower quickly.
Spirit took a deep breath, then turned to look at him. She almost gasped as she stared at the pale face, the red hair, into the green eyes.
But she didn't. Spirit kept her cool.
"What do you want, Virginia?"
Dracula's daughter bared her teeth in a sharp hiss. "My father sends a message to Count Inferno."
"Really. Well, he's getting kind of sick of those," Spirit answered flatly.
Virginia almost answered if a voice hadn't panted "Spirit- wait up!"
"You must be Inferno Junior," Virginia said, looking Jeiklee up and down as he finally reached Spirit. Jeiklee eyed her curiously, saying "You're the girl I saw on the way to the Wal-Mart."
Virginia nodded.
"That's why I didn't feel her presence," scowled Spirit. "She and her father have the power not to be traced or felt by us magical beings."
"Really," said Jeiklee flatly as he looked at the red-haired girl. "Well, what's your name then?"
"I am Virginia," she answered, holding out a hand. "Daughter of Dracula."
Jeiklee stared at her fangs, unnerved but still shaking her hand.
"I'm Jeiklee Inferno. It's nice to meet you, Virginia."
Spirit shook her head disgustedly, turning and walking away with her bow and arrow. Jeiklee started and took after her, but before he could catch up with her she vanished.
Jeiklee skidded, turning to look at Virginia, but she too had disappeared.

* * *

"One… two… three." Spirit ducked as Jeiklee pounced, grabbing his arm while he was in the air and catapulting him over her shoulder.

"Aaargh!!"

Jeiklee tumbled down the hill they were on, making so much noise he caused the flock of birds Spirit was eying hungrily to take flight. Spirit groaned, glaring at the spot where Jeiklee landed.

Jeiklee dusted himself off as he stood, walking back up the hill.

"Hi." she glared in answer. "You uh… you heard me."

"And so did my prey," snapped Spirit. "Thanks a lot."

"Well… maybe you can teach me the elements of hunting rather than go after them today," suggested Jeiklee, and she looked at him.

"First, you shouldn't even be wearing any shoes." Jeiklee glanced down: Spirit's feet were bare. "You need to relax, but keep silent but focused at the same time… feel the earth under your feet…"

Jeiklee didn't answer that, removing his trainers and socks. He relaxed, looking down at his feet. The soil was soft and warm under them.

Spirit watched as the flock of birds slowly returned to their feeding spot.

Jeiklee joined her side but she pushed him back, annoyed.

"You're breathing too hard. You need to relax."

"Can I try with the bow and arrow?" asked Jeiklee, and she scowled.

"I don't think so. Maybe after you learn how to use one- watch." Spirit aimed slowly, muttering "Silence, Jeiklee. Watch and learn."

Spirit pulled back, then released the arrow. Jeiklee wowed as it whistled through the air, piercing it's target. The bird rasped, caught by the neck. Spirit raised the bow again.

"Watch an expert at work."

The arrow struck again, directly in the bird's heart.

"Ooh, you go girl. Work it," said Jeiklee impressively, and she smiled.

"Westley taught me every evening after high school."

"You've been hunting with my father that long?" he said, impressed. "Go girl, do your thang."

Spirit laughed, then caught herself. Jeiklee frowned at her.

"You seem different since I got used to here. Sharper, colder."

"That's how I am," Spirit replied. "I put on a front to gain your trust."

"Hmm. I'm not sure I like this colder Spirit. It'll take longer to break the ice with you now that you're back to your old self."

"And why would you want to break the ice?" she asked softly, walking down the hill towards her target. The bird was dead, as she expected. It only took two arrows, three if the bird was a strong one. Spirit knelt down, looking at it. "Why?"

Jeiklee swallowed as she stood, walking back to him. He didn't miss the

fact that her gaze lingered on his lips. Then her eyes locked on his.
"Well?"
"I don't! Well, it's just that-"
"Yes?" she asked softly, as she looked up at him through her lashes.
"Damn, Spirit, don't look at me that way…" Jeiklee moved closer to her, raising a hand to caress her cheek. Her skin felt so soft! Spirit closed her eyes at his touch, a soft sigh escaping her as she whispered "Jeiklee…"
The feeling was so intense, Jeiklee didn't know what to do about it. He caressed her cheek, murmuring "I want to break the ice because… I… I… Spirit-"
"Yes?"
Then he saw his father appear, not far off, within earshot.
"I'd like to hunt," he said clearly as he lowered his hand, and she gaped, then regained composure as she stared at him.
"You'd like to hunt," she said coolly, and Jeiklee nodded. "Well, that won't be a problem. You can come hunting with your father, if that's the reason. Father-son time. Bonding and whatever."
Damn. She's mad, thought Jeiklee, as she pulled the arrows out of the exotic looking bird, hauling it over her shoulder.
Westley nodded at them, Leticia appearing at his side. Both seemed to be walking away from them.
"Where're they going?" asked Jeiklee, and Spirit answered icily "Away. Leticia and Westley leave at daybreak and return after nightfall at the weekend. I don't know where they go. They don't tell me or anyone else, for that matter. We'd better head on home and give this bird to Cook."
"Hmm, ok. Spirit, about what happened back there, I-"
"Nothing happened," she cut across. "I asked you a question, you gave me an answer. So-"
"Well well well, Inferno Junior," said a smooth voice; they turned. Jeiklee's jaw dropped: she looked amazing. "And his chauffer."
"Clarissa." Spirit showed no sign of liking. "How are you?"
"Fine, fine."
Jeiklee took in the tight red dress with the matching shoes and handbag, the sleek blonde hair, which complimented her bright blue eyes. He wondered which lucky guy had the courtesy of dating Clarissa.
"What are you doing out so early?" Spirit asked, and Clarissa smiled.
"Sometimes I need a little fresh air, and I go out very early."
"Dressed like *that?*" Spirit looked her up and down. "It seems more like you dressed like that to capture Jeiklee's attention."
"And so what if I did," snapped Clarissa. "Better this than a sexy pair of jeans and an oh so tight top. Don't be a hypocrite, Spirit."
"I'm hunting," Spirit said, stung. "These are my usual clothes."
"Liar."

"Anyway, I'm coaching Jeiklee right now, so if you'll excuse us?"
Clarissa scowled. "You won't always be able to keep him to yourself, Spirit McKenzie."
"I'm not trying to," snapped Spirit, temper rising. Jeiklee saw the friend he'd grown to know and like a lot about to surface again. "Why is everyone saying that?"
"Because it's true," Clarissa shot back. "Everyone's talking about how you want-"
"Everyone can get stuffed," Spirit said angrily, Jeiklee adding "Seriously, people need to get a life. If all you guys can do is gossip about Spirit- well, I can see why she keeps to herself and away from you."
"Jeiklee, it's not like that," said Clarissa softly: her tone licked every one of his senses. "I'm just repeating what I heard."
"Well, you need to stop doing it," Jeiklee answered, rubbing his neck as the hairs rose on the back of it. "We going, Spirit?"
"Why don't you stay with Clarissa?" Spirit answered, and Clarissa gaped.
"You mean that?" she asked, and Jeiklee looked at her.
"Sure," Spirit said loftily. "I mean, I don't want to keep him to myself now, do I Clarissa?"
Clarissa flushed rose red. "I- I- well, if he wants to stay-"
"Oh, he looks like he does. Jeiklee?"
"Huh? Oh- right. Well, I'd rather go back home with you, Spirit. Me and you can spend some time together."
Spirit raised an eyebrow. Clearly she was still annoyed at his reason to break the ice with her. And that wasn't even the real reason!
"You know, just chill at home watching TV?"
"Wouldn't you rather walk around and see the sights?" asked Spirit, voice laden with sarcasm. "I mean, Clarissa *is* a romantic, after all."
"No- I don't think so," Jeiklee said, warning her with his eyes not to play games with him. "Clarissa was just going on her way, right Clarissa?"
Clarissa blinked, then turned and walked away. They watched her walk so far, then she turned back and looked at them.
"When he starts Thrill you won't still have him just for yourself, Spirit."
And with that she turned and flounced off.
"So... are we going home to chill?" asked Jeiklee, and Spirit sighed.
"We may as well."

* * *

Jeiklee faked a yawn, then put his arm around Spirit. "Still mad at me?"
Spirit rested her head on his shoulder as she murmured "No."
"Good," he said, relieved. "Because I'd be mad at myself. Spirit, I only
said I wanted to hunt because my father was nearby, I never-"
"Shh," Spirit said softly. "It's ok."
"Are you sure?"
"I'm sure." Spirit looked up at him through her lashes again. Jeiklee swore
she never looked so pretty before he arrived in Severna. Before he knew
what he was doing he was tilting his head, and she tilted hers- the giant
doors burst open.
"Time to eat, Master In- oh!"
Antonio looked from Jeiklee to Spirit and back, then hurriedly left again.
Spirit flicked her hand, the doors closing again.
They sat looking at the television, Jeiklee wringing his hands.
They had almost kissed just then. What was wrong with him? Spirit...
She's like a sister, he thought desperately. A sister!
He was at war with two opinions of Spirit. A part of him wanted to love
her, have her at his side as his girlfriend. Another part wanted to stick to
what his parents had implied: a new sister.
But when he reached and turned her face gently, making her look at him
through those beautiful grey eyes... he thought he'd drown in them.
"Spirit?"
"Yes?"
"I... well... I just..." She was gazing at him. "Spirit, please don't look at
me like that..."
"Why?" she said softly, and Jeiklee swallowed.
"I... uh... we-"
"We're a *we* now?" she asked softly- Jeiklee groaned. All thoughts of Spirit
as his sister vanished from his head as he leaned in, she tilted her head- and
they were pressed mouth to mouth furiously, Spirit moaning as she moved
closer to him, arms rising to snake around him, pulling him closer.
Jeiklee didn't know he could feel bliss like this- all he knew was bliss was
here with him. Spirit deepened the kiss as she climbed atop him, then,
breaking away reluctantly, she gazed down at him. Jeiklee didn't want to
beg, but he found his mouth had the opposite thought.
"Spirit... *Spirit...*"
"Spirit indeed," said a reproving voice, and he leapt up.
Leticia was standing there, an eyebrow raised. "I take it you had a good
sleep? Spirit is waiting for you."
"Huh- what?" Jeiklee looked around: he was in his bed. "What happened?"
"Spirit says you fainted," Westley answered for Leticia as he appeared by

her side. "Soon after you returned from your hunt. I wonder what caused such a thing, Leticia?"

"As to that I have no clue," Leticia said thoughtfully. "Spirit says you play-duelled. You kept yelling her name in your… sleep, which explains," she said amusedly, "Why you were saying her name just now."

"Erm… yeah," said Jeiklee, standing up. His legs felt shaky. "Where is Spirit, anyway?"

Westley smiled. "Get dressed, son. Then, come and have lunch."

"Ok."

* * *

Spirit avoided Jeiklee's eye as they ate. Jeiklee was frowning as he thought, well confused by now. They were kissing on the sofa, then he woke up to his mother in his bedroom. How…?

Kissing… bedroom. Jeiklee scratched his head, picking up his fork. Kissing… bedroom. Seriously, how did that happen?

Spirit says you play-duelled…

Spirit lied obviously, but that still didn't explain how he woke up shaky in his bedroom.

What if he'd imagined the kissing? What if he didn't kiss Spirit at all?

"Jeiklee?" Leticia looked at him, concerned. "What's the matter?"

"Nothing. Well… I'm just nervous, I guess, about my first day at Thrill tomorrow."

"It's Saturday," Westley told him gently. "Thrill starts at noon on Monday. Are you sure you're ready for this, son? We could ask for an extra week off."

"He looks ill," said Leticia worriedly. "Westley, I really think he should have an extra week off- a few days here isn't enough to ready him for Thrill. He hasn't been here that long-"

"May I be excused?" asked Jeiklee; they both nodded. Spirit picked at her food, keeping her eyes on her plate. Jeiklee looked at her, but she didn't look up. So he turned and left the dining area, fuming inside his head.

She did something to me.

* * *

It was midnight.

Spirit laid in bed, thinking about the kiss she and Jeiklee shared. She hadn't meant for it to happen, it never should have happened… that's why she had to make it stop… even if she didn't want it to.

She needed some fresh air. She could hardly eat with Jeiklee sat opposite her, after what happened. A walk around in the garden would do.

She got up slowly, thinking about dipping her feet in the pool. Not that it would extinguish the desire burning inside of her, all for Jeiklee.

As soon as she'd taken two steps into the corridor a hand clapped over her mouth and dragged her along the wall back towards her bedroom.

"Jeiklee!" she gasped, when he released her.

"All right, explain. Now!"

"Shh!" she hissed, closing her door behind her. "All right, I used a sleeping spell on you the minute I heard Westley and Leticia come back so soon. Real soon, in fact. It gave me time to figure out what to do, time to think- don't look at me like that!"

Jeiklee was glaring at her. Spirit averted her gaze, saying "It was the quickest thing I could think of. I heard them outside when we were… you know. So I cast the spell, jumped off you and called Antonio."

"You told him I passed out?"

"Duh."

"Well, wasn't that smart and stupid of you," he said furiously, and Spirit frowned at him, asking "Smart *and* stupid?"

"It was smart because that took quick thinking. It was stupid because I missed out on the rest of the morning- which could have been with you."

Spirit looked away from him. "I think we should forget about the ki-"

She knew her reaction time had slowed when she found she was against the wall. Jeiklee's hand trailed her woolly pyjama top as he stared deep into her eyes, murmuring "Are you tired, Spirit?"

"I- no, not anymore. Jeiklee…"

She closed her eyes; his hand had found the hem of her pyjama top. Jeiklee sighed as his hand ran over her smooth skin, higher and higher-

"Not out here," she gasped, placing a hand over his. "Not out here."

"Well, either we go in there-" Jeiklee nodded at her door. "Or we take it to my room instead."

"Jeiklee, we can't," she hissed. "What if Westley or Leticia-?"

Jeiklee kissed her, long and hard. Spirit raised her hands to his chest and pushed him back, heart racing as she whispered "We mustn't do this. It's not right- Leticia would never forgive me if I-"

"Can you focus on the present and not the future?" Jeiklee whispered back. Spirit froze.

"What?"

"What's what?" he asked, as she detangled herself. "What is it?"

"Bruce," she muttered, stepping back. "He said the same when we… when I wanted to get more serious. I asked if we had a future, and he said exactly what you said. Focus on the present and not the future."

"Spirit-"

"I think we should forget about… this. All of it. And just be friends." Spirit took a deep breath. "We'd be better off with someone else."

Jeiklee stared at her. She looked deadly serious.

"That's what you want?"

Spirit nodded. "That's what I want."

Jeiklee took a deep breath. "Then… that's what you'll get. But don't expect me to get used to it quickly."

"Jeiklee, what we're doing… it's incest."

"How? You're not my real sister."

"I am," she shot back, hurt. "You'd better think of me as that from now on. A relative. Because that's all I want to be."

"Where the hell did this come from?" spat Jeiklee. "Are you that in love with Bruce Finnegan, you're all unsure now?"

Spirit didn't answer. Jeiklee took that as a whopping yes.

"Well thanks for letting me know. I'll just go back to my room and sulk like a little boy who got told he can't have any candy."

Spirit smiled. "Oh, so now I'm candy?"

"Oh hell yes. Can I have one last kiss goodnight?"

"No."

"Why not?"

"Because," she said heavily, "I'm your sister."

Element Three: Dracula

* * *

Spirit packed her lunch in her bag, Jeiklee jogging down the stairs.

"Morning Spirit." She said morning. "Where're you going?"

"To college, why? Or school. Whatever you want to call it."

"College?"

"Thrill," Leticia said as she appeared, and Jeiklee pouted.

"Aw Mum, can't I go?"

"No, you- what?" Leticia did a double take, staring at her son. Westley appeared by her side, pouting as he said "Well, if you're calling Leticia 'Mum' now, you'd better start calling me 'Dad.'"

"Okay Dad. I- wait," Jeiklee said, frowning. "How did I just fall into that? I feel like I've been calling you Mum and Dad all my life!"

"You're used to us now, I presume," Leticia said thoughtfully, and Jeiklee nodded.

"So can I please start college today?"

"We've already agreed with your tutor next week, Jeiklee."

"That's a kind no," Spirit added with a smirk, slinging her bag over her shoulder. "See you later. Bye Leticia, Westley."

"Bye darling."

Leticia blew her a kiss: Jeiklee's jaw dropped as smoke furled from his mother's lips, forming and taking shape of his mother's mouth. Spirit smiled as the kiss flitted through the air and planted itself on her cheek before vanishing. Then she walked through the giant doors and was gone.

* * *

Jeiklee laid on his bed, staring up at the ceiling as he thought of Spirit and what he could do to break the new slab of ice that was between them romantically.

Bruce Finnegan really messed her up, he thought angrily. She wouldn't have kissed him the way she did if she really wanted to be just friends, or like a sister to him. No way.

"Now I have to figure out how to get her to stop being in denial," he muttered, as there was a knock on the door.

"Master Inferno?"

"Yes Antonio," he called, and Antonio said "Lunch is ready, sir."

"Ok. I'm coming."

Leticia sensed her son's frustration as he sat at the table. "Jeiklee? Is everything all right?"

"Yes Mum. Well... um... I was thinking about Thrill and was a bit worried about not learning the spells on time. I might get picked on."

"You got the gist of the Hovering and Lowering Charms almost immediately," Westley said, amused at his son's worried face. "That's all that's being taught in September, son. You're not behind on anything, I promise."

Jeiklee nodded. "Yes sir."

"Are you sure that's all that's bothering you, Jeiklee?" asked Leticia, and Jeiklee said yes. "Well don't let it bother you. You're not behind."

"Ok."

* * *

Spirit sat alone in the cafeteria, gazing out the large windows at the river next to the massive building. She sighed, picking up her sandwich and taking a bite.

Jeiklee was on her mind. Telling him she wanted to forget the kiss and everything else and remain like a sister was a big fat lie. She had strong feelings for him, and she'd had them for a while.

A hiss made her glance round, startled.

Dracula's daughter Virginia was sat at her table, a smirk on her face as she said "The Count and Countess of Severna can't protect you here at Thrill, Spirit McKenzie."

Spirit's body erupted in a burst of scarlet light as her fury exploded within her.

"You think you can keep hexing me at every chance you get?!"

"I do," smirked Virginia, her hand glowing. "You never retaliate anyway."

"Don't think I won't this time," spat Spirit. "I've got a lot on my mind and I don't need a flipping hex right now, ok?!"

"Ricato!!"

BANG!!

Spirit was blasted off her feet, everyone whipping round to see Virginia smirking, Spirit on the ground.

"Spirit! Are you ok??" some people called, while others burst out laughing.

"Virginia, give the girl a break!"

Spirit unsteadily got to her feet, livid. She was sick of being embarrassed like this- sick of it!

Spirit's arm lit bright orange as she cried *"Mordzmorda!!"*

BAAAANG!!!

Everyone gasped as Virginia slammed through the cafeteria windows, glass shattering everywhere as she tumbled down the hill into the river.

SPLASH!!!

Loads cheered, Spirit dusting herself off as the college professors came running.

"What on earth is going on?!"

Soaked and in terrible pain, Virginia unsteadily climbed out of the river, screaming *"Spirit McKenzie!!"*

"Try me again!" Spirit screamed back. "You'll be in your coffin permanently the next time I have to deal with you, Daughter of Dracula!"

"Spirit, calm down," Professor Gene said gently, taking her arm, then Spirit gasped in pain. She lifted her sleeves to find raw burns all over her arms-immediately her body lit scarlet again.

"You little-!!"

"Spirit," Professor Gene said firmly. "Calm down and come with me to the nurse's office. She can remove the Burn Hex easily."

As Spirit left with Professor Gene, everyone started cheering and calling her name.

"Good for you, Spirit!"

Spirit glanced back in time to see Virginia dissolve into nothingness, gone. Probably back to Castle Dracula, she thought bitterly, though she smiled and waved as Professor Gene led her out of the cafeteria.

* * *

"She always hexes me," Spirit said bitterly. "And not one professor ever does anything about it! She hexes me and vanishes, and comes back to class when everything dies down- and I'm the one who gets told to keep out of her way!"

"Spirit, you know we don't involve ourselves when the students play duel," Professor Gene said gently. "It's harmless fun."

Spirit shook her head angrily: didn't any teacher get it??

"We're not play duelling, Professor! This is real!"

"If you hadn't responded there may have been a problem, especially if she hexed you again," Professor Gene said. "Spirit, if you want to report an issue of bullying-"

Spirit cringed: Virginia could never bully her. Well, not anymore anyway.

"Forget it, Professor. May I go home for the rest of the day?"

"Yes, and three more days," Professor Gene said kindly. "Take some time to calm down."

Spirit heard the bell for afternoon lessons sound. Sighing, she picked up her bag and said "Thanks, Professor. See you on Thursday."

* * *

"What happened to *you?*" said Jeiklee, surprised when Spirit stormed into the living area and flopped down on one of the sofas.

Leticia frowned at her as well. "Spirit, you're not due home for another three hours."

"Virginia hexed me in the cafeteria, Leticia," Spirit said angrily. "With a Burn Hex. So I blasted her through the windows down the hill and into the river with a Fire Bone Hex-"

"Nice," said Jeiklee impressively, and Spirit concluded "I got told to cool off at home and come back on Thursday. But I wasn't expelled, Leticia. I promise."

Westley smiled. "You finally retaliated."

"She had it coming," Spirit said as she smiled back. "I'm going to go hunting in a bit. It'll take my mind off that Spawn of Satan."

"Can I come with you?" Jeiklee asked, and Spirit said "Sure."

Relieved, Jeiklee smiled at her. Spirit smiled back briefly before she left the living area.

* * *

Castle Dracula…

"What happened to you?" Dracula asked sharply, as his servants crowded Virginia in the lounge. Her skin was a burning red colour. "Speak!"

"Spirit McKenzie," hissed Virginia. "She hit me with a Fire Bone Hex."

Dracula frowned. "That's a cruel hex for a simple play duel."

"It was no play duel Father," Virginia said angrily. "I didn't expect her to retaliate. She never does when I hex her normally."

"Well what would you expect when you constantly attack her?" Dracula replied flatly. "Ready yourself for dinner and afterwards rest. The pain from the Fire Bone Hex should wear off in the next six to eight hours. Succumb to sleep in your coffin while it does. You will be of no use in the meantime."

"What will *you* do, Father?"

"I will think of a way to see the Countess of Severna. Maybe I will have a word with her about that Spirit McKenzie," Dracula said thoughtfully. "A pitiful excuse to see her, but it's still an excuse."

Virginia sighed as the servants pressed ice packs to her body. "Won't you let her go, Father? You and Leticia Inferno were a real long time ago."

"We were *everything* a real long time ago," Dracula corrected. "And no, I'm not going to let her go. I did that once when she met that idiot Westley. I'm not going to do it again."

"But Father-"

"But nothing," he said sharply. "Ready yourself for dinner and then rest."

Virginia sighed. "Yes Father."

* * *

Spirit sat in the garden, gazing down at the pool water.

Jeiklee watched her from his bedroom balcony. The moon was shining down on the grass, stars sparkling. Jeiklee wondered if he should go down to her.

"Should I?" he asked himself as he came back into the bedroom. She seemed fine when they were out together, real casual when he watched her hunt and spoke to her. If she was thinking about him the way he was thinking about her, she was hiding that fact very well.

Jeiklee threw on his dressing gown and left his bedroom quietly. The main lights were off in the mansion, soothing lamps on instead.

Jeiklee sighed contentedly. He'd never felt so at home. Like he belonged. It was great.

Spirit's back was towards Jeiklee as he walked towards her quietly. He stopped for a moment, hesitating, before he said her name gently.

"Spirit."

She glanced around, startled. Then she softly said "Hey."

"Hey," said Jeiklee. "Um- it's midnight. What are you doing out here?"

"I couldn't sleep," Spirit said quietly. "I… I have a lot on my mind."

"Virginia?"

"Kind of."

"Did she hurt you real bad?" asked Jeiklee, sitting down next to her. "The Burn Hex, I mean."

"It killed," admitted Spirit. "But the nurse healed me. The Fire Bone Hex would only have worn off Virginia at around this time."

"Wow. So what does it do?"

"It causes terrible pain, from the insides of bones outwards through the flesh and onto the surface of the skin," Spirit replied, and his jaw dropped. "Normally it hurts so much you can't move, for hours. The best thing to do is sleep it off."

"Serves her right if she hexed you," Jeiklee said. "Um… can you teach me the Fire Bone Hex? It sounds like a real useful one."

"Sure," said Spirit, getting to her feet. "You already know how to do the Burn Hex, right?"

Jeiklee nodded, smiling as he got up as well.

"Ok. I'll teach you. It's not an easy one to learn," Spirit told him. "But the better you get at it, the worse it is on the receiving end."

"Cool!"

"All right. Repeat after me," she said, and Jeiklee nodded, waiting. "Mordzmorda."

"Mordzmorda!!"

BANG!!

Spirit ducked, the hex whooshing over her head, through some trees and out of sight.

"I didn't say perform the hex, idiot! I said repeat the word!"

"Sorry," grinned Jeiklee, and she couldn't help but smile back. "What can I practise the hex on?"

"Shoot it at the sky," Spirit replied, "And pray you don't hit a flying creature. Or practise on some vases or wooden stakes out here in the garden."

"How will I know if I'm getting better unless I perform it on a person?" asked Jeiklee curiously, and Spirit said "You see how the colour of the hex was white when you performed it?"

Jeiklee nodded, eager to learn.

"Well, the colour will change as it gets stronger. It will go from white to blue to green then yellow, and finally to orange. Orange is the most powerful. Once you master the Fire Bone Hex and it reaches maximum power, that's the colour it will become."

"Awesome," Jeiklee said admiringly. "Who taught you the hex?"

"Westley and Leticia," smiled Spirit. "About three years ago. I've had plenty of time to practise and perfect it. But they said not to use it unless it's totally necessary."

"You got hexed for no reason by Virginia," scowled Jeiklee. "It was definitely totally necessary."

Spirit smiled at him. "Glad we agree."

Jeiklee smiled back.

Spirit averted her gaze to the swimming pool, then she sat down again. Jeiklee joined her.

"Are we ok, Spirit?"

"Of course we are," she said softly. "Why would you even ask that?"

"Because-"

"Psst! Spirit!"

Jeiklee and Spirit whipped round, startled. Someone was climbing over the giant garden wall.

"Bruce??" said Spirit disbelievingly. "What are you doing here?"

"I knew you'd be in the garden," grinned Bruce Finnegan as he walked up to her. "Everyone's talking about the way you blasted Virginia with a Fire Bone Hex."

"Ok," said Spirit curiously, Jeiklee scowling. "That doesn't explain why you're in our garden."

"Well, I was wondering if we could like… chill sometime? Me and you. Like we used to," smiled Bruce, and Spirit's jaw dropped.

"Are you serious?"

"Yeah," said Bruce. "Like, I know we had words in the crowd the last time- I was out of order. But the way you hexed Virginia was brilliant! It made me realise I could do with you in my life after all."

Jeiklee saw red as Spirit stared at him. Couldn't she see he was trying to use her?!

Spirit wasn't stupid. "You know what, Bruce? I don't think so."

Bruce blinked. "Excuse me?"

"You heard me," Spirit said flatly. "You think I've forgotten about the rumours you spread about me with Virginia of Dracula? The way you treated me? And how you treated me in front of Jeiklee? You said I have the IQ of a raisin, remember that? You told Jeiklee you was preparing him for what lived in his own home. You honestly think I forgot?!"

"Well, uh…"

"Well uh what? You've got some nerve coming here," spat Spirit. "Get lost, Bruce. And don't come near me again."

"What, so you're going to forget everything we had?!" Bruce was furious, Jeiklee not saying a word. He knew Spirit could handle him.

"I forgot everything we had a long time ago," Spirit said coldly. "Can you leave before I wake up the mansion's defences and it *forces* you to leave? It won't be pretty."

Bruce stared at her angrily, then he spat "You had a chance with me again and you blew it! Don't come crawling back to me when things don't go your way, Spirit McKenzie!"

"Crawling back to you?" Spirit was amused now. "Who's the one scrambling over garden walls to beg to be together again? Me or you?"

Bruce didn't answer.

"Now get out of here and don't come back," Spirit said flatly. "Don't come up to me when I'm out or at Thrill. We're done."

"Bye," Jeiklee added coldly, and Bruce stormed away.

Spirit waited until he hauled himself over the garden wall and was gone before she shook her head and sat by the pool again.

Jeiklee joined her. "You ok?"

"I'm fine," smiled Spirit. "I feel great."

"I'm glad," said Jeiklee, smiling back. "Hey. Fancy a hot chocolate in the living area? Cookie won't mind us being in the kitchen."

"She will," said Spirit, amused. "If anything's out of place she'll have our heads. Let's make it at the bar."

* * *

Leticia snapped awake, startled as she stared at the figure at the foot of her giant bed, then she whispered "Dracula."

Westley slept on, Dracula smiling.

"Hello Leticia."

"What are you doing here, Dracula?" she asked quietly as she slid out of bed, and he smiled at her, his fangs glimmering.

"You removed the protective charms on the mansion. And the defences of the Force from yourself. So I entered. Though the charms have no effect on me, the Force definitely has. I wasn't sure you'd dropped your defences until I morphed in the garden," Dracula added as she looked at him.

"What are you doing here?" Leticia repeated, and he pouted at her.

"I cannot see you when Westley is awake. This was the only way."

"That doesn't explain why you're here," Leticia replied as she reached for her robe, slipping it on. "And at this time."

"I wanted to see you," Dracula said softly. "Even for a split second."

"Well you've been here for more than a split second, Dracula."

"Yes. I know. I also wanted to talk to you about the on-going dispute between my daughter and Spirit McKenzie."

"Virginia is obsessed with Spirit," Leticia replied flatly. "She has been since they were in high school. When Spirit and Bruce Finnegan grew close two years ago, Virginia became madly jealous, and that's when everything started. The hexing, the spells. The duelling and the filthy rumours, all from your daughter. Spirit had no problem with her at all before then. It was Virginia who started everything, Dracula. Not Spirit."

Dracula opened his mouth, then closed it. "I had no idea."

"I did."

"How could you not," Dracula said, shrugging a shoulder. "Your senses are extraordinary."

Leticia glanced at Westley, then she quietly said "You have to go, Dracula."

"But I've only just arrived." Disappointed, he looked at her. "Can we not share a drink at the bar together?"

"No," she said flatly, and Dracula sighed.

"Are you afraid of being alone with me, Leticia?"

"I'm not afraid of anything," Leticia tossed back. "But I am wary of Westley realising you're here and murdering you."

"He couldn't do a thing," Dracula snarled angrily, and Leticia shrugged.

"If you stay and he wakes up, he will definitely do *something.* Are you going to risk being attacked by my husband just for some time alone with me?"

Dracula didn't reply.

"You should go," Leticia said quietly. "I don't want a confrontation,

Dracula. Westley's going to wake up in less than five minutes, when he realises I'm not asleep or in bed. Go."

Dracula took her hand. "Promise me I may see you again."

"I don't have to promise. You already know we'll see each other," Leticia replied, and Dracula smiled and pressed her hand to his mouth in a kiss before he dissolved into thin air, gone.

Westley mumbled in his sleep, rolling over. "Leticia…"

"I'm here," she said softly, and he lifted his head to look at her.

"What woke you?"

"Count Dracula," she replied honestly, and Westley said "What!"

He got out of bed, furious. "Where is he now?"

"Gone," Leticia said gently. "He wanted to talk about Spirit and Virginia."

"And he chose to come when you were pretty much alone," Westley said, annoyed. "If anything happened to you-"

"Dracula wouldn't harm me, Westley." Leticia sighed and got back into bed. "Let's go back to sleep."

* * *

It was nearly five in the morning.

Jeiklee walked Spirit back to her bedroom, Spirit stifling a yawn behind her hand before she said "We're going to be exhausted."

"Good thing we don't have to go to Thrill," Jeiklee agreed, and they stopped at her bedroom door. "Well… um…"

Spirit smiled as he struggled to say something else. Taking his hand gently, she said "Good night, Jeiklee."

"Yeah. Night," he said embarrassedly, then he kissed her gently on the cheek, making her shiver as he said "Sleep tight, Spirit."

"You too," she said softly, then she stepped inside her room and closed the door.

Jeiklee smiled and made his way to his room, his smile growing as he slipped into bed. He knew Spirit felt something for him, even if it was a little something.

Still smiling, he fell asleep.

* * *

Leticia smiled at Westley over her cup of tea. "Spirit and Jeiklee are practically passed out. They must have been up until-"
"Almost five a.m., My Lady," Antonio said amusedly as some maids entered the dining area with platters holding their lunch. "I was up for a moment when I heard them go to bed, before I fell asleep again. I checked the time. It was past four in the morning."
Westley laughed, Leticia smiling amusedly as he said "Wake them at two, Antonio."
"Yes sir."

* * *

Jeiklee snapped awake at the sound of a horn blowing. "What the-!!"
"Apologies Master Inferno," Antonio said, though he looked highly amused. "Your parents ordered me to wake you and Miss McKenzie at two p.m. It's five past."
"Ok," muttered Jeiklee as he slumped back on his pillow, closing his eyes. "I'm up…"
The horn blew again, Jeiklee startled as he tumbled out of bed.
"I said I'm up, Antonio!"
"Good, sir. Ready yourself and come down for something to eat."
"All right. I'm coming."

* * *

Spirit smiled as Jeiklee sauntered into the dining hall, rubbing his ears.
"You got the horn, didn't you?"
"Yeah," pouted Jeiklee. "Like six times."
"You should have got up the first time," said Spirit amusedly. "I learnt that the hard way."
Jeiklee smiled back, sitting at the table. "I'm starving."
"Me too. Mmm, bacon."
Jeiklee helped himself to the food set before them, Spirit as well. They ate in silence for a bit, then Jeiklee asked "Do you really think Bruce Finnegan will leave you alone now?"
"No," shrugged Spirit. "He'll probably be as twice as cruel as he was before. You saw how he was in the crowd that time."
Jeiklee scowled. "Yeah."
"Him and his stupid group of friends will probably pick on me at Thrill, and Virginia of Dracula will as well. But I don't think she'll hex me for a while."

Jeiklee nodded as he helped himself to baked beans. "If it gets out of hand-"

"I can handle myself," smiled Spirit. "Don't worry."

Jeiklee smiled back. "All right, if you're sure."

Westley and Leticia entered the dining hall, smiling at them.

"Good afternoon."

"Good afternoon," Jeiklee and Spirit responded, Leticia saying "Jeiklee, I want you to practise every spell or charm you know in the garden. You must strengthen all of them. The students at Thrill have had all month to do so, so for the rest of this week you must practise."

"Yes Mum."

"Spirit can help you," Leticia replied, "And I will also supervise."

"Ok. Dad?" said Jeiklee, noticing the sword in Westley's belt as he stood. "Are you going hunting?"

"I am, son. In the Forest of Fear."

"Whoa!" said Spirit, impressed. "Can I come, Westley? Please? I won't slow you down."

"Spirit, you're not ready for this kind of hunting-"

"Ok, I won't hunt! I'll just be there," Spirit said eagerly. "Please let me come, Westley!"

"Well it won't be fair if you come on a hunting trip with me and Jeiklee has to stay at home," Westley said, pondering the idea. "Jeiklee? Would you like to come also?"

"Yes please!" gushed Jeiklee, and Leticia laughed.

"You will need your own weapon and armour, Jeiklee, if you want to enter the Forest of Fear."

"I'll get my bow and arrow," Spirit said excitedly. "Jeiklee, maybe you should get a sword."

Jeiklee gaped. "My own sword??"

"Of course," smiled Westley. "You are an Inferno, and Spirit is as good as. She is very skilled with her bow and arrow and other weapons, due to my and Leticia's training her."

Jeiklee nodded. "I know, sir."

"If you were raised in Severna we would have trained you just as we trained Spirit," smiled Leticia, and Jeiklee quickly said "I want to be trained with weapons too! Can I be trained?"

"Of course you can," Leticia replied, "When the weapon chooses you."

"I- what?"

"The weapon chooses you," explained Spirit. "Like, I used to practise with swords and I was really good, but something about the bow and arrow hooked me the moment I laid eyes on it. And when I felt the bow, touched the arrows, I knew it was the weapon for me."

"Wow." Jeiklee was amazed. "Mum? What about you?"

"Any weapon I come into contact with I am the master of," smiled Leticia, and Jeiklee's jaw dropped.

"Any weapon?? Seriously?!"

Westley and Leticia burst out laughing, Spirit saying "Nobody would want to get on the wrong side of your mother or father, Jeiklee."

"This is nuts," Jeiklee said amazedly. "So… will I be skilled with weapons like you and Dad, Mum? Did I inherit that power?"

"I'm not sure just by looking at you, sweetie. Come here, take my hands." Jeiklee got up nervously, Leticia holding out her hands, which lit bright blue as he neared her. Jeiklee stopped, staring at her hands.

"Don't be afraid," Leticia said gently. "You have a combined aura of both mermaid and dragon, from me and your father. You are powerful, Jeiklee."

"I am?"

"You are," said Westley, nodding. "Take your mother's hands."

Jeiklee took Leticia's hands in his, then he gasped as the blue light ran up his arms, circling them until his arms were glowing bright blue.

"You have indeed inherited great power from myself and Westley," Leticia said softly. "I sense my father's power in you also, Jeiklee. A strange power which made many fear and adore him, and I also."

"The Force?" Westley asked amazedly. "Jeiklee has the Force within him? Like you?"

"Yes," Leticia said softly, letting her son's hands go. "He is powerful."

Jeiklee took a step back, a little lost. "I'm powerful?"

His parents and Spirit nodded, smiling.

"Wait. So… will I need to train? And what's the Force?"

"Well, you will have to stay at Thrill for an hour longer than usual to learn about the Force and also learn to use it," Leticia replied. "I had to do the same thing until the Elders thought I was ready to continue without their guidance."

"The Elders?"

"These wise folk," Spirit said. "They're immortal. They live above us, far up in the sky. I guess one will come down to guide you and teach you everything you need to know about the Force."

"You know a lot," pouted Jeiklee, and Spirit laughed, Leticia saying "Many have tried to develop the power of the Force within them, Jeiklee. Sometimes they succeed, but not many do. Either you are born with the power, or you spend a very long time attaining it. It's very fascinating to many in Severna."

"Wow," said Jeiklee. "Um… so… *wow.*"

Everyone laughed, Westley saying "Come, son. Time to let a weapon choose you."

* * *

Jeiklee stared around at many weapons, but none of them seemed to pull him.

"The bow and arrow is handy," Leticia told him softly. "Especially if you are being attacked from far."

Jeiklee cautiously touched the bow, and suddenly his hands grew lukewarm. He looked at Leticia and Westley, saying "I think it wants me to choose it. My hands are warmer."

"Put your hands over the arrows," Spirit told him, "But don't touch them." Jeiklee obeyed, holding his hands over the arrows. His hands grew warmer, and he said "Yep, it definitely wants me."

"Ask if they do," Spirit said, and he frowned at her. "Whisper it. If you have a connection with the bow and arrow, you'll know the answer."

Jeiklee took a deep breath, then he whispered "Have you chosen me?"

The arrows shot up into his hands, the bow rising into the air and coming to him as well.

"Great!" said Spirit happily. "I'll teach you everything to do with the bow and arrow, Jeiklee."

"I feel like I already know everything," Jeiklee said amazedly, and Leticia said "Maybe you are already skilled because I am automatically the master of any weapon. You truly have inherited a lot from myself and your father."

Jeiklee smiled at her, and she smiled back, love in her eyes for her only son. Westley was proud too, his eyes twinkling though his face was calm.

"Choose your secondary weapon, son."

"Yes Dad."

Jeiklee looked around, then he saw it. "Whoa!"

The sword seemed to glow as he stared at it, brighter and brighter.

"It definitely chose you," said Spirit, amused. "Go and touch it."

Jeiklee obeyed, walking towards the weapon slowly. He ran his hands over the sword, smiling as he said "I like this sword."

"Pick it up," Westley replied, and Jeiklee lifted the sword up, then he demonstrated some acts of fighting with it, Leticia impressed. So were Spirit and Westley.

"You already know how to use it?"

"Yes Dad," Jeiklee said, "But I still want to train with it. And with the bow and arrow."

"And with spells and hexes," Leticia reminded him, Spirit saying "We can stay here if you like, Jeiklee. You can train with me in the garden."

"That's a good idea," Westley said, nodding. "When you're ready, I will take both of you with me into the Forest. For now, stay and train."

Jeiklee and Spirit nodded. "Yes sir."

Westley smiled and vanished, Leticia saying "Take your weapons, Jeiklee.

Keep them in your room until you're ready to practice with them. For now, focus on strengthening your powers."

"Ok."

* * *

"Steady, Jeiklee," Leticia said softly, Jeiklee holding both hands up. They were glowing bright yellow. "Stay focused."

Jeiklee concentrated on the hovering piano, trying to keep his mind on it, but he could smell Spirit's flowery scent as he made the piano remain in the air.

He shut the thought of her out completely, and the piano stopped leaning to one side, becoming steady in the air.

"Good," Leticia said approvingly. "Now, gently lower your hands."

Jeiklee obeyed, the piano sinking.

"Slowly," Leticia said gently, and Jeiklee lowered his hands bit by bit until the piano hit the grounds of the garden with a soft *clunk.* "Excellent."

Spirit smiled. "Piece of cake, right Jeiklee?"

"It is when I shut out all distractions," Jeiklee replied as he smiled back, and she averted her gaze self consciously, Leticia saying "Repeat the Hovering and Lowering Charms a few more times, then you can take a break, Jeiklee. Afterwards you can start practicing spells and hexes with Spirit."

"It's crunch time," Spirit added with a grin, and Jeiklee grinned back. "I'm ready."

"Good," Leticia said, amused. "Now I'm going into my Chamber of Serenity, and I will be there for the rest of the afternoon until dinner. Both of you keep out of trouble."

Spirit nodded. "Yes Leticia."

"Yes Mum," said Jeiklee, and Leticia vanished on the spot, Spirit saying "Ok, time to make the piano hover again. We need your hands to glow a deep orange or even red."

Jeiklee nodded. "Ok."

"Yellow isn't bad though," Spirit said reassuringly. "If it was white I'd be worried."

Jeiklee smiled at her, then he focused on the piano his mother summoned.

"This isn't hard, you know. It's all about control," Jeiklee said, as he levitated the piano.

Spirit nodded, answering "You just need to learn to fully block out all distractions. Everything else aside from your target is minor."

"You're not minor," Jeiklee said before he could stop himself, and Spirit smiled at him.

"Thanks, Jeiklee."

"Actually I take that back," Jeiklee said softly. *"You're* my target, Spirit...
so everything else really is minor."

Spirit gazed at him, grey eyes on green eyes. Jeiklee dropped the force he
had on the piano, and it clunked to the ground as he slowly walked towards
her.

Spirit backed three or four steps, then she nervously stood her ground as
Jeiklee came closer.

"We um... we should keep training," she mumbled, when he stopped in
front of her, then he gently lifted a hand to caress her cheek. "Jeiklee-"

"Shh," he said softly. "Do you really want to be just friends, Spirit?"

"Well... I... um-"

"If it's yes," Jeiklee said just as softly, "I'll back off. But I don't think you
really do. I see the way you look at me when you think no one's looking."

"I see the way you look at me too," Spirit said quietly, and he smiled. "But
people at Thrill and out of it will know-"

"Know what?"

"Know if we get involved with each other," Spirit said softly. "And they'll
talk-"

"Let them talk," whispered Jeiklee, and he lowered his mouth to hers in a
slow, drugged kiss before she could reply. Spirit pulled him closer urgently,
and Jeiklee knew she was dying to be kissed by him, held by him. He could
feel it.

Spirit gasped and pulled away, sensing something. She whipped round to
stare at the garden wall curiously, wondering if Bruce Finnegan had come
back.

"What's wrong?" asked Jeiklee, and Spirit replied "Someone was there. I
could feel... something. Not their presence, but... something else. I know
someone was definitely there. Or something."

"I know," shrugged Jeiklee, and she gaped at him.

"You know??"

"Well, I could sense it," shrugged Jeiklee, "But I didn't care."

"But whoever it was could tell everyone we were kissing-"

"All right. Let's go back in time and see who it was," said Jeiklee, and this
time she said nothing, just stared at him. Then she said "Go back in time."

"Yep."

"You know how to travel back in time."

"Well... sort of. It's the Force within me," shrugged Jeiklee, and Spirit
started pacing the garden.

"You know people who have the power of the Force are feared for their
knack of being able to travel back and forward in time as well as loads of
other things?"

"Yes," said Jeiklee with a pout. "Don't tell me you're scared of me? My
mother already said I have the power of the Force and you even said who

the Elders were."

"I know, but-"

"So come on. Let's do it," said Jeiklee with a smile. "We can go back about ten minutes-"

"Too far back."

"Okay, seven or six minutes," said Jeiklee. "Then we'll see whoever it was."

"And then what?" said Spirit, amused. "We grab them and make them swear not to talk?"

"We can't do that. It's tampering with time," Jeiklee replied. "I mean, they can't spot us kissing in the garden and turn and find us next to them. It wouldn't make sense- and it would be real confusing."

"That's why you can't tell anyone you have the power of the Force," Spirit said. "The Elders won't be able to protect you from the people of Severna, and neither will Westley or Leticia."

"Don't people know my mother has the power of the Force??"

"They know. And that's one reason they wouldn't want to get on the wrong side of her," smiled Spirit, and Jeiklee nodded. "Are we doing this or not?"

"I'm not sure. What if I get it wrong?"

"The power of the Force never goes wrong," Spirit replied, and Jeiklee shrugged and took her hand.

Antonio came into the garden just as they vanished in a flash of yellow light, making him gasp and stop dead, staring at the spot they disappeared.

"Oh no. Oh no oh no oh no- My Lady must know-"

Antonio knew what just happened, hurrying back into the mansion and down the massive corridors, down to the basement floor and down more corridors, until he reached the Chamber of Serenity.

He banged on the door, crying "My Lady! My Lady, come quickly!"

Leticia morphed in front of him, eyebrow raised. "What is it, Antonio?"

"Time," panted Antonio. "Master Inferno used the power of the Force and went back in time with Miss McKenzie!"

Leticia stared at him, then she teleported to the garden, looking around curiously.

Spirit and Jeiklee were gone.

"Antonio, fetch my travelling cloak," she said firmly, when Antonio caught up with her, out of breath. "Also bring my sword and dagger. Jeiklee and Spirit are most likely in trouble."

* * *

"This isn't the garden," Spirit said, unnerved as she looked at the thick tangled trees surrounding them. "And this isn't safe either. I can feel dark energy."

"Me too," said Jeiklee. "What should we do?"

"Find a way out of here," Spirit replied, "Before nightfall."

"Why before nightfall?"

"Because I think we're in the Forest of Fear," Spirit said quietly. "And all the animals and dark creatures come out after dark. Even the trees come alive."

"What kind of dark creatures?" Jeiklee asked nervously. "Demons?"

"Demons, goblins, giant bugs. Snakes, rhinos, jaguars and wolves. Pretty much anything."

Jeiklee swallowed, then he said "Maybe we should find the mansion when we get out so we can see who was watching us-"

"That's all you're thinking?? Jeiklee, we're not in that time zone. Everything feels different," Spirit said as she looked at their surroundings. "I think you pulled us back years instead of just minutes. But we won't know for sure until we get out of here."

"All right, let's find a way out."

Spirit and Jeiklee started walking, for the first half hour in silence, then Jeiklee asked "Shouldn't we summon our weapons in case of anything?"

"Well-"

"Leticia!" called a voice, making them freeze. "Leticia, where are you?"

"I'm here, Father!"

Spirit pulled Jeiklee into the trees as plenty of men charged forwards from in front of them, then they saw a little girl run towards a man happily, her long black hair flowing behind her.

The man swept her up into his arms and cuddled her, then he scolded "Stay where I can see you, Leticia. It's getting dark- and we're in the Forest of Fear. Your mother would kill me if any harm came to you."

"Yes Father."

The man smiled and set Leticia down again, Spirit whispering "She's only ten! And that must be your grandfather!"

Jeiklee nodded, pulling Spirit farther back into darkness as another voice whispered "Hey!"

Ten year old Leticia whipped round, staring around. "Who said that?"

"It's me," the voice whispered, then Spirit and Jeiklee saw a pale boy appear before walking towards them.

"Dracula!" Overjoyed, Leticia ran towards him and hugged him tightly. "I missed you so much!"

"I missed you too," the eleven year old Dracula said shyly, and Leticia smiled before she said "Say aaah."

Dracula obeyed. "Aaah."

"Your fangs are getting longer!" exclaimed Leticia, and Dracula said "I know. My father will teach me how to make them look ordinary. But I can't for now because they're still growing, he said."

"Oh," said Leticia. "What are you doing here all by yourself?"

"Looking for you," Dracula said, and he sort of blushed. Jeiklee swore his snow white cheeks had turned a little pink.

"He had a crush on my mother since then??"

"Shut up!" hissed Spirit, and he closed his mouth as Dracula said "I came and knocked for you, and your mother said you was hunting with your father."

"Father let me come just this once," Leticia said, smiling at him. "And the Forest of Fear is massive! How did you find me?"

"You're my soul mate, remember? I always know where you are," Dracula said shyly, and Leticia's father called "Leticia! Time to go!"

Dracula smiled. "See you later, Leticia."

"Bye," smiled Leticia, then she stood on tiptoe and kissed him on the cheek before she turned and ran back to the crowd of men.

Spirit waited until Dracula dissolved into thin air before she said "This is crazy. We've definitely gone plenty of years back."

"Should I try and bring us a few years forward?"

"I'm not sure," Spirit said cautiously. "You might bring us too far forward just how you brought us too far back."

"Well what do you want to do?"

"I'm not sure," Spirit repeated, then Jeiklee frowned as a thought hit him. "Jeiklee? What's up?"

"You said the power of the Force never goes wrong," Jeiklee said, and Spirit nodded. "How sure are you about that?"

"Ninety five percent," Spirit replied. "I was a hundred percent sure before we ended up here."

"Right, so what if it didn't go wrong at all?" asked Jeiklee, and she frowned at him.

"What do you mean?"

"I mean what if we're *meant* to be here. What if for some reason we were brought here?"

"What possible reason could there be for being brought here?" demanded Spirit, and Jeiklee said "I'm not sure, but I feel like it was meant to happen."

"We should find shelter," Spirit said, deciding not to answer that. "I'll find some firewood."

"Want me to do anything?"

"Summon our weapons," Spirit replied as she looked around. "I'll need to chop some tree branches before they come alive. It's soon going to get dark."

"You weren't joking about the trees coming alive?" Jeiklee said nervously, and Spirit said "No I wasn't. Now summon our weapons."

* * *

Leticia appeared in the Entrance Hall, panting.

Westley stood and teleported to her, Antonio hurrying towards her as well.

"Did you find them, Leticia?" Westley asked urgently, and she took a deep breath before she managed "Water, Antonio."

"Yes My Lady." Antonio waved his hand and a goblet of ice cold water appeared, Leticia taking it with a weak thank you.

Westley waited anxiously as she drank, then she gave the goblet to Antonio before she said to Westley "I found nothing. Not a trace of them. I jumped years forward, years back- it was hopeless. I need to know the exact year they travelled to before I will be able to find them."

"Are there no clues?" asked Westley. "Maybe we should ask around. Someone near the garden side of the mansion may have heard their conversation before Jeiklee used the power of the Force."

"That's a good idea," Leticia said, and Antonio said "I will run the errand, My Lord and Lady. My Lady, you must rest. I can tell you are very weak."

"My power is drained," Leticia said softly. "I'm afraid I won't be of much use psychically, Westley. I'm sorry."

Westley drew her into his arms and kissed her forehead.

"Don't apologise, Leticia. Just rest," he murmured. "Let me take you to our suite. Antonio will tell us of his findings later."

* * *

"It's getting dark," Jeiklee said nervously. "Do we have enough firewood?"

"Yep. Of course." Spirit smiled at him. "Thanks for summoning our weapons. I didn't think you'd be able to."

Jeiklee grinned. "Don't underestimate me, Spirit McKenzie."

Spirit couldn't help thinking he looked gorgeous. "Um… this clearing should be ok for us. We'd better light the fire and get warm."

"What about food?" asked Jeiklee. "We're going to be starving by this time tomorrow."

"Well we can't eat anything from the Forest. Unless it's fruit."

"Are you sure?"

"I'm sure," said Spirit, nodding. "The trees grow things at night to entice you. Bread, hot dogs, burgers. Whatever appeals to you."

Jeiklee frowned. "Isn't that a good thing?"

"Not when they're laced with poison," Spirit said, amused. "Think, Jeiklee. Do you really think a tree would grow a hot dog you could eat?"

"I have no idea," said Jeiklee honestly. "In Severna, everything is magical. So I wouldn't be surprised if a tree did grow a tasty hot dog."

"Well you're right in a sense. The food is fine but only in the light of day. The moon will soon be out," Spirit said, placing another branch on top of the pile of wood they gathered. *"When darkness comes and it is night, pray to be safe until the coming of light."*

Jeiklee frowned at her. "Where did you get that from?"

"It's an old warning about the Forest of Fear," Spirit replied, "For those brave enough to enter here."

"Oh. That doesn't make me feel good at all," admitted Jeiklee, then a gentle breeze blew, ruffling his clothes and making him shiver. "It's getting cold."

"Sit down," Spirit said gently, and he obeyed. "I'll light the fire."

"Great."

* * *

Leticia mumbled something in her sleep, Westley watching her anxiously. She was glowing a deep yellow as she laid in slumber.

Antonio knocked on the door of their suite timidly. "My Lord and Lady?" Leticia snapped awake, and Westley uttered a curse word as he stood and opened the door to their vizier.

"You woke Leticia, Antonio. This had better be good."

Leticia stood, rubbing her forehead. "How long have I been asleep?"

"For about six hours," Westley replied, and she nodded. "How do you feel?"

"Still a little drained. What did you find, Antonio?"

"My Lady, Julius Charter told me he heard Master Inferno and Miss McKenzie speaking of going back in time to find a spy."

Leticia frowned, Westley as well. "Find a spy?"

"Someone who was watching them, apparently," Antonio said thoughtfully. "He came to see how they were doing, and that's what he overheard. I asked if he actually saw anything, and he said no. He said he popped his head over the wall just as they vanished into thin air."

Westley cursed again. "So now we have to find this spy Spirit and Jeiklee went searching for. Didn't Julius hear why they had to find them?"

"He said Master Inferno and Spirit meant to go back roughly ten minutes to stop the spy from spying," Antonio said, and Leticia frowned again.

"Did Julius say what time that was?"

"No My Lady."

"If they were planning to go back in time for ten minutes then it was roughly ten minutes before they vanished," Westley said, and Leticia nodded. "Do you think you could go back to then, Leticia?"

"I could, but I warn you I will be weak again. My powers aren't fully restored," Leticia said, and Westley said ok. Leticia took a deep breath, then she vanished.

* * *

Jeiklee snapped awake, reaching for his sword. "Spirit?"

Spirit slept on, her bow and arrow close by. Jeiklee could hear growling.

"Spirit!" he hissed, and Spirit stirred. "Spirit, wake up!"

"What's the matter?" she mumbled, and he whispered "There's something out there!"

"You think? We're in the Forest of Fear, Jeiklee." Spirit yawned, sitting up. "There's *always* something out there."

"Well I don't like it. We'd better get out of here."

"We're fine," Spirit replied, and Jeiklee noticed a pair of gleaming red eyes staring at them through the gloom of the shadows.

"Look! Those eyes!"

"Jeiklee, relax, ok? The dark preys on fear. Take a deep breath and just chill. Look deep into those red eyes and firmly say you're not afraid."

Jeiklee obeyed, looking straight into the gleaming eyes and hesitantly saying "I'm not afraid of you."

The eyes gleamed brighter, and he saw the whites of razor sharp teeth.

"I don't think it's working, Spirit-"

"Pick up your sword and say it again."

Jeiklee picked up his sword, which began to glow at his touch. Feeling bolder, he repeated himself: "I'm not afraid of you."

The eyes vanished, and they heard the pounding of paws as whatever it was went away. Jeiklee breathed out, Spirit saying "See?"

Jeiklee nodded. "So I can't be fearful because the dark preys on fear."

"Pretty much."

Jeiklee nodded, placing his sword down. "Ok. You don't think I'm a wimp?"

"Of course not," Spirit said softly. "Want some fruit to keep you until daylight?"

"Yes please."

Spirit handed him some fruit before she settled back down by the fire, on her side. Jeiklee peeled an orange thoughtfully, then he said "So why do you think we've been brought to the past?"

"Because you weren't trained and you brought us accidently," Spirit replied, and he pouted at her.

"I don't think it was an accident. I told you that."

"Ok, so if we're in the past for a reason," Spirit said, "What the hell is the reason? All we saw was Count Dracula and Leticia-"

"That's it," Jeiklee said, realising. "We've been brought here because of them."

"What about them exactly?" asked Spirit, frowning. "Leticia has nothing to do with Count Dracula. At all."

"But she did once," Jeiklee pointed out. "When they were kids. I think we might find out a few things about him-"
"Or her."
"Or both," agreed Jeiklee. "I know we're here for a reason."
Spirit sighed her ok. "Let's go back to sleep."

* * *

"Nothing," sighed Leticia. "At all."

Westley swore frustratedly. "Anything could have happened to them! We need to call upon the Elders. They could locate Spirit and Jeiklee wherever in time they are and bring them home."

"No word on the spy, My Lady?" asked Antonio, and Leticia said "Spirit and Jeiklee were talking about it, like Julius said. Then they were gone."

"And you didn't see or hear the spy's name?" asked Westley, and Leticia said no. "All right. Antonio, tell the Chef we're ready to eat."

"Yes sir."

"I'm so worried about them, Westley," said Leticia, eyes filling over. "We've only just got our son back. To lose him again-"

"Don't worry too much, Leticia." Westley pulled his wife into his arms and held her close. "Jeiklee is tougher than you think. And so is Spirit. If the worst comes to the worst, we'll call upon the Elders."

Leticia nodded her ok.

* * *

"Jeiklee!!"

Jeiklee snapped awake, reaching for his sword immediately. "What??"

"You're glowing," Spirit said, unnerved. "Glowing yellow!"

Jeiklee glanced down at himself, then he scrambled to his feet, feeling something odd was about to happen.

"Spirit, grab your stuff and take my hand."

"What?"

"Quickly! I think I'm about to jump through time again-"

Spirit quickly grabbed her bow and arrow and joined him, Jeiklee taking her hand.

A gentle breeze passed through the clearing, and Spirit closed her eyes, Jeiklee as well as they waited for the breeze to pass. When it did, they opened their eyes and looked around curiously.

"There," hissed Spirit as she spotted Leticia, thirteen years of age, and they saw fourteen year old Dracula appear in front of her. Jeiklee and Spirit backed into the trees as he smiled at Leticia, saying "What was he like?"

"Who?"

"The Count of Severna's son," Dracula said amusedly. "You was meant to meet him today, remember? At the Severna mansion with your parents. Didn't you go?"

"I did," said Leticia, biting her lip, and Dracula said "So what was he like? Won't you say?"

"He's really nice," Leticia admitted. "I thought he'd be a bit…"

"Big headed?" smiled Dracula, and Leticia said "Yes. Everyone knows his family and he's always having dinner with the King and Queen and his parents."

"Everyone knows you too," Dracula pointed out. "You're practically royalty just like the Count and Countess of Severna. Your family name enhances you and is one to be proud of. That's why the Count wants you to be his son's wife just like many other families do." Leticia nodded, and Dracula added "Loads of men have come forward offering their sons to be your future husband."

"I know."

There was silence for a minute, then Dracula said "So Westley Inferno is really nice?"

"Yes," Leticia said. "Me and my parents will start having family meetings with his family, at least twice a week. Mother said this is what she's been waiting for my whole life."

"But it's years before you have to marry him," shrugged Dracula. "And you don't have to anyway, not if you don't want to."

Outraged, Jeiklee whispered "She's just a kid!"

"Shh!" Spirit whispered back, and they saw Dracula put his arm around Leticia.

"We won't stop being friends because of him, will we?"

"No way," smiled Leticia. "We'll always be best friends."

Dracula smiled back, and Leticia laid her head on his shoulder.

"Dracula?"

"Mmm?"

"You won't be like your family, will you?"

Dracula looked down at her. "You mean… evil?"

Leticia nodded, and Dracula shrugged.

"I haven't any reason to be."

"People already think you're evil," Leticia told him, and Dracula replied "People are quick to judge me because of my family's actions in the past."

"But what about the future? Will you be like the other vampires?"

"No," he said firmly, and Leticia said "You're just fourteen, though. You might when you're older."

"Even so, I wouldn't do a thing to harm you." Dracula stroked her hair. "I promise."

Jeiklee was moved. Spirit wasn't impressed.

"We'll always be friends," Dracula added softly, and Leticia nodded.

"We'll be friends forever."

That magical breeze passed again, and Spirit and Jeiklee were back in their clearing.

The sun was out.

"So they were friends when they were kids," Jeiklee said thoughtfully.

"When did they become enemies?"

"Leticia doesn't see him as an enemy," shrugged Spirit, and Jeiklee said "Well he's definitely my Dad's enemy."

"I know."

Jeiklee looked around before he sat down, getting comfortable in the clearing. Spirit did the same, placing her bow and arrow down.

"So what do we do now?"

"Train?" Jeiklee suggested, and she looked at him.

"Train?" He said yes. "Here in the Forest?"

"We may as well strengthen our powers while we're out here," shrugged Jeiklee, and she smiled at him.

"You mean strengthen *your* powers."

"Yep. You can be my coach," smiled Jeiklee, and Spirit laughed.

"I was pretty much your coach anyway."

"All right." Jeiklee smiled broadly. "Coach me."

* * *

Almost five hours later, Jeiklee was exhausted.

Spirit had coached him and pushed him further and further until every spell and hex he casted was the colour orange, the Fire Bone and Burn hexes such a deep orange Spirit said they could pass as red.

"We'd better get food," she said, and Jeiklee shook his head. "What's up?"

"I don't think I can move," he muttered as he laid down by the fire. "I feel real drained."

"All right, I'll go get us something. Don't move and stay on your guard." Jeiklee said ok, and Spirit left the clearing.

Jeiklee stared at the flames of the fire flickering, wondering how his parents were- his *real* parents. Leticia and Westley Inferno.

He hoped they weren't worrying too much about where he and Spirit were. Ten minutes later Spirit came back into the clearing, saying "There were bottles of soda and juice on one tree, and bread and meat on the others."

"No butter?" smiled Jeiklee, and she smiled back. "Bread and meat is fine, Spirit."

"Ok." Spirit handed him his food and drink before she sat opposite him, looking deep in thought as she ate.

"What are you thinking?" asked Jeiklee, and Spirit said "Nothing, I…"

She trailed off, and Jeiklee asked "Are you worried about the person who saw us kissing?"

"It's probably around the whole of Severna now," Spirit said quietly, "And that means Leticia and Westley know too. They'll be real disappointed with me."

"No they won't," Jeiklee said reassuringly. "And if they are, I'll tell them

I made the first move and it's what I want."

Spirit glanced at him. "What is?"

Suddenly Jeiklee felt shy, Spirit looking at him curiously.

"Jeiklee?"

Jeiklee swallowed, then he quietly said "I want to be with you."

Spirit stared at him, but before she could say something he said "Don't start giving me the cold shoulder by saying you want to be friends and it's incest. I know you want me and you have done for a while." He smiled at her as he said "I want you as well. Just don't shut me out, Spirit. Please."

Spirit's eyes filled over and she quickly glanced at the fire before she nodded. Jeiklee's heart leapt as she said "We'll see how it goes. I'm not saying we're together, but…"

She smiled at him, but Jeiklee's heart was pounding as he asked "But what?"

"But I'm not saying I want to be just friends."

"Good," smiled Jeiklee. "Let's have dinner and rest."

An hour later they were laying looking up at the stars, Jeiklee holding Spirit's hand. Spirit snuggled up to him in a surprising move, and Jeiklee smiled and put his arm around her.

"You still worried about what people will say about me and you?"

"No," Spirit said softly. "I'm worried about what Westley and Leticia will think. I love them so much, I… I don't want to hurt or upset them."

Jeiklee was moved. "Is that why you don't want us to rush into anything? Because you're scared of their reaction?"

Spirit nodded. "A little. But I want us to take it slow. I rushed into things with Bruce Finnegan and ended up heartbroken. I'm not going through that again."

Bruce Finnegan again, Jeiklee thought to himself, then he said "I'm nothing like Bruce Finnegan, Spirit."

"I know," she said, "But you're just as popular."

Jeiklee was surprised. "Since when??"

"Since the mortals stole you," Spirit said, amused. "Years back. Everyone knows your story- I'm sure I told you that. And now you're back where you belong, everyone is dying to know you- and the young adults like us at Thrill can't wait for you to start."

"Well I'm not going to let popularity turn me into a jerk like that idiot Bruce Finnegan," Jeiklee said flatly, and Spirit smiled, closing her eyes.

"That's good to know."

"You going to sleep?" asked Jeiklee; she said yes. "Ok. Sweet Dreams, Spirit."

"Same to you."

* * *

Leticia woke up revitalised. "Westley?"

"Yes Leticia?" he said softly: he was sitting in a chair facing their bed. Leticia smiled at him, slightly amused.

"You were watching me sleep?"

"Of course." Westley smiled back, then he said "I don't want you to jump through time again. Not yet. You've only just restored your powers to the maximum."

"How can you tell?"

"Because you're glowing pure white," Westley replied, standing up. "Let's have something to eat, then we can put our heads together and figure out how to get our son and Spirit back."

* * *

Spirit grabbed her weapons and Jeiklee as he started to glow yellow, and Jeiklee put his arm around her as they waited to be pulled through time again.

Suddenly they were in dark tangled trees, Jeiklee backing away and pulling Spirit with him as a group of hunters traipsed past them, but they didn't seem to notice Spirit or Jeiklee.

"We're invisible," Spirit said quietly, and she took Jeiklee's hand. Jeiklee squeezed it gently as they heard a soft voice call "Dracula?"

They saw Leticia walk through some trees, looking stunning in a silver gown.

"Dracula, are you here?"

"I'm here," a voice said just as softly, and they saw Dracula materialise, arms open. "Come to me."

Leticia ran and hugged him, Dracula holding her tightly. He dropped a kiss on her forehead, eyes glimmering.

"I know we've been forbidden to see each other, but I had to see you," Leticia whispered. "Even for a small while."

"It's unfair," Dracula said angrily. "I'm not doing anything to hurt anyone, I just-"

"I know," Leticia said softly. "The Count and Countess are worried about our relationship. So is my mother. She's been preparing me for this my whole life."

"You don't have to go through with it, you know."

"Everyone expects me to. I can't just say I refuse to marry him-"

"Why not?" said Dracula, Leticia still in his arms. "If it's not what you want, Leticia-"

"I don't know what I want anymore," Leticia said miserably. "Me and Westley are close, but..."

"It's nothing like me and you," Dracula said quietly, and she nodded, eyes filling over. "Hey. Don't cry."

"I can't help it," Leticia said, weeping now. "I love you."

Jeiklee gasped, and Spirit hissed "Quiet, Jeiklee!"

"And I'll always love *you*, no matter what you choose," Dracula said, gently wiping her tears away. "I know you really like him. He's the future Count of Severna. And you're always together at Thrill. He makes you laugh, makes your eyes sparkle. He makes you happy."

"But-"

"I'll always be the outsider, the danger to you. The one who could ruin everything," Dracula said sadly. "They forget we grew up together. But your mother always wanted you to be with him."

Tears coursed down Leticia's face again.

"We could run away."

Dracula stared at her blankly as if she'd spoken another language. Then he said "Run away?"

"Yes," Leticia said, and Dracula sighed.

"Your father would find you easily. He has the power of the Force, remember?"

"Well I don't care. I have the power of the Force too," Leticia said angrily. "I'll use it against him if I have to."

"Your mother would never forgive me."

"You??"

"She would blame me," Dracula said. "She always does when you do something she doesn't like. 'That boy is a bad influence, Leticia. Cut all ties to him at once!'"

Leticia smiled through her tears. "She always says that. I never listen to her."

"Well I don't think we should run away," Dracula said as he put an arm around her. "It would stir things."

"But I want-"

"You're confused," Dracula said softly. "I love you too, more than you could imagine. And I know you love me. But I don't want you to be an outcast or ill spoken of because of me."

"But I don't care about that," Leticia said angrily. "I love Westley, I do. But I love you so much more."

"You'll love him just as much or even more over time," sighed Dracula. "I know you will."

He pulled Leticia into his arms before she could reply, gazing down at her. Leticia stared up at him, then suddenly they were mouth to mouth in a passionate kiss, arms around each other.

Around fifteen seconds later a voice yelled "Leticia!"

Leticia broke away quickly, both of them whipping round to stare as Westley Inferno and her father emerged from the trees, more men in tow.

"Leticia, you're safe," said her father, relieved as he pulled his child into his arms. "Your mother was mad with worry."

"I'm fine, Father. I promise," mumbled Leticia, and he kissed her forehead. "Thank you for keeping her safe, Dracula."

"Yeah," Westley said reluctantly, and Dracula said "I'll always keep her safe, sir. Um... I know we aren't allowed to see each other, but-"

"Nonsense," smiled Leticia's father. "I know you and I trust you. I always have. I don't know why everyone is suddenly wary of you being around my daughter."

Westley took Leticia's hand. "Are you all right?" Leticia nodded. "You're shaking."

"I'm a little cold," she said softly; immediately Westley took off his jacket and put it around her shoulders.

"Is that better?"

"Yes thank you. I'm fine." Leticia spoke quietly, not making eye contact.

"Are you sure you're all right?" Westley said uncertainly, and Dracula curtly said "She said she's fine, Inferno."

"Slink back to your castle, Dracula," Westley said icily in reply, and Leticia's father said "Don't start, you two. Leticia, let's get you home."

"Yes Father."

Westley took Leticia's hand as she quietly said "Goodbye Dracula."

"Goodbye Leticia," Dracula said just as quietly, and Leticia went away with her father and husband to be. Dracula sighed before he dissolved into nothing, gone.

A gentle breeze blew through the trees, and suddenly Jeiklee and Spirit were visible again.

Jeiklee was gaping. "My mother was in love with Count Dracula?"

"I always had a feeling," Spirit said, intrigued. "Not that they loved each other, but I always knew there was more to their relationship."

"Have you ever spoken to or asked her anything about it?"

"No," shrugged Spirit. "I never dared."

"Well we're being shown my mother's relationship with him," Jeiklee said. "For a reason, I think. Maybe when we get back to the present we can ask her about it."

"I think she shut out the memory of him," Spirit said gently. "It wouldn't be a good idea to bring everything back, Jeiklee."

"Ok, then we'll ask Dracula."

Spirit's jaw dropped. "Are you serious??"

Jeiklee said yes.

"We can't ask either of them," Spirit said flatly. "At least not for a while."

"Spirit, we're stuck in the past," Jeiklee said, "And we're finding out so much. We can't keep it to ourselves and we can't tell my mother or father about it. Not yet, anyway. Dracula's been made out to be this cruel, twisted, evil guy. By everyone. But after seeing how he was with my mother, I don't think he is at all."

"His daughter is," Spirit retorted, "And Count Dracula has ancestors who made history they were so evil. They all have some kind of link to Satan himself. They're cursed, Jeiklee. I can see why everyone wanted Leticia to keep away from him."

"But-"

Another gentle breeze blew, and Spirit quickly grabbed Jeiklee as he started to glow bright yellow. Jeiklee put an arm around her, saying "Here we go."

Westley Inferno sat talking to Leticia, in some kind of park or garden.

"Leticia, are you sure you're ok?"

"I'm fine," Leticia said softly. "It's just..."

"Dracula?" said Westley, and Leticia didn't reply. "I know you've been thinking about him."

"I just don't see why he's loathed," Leticia said quietly. "He hasn't done a thing to hurt anyone."

"His family has," Westley said gently. "And I know everyone shouldn't judge him based on that. But it's hard to forget. His grandfather murdered mine, you know. And my grandmother died of a broken heart."

"I know." Leticia sighed. "Forgetting him won't be as easy as my mother says it will."

Westley looked at her, surprised. "You mean you'll stop contact with Dracula after all?"

"Yes," Leticia said quietly. "I'll find it hard at first, but I suppose it's for the best."

"Are you sure that's what you want, Leticia?"

Leticia looked at Westley. "Why do you ask?"

"Because he means a lot to you. You grew up together," Westley said. "You're best friends."

"You're my best friend too," Leticia said softly, taking his hand. "I'm not saying I won't be a little sad. I will be. But it's you I want."

Westley lifted her hand to his mouth in a gentle kiss. "You're sure?"

"I'm sure."

"Well I'm going to do everything to keep you happy," Westley told her. "I'm in love with you and I probably will never fall out of it. You're amazing."

Leticia kissed him, touched. "I hope you think I'll be a reasonably good wife."

"I already think you'll be an excellent wife," smiled Westley. "Everyone does."

"I'll always be loyal to you," Leticia said before kissing him again. "I promise."

Jeiklee heard a sharp intake of breath behind them, and he turned curiously. His jaw dropped as he saw Dracula dissolve into thin air in the trees, hidden.

That magical breeze blew again, and they were back in the Forest of Fear. "Dracula heard everything," he said, before Spirit could say anything. "I really feel sorry for him. Maybe that's why he's the way he is. Because Mum chose Dad after all."

"We should rest," Spirit said, yawning. "I'm tired, hungry and cold. Let's get back to the clearing and light a fire."

"The sun's still out," Jeiklee said as his stomach grumbled. "We can pick some food off the trees, right? They won't be full of poison until after dark."

Spirit nodded, and Jeiklee immediately seized about six meat samosas dangling from a tree branch.

"I'm starving."

Spirit smiled as she said "Collect as much food as you can, ok? I'm going to get some firewood. And be quick, Jeiklee. The sun will go down real fast."

Jeiklee nodded. "Meet you at the clearing."

* * *

Jeiklee walked into the clearing half an hour later, arms laden with food. "Here we go. Dinner is served!"

Spirit smiled as he sat down, the fire crackling merrily. "I'm starving."

"Well there you go. Hot dogs, samosas, fruit and some sandwiches for later tonight. I wasn't sure what you wanted," he added cautiously. "So I grabbed filling food."

"No problem," smiled Spirit. "We can talk about what we saw after we eat."

"And rest," Jeiklee added, and she nodded.

"Yep. I'm worn. Jumping through time wears you out."

"I hope Mum hasn't been jumping through time looking for us," Jeiklee said worriedly. "If she has, she must be exhausted."

"Sometimes Leticia goes back in time to view her memories," Spirit said, reaching for a hot dog. "It does make her a little tired. I hope she's all right. Leticia and Westley- they must be so worried."

"Well I'll find a way for us to get back," Jeiklee said before he bit a samosa. Swallowing after a moment of thoughtful chewing, he added "I promise."

Spirit smiled a little pityingly. "Jeiklee, you have no idea how to control the Force. You haven't had one lesson with an Elder or your mother. You don't know how to get back to the present and this time I can't help you. I feel bad about that."

"Don't feel bad, Spirit. I'm the dumb one," Jeiklee said, sighing. "I never should have used the Force. I didn't even know what I was doing," he admitted. "Not really. I just wanted to impress you and ease your mind about whoever saw us kissing."

Spirit sighed too. "I'm not bothered about that anymore. I just want to get back home."

Jeiklee nodded. They both ate in silence for a while, then Spirit said "I'll start the fire. It's getting dark and chilly."

Jeiklee said ok, and she said "We're running low on firewood. I'd better go get some more before the trees awaken."

"All right, I'll wait here."

Spirit smiled at him, then she caught herself and quickly left the clearing.

Jeiklee rolled onto his back, looking up at the sky. It was getting darker by the minute. He thought for a split second about life in England, his adopted parents, his friends. And as soon as he thought about them, Jeiklee knew he wouldn't go back even if he was paid a million.

"I belong in Severna," he muttered. "I always have."

"Indeed you have," a voice said, and Jeiklee leapt up, startled.

A woman in a white cloak was standing in the clearing, looking at him. Her golden hair fell around her shoulders, her blue eyes twinkling as she looked at him. She seemed to be glowing brightly.

Jeiklee stared at her, then he swallowed and asked "Who are you?"

"I am the Elder Samantha," she replied, as Spirit came back into the clearing with firewood. Spirit gasped when she saw the Elder, who said "Spirit McKenzie, you doubt the power of the Force."

"No," Spirit said quickly. "I was just unsure about why we've been brought here and why we're being shown things about Leticia and Count Dracula."

"Unsure is still a form of doubt," Samantha replied. "You were brought here for a reason."

"Told you," Jeiklee said triumphantly, and Spirit scowled at him. "Please Samantha, can you tell us the reason? And how can we get back to the present?"

"You will be brought back to the present in five days," Samantha said, a small smile on her face. "After you have seen what must be seen, realise what must be realised, and confront the situation."

"But Leticia has nothing to do with Dracula," Spirit said uncertainly. "I don't want her hurt or confused if we tell her or Westley what we saw."

"You love them, and I understand that," Samantha said kindly. "But Leticia and Westley Inferno are strong beings. They will not be hurt if you decide to tell them."

"Promise?" said Spirit, and the Elder replied "I promise."

Jeiklee nodded, then he asked "Will it be you who trains and teaches me about the power of the Force?"

"Yes," Samantha said, nodding. "Your mother will also guide you."

"Ok. Um… can you tell her I miss her and my Dad?" Jeiklee asked humbly. "And we'll be back in five days? I don't want them worrying."

"Of course," Samantha said. "Also, you needn't hide. You will not be sensed by anyone in the past nor will you be seen. Make sure you eat before nightfall and collect food. Try not to disturb the creatures here in the Forest and keep out of harm's way."

Spirit and Jeiklee nodded.

"That is all," the Elder Samantha said, and suddenly she was gone.

Spirit and Jeiklee looked at each other, and Jeiklee said "I knew we were here for a reason."

Spirit nodded. "Now I know it wasn't you who messed up. The Elders

brought us here. It's kind of an adventure, isn't it?"
"Yep."
"We'd better eat a bit more before we get pulled through time again," Spirit said, and he nodded. "Then we definitely should get some sleep."
"Ok."

* * *

"Five days?" said Westley, and the Elder Samantha nodded.

"Yes."

"Why so long?"

"Your son is learning whilst being away," Samantha said gently. "Also, he is with Spirit McKenzie. She has been of great help to Jeiklee."

"In what way?" asked Leticia quietly, and Samantha said "The animals in the Forest made him fearful. Spirit explained to him that the dark preys on fear, and Jeiklee understood. She has also been training him and making him practice the spells he knows. Now, he has mastered them all."

Leticia nodded, Westley still unsure about the situation.

"No longer than five days."

"No longer. You have my word," Samantha replied. "Jeiklee also wanted me to tell you both that he is missing you. Also, he doesn't want you to worry."

Leticia smiled, and so did Westley.

"Thank you, Samantha."

"You are most welcome," the Elder replied, and then she was gone.

Westley and Leticia looked at each other, then Leticia said "I feel more at ease knowing they are all right. I know Spirit won't let anything happen to Jeiklee and vice versa."

Westley nodded, then he smiled at her. "We have five days to spend together, alone. What would you like to do?"

"For now, spend time with my husband." Leticia smiled back. "Would you like to come with me to the spa? I was going to relax in the Jacuzzi and soak my aching bones. You can join me if you'd like."

Westley nodded. "I'd love."

* * *

Castle Dracula…

Count Dracula sat in an armchair, brooding. He was wondering what to do for the remainder of the day. He could go out for a walk and be thrown filthy looks from all over, he could meet with fellow vampires, or he could stay home and relax.

Before he could decide what do Virginia entered his study. "Father, I was reading about our kind in the library."

Dracula glanced at her. "And what are you curious about?"

"I'm curious about you and I not being affected by the sun," Virginia said, intrigued. "We don't burst into flames like the vampires in our history. Why is that?"

"Because we aren't like them," Dracula replied. "Our blood is much stronger, we are more powerful than regular vampires. We have a direct link to Satan himself. Do you think Satan would allow his blood to be destroyed by something so simple as the rays of the sun?"

Virginia shook her head. "No Father."

"Good. Now I hope that my answer has fed your curiosity. We cannot be destroyed by a simple crucifix, a splash of holy water, the rays of the sun, or a stake through the heart. So if you are worrying, you need not worry."

"Yes Father. What will you do today?"

"I'm not certain," Dracula said thoughtfully, and Virginia said "We could go to the Forest of Fear and meet the other vampires."

"I thought of that, but I'm not sure about it," Dracula said, and Virginia said "After I come back from Thrill, can we go Father?"

"Why don't you spend time with some of your friends in town after Thrill?" was Dracula's reply, and Virginia pouted. "We can go and see the other vampires at the weekend."

"You promise?"

"I promise," Dracula said with a smile, and Virginia smiled back before she left the study.

Dracula sighed, wishing things were how they used to be, years ago. He and Leticia were inseparable then. Even when they attended Thrill when they reached eighteen, she'd always make time for him. And now…

Anger surged through Dracula as he thought of Westley Inferno and how popular he was, how loved he was. Dracula knew it would never be the same for him back then, and he knew it wouldn't be the same now.

Leticia had shut the thoughts and memories of Dracula out completely, and was devoted to her husband… the husband she chose over him.

Dracula stood and walked to gaze out of his study window. He remembered Leticia's reaction to the fact he had met someone, another vampire like him, a female vampire with bright red hair and brown eyes, a vampire who loved him and gave him the love and attention he craved- but from Leticia. Leticia had wished Dracula all the best with Malinda the vampire with a smile on her face, she told him she was glad he had found someone, that she was happy for him.

But Dracula saw her eyes fill as she turned and walked away. He should have ran after her, wiped her tears away, held her in his arms and told her he loved her and would stop seeing Malinda if that's what she wanted.

But then he thought *why should I?* Leticia was with Westley Inferno, the future Count of Severna- she was going to marry him when they came of age regardless of what he felt for her. She chose Westley over Dracula, and that was that. So why shouldn't he be with Malinda of Brubeck? She was beautiful, and Brubeck the vampire, her father, insisted on them being together.

Dracula's father was unsure at first; he knew how his son felt about Leticia. Then he called Dracula down to meet the stunning girl. At first Dracula was very neutral, then Malinda took charge of the meeting, asking him a ton of questions and then telling him about herself.

And at the end of it, Dracula was very comfortable and could see no reason why Malinda couldn't be his bride. Dracula could have up to three brides if he wanted, but he wanted one.

"Just one?" his father had exclaimed, and Dracula had said "Yes. I don't want three Brides of Dracula. It won't look good, especially through the eyes of Leticia."

Dracula's father sighed. "How can you fully love Malinda of Brubeck if you're still thinking about Leticia of Sampson?"

"Sampson liked me," Dracula retorted, "And I do love Malinda, but why should I wear my heart on a sleeve with her? I did that once and look where it got me. Leticia is marrying that hotshot Westley and there is nothing I can do about it. Now drop the subject, Father. I beg you."

His father nodded then, but Dracula knew thoughts of the subject were whirring around his head still. He'd gone to Brubeck and he'd told him everything about Dracula and Leticia- and in a rage Brubeck had murdered him with a mix of serpent and scorpion venom, planted in his drink before beheading him, and swept Malinda away from Dracula just like that.

Only to return a year later with a bundle in a Moses basket, banging on the castle doors and forcing the basket into Dracula's servant's arms- Dracula never answered his castle doors himself.

The basket was carried to Dracula, and a curious Dracula read the note from Brubeck:

This belongs to you. My daughter is having

nothing to do with it or you, so take it or
throw it into the ocean, we do not care at all.
You are not to contact us about it.
We don't want to know.

Brubeck.

Curious, Dracula lifted the bundle of cloths- and screamed aloud, making the baby girl start crying, her green eyes startling, her red hair bright as the fire burning in the fireplace.

His servants came running as he stared at the baby, who stopped crying as soon as she locked eyes with him- and Dracula knew then that although his heart belonged to Leticia, a slice of it now belonged to his daughter.

"Buy everything you can for babies," he ordered his servants. "Milk, bottles- everything. Ready a room for her. She is my child and she must be comfortable."

"Yes Master."

A female servant named Nancy, one that had seen to Dracula when he was a child, asked "What will you call her, Sir?"

"Well I won't name her after her mother," Dracula said, heat rising. "Who abandons a child? A baby? Just because her father hates me? Malinda should have stood up to him- but she didn't. Coward!" he spat, his servants bristling nervously as the baby gurgled. Dracula gently picked her up and held her, saying "If she is not wanted by Malinda or Brubeck then she will have nothing to do with either of them. She is my responsibility."

"Yes sir," his servants responded, and Nancy said "And also mine, sir."

Dracula smiled at her. Nancy, a vampire, had even seen to his great grandfather when he was a baby. Centuries had passed but her age had not, and she was still fit as ever, a beautiful vampire of thirty five.

"Thank you, Nancy."

He stood deep in thought for while, still holding the baby. He remembered a time when he and Leticia were young, thirteen and fourteen, talking about children of their own one day.

"If I have a son I'm calling him Spartan," Dracula told Leticia as she swivelled a lolly in her mouth, and she smiled at him.

"If I have a daughter, I'm calling her Virginia."

Dracula frowned at her. "Virginia?"

"Yes," Leticia said, still smiling. "It's one of my favourite names now."

"Because of the Elder Virginia?" Dracula asked, and Leticia nodded.

"She's so pretty, Dracula. And she's a great teacher of the Force."

"I hope you take her back in time to see our discussion," smiled Dracula as he put an arm around her, their backs to a giant boulder. "She'll be pleased you want to name your baby after her."

"I hope so."

Dracula smiled as he remembered that, saying "I will call her Virginia."

His servants cheered, Nancy smiling as she said "Virginia of Dracula."

"Yes," Dracula said, smiling back. "She has her mother's hair, but my green eyes. I love her already and it hasn't even been three hours."

"Well she is yours, sir. You couldn't possibly feel anything aside from love."

And then three days later he heard.

The news was all over Severna- he couldn't possibly have missed it. Mortals had stolen Leticia and Westley's baby and for the safety of their world, they were powerless to get him back. The King had put his foot down about them taking the baby by force, and had told them to let the mortals raise the boy. Everyone was talking about it, furious. The King had forbidden any form of rescue mission from anyone in Severna, saying that the boy would come home when the time was right.

A tear fell from Dracula's eye that day. He wanted to comfort Leticia, assure her everything would be all right, that she could watch him in her Chamber of Serenity through her crystal ball, and go back in time using her powers to view his first moments, like walking, talking, going to school.

But he couldn't go near her, not with Westley hot on his heels. So he kept away for another year, tending to his own child, until he was sure the anger and sadness of what had happened had faded a little. Then, he visited her.

Leticia was in the garden, staring down at the pool thoughtfully. She looked even more stunning than he remembered, he had thought amazedly, then he took a deep breath and said "Leticia."

Leticia had glanced up, startled as he appeared, then she gasped "Dracula!"

"Come here," he said softly as he held his arms out; she didn't think twice about it as she ran to him, just like she did when they were children, and he pulled her into his arms, holding her to him and dropping a kiss on her forehead.

"It has been almost two years since I last saw you alone," he murmured, and she asked "Why didn't the manor's defences stop you from entering?"

"Because I am powerful," Dracula replied with a smile. "Did you forget?"

"I've had a lot going on," Leticia said quietly, and Dracula nodded.

"I know. I heard about what happened to your son."

"And I also heard about Malinda of Brubeck leaving you a daughter to raise alone," Leticia answered. "You must have been shocked."

"I was," admitted Dracula. "And I was angry with her and her father. I haven't heard from either since the baby was dropped on my doorstep. They truly want nothing to do with her."

"That is awful."

"I know."

They stood in silence, Leticia still in Dracula's arms. Then she softly admitted "I wanted to come and see you when I heard."

"I felt the same about you when I heard about your son," Dracula replied gently. "But I knew the anger with those mortals and the King's foolish law hadn't passed. You may have been too distressed to see me and Westley definitely would have taken his anger out on me."

Leticia nodded, and Dracula asked "Would you like to meet her?"

"Who?"

"My daughter."

Leticia opened her mouth, then she closed it and nodded. Smiling, Dracula held her closer before teleporting to his castle.

Baby Virginia was cuddling her doll, sitting up on a green mat. She beamed when Dracula appeared, saying "Daddy!"

Leticia stared at her, eyes filling over. "She has your eyes."

Dracula smiled and nodded. "She doesn't have my jet black hair, unfortunately. But she's still my beautiful baby vampire."

Leticia nodded, and the toddler got up unsteadily before tottering over to Dracula, lifting her arms.

Dracula picked her up gently, and Virginia looked at Leticia curiously, Dracula saying "Say hello, Virginia."

"Hello," Virginia said shyly, and Leticia whispered hello, before tears fell down her face.

Startled, Dracula handed the toddler to Nancy, who took her out of the room.

"Leticia?" She didn't reply. "Leticia, sweetheart. What's the matter?"

"I wish things were different," wept Leticia. "I wish I could have my own toddler back. He should be walking by now, just like Virginia. They may even have been friends like you and I were."

Dracula bit his tongue as he almost said he would go to the mortal realm and get her son back. But he didn't, because he couldn't. He was feared so he had no problem with breaking the law, because the King turned a blind eye where he was concerned- but the boy would be an outcast... because of him. Dracula couldn't let that happen. So he said nothing, and kissed Leticia on the forehead before gently wiping her tears away.

"Everything will be ok, Leticia. I promise."

Leticia nodded, then she said "I must get back. Thrill starts in two hours."

"Have lunch with me at Thrill," Dracula replied, and she said ok. Then she kissed him on the cheek before she whispered goodbye, and vanished.

Dracula dragged himself out of the reverie he was having as Nancy entered the room.

"Brooding again, Master?"

"Sometimes I cannot help but brood," Dracula replied with a smile, and Nancy smiled back. "What can I help you with?"

"Nothing, sir. I was just making sure you are all right."

"As you have been for how many years." Dracula's smile grew. "Would you mind making sure Virginia has supper when she returns from Thrill? I know she will be out later than usual, and I want her to eat well before she goes to sleep."

"Yes sir." Nancy bowed and left the room.

Dracula sighed and stood, deciding to go for a walk through the Forest of Fear. The cool air would clear his head a little.

He summoned his cloak and put it on, then two of his servants joined him as he left the castle, deep in thought about Leticia.

* * *

"Was we meant to see or hear that?" Spirit asked uncertainly as they appeared back in their clearing. "Dracula's thoughts and memories?"

"He really loved my mother," Jeiklee said, thoughtful as he sat down. "I think we need to understand that a bit more."

"We've got five days to come to some kind of realisation," Spirit said thoughtfully. "But I still don't think we should tell Leticia or Westley about it. Not until we figure out what to do."

"Ok," Jeiklee said, then he scowled. "Malinda of Brubeck is a heartless-"

"Maybe she knew her baby was evil," shrugged Spirit. "Or she knew she'd become evil. I'd have given her up too."

"Virginia was totally innocent," argued Jeiklee, "And even if Malinda *did* know she'd be evil it doesn't excuse her abandoning her baby. That's sick. If Virginia had a mother, she wouldn't be as cruel as she is. I know it."

"Are you done defending Virginia of Dracula?" Spirit asked coldly. "Because I'm done listening."

"You really hate her, don't you?" Jeiklee was annoyed at her attitude. "And you hate Count Dracula as well when you have no reason to!"

"They're evil, Jeiklee!"

"Did you not see all that?" Jeiklee demanded. "If Dracula was so evil he really *would* have tossed Virginia into the ocean when she was a baby. If he was evil, he wouldn't care so much about my mother!"

"And Virginia?" Spirit shot back. "What counter comment do you have to make about *her* being evil?"

"I think she's messed up, that's all," shrugged Jeiklee. "She needs a friend."

"Virginia has a ton of followers and admirers," Spirit said coldly, and Jeiklee said "Yeah, but do they know the real her?"

"Who would want to?!"

"You're just sore about her performing hexes on you and spreading rumours about you," Jeiklee said dismissively. "She needs a mate just like Dracula did when everyone turned away from him. My mother was his closest friend."

Spirit sighed. "You need to take off your sympathy goggles."

Jeiklee laughed; she smiled grudgingly.

"Well it's true."

"You think I'm too sympathetic about them?"

"Yep."

"Well I don't think that. I think they both need-"

"Help," Spirit cut across before he could finish. "They both need help. If Count Dracula loved Leticia, ok. But she didn't feel the same way-"

"She did and you know she did. You heard her say it," Jeiklee pointed out, Spirit pouting. "You saw that kiss. They loved each other."

"Well Leticia doesn't love him now."

"You don't know that," Jeiklee said flatly. "A woman's heart is an ocean of secrets."

"Stop quoting epic movies, Jeiklee!" Spirit burst out laughing. "Jeez!"

"All right, sorry. I'm just saying we have no idea how my mother felt or how she feels now. Maybe that's what we're going to figure out."

* * *

"Count Dracula, My Lord," a female vampire whispered from the trees, and Dracula stopped to look at her. "Have you come to join us for the night?"

"No. I'm just taking a walk," was Dracula's reply, and she smiled as he said "I will return at the weekend with my daughter."

"Yes sir."

Dracula continued to walk, raising a hand in reply when he was greeted by vampires and other creatures in the Forest.

He wanted to visit Leticia again. She had to face him at some point and address the situation, he thought to himself. She had shut him out for far too long just for the approval of her husband and the people of Severna. They had told her for years it was the right thing to do. But it wasn't.

Dracula sighed and stopped, his servants stopping with him.

"Sir?"

"Go back to the castle," Dracula told them. "I wish to be alone."

His servants hesitated, and he said "Do as I say."

"Yes my Lord."

His servants turned and walked back into the depths of the forest, Dracula sighing as he found the clearing he and Leticia always used to sit in together.

Dracula sat down, sighing again. "If only I could turn back time."

* * *

Leticia's stunning grey eyes suddenly turned bright blue, startling Antonio as he said "My Lady?" She didn't reply. "My Lady, are you all right?"

"Leticia," said Westley, and she looked at him, but she didn't speak. "Leticia, what's wrong? What can you see?"

Leticia could see Count Dracula, in their special clearing. But she wasn't going to tell her husband that. He wouldn't understand her need to see him. "Leticia," said Westley firmly, and she blinked, her eyes grey again. "Is everything ok?"

"Yes," she said quietly. "Antonio, fetch my cloak."

"Yes My Lady."

"Westley, I'm going for a walk. I have a slight headache and need to clear my head."

"You usually go into your Chamber of Serenity when you want to clear your head," frowned Westley, and she pouted at him.

"I'm not about to stay in on such a lovely day, Westley."

"Would you like me to come with you?"

"No," smiled Leticia, and Westley smiled back at her. "I won't be longer than two hours."

"All right."

Leticia smiled again as Antonio brought her cloak, and she put it on, saying "Are you still going to visit King Harlot this evening for dinner?"

"I was hoping to go with you," Westley admitted; Leticia laughed.

"All right. I'll see you soon."

She walked through the giant doors and was gone, Westley smiling dreamily.

"Sir?" said Antonio amusedly, and Westley looked at him. "My Lady still has a tremendous effect on you, doesn't she?"

"Yes," smiled Westley as he started to glow pink: a sign of how deeply in love he was. "My heart races when Leticia smiles at me, her voice calms me. I'd do anything for her."

* * *

Leticia walked through the tangled trees, glowing a soft baby blue. She hadn't been to the clearing in a long time, but she never forgot the way. It was her escape from everything, a place she found peace and comfort- because of the man sitting by their special boulder.

"Dracula," she said quietly; startled, he glanced up.

Dracula's jaw dropped and he quickly stood, saying "Hello Leticia."

"Hello."

They stared at each other for a moment, then Dracula asked "What brings you here?"

"I… I needed to clear my head."

And I needed to see you.

Dracula was amused. "You usually go into your Chamber of Serenity for such a thing."

Leticia opened her mouth to retort, then she closed it. "I know."

"So what really brings you here?" Dracula asked, and she replied "I had to get away for a while. And this is where I used to go as a child and teenager. It gives me comfort."

Dracula nodded. "I feel the same. Sometimes, when I come here, I half expect to hear you call my name."

Leticia smiled sadly. "If I could change everything, I would."

"You needn't change a thing," Dracula said softly. "Come, let me hold you. You always liked my cuddles, Leticia."

Leticia stared at him, then she walked towards him. Dracula pulled her into his arms and held her, lifting a hand and stroking her hair gently. Leticia closed her eyes as he murmured "I have missed you terribly."

"And I you," she whispered, and he smiled sadly.

"We were so close, Leticia."

"I know."

"Do you think if you hadn't obeyed your mother and the people of Severna things would have been different?"

"Yes," she admitted. "I did everything that was expected of me."

"I don't forget how trapped you felt," Dracula told her. "The pressure of everyone's orders and expectations. And I wouldn't have seen Malinda of Brubeck if only you told me how you felt about that."

"You knew how I felt, Dracula."

"Yes, but I wanted to hear it from you."

"And vice versa," Leticia replied, and he frowned at her. "I knew how you felt about me and Westley but I wanted to hear it from you also."

"And if we did tell each other?" asked Dracula, and Leticia sighed.

"Things definitely would have been different."

She closed her eyes as Dracula held her closer, and he whispered "I always thought of you."

"I know," Leticia said softly. "Dracula, I-"

"Shh." Dracula put a finger to her mouth. "What's done is done. So shall we pick up where we left off so long ago? Be close friends like before and more?"

Leticia didn't reply.

"I know it's what you want," Dracula said gently. "We could be like that again."

"We couldn't," Leticia said uncertainly, and he sighed.

"Leticia, stop thinking about what people will think of you. You are the Countess of Severna, did you forget? It matters not what people will say."

"I know, but my husband will be furious. You and Westley aren't exactly the best of friends, Dracula."

"If it's what you want, Westley will comply. You have my word," Dracula said as he stroked her hair, and Leticia said "He will be shocked. I don't think it would be a good idea if we-"

"You're worrying again." Dracula smiled at her, and she pouted at him. "How can you tell?"

"Because you've got that cute little frown on your face."

Leticia smiled at him. "You still remember everything about me."

"Well we're best friends. What do you expect," shrugged Dracula, and her smile grew. "I doubt you remember everything about me also."

"Of course I do," Leticia said, amused. "What do you want to do now?"

"We could walk by the lake," suggested Dracula, and she said "We'll be spotted by others."

"It matters not," said Dracula, taking her hand. "We used to walk by the lake often. And many saw us."

"Yes, and Westley heard," Leticia said, shaking her head. "He wasn't happy about that, you know."

"Well he's not the boy he was," Dracula answered. "He would move mountains to make you happy. As would I," he added after pausing, and Leticia smiled at him, touched.

"Thank you."

* * *

"Jeiklee, wake up."

Jeiklee mumbled something before rolling onto his side, and Spirit nudged him, whispering "Jeiklee."

"What's the matter?" he muttered, then he opened his eyes, sensing something. Jeiklee sat up, then he saw they were being watched by something about to strike behind Spirit- "Spirit, get down!!"

Spirit ducked as Jeiklee's arm lit bright orange-

"Ricato!!"

BANG!!

The creature was blasted into the trees with a howl of pain, Spirit saying "Thanks for that!"

"No problem," Jeiklee said, reaching for his sword and standing. "What was you waking me for?"

"You was glowing," Spirit said, as he shook his head to clear it.

"Glowing yellow?"

"Glowing blue," Spirit replied. "I thought you were having some kind of vision. Leticia's eyes turn blue when she has visions. I thought it may be the same with you."

"My body was glowing, not my eyes." Jeiklee yawned, Spirit saying "I'm sorry. You can go back to sleep if you want."

"No chance of that now. I'm hungry," said Jeiklee, and Spirit said "I'll go find us something to eat."

"Isn't it my turn?" smiled Jeiklee, and she smiled back.

"Yeah it is, but you just saved my skin. I don't mind going."

"Ok."

Spirit picked up her bow and arrow and slung it over her shoulder before she left the clearing, Jeiklee smiling as he sat down.

"Four days to go."

* * *

"I must head back," Leticia said softly, Dracula's arm around her as they gazed across the water. Dracula nodded, then he said "Brubeck's accommodation is further into the ocean. Beyond this lake."

Leticia looked up at him. She could see the hurt etched across his face as she asked "Do you still think of Malinda?"

"No," Dracula replied honestly. "I do think of Brubeck and his cruelty, though."

Leticia nodded, saying "Had my parents been around, I'm sure we would have gotten Jeiklee back sooner. I know how it feels to have 'what ifs' rushing around the brain. It's not a nice feeling."

"The King should never have insisted they take part in the war," Dracula said, shaking his head. "That's why I had to take you away from the war against dragons, Leticia. I had to keep you safe. I didn't want to lose you just how you lost your parents in previous years. But as usual my actions were poorly judged and it was assumed by everyone in Severna that I kidnapped you."

Leticia smiled. "You don't pay attention to the people in Severna anyway, Dracula. You never have."

"I know." Dracula smiled back. "If I had, you may not have liked me as much as you did."

Leticia glanced up at the sky: the sun was setting. "I have to get back, Dracula. I'm meant to be going to dinner with Westley and the King."

"He can't go alone?" pouted Dracula, and Leticia replied "He could, but he wants me at his side."

"As if you are a trophy," scowled Dracula, Leticia standing. "When will I see you again, Leticia of Sampson?"

Leticia smiled at the use of the name everyone knew her by from the day she was born.

"In two days. In our clearing, at five."

Dracula stood as well. "You promise?"

"I promise," smiled Leticia, and he nodded as she softly said "Goodbye Dracula."

"Goodbye Leticia," he said just as softly, and she vanished. Dracula sighed and sat back down, looking across the lake thoughtfully. Maybe things were looking up for once in so long.

Maybe.

After brooding for another half hour Dracula stood, teleporting to his castle.

* * *

"Here we go," said Jeiklee as he began to glow yellow, and Spirit smiled and took his hand.

They appeared in a fine dining area, and they saw Westley standing there, looking anxious.

"We're in the Palace of Severna," whispered Spirit, and Jeiklee nodded, watching his father.

"Stop fretting," a woman said to him gently. "Why are you so nervous?"

"I'm nervous because I'm not sure if Leticia's ready to be married," Westley replied. "Please Cookie, can you talk to her before this goes ahead?"

"You know Leticia's mother won't let me near her," smiled their chef, Spirit and Jeiklee listening hard. "She doesn't think her daughter should be around riff raff like a servant. Or certain friends," she added, looking at Westley knowingly. "You agree with her mother on that part."

Westley sighed. "Do you think it was harsh to ban Leticia from seeing Count Dracula?"

"Well it's not my place to say sir," Cookie replied, "Although you could make things right by talking to her mother about it. Dracula and Leticia of Sampson grew up together, did you forget? That's like snatching George away from you for no apparent reason. How would *you* feel?"

Westley scowled. "I'd hate my parents and whoever else didn't want George in my life."

"Exactly," the chef said. "So think of how poor Leticia must feel."

Westley nodded.

"Who's George?" hissed Jeiklee, and Spirit whispered "A servant at the mansion. George and Westley grew up together too. They're best friends."

"How come I haven't met him??"

"Because we've been wrapped up in other stuff," Spirit replied. "George probably cleaned your room a few times."

"Oh."

Westley shook his head. "She says she wants to be my wife, but I feel like she's putting on a brave face for my benefit. Maybe we should wait a while longer-"

"Sir, a lot has happened. You lost your son to deranged mortals," Cookie said, placing a hand on his shoulder. "And you are of age now. A wedding may be just what everyone needs, something positive."

"But-"

"Leticia of Sampson," said an adoring voice, making Westley turn quickly. Leticia was walking towards them, servants in the Palace bowing to her as she passed them, her beautiful eyes on Westley. Westley took a sharp breath before he said "Are you all right, Leticia?"

"Yes," Leticia said softly, and Cookie greeted her before quickly leaving them alone. Westley took Leticia's hand and kissed it as she asked "Are we still to dine with the King, Westley?"

"Yes," Westley said, leading her out of the dining hall. "But I want to be alone with you. The King will understand."

Leticia nodded, and he led her outside.

"I want to talk to you."

"About what?"

"About the wedding," Westley said. "Are you sure it's what you want?"

Leticia didn't answer that. "Is it what *you* want, Westley?"

"Of course it is."

"Then shouldn't that be enough?" asked Leticia. "My mind is full of so many things right now. I can't take my mind off our son."

"I feel the same," Westley said sadly. "That's why I wanted to know if you'd rather wait. We're of age now, so everyone is expecting a wedding. But if it's not what you want, we could wait. I promise I don't mind."

"Leticia," called a firm voice before she could answer, and they turned and saw an elegantly dressed woman who looked a little haughty. Leticia sighed before she said "Yes Mother?"

"What nonsense are you telling your future husband, Leticia?" scolded the woman as she walked towards her daughter, and Jeiklee stared at his grandmother. "Are you postponing the wedding just because you lost your son how long ago? It isn't something that has just happened! You've had plenty of time to mourn and move on."

Anger flashed across Leticia's face as she said "You wouldn't understand how I feel, Mother."

"No I wouldn't," the woman snapped. "Get your head screwed back on, Leticia of Sampson. I won't be the talk of the land, do you understand me?"

"If the wedding is so important to you why don't *you* marry Westley?" spat Leticia, and her mother said "How dare you speak to your mother that way! All I want is what's best for you-"

"Leaving me alone would be best for me!"

"Don't be ridiculous," her mother snapped. "Now prepare yourself for dinner with the King, and for Heaven's sake put a smile on your face. Your scowling would make fresh milk sour in an instant."

"I don't want to go to dinner with the King," spat Leticia. "I'm going for a walk!"

"Well if I find you're not back in ten minutes for dinner or you've gone into the Forest of Fear to see that scoundrel Count Dracula, I'll-"

"You'll what!" Leticia was glowing scarlet now. "Ground me for eternity? You don't have a say in what I do and where I go!"

"If you think that I feel sorry for you," was her mother's cold reply. "I am your *mother,* did you forget?! You will respect me, Leticia, and you will be back for dinner in ten minutes!"

Westley hovered uncertainly, not knowing whether to get involved as Leticia said "I won't be like you, do you not understand that?! I will *never* be like you!!"

Before anyone could answer or stop her she vanished in a flash of scarlet light, gone.

"Wow," said Jeiklee, as his father's mouth hung open. "I've never seen my mother lose her cool like that-"

"I'll go and find her," Westley told Leticia's mother, but she shook her head.

"If Leticia has used the Force and jumped through time then you won't find her, Westley. I'll send her father if she isn't back in ten minutes."

Westley nodded. "Yes Ma'am."

Jeiklee started to glow again, Spirit slipping her hand in his. They were pulled to a massive cliff, where they saw Leticia staring down at the roaring ocean water, taking steady breaths.

"Well at least she hasn't gone to see Dracula," started Spirit, and a voice shouted "Leticia!!"

They turned and saw Count Dracula, and Spirit scowled.

"I spoke too soon."

"Stay back, Dracula!" said Leticia angrily, and Dracula cried "What are you doing?!"

"What does it look like!"

"Don't jump, Leticia! Please!"

Leticia ignored him, her hair being blown back with the wind. Dracula cautiously took a step closer, and her body lit scarlet as she looked back.

"Did I not say to stay back?!"

"Things can't be this bad for you to want to do this, Leticia!" said Dracula angrily. "What happened??"

"I can't do it anymore!"

"Do what?!"

"Everything! My life is one big upper-class mess! My son- my son is gone- and I cannot see you- I have to get married as I'm now of age- and my mother orders every single thing!" said Leticia, tears falling now. "I must obey her! Everything is rules and perfection- *stay back!!"*

Dracula stopped again, Leticia saying "Not once has anyone thought about how *I* feel, how I'm feeling inside! Only Westley and my father take the time to consider it- I've had enough! I have to be the good woman everyone expects me to be! And I feel like a caged animal being ogled without an ounce of freedom! Have you any idea how that feels?!"

Jeiklee realised Spirit was crying too. Putting an arm around her, he whispered "It's ok, Spirit!"

"Look at how distressed she is," wept Spirit. "And nobody had a clue-"

Jeiklee held her closer as his mother took another step towards the edge of the cliff, and Dracula did something very brave and risky- he ran towards her.

"No!" cried Leticia as he got closer, and the wind blew- Spirit screamed as Leticia lost her balance and tumbled off the edge of the cliff, Dracula shouting her name the same time Spirit screamed it.

"LETICA!!"

Without thinking he dived after her, and Jeiklee and Spirit were suddenly hovering over the surface of the water, looking around desperately.

Dracula burst out of the water moments later with Leticia in his arms, swimming for the shore desperately. Leticia was unconscious, her face and arms cut as they washed onto the sand, her dress torn. Dracula shook Leticia desperately.

"Leticia!"

She didn't reply, eyes closed. Dracula took a deep breath before his hands started to glow a deep violet, and he placed them on Leticia, the violet light running along her body and swirling around her.

"What's he doing?" hissed Jeiklee, and Spirit whispered "Healing her. Count Dracula has healing powers. Leticia said so once."

Leticia's cuts and gashes faded away, her skin smooth again, and her eyes flickered open, locking on his as she whispered "Dracula…"

Relieved, Dracula whispered "Don't ever do that again, Leticia…"

Leticia's gaze lingered on his mouth, and Jeiklee knew they were going to kiss again. He could tell, and he wasn't surprised when they were mouth to mouth moments later, Dracula pulling Leticia up into his arms.

"You can't go back like this," Dracula said breathlessly, when they broke apart. "Your gown is ruined. Come back to my castle with me. You can spend the night if you'd like."

Leticia nodded, and he kissed her again.

Suddenly Jeiklee and Spirit were back in the clearing, in the Forest of Fear. Spirit was looking scandalised, and Jeiklee said to her "What more proof do you need that Mum was in love with Count Dracula?"

"All right," Spirit snapped, when he smirked at her. "But she doesn't love him now. She's grown up from all of that."

It was dark, Jeiklee saying "No chance of food for tonight, then. We'd better get a fire started."

* * *

"Marvellous to have your boy back where he belongs at last," King Harlot said at the table, smiling at Leticia, who smiled back stiffly. "I hope you bear no ill will towards me anymore, Countess."

Leticia took a sip from her glass of wine before she replied "I came to terms with your decision a long time ago, Your Majesty. And yes, it is lovely to have Jeiklee back after so long. He is a treasure."

"I would like to meet him at some point."

"As would many in Severna," Leticia replied, "But I leave the decision up to Jeiklee about meeting you."

"Come now Leticia, the boy is royalty. He should meet the King of this land, don't you agree?" Leticia didn't reply. "Westley met me and the rest of the Royal Family when he was a small boy. Surely you want the same for your son."

Westley said nothing, knowing his wife was fuming inside as she said "I want my son to have the freedom I was barely allowed to have growing up. I won't do to him what my mother did to me, King Harlot."

"Your mother knew what was best for you," the King started, and Leticia said "She *thought* she knew what was best for me. There's a difference."

King Harlot pouted. "You're a stunning woman, beautiful to lay eyes upon. And you are still as headstrong as you ever were, Countess."

"And that will not change," Leticia replied, glancing at Westley. "I'm ready to leave. You may stay here with the King if you wish, Westley."

"No, I'm coming with you," Westley said, standing. "Thank you for dinner, Your Majesty."

"Anytime, my boy. Come again soon. You too, Countess."

Leticia merely nodded, Westley taking her hand.

Both of them vanished.

* * *

Castle Dracula…

Dracula hummed a tune as he walked about the castle, making his servants including Nancy smile, and making Virginia curious.

"Why are you in such a good mood, Father?"

"Because I woke up in good spirits," Dracula replied with a smile, and Virginia said "You never sing songs. This has something to do with Leticia of Sampson, right Father?"

"Maybe," Dracula said, his smile broad now as Virginia asked "Are you back in contact with her?"

Nancy looked at Dracula as well, glad Virginia asked the question so she didn't have to.

Dracula wondered whether to reply honestly, or lie. Virginia waited, and he decided to tell the truth: "Yes. I went to our clearing to brood as I always do, and reminisce about Leticia and my relationship."

"And what happened?" asked Virginia, very curious now. "How are you back in contact with her? You always go to that clearing and return very calm with a lot to think about, Father. But this time you're smiling and singing."

"Leticia knew I was in the clearing and she came to me." Dracula sighed a little dreamily. "I did not summon her. I did not contact her in any way. She came to me on her own, and I held her in my arms just like I used to. Her scent, her hair, her smile- everything- is still so breath-taking. It felt like nothing had changed, no time had passed. I loved every moment of it."

"And will you see her again?" demanded Virginia. "Father, please don't read too much into this. I don't want you hurt."

"Nothing Westley does will affect me, Virginia. I'm past that. And Leticia will never hurt me."

"She married the Count of Severna! Are you saying that didn't hurt you?? Because if you are, you're lying," Virginia said, scowling now. "I *know* it hurt you. And just because you saw her the one time, it doesn't mean anything will change-"

"Everything remained the same between us, Virginia. We didn't see much of each other at one point, but our relationship didn't waver," Dracula told his daughter. "You saw Leticia a few times in the castle after she married Westley Inferno, did you not?"

"I did Father, but I'm still a little wary."

Dracula smiled and pulled Virginia into his arms, dropping a kiss on her forehead.

"I love you, my daughter."

"I love you too Father," smiled Virginia. "Whatever happens you will always have me."

"And you will always have me too," Dracula said, touched. "Have you packed your bag for Thrill?"

"Yes Father."

"Then make your way. I don't want you to be late."

Virginia smiled. "Ok. I will see you this evening. Don't spend the day daydreaming, Father."

Dracula chuckled. "All right. I won't."

Virginia smiled back before she summoned her bag and left the castle. Nancy looked at Dracula, saying "Virginia asked all the questions I wanted to, sir."

"I know, Nancy." Dracula smiled at her, and she said "If Leticia of Sampson is toying with you, I will be most displeased."

"Leticia has never toyed with me and you know that," Dracula said, and Nancy nodded. "She always told me everything just like I told her everything. And she never once deceived me."

"Yes My Lord."

"We will see each other at five tomorrow." Dracula smiled again. "I can't wait."

* * *

Jeiklee woke up, looking around. "Spirit?"

"I'm here," she said, smiling at him. "Good afternoon."

Jeiklee yawned, getting up. "Why didn't you wake me?"

"Because I know you need your energy," Spirit replied. "I got you some sandwiches. Ham, tuna and chicken."

"Thanks," smiled Jeiklee. "I need to get to the lake to bathe. It's through the Forest, right?"

"Right," said Spirit, standing. "I'll come with you. I need to bathe too."

Jeiklee swallowed before he nodded, and she burst out laughing.

"Don't worry, you won't see me. The lake joins a river that leads right past Thrill. The water is cool, clean and refreshing. I'll go to the riverside and you can go to the lake."

Relieved, Jeiklee said "Great. I'll meet you back here in about an hour?"

"An hour and a half," Spirit said amusedly. "It takes half an hour to reach the lake and river from here, we'll bathe for half an hour, and it'll take another half hour to reach back."

"Should I eat first?" asked Jeiklee, but Spirit said no.

"Never eat before you swim, Jeiklee. You don't want to chuck up, do you?"

"Oh- right. I totally forgot," smiled Jeiklee. "I'm starving though."

"I know." Spirit picked up her bow and arrow and slung it over her shoulder, Jeiklee doing the same with his weapons. "See you in a bit."

* * *

Jeiklee stripped off, staring down at the clear blue water. He couldn't see any fish, so that was ok.

"No body wash," he muttered, then he scowled. Spirit would have conjured everything she needed to bathe, he didn't doubt that at all.

"Do you require help, Jeiklee?" a voice asked, and he whipped round. The Elder Samantha was standing there, glowing brightly as he gasped "Samantha!"

"Do you require help?" she asked again, and he said "Um… I need a fresh set of clothes and body wash and deodorant. And maybe a spare T-shirt, and a toothbrush and toothpaste, please."

The Elder Samantha waved her hand and everything Jeiklee asked for was on the ground beside him. His dirty clothes vanished, Jeiklee saying "Thank you so much."

"You're welcome, Jeiklee. What have you discovered so far?" smiled Samantha, and Jeiklee replied "My mother and Count Dracula loved each other. But she did what was expected of her instead of following her heart."

"Yes, you are correct."

"And I know Dracula still loves her," Jeiklee said as he dipped a toe into the cool water, testing the temperature, and the Elder nodded. "He isn't evil at all, is he? His ancestors were, and he may be linked to the Devil, but where my mother is concerned he has the purest heart."

"You understand greatly," smiled Samantha. "I am glad you have not judged Count Dracula like everyone in Severna have, including Spirit McKenzie."

"Spirit just won't accept the truth about him," Jeiklee said as he eased into the water. "Count Dracula isn't evil. And I don't think his daughter is evil either."

"You have reached the right conclusion, Jeiklee, and I am glad," said the Elder. "You will be back in the present in two days. Do what you have been doing, which is understanding. You have done well."

Before Jeiklee could reply she was gone.

Jeiklee smiled and swam around for a while, before reaching for his body wash and soaping himself slowly, thinking. Then he realised.

"I'm being tested."

* * *

"Tested?" said Spirit, puzzled. "Tested about what? How to survive?"

"Tested to see if I'll think the same as everyone about Count Dracula, if I'm like everyone else. And I'm not," shrugged Jeiklee. "I'm not going to judge him or Virginia. I really don't think they're evil."

Spirit scowled. "Did the lake water drench your brain as well as everything else, Jeiklee?"

"You're just like everyone else," sighed Jeiklee. "Won't you even *try* to understand, Spirit?"

"I understand Leticia was confused growing up. Dracula took advantage of that," Spirit said, glaring at Jeiklee as if he was Count Dracula. "When we get back we'll tell Leticia and Westley, and I bet you they will both say the same thing."

"Don't count on it," Jeiklee said. "Where's those sandwiches?"

"We can get fresh lunch, Jeiklee. There's tons of food on the trees."

"All right. Can we cuddle before we get pulled through time again?"

Spirit smiled at him, and Jeiklee smiled back as she said "Sure."

* * *

Leticia walked about the mansion deep in thought, her gown flowing behind her.

"Good afternoon My Lady," the servants said respectfully, and Leticia responded "Good afternoon to you all. Where is Westley?"

"In the garden with George, My Lady."

"Thank you."

Leticia walked into the garden, where the servant George and Westley were deep in conversation in recliners by the pool.

"I must introduce you properly to Jeiklee," Westley was telling his friend. "I am sorry I didn't before."

"It's no problem," smiled George, and Westley smiled back. "He is a very smart young man, just like his parents. I saw the way he took everything on board and adapted to Severna. He didn't falter at the spells and everything else he had to learn. It's quite amazing. Your son should have come to Severna much sooner."

"I know." Westley nodded. "Leticia still hasn't forgiven the King for passing that law about our son. She was most displeased at dinner last night with him."

"I would be too," shrugged George. "Those mortals weren't police or politicians. They couldn't possibly have burnt My Lady at stake. I would have taken Jeiklee back regardless of what they said. After all, they were mortal."

"I agree, George."

"Good afternoon My Lady," George said, standing as soon as he saw Leticia. "Is everything all right? Do you need anything?"

"No, George. Thank you," smiled Leticia, Westley standing as well. "Westley, would you like to go for a ride in the chariot? The Magenta Birds are growing restless, I can feel it from here. We could fly around Severna for an hour or so."

"Of course, Leticia." Westley smiled back. "We have two days left before our son comes home with Spirit. I am very glad."

"As am I," Leticia said, George leaving them alone with a smile. "I miss them dearly."

"Shall we feed the Magenta Birds?" asked Westley, and Leticia said "They were fed earlier today. Embers and liquor. They're ready to spread their wings and fly for hours."

"Then let's go," Westley said, kissing her. "Let's take some food with us with champagne. An airborne picnic sounds wonderful."

"All right. I'll meet you at the chariot," Leticia said, and Westley nodded and said ok.

Leticia walked to the stables of the mansion where the Magenta Birds were, their bodies ablaze as they walked around, singeing the ground. They screeched happily when they saw Leticia, and she smiled as she asked "Are you ready to fly?"

The giant birds blew fire happily, the servants who saw to the animals running to attach them to the chariot.

"My Lady, stand back!"

"I'm fine," smiled Leticia, as they cautiously approached the birds. "The Magenta Birds are harmless. It's only because they are on fire people are wary. But they're the most gentle birds in Severna."

"Stand back anyway, My Lady. We don't want you burnt."

Leticia sighed and obeyed, Westley joining her holding a large basket. As soon as the birds were attached to the chariot and were ready, he said "This will be very nice, provided it doesn't rain."

Leticia agreed. "I know. Let us go."

As the chariot took off the servants waved and shouted goodbye, Leticia and Westley waving back before they settled down, flying into the horizon without a worry in the world.

* * *

Virginia glanced about the cafeteria before she sat with her group of friends outside, under a tree by the river. She reached in her bag for her lunch, sighing a little.

"What's that, Virginia?" Clarissa asked, as Virginia unwrapped her sandwich. Virginia glanced at her, answering "It's a sandwich. Does it look like a piece of fruit to you?"

Clarissa blushed as the group sniggered, then she said "I meant what flavour sandwich."

"Spicy chicken," Virginia said, amused now. Clarissa smiled back, a little relieved before she said "Virginia, you're my best friend."

"You tell me all the time," smiled Virginia. "Can I eat my sandwich?"

"Oh- sure. I just wanted you to know how much you mean to me. And hopefully you feel the same about me, that we're best friends," Clarissa told her. "We've been friends since the beginning of high school."

Virginia nodded, taking a bite of her sandwich. Swallowing after a moment of thoughtful chewing, she said "Where is Jeiklee Inferno and Spirit McKenzie? Spirit was due back days ago and Jeiklee was meant to start Thrill this week."

"The Count and Countess of Severna have spoken to the Headmaster about that," a voice said, and everyone turned to see Professor Gene standing there. "Jeiklee Inferno and Spirit McKenzie will be here next week."

"Yes Professor," everyone said, and Professor Gene said "Virginia, can I talk to you?"

"What about, Professor?" asked Virginia, and Professor Gene said "About the duelling between yourself and Spirit McKenzie."

"Oh," said Virginia, while her crowd smirked. "We're just play-duelling, Professor-"

"I have asked around Thrill and some students including Spirit say otherwise," Professor Gene said, frowning at her. "They seem to think you attack Spirit whenever you have the chance to."

"That's not true," lied Virginia, and this time Professor Gene didn't even answer, staring her out as she waited for the truth. Virginia sighed before saying "Professor, you don't have to worry. I won't hex Spirit again."

"Good," said Professor Gene. "If I have to alert your father-"

"Don't!" Virginia said quickly. "I won't trouble Spirit anymore. I promise!"

"I'll take your word and no further action, Virginia. Don't make me regret it."

Virginia nodded, and Professor Gene turned and walked back into the building. Virginia scowled as she saw Bruce Finnegan walking, saying "Who snitched on me aside from Spirit?"

"Whoever says to leave her alone when you hex her," shrugged Clarissa. "Spirit's defenders. Anyway, are you looking forward to Jeiklee Inferno coming? I expect he'll be in our class."

Virginia frowned. "Why *our* class?"

"Because Spirit's in our class," said Clarissa, "And he knows her. He met us too, but he lives with her. Or she lives with *him,* should I say. I don't know why Countess Leticia didn't take her to the orphanage when she lost her parents."

"Don't be mean, Clarissa." Virginia finished her sandwich. "I think Countess Leticia is amazing. She's so kind. And she was friends with Spirit's parents, don't forget. So she definitely wouldn't have allowed Spirit to be taken into care."

"I guess," Clarissa said. "Spirit wants Jeiklee to herself."

Virginia glanced at her. "What makes you say that?"

"She's kept him away from everyone since he arrived in Severna," Clarissa pointed out. "Once I woke up early and went out to meet him. He was out with Spirit, learning to hunt or something. I dressed up in my sexy red outfit to get his attention, and I didn't even get a chance to flirt. Spirit couldn't wait to get rid of me."

"Well you did make yourself a little available," Virginia pointed out. "I met Jeiklee Inferno too. He seems like a nice guy. But I didn't dress up and get up early and all of that mess. I was myself. And he didn't seem that bothered by me, even though I am the Daughter of Dracula."

"Because Spirit is poisoning his mind," Clarissa pressed. "Everyone thinks so."

"But I don't go by what everyone says, Clarissa." Virginia shrugged a shoulder. "He lives with her and they hang out. Big deal."

Before Clarissa could answer the bell for afternoon lessons went, Virginia standing. Her group stood with her as she said "Come on, let's go."

* * *

Jeiklee began to glow yellow, Spirit quickly linking arms with him.

They saw Leticia fast asleep in a massive bed, someone knocking on the door gently.

"Leticia of Sampson? Are you awake?" a voice asked gently, Leticia stirring. "Are you up?"

"Yes," Leticia mumbled, and the door opened, a woman coming in.

"She's a vampire," whispered Spirit, as the woman said "Good morning Leticia."

"Good morning," Leticia responded warily, and the woman gently said "Don't be afraid. My name is Nancy. You may have heard of me."

"I have," Leticia said truthfully, and Nancy said "Would you like some breakfast? The table in the dining hall has been set for you especially."

"Oh," said Leticia. "Um… ok. I'll be down soon."

Nancy pointed to a wardrobe. "Your gown has been washed and is in there, but it is ruined. Count Dracula has a new gown for you."

"Where is Count Dracula?" asked Leticia curiously, and Nancy replied "He has taken Virginia to school. Something has come up regarding his daughter, and they requested he come for a meeting."

"Ok. Well… I'll get dressed and then I'll come down to breakfast. I need to shower first." Nancy nodded. "Thank you, Nancy."

"You're welcome."

Nancy left the room. Leticia sighed before she slid out of bed and walked into the bathroom suite.

Jeiklee and Spirit were suddenly in the dining hall, where they saw Count Dracula sitting anxiously, glancing at the clock.

"She hasn't come down yet?"

"No sir," one of his servants said, and Nancy entered the hall with a smile. "She's coming, sir. And she looks beautiful."

Dracula stood as Leticia entered the dining hall, inhaling sharply. Jeiklee and Spirit did too: Leticia looked amazing.

Her gown was studded with diamonds and was the colour silver, as were her shoes and the rose in her hair, her jewellery. She smiled as she walked towards Dracula, and he smiled back.

"I know you have always loved that gown. You asked your mother for it a month ago and she declined, do you remember?"

"You knew about that?" said Leticia, surprised when he nodded.

"I knew."

Leticia's expression grew so warm as she looked at him. "Thank you."

"You're welcome," Dracula said, his expression mirroring hers. "Shall we eat?"

Leticia nodded, a servant pulling a chair out for her. She sat down, eyes on the food.

"Everything looks delicious."

Dracula nodded. "Tuck in."

"What happened with Virginia?" asked Leticia as she helped herself to some fruit juice. "Nancy said the school needed you?"

"She was being picked on, and for a while," Dracula replied as he reached for some bacon. "I wasn't aware of that until today. Virginia reacted yesterday in a pretty big way. The boy is now in hospital."

Leticia's jaw dropped. "Was it a hex?"

"A curse," said Dracula, shaking his head. "The Tongue-Tie Curse. His tongue stretched and tied itself into a knot and his voice has vanished."

Leticia gaped, and Dracula sighed before continuing "He won't be able to speak for six months. I offered to go to the hospital and remove the curse but his parents are so afraid of me they declined immediately. Which is a real shame."

"I could go," Leticia said, shrugging a shoulder. "Unless you want me to keep away?"

"No," Dracula said, a small smile on his face. "Please go, Leticia. This is going to be another thing for Severna to speculate about and something to add to their fear of me."

"They will say Dracula's daughter is following in his footsteps or something of the sort," Leticia said as she smiled back. "I don't understand how people can be so judgemental without knowing the full story."

"The fact that he was bullying Virginia will skip over their heads," Dracula answered, "But I am used to the way people think of me."

"I will contact the boy's parents and go to the hospital," Leticia replied, "This evening before I go home. My mother must be furious with me."

"Would you like me to take you home?" asked Dracula, but she shook her head.

"That will spark anger and you know that, Dracula. I'm forbidden to see you, did you forget?"

"But if Sampson is there-"

"I can't risk it. My father might be out looking for me by the time I get back," said Leticia, sighing a little. "I don't plan on going straight home."

Dracula said ok.

Suddenly Jeiklee and Spirit were pulled to the castle entrance, where they saw Count Dracula and Leticia saying their goodbyes.

"I will meet the parents of the boy tonight," Leticia told Dracula, and he nodded. "Thank you, Dracula. For... for everything you did yesterday and today."

"I couldn't have done anything else," Dracula said quietly, and she kissed him on the cheek. "Goodbye Leticia."

"Goodbye," she whispered, and she vanished. Dracula dissolved into thin air, and suddenly Jeiklee and Spirit were back in their clearing.

"I knew Virginia was evil," Spirit said flatly. "The Tongue-Tie Curse?? Seriously? She was a little kid for Pete's sake!"

"She was getting bullied and she didn't tell anyone," Jeiklee said in Virginia's defence. "She couldn't take it anymore and she reacted. Just like you did when you hit her with a Fire Bone hex."

"I wasn't in primary school," Spirit reminded him irritably. "I'm a young adult. You'd expect me to react at this age, not go into a rage and curse the bully when I'm not even eleven. Virginia of Dracula is evil and always has been. We saw the proof right there."

Jeiklee sighed, not wanting to argue. "I'm going to sleep until the next time we get pulled through time. I want to be fully alert."

Spirit nodded. "Ok."

* * *

When Jeiklee woke again, the moon was shining on their clearing, a fire was burning. Spirit was snuggled next to him, fast asleep.

Jeiklee gently eased away from her and stood, yawning. There was food set by the fire, Jeiklee frowning at it before he whispered "Spirit."

"Mmm?"

"Did you set that food by the fire?"

"Before I fell asleep I got food for tonight," she mumbled, and Jeiklee relaxed, his stomach grumbling.

"Can I eat it then?"

Spirit opened her eyes to look at the food, then she frowned and sat up.

"I didn't get pizza. I didn't even see any pizza on the trees."

"So where did this pizza come from?" said Jeiklee curiously, then a croaky voice replied "From me."

Jeiklee reached for his sword the same time Spirit leapt up, Jeiklee demanding "Who said that?"

"A humble tree, Master Inferno."

"Which tree?" said Jeiklee angrily. "Raise a branch before I light all of you!"

The tree lifted a branch immediately, Spirit saying "Were you spying on us?"

"Not spying, Miss McKenzie… watching." The tree's glowing eyes could now be seen. "I knew you would wake soon so I grew a meal for you."

"How did you place it by the fire?" Spirit demanded. "And are you a tree for good or evil?"

"A good tree. There are still some good trees left here in the Forest of Fear."

"Right," said Jeiklee. "Well… I'm not chancing eating a sizzling pizza that grew at night. I'll just have some fruit."

"But sir, I grew that meal for the pair of you-"

"Why?" demanded Jeiklee, and the tree replied "Because I know you must be sick of sandwiches."

Spirit smiled. "Thank you, Mr Tree."

"Spirit, don't trust it," hissed Jeiklee, and Spirit said "Come on Jeiklee, we'd sense dark energy. I can't feel any at all coming from this tree."

Jeiklee frowned as he realised that, then he smiled. "I don't sense any from Virginia of Dracula either."

"This again?" sighed Spirit. "Come on, let's eat before it gets cold."

Jeiklee still didn't trust the tree, but he did trust Spirit. "All right."

"Mmm," sighed Spirit as she bit into a slice of pizza. "Gorgeous."

"Any poison?" asked Jeiklee, and she laughed.

"You ask me that after I put it in my mouth??"

"Sorry," grinned Jeiklee, and she laughed again, the tree chuckling as well. "Eat, Master Inferno."

Jeiklee sighed as he joined Spirit by the fire and picked up a slice, biting into it. He scowled as he chewed, not wanting to show how much he liked the taste of the pizza, but Spirit knew.

"Any poison?" she said amusedly, and Jeiklee smiled before he said "I don't think so."

"Neither do I. Have some juice."

Jeiklee smiled as he reached for the jug of ice cold juice and a cup, saying "This is really nice. Thanks, Tree."

"You're most welcome. I believe you will be dragged through time in ten minutes," the tree told them. "So eat quickly."

Jeiklee and Spirit obeyed, feeling warm and lazy after they drank their juice.

"I almost don't want to be dragged through time," Jeiklee said as he leant back. "That must have been the best pizza I've had since I left London."

The tree chuckled. "Thank you for the compliment."

Spirit smiled and laid her head on Jeiklee's shoulder. "I hope we'll still be like this after you start Thrill, Jeiklee."

Jeiklee glanced down at her. "What do you mean?"

"There's tons of girls who want your attention," Spirit pointed out as she looked up at him. "I just… what if you change your mind about me? Like you stop being attracted to me?"

"Like Bruce Finnegan?" Spirit averted her gaze, and Jeiklee said "I'm not a jerk like him. And I don't just hop from one girl to the next either."

Spirit nodded. "If you're sure?"

"Of course I am," smiled Jeiklee. "But you said we're not in a relationship, right? So if I went with someone else, how would you take it?"

Anger flashed across Spirit's face before she lied "I wouldn't be bothered."

"Yeah right," smirked Jeiklee. "I saw that look just now. If I was you I'd claim me, Spirit McKenzie."

Spirit glared at him before she said "No. You're just trying to wind me up."

"And it's working," smiled Jeiklee. "You don't want us to be together but you don't want me with someone else. Is there logic in that?"

"Well… I-"

"Why don't you just admit that-"

Jeiklee began to glow bright yellow, Spirit relieved as she muttered "Saved by the vision."

"I heard that," Jeiklee said amusedly as he held a hand out, Spirit taking it. "This conversation isn't over."

"It is for me," Spirit retorted, but before Jeiklee could reply they were pulled through time.

Leticia's father stood as Leticia appeared in their front garden. Westley stood too, and so did many others including her mother.

"Leticia, where have you been?!" her father was relieved and angry at the same time. "Are you all right?"

"Yes Father. I'm perfectly fine."

"Where were you, Leticia?" her mother asked curtly, and Leticia glared at her. "And where did you get that gown from??"

"I spent the night at Castle Dracula."

"You did WHAT?!" Leticia repeated herself stonily, her mother saying "What have we told you about that boy, Leticia?! What did your father tell you?!"

"Father has no problem with me being friends with Dracula," Leticia said flatly, Westley's face furious as he stared at his wife to be. "I was in a state and Dracula calmed me down. He took me to his castle and I stayed there for the night. He got me this beautiful gown."

Westley spoke quietly. "You said you'd have nothing to do with Dracula, Leticia- you promised."

"He came to me when I was in need," Leticia said, looking at him while her mother seethed. "If it wasn't for Dracula I may not even be here."

"What do you mean?" her father asked sharply. "Were you in danger?"

"You could say that, Father. Dracula saved me, pretty much."

"Well if I have to put a Binding Charm on you so you keep away from that boy, I will!" her mother said angrily. "Why do you never listen!"

"I do listen," snapped Leticia. "I've been listening all my life. Now if you'll excuse me, I'm going for a shower. I've just come back from the hospital."

"The hospital??"

"What were you doing there?" asked Westley, and Leticia replied "I was doing a favour for Count Dracula. I expect you'll hear about it in the news tomorrow. Everything negative about him somehow reaches everyone's ears yet the good things he does, like saving my life, is ignored."

Westley opened his mouth, then he closed it and nodded. Leticia walked

inside her family home without another word, the doors closing behind her.
"Sampson, go and tell that wretched boy to keep away from my daughter,"
Leticia's mother said angrily. "At this rate there will be no wedding!"
"There's no harm in their relationship," Leticia's father said wearily. "I
have nothing against Leticia being friends with Dracula. I'm not going to
tell him to keep away when I have no reason to."
"Then *I* will tell him," snapped Leticia's mother angrily. "If I want
something done I may as well do it myself!"
"I'll come with you," Westley said, and she nodded.
"Sampson, stay with Leticia and make sure she doesn't run off again."
Leticia's father sighed, saying "You're going to make things much worse,
woman."
"I don't care. Something must be done. Come, Westley."
Westley followed his future mother-in-law through the garden gates and
into the open.
"Guards, come also. I don't know how that boy will react to me coming to
his castle."
"Yes Ma'am."
Leticia's father sighed again, shaking his head before he went indoors.
Suddenly Jeiklee and Spirit were at the doors of Dracula's castle, Westley
pounding on them furiously.
"Dracula! Get down here right now!"
The doors creaked open, and they saw Nancy the vampire servant, little
Virginia holding her hand nervously.
"What do you want with Count Dracula, Westley Inferno?" Nancy asked
coldly, and Westley spat "That's between me, Dracula, and Leticia's
mother. Where is he?"
"He needs not be seen by you. I suggest you leave."
"We are not going anywhere," Leticia's mother said icily. "Call the boy
down right now, or I will have my guards seize you."
"Nancy, I'm tired," Virginia said, looking up at her. "I want to sleep."
 Westley scowled at Virginia before he said "Take her to bed and call
Dracula down while you're at it."
Before Nancy could retort Count Dracula morphed in front of them,
glowing scarlet. You could tell he was furious.
"What can I do for you both?"
"You can keep away from Leticia," spat Westley, and Dracula said "Why
should I? I haven't done anything wrong."
"That's neither here nor there," snapped Leticia's mother. "I always
thought you were an odd little boy and now you're an even more odd older
boy. Stay away from my daughter or I will not rest until you go the same
way as your father, do you understand me?"
"Does Leticia know you're here?" was Dracula's cold reply, and she spat

"No. You'd better obey me and keep away from my child."

"Or else," Westley added furiously, and Dracula glanced at him.

"Or else what, Inferno?" Now his eyes were burning bright red as well. "I haven't done a thing to hurt Leticia. If you listened to what she wanted instead of trying to force rules down her throat, maybe she'd open up to you properly instead of running to me all the time."

"Do you want my fist replacing your teeth?!"

"Touch me if you dare," shrugged Dracula, then he glanced skyward. "You see that fork at the top of the castle?"

Westley and Leticia's mother looked up, Leticia's mother snapping "What about it?"

"If Inferno lays a finger on me I will kill him," shrugged Dracula, and they stared at him. "And I will hang his body on that fork for the vultures to snack on. Do you want that, Inferno?"

Westley didn't reply, Leticia's mother hissing "You're a monster."

"Call me what you like," Dracula replied coldly. "I didn't come to your accommodation to cause trouble. It was you and your suck up future son-in-law who came to mine. So I have every right to remove you from my premises- alive or dead."

Westley took a step back, then he spat "I don't know what the hell Leticia sees in a creep like you."

Spirit nodded angrily, and Jeiklee scowled at her as his grandmother said "I don't know either. Fine. We will go. But this isn't the last you've heard of me, Count Dracula."

"Nor me," snarled Westley, and Dracula laughed.

"I don't lay a hand on you only because I think of Leticia. Push me over the edge and she will vanish from my mind, Westley Inferno."

Westley took another step back, then he turned and stormed away. Leticia's mother glared at Dracula before she snapped "Come, guards."

She turned and walked away, the guards behind her. Dracula dissolved into thin air, Nancy lifting a half awake Virginia into her arms before she signalled the close of the castle doors.

Jeiklee and Spirit were pulled to Dracula and Leticia's clearing, where Dracula sat by a boulder, staring at the ground deep in thought.

"Dracula," Leticia said quietly as she entered the clearing, but he didn't react this time. "Dracula, please look at me."

Dracula sighed before he stood and looked at her. "I'm looking, Leticia."

Leticia hesitated, then she said "You're all over the news. You have been for the past three days."

Dracula didn't reply, and Leticia took a cautious step closer before she asked "Did you really threaten Westley's life, Dracula?"

"I did," shrugged Dracula. "I was prepared to murder him if he laid a hand on me."

Leticia opened her mouth, then closed it. "But he didn't."

"Well he was going to."

"And you threatened to hang him on a fork? Dracula, this whole thing has fuelled more rage at you-"

"I'm past caring."

"But-"

"Did you come here to lecture me, Leticia?" Dracula looked at her stonily. "You already know I care not what the people of this land think of me."

"I came here to make sure you're all right," Leticia said softly. "I know you must be angry, and I know I'm probably the last person you want to see right now. All of this is because of me."

Dracula sighed before he said "Come here." Leticia hesitated, and he smiled at her. "Come on, Leticia. Come to me."

Leticia walked towards him, and Dracula gently pulled her into his arms. "Your mother has told the press everything, am I right?"

"Yes," Leticia said, "And so has Westley. I'm sure they're exaggerating a little. You didn't do much." She paused, looking up at him. "Did you?"

"No I did not. And it was Westley who threatened me first," Dracula said, stroking her hair gently. "I retaliated and it scared him. I doubt he'll confront me again anytime soon."

Leticia closed her eyes at his touch, arms creeping around his waist. They held each other in silence for a while, then Dracula quietly asked "Shall we stop?"

Leticia didn't reply, lost in sensations as his fingers combed through her hair. Dracula smiled a little as he dropped a kiss on her forehead, and Leticia whispered something inaudible, Dracula murmuring "What was that, Leticia?"

"I said... I said I love-"

"Leticia!!"

Leticia gasped as her mother and father appeared with Westley and some guards; Westley reacted big time in a rush of fury, diving at Dracula as he released Leticia and slamming him to the ground.

Cameras flashed as the press appeared with many others as Dracula and Westley fought furiously, Leticia crying "Stop- Westley, don't!!"

Westley drew a dagger from his belt, snarling "I'll have your heart, Dracula!"

"No!" cried Leticia as he swiped furiously, a gash appearing on Dracula's face. "Father, tell him to stop!"

"Kill him!" everyone else shouted, and Dracula's body lit scarlet as he blasted Westley off him with a brilliant green hex- or was it a curse? Jeiklee thought amazedly, as his father crashed through the trees and fell to the ground, lifeless.

"Oh my God," whispered Spirit, as everyone cried "Westley!!"

Panting, Dracula stood. His face was bleeding, as were his hands and arms. Leticia made to go to him but her mother grabbed her, snapping "Whose side are you on exactly, Leticia?!"

Dracula looked at Leticia, and she whispered "Go. I'll deal with it- just go."

Dracula nodded and dissolved into thin air as someone said "We've got to get Westley to the hospital- now. His pulse is very weak."

Leticia was staring at the spot Dracula vanished, her mother grabbing her by the chin and forcing her to look in Westley's direction.

"Westley is your priority, Leticia! Not that monster!"

"Dracula isn't a monster," Leticia said quietly as she pulled away. "And Westley attacked Dracula, not the other way round."

Her mother gaped at her before she spat "Have you gone *mad,* Leticia?!"

Leticia didn't reply, watching as an unconscious Westley was lifted and carried away, cameras flashing at him again, journalists scribbling on notepads.

Leticia turned and walked in the opposite direction, her mother saying "Leticia? Leticia! Where are you going?!"

"I'm going to Castle Dracula. I have to make sure he's ok."

"But-"

"I will meet you at the hospital, Mother." Leticia stopped and looked back. "Make sure Westley is all right and alert his parents. Please let me go."

Leticia's mother looked like she was about to explode. Then she quietly said "You love that boy, don't you? You're in love with Count Dracula!"

"I never once told you I love Count Dracula nor have I ever implied that," Leticia said coldly. "Now go to the hospital. I will meet you there."

Before her mother could stop her she vanished.

The wind blew and Jeiklee and Spirit were back in their clearing.

"What the hell did we just see?" said Spirit amazedly, and Jeiklee looked at her. "Leticia chose Count Dracula? Seriously??"

"She went to make sure he's ok," Jeiklee said, shrugging. "If I were in that position I would have done the same."

"But-"

"Dad attacked Dracula, Spirit. That's what we saw. Dracula retaliated. That's it." Jeiklee sat down, then he remembered the talking tree. "Tree! Are you here?"

"I am, sir. Would you like a beverage of some kind?"

"Juice please. Ice cold."

He watched amazedly as a jug appeared with two cups on the tree branch, dangling. Spirit reached for them quickly, her throat dry.

"Thank you Mr Tree. I'll start a fire, Jeiklee."

"All right. Tree, can you grow me a chicken sandwich? I'm starving," smiled Jeiklee, and the tree chuckled.

"Yes sir. And I would prefer to be called Bari, sir. That is my name."
"Oh," said Jeiklee. "Sorry Bari. I'll call you that from now on."
"Thank you sir."

* * *

"What a lovely day," sighed Leticia, as Westley lifted her out of the chariot.
"I could have stayed airborne for hours more."
Westley smiled as he held her in his arms. "It's ten at night, Leticia. The
Magenta birds couldn't possibly have stayed in the air for more than
another two hours."
"I know. But the thought of it is appealing."
Amused, Westley set his wife on her feet. "Come, let us go to bed. Our son
returns to us tomorrow. We must be alert and ready to welcome him and
Spirit."
Leticia nodded her ok, servants running towards them to lead the Magenta
birds back to their enclosure.
Leticia sighed happily. "It feels like we have had Jeiklee all our lives. The
gaping hole of loss I have felt for years has truly vanished, Westley. Jeiklee
isn't here, but I know he will return. And that is a very nice feeling."
Westley smiled and took her hand, making her stop. "I do love you so
much, Leticia of Sampson."
"I know, Westley Inferno. I love you too."

* * *

Spirit and Jeiklee linked hands as he started to glow again, and Bari the Tree said "Not much rest I presume now that it's your last night."
Spirit and Jeiklee nodded before they vanished from the clearing, and suddenly they were at Castle Dracula, in a study with a fireplace.
Dracula sat staring into the flames, his face still cut. Nancy knocked, saying "Sir? Leticia of Sampson has arrived."
Dracula stood, surprised. "She didn't go with Westley Inferno?"
"It seems not, sir. Shall I bring her to you?"
"Please," said Dracula, and he took a deep breath as Leticia entered his study. "Leticia, what are you doing here? Shouldn't you be with-"
Leticia ran and hugged him before he could finish, and he hugged her back tightly. Leticia looked up at him, whispering "You're hurt."
"I'll heal myself," shrugged Dracula. "Don't worry about me, Leticia."
"Heal yourself now," Leticia said softly, "Or I will."
Dracula smiled a little. "Does your mother know you have the power to heal wounds and vanquish curses hexes and all injuries and illnesses?"
"No," shrugged Leticia. "Neither does my father. Not many know."
Spirit gasped. "She's a Healer?!"
"Not surprised," Jeiklee said admiringly, and Dracula said "Is that why you didn't go with Westley? Because you know he'll be ok once you heal him from my attack?"
"No," Leticia said quietly. "I came to make sure you're all right."
"I always am." Dracula smiled a little as his cuts and bruises faded away, the gash on his face thinning until she saw his smooth skin again. "See?"
Leticia nodded. "I see. Dracula… I apologise."
"For what?"
"For Westley attacking you and the press coming and my mother spurring it on. I know you haven't done anything wrong."
"He saw you in my arms, Leticia." Dracula shook his head. "I expected some kind of attack. Especially after threatening him."
Leticia sighed. "I'd better go to the hospital. But I had to make sure you were ok first."
"And I thank you for that." Dracula pulled her to him gently and kissed her forehead. "Go, Leticia. We will see each other again soon."
"You promise?"
Dracula smiled into her hair. "I promise."
Leticia sighed her ok and vanished; Dracula sat back down by the fire. Nancy knocked and entered, little Virginia trailing in behind her.
"Daddy, what the matter?" she asked before she popped her thumb in her mouth, and Dracula smiled at her.
"Nothing, Virginia. What did Daddy tell you about sucking your thumb?"

"You said a donkey will bite it off," giggled Virginia, and Dracula laughed as well. "Not true, Daddy!"

"It certainly is," chuckled Dracula. "Have you had your hot milk and cookies already?"

"Yes Daddy."

"Then it's time for you to sleep, little one. You have school tomorrow."

"Can I stay with you, Daddy?" asked Virginia, and Dracula said "You can stay up an extra hour on Friday. I promise. Now come and give Daddy a hug goodnight."

Virginia ran and hugged him. "Goodnight Daddy!"

"Goodnight sweetheart." Dracula hugged her back, Virginia's bright red hair glimmering from the light of the fireplace. "Dream good dreams."

Jeiklee was moved. Spirit was scowling.

They were pulled to a room with white walls, Westley still lifeless in a bed with white sheets. Jeiklee assumed they were in the hospital.

Westley's parents were there, looking grim as they stared at their unconscious son. Leticia's parents were there too.

The press were just outside the door, getting information from the nurses- probably for their next big story, Jeiklee thought with a scowl, as Westley's mother said "Where is Leticia?"

"She should be here soon," Leticia's father said, and right on cue they heard the clicking of cameras and the press calling Leticia's name.

"Leticia of Sampson! What have you to say about the duel between Westley Inferno and Count Dracula??"

"Not one word," Leticia replied stonily, and a journalist said "Is it true you are in love with Count Dracula? Were you about to tell him you love him?"

"Get out of my way," Leticia said quietly, and another journalist said "Please Leticia, give us a moment. Why were you in Count Dracula's arms? Hidden in the Forest of Fear?"

"You were alone with him," another journalist pressed. "What were you talking about? Why was he holding you when we arrived?"

"Would you like me to perform the Tongue-Tie curse on all of you at the same time?" Leticia asked sweetly. "Six months without hearing you wittering on about Count Dracula sounds very appealing to me."

"No- please! We don't want that Leticia, we just want a few questions answered-"

"Then go to Castle Dracula and ask the Count your questions," Leticia said icily. "And if any of you come back alive I would have to applaud Dracula for not slaughtering the lot of you."

Silence, Westley and Leticia's parents gaping.

Not even a camera clicked outside as Leticia said "Now get out of my way. I need to make sure Westley is ok."

"Yes Leticia," the journalists said humbly, and she said "Thank you."

"Damn. Mum doesn't play," Jeiklee said admiringly, and Spirit nodded.

Leticia entered Westley's room, all eyes on her as she walked towards his bed. Westley's brown skin looked pale and dry, life slowly leaving him. Leticia reached out and touched his forehead, then she looked at everyone. "He's so cold."

"They say Dracula's curse won't leave him for at least a month," Westley's mother said, eyes filling. "Why did Westley have to attack him?? He knew what Count Dracula was! Dracula shows no mercy! We've told Westley so many times yet he still thought he'd have Count Dracula's heart!"

"I can heal him," Leticia said quietly, "But not right now. I need time to think. Will you give me three days? I promise you Westley will be ok."

Everyone looked at each other, and Leticia said "You have to trust me. I've never deceived any of you before. Trust me when I say he will be fit and healthy in three days. I just need to sort some things out before Westley is better."

They nodded, Westley's father saying "We trust you, Leticia."

Leticia smiled briefly before she vanished.

"Sampson, what say you about this?" Westley's father asked, and Sampson replied "I have always said banning Leticia from seeing Count Dracula was a bad idea. And now because of that, your son is lying near dead in a hospital bed. I've said countless times to my wife that banning Leticia from seeing Count Dracula won't do any good for anyone. And now the proof is right here. I expect Leticia has gone to Castle Dracula to make sure he is all right if she hasn't done so already. They grew up together, and he makes her happy. Leticia is growing more and more miserable as time goes on. If she refuses to marry Westley, I won't be surprised. Dracula is her closest friend."

Leticia and Westley's mother scowled, Leticia's mother saying "She won't refuse to marry Westley. I won't allow it."

"Well good luck in making her walk down the aisle," Sampson said, scowling at his wife. "This is your fault, woman. I told you to let our daughter be, but you won't have it. And now you've made even more hate Count Dracula."

"Count Dracula is an outcast," she snapped back, "And he always will be. I was right in banning our daughter from seeing him, and if you had more of a backbone you would have done the same thing instead of thinking of what she wants. This friendship between them is not healthy and everyone agrees! Why are you defending Dracula even after what he did today??"

"I'm not defending him," Sampson said calmly, "And I don't agree with Westley's attempt to murder him either. They were both in the wrong and they will both learn from their mistakes. Leticia has gone to Dracula, yes. We know she has, it's not rocket science. But she also promised Westley would be fine in three days, promised she'd make sure of it. Our daughter has great power, we all know this. I believe she knows exactly what she is doing."

"Go Granddad," said Jeiklee happily, and Spirit said "Shut up, idiot."

They were pulled to Castle Dracula, back in his study.

Dracula and Leticia sat on the carpet, eyes on the fireplace. Dracula's arm was around Leticia, her head on his shoulder. Her eyes were closed as he stroked her hair.

"Would you like to stay with me tonight, Leticia?" he murmured, and she quietly said "Yes please." She paused, then said "I want to stay with you... in your chamber."

Dracula glanced down at her, surprised. "If you're sure?"

"Of course I am," Leticia said, taking his other hand. She lifted it to her mouth and gently kissed his fingertips. "If I wasn't sure I wouldn't have asked."

Dracula drew a deep breath, and they saw his fangs were unsheathed as he said "Leticia..."

Leticia tilted her head and pulled him down so his lips met hers. Dracula kissed her back, reaching for her blouse and unbuttoning it so fast it couldn't have been more than twenty seconds, Jeiklee thought amazedly as he all but tore the blouse off her body, both of them still lip-locked.

Everything went blurry, Jeiklee and Spirit hovering in an abyss of nothing, holding hands as they looked about curiously, then the scene became sharp as anything again, Dracula and Leticia fast asleep in his gigantic bed, Leticia's head on Dracula's muscular chest, his arms around her.

It was daytime, probably the next day.

Spirit couldn't believe it. "Did they sleep together??"

"We really don't need to know that," Jeiklee said, looking at her disdainfully. "It's none of our business, Spirit."

"But-"

There was a timid knock on the door. "Daddy?"

Leticia snapped awake, Dracula as well as Virginia called him earnestly.

"Daddy? Are you up yet? Nancy said to say bye before I go to school!"

"Goodbye Princess," Dracula called, and Virginia giggled before she said "Bye Daddy! Bye Miss Leticia of Sampson!"

"Goodbye Virginia," Leticia called with a smile, and they heard Virginia's little feet pattering as she ran back down the hall to Nancy.

Dracula looked at Leticia. "Good morning."

"Good morning," Leticia replied with a smile. "I feel amazing."

"As do I," Dracula said, putting an arm around her. "I love you, Leticia of Sampson."

Leticia kissed him. "And I love you."

"No matter what happens," Dracula said seriously, "You will always have a place in my heart."

Leticia's eyes filled over. "Why do you say that?"

"Because I know something will happen," Dracula said quietly, as there was a high pitched scream from below.

"DADDY!!!"

Dracula leapt up with Leticia. "Virginia!"

"Oh hell," muttered Jeiklee, Spirit gripping his arm as they were pulled to the castle entrance.

Soldiers held little Virginia and Nancy as Dracula appeared with Leticia, Leticia and Westley's parents with them.

"Father, what is the meaning of this??" cried Leticia, as tears poured down Virginia's little face.

"Leticia, I have no part in this," her father said, glaring at his wife. "This was your mother and Westley's parent's decision."

Leticia's mother pointed to her guards, who all held giant jars as they surrounded Virginia.

"Do you know what is in those jars, Count Dracula?"

"No," spat Dracula. "Release my daughter at once!"

"Acid," spat Leticia's mother, "Is in those jars. And on my word those jars will be opened and the acid shall be thrown all over your daughter."

Leticia gasped as Dracula's body erupted in a scarlet glow.

"Mother, you can't be serious!"

"It shouldn't have come to this but it has," snapped Leticia's mother. "You will marry Westley, Leticia, and you will not see Count Dracula again!"

"You can't do this!!" screamed Leticia, tears coursing down her face now as Dracula put an arm around her protectively. "You can't!"

"So you think. Now I think Dracula will make the right choice and agree that you will do as I say, Leticia. Or his daughter is off the face of Severna."

"You're evil!!" screamed Leticia. "I hate you, do you understand me?! *I HATE YOU!!!"*

Her mother didn't even blink as she nodded, and the guards began unscrewing the lids of the jars-

"No!" shouted Dracula, Leticia crying "Fine! I will do as you say and marry Westley! Don't hurt Virginia- please! Don't hurt her!"

Dracula glanced at Leticia, a little surprised as Virginia shakily asked "Do you like me, Miss Leticia?"

"Of course I do, Virginia- and I am so sorry for all of this, I swear to you," whispered Leticia. "I'm sorry."

Virginia swallowed as her eyes filled again, and she nodded. Leticia glared at her mother before she said "Release the child this instant."

The guards hesitated, and both Leticia's hands erupted in a scarlet glow as she spat "Now!"

The guards holding Virginia immediately let her go, and Virginia ran towards her father, still frightened as she said "Daddy!"

Dracula scooped his daughter up into his arms and held her, whispering "Thank you, Leticia. You didn't have to do this."

"I know. I'm so sorry," Leticia said quietly, eyes filling over as her mother said "Come, Leticia! We had a deal. Now you will heal your husband to be and you will get married!"

Leticia turned to look up at Dracula, eyes brimming with tears. There were tears in Dracula's eyes also as he stared down at her. He nodded, and the tears fell down Leticia's face as she reached up and kissed his cheek, whispering "You will always have my heart also."

"And you mine. Always," Dracula whispered back, and Leticia's father's jaw dropped as Leticia walked towards her mother.

Triumphant, her mother said "Good! Now let us go. Farewell, evil odd Spawn of Satan, or should I say Count Dracula!"

"I'll see you in Hell," was Dracula's cold reply, and gasps went up. Not fazed, Leticia's mother said "Let him be. I have what I want! Let us go!"

They all vanished, Dracula still holding Virginia.

Tears fell from his eyes, and Jeiklee's eyes welled up as Nancy said "Sir?"

"She sacrificed her way of life," Dracula said quietly. "For my daughter."

He placed Virginia down, then he knelt next to her, looking into her green eyes as he seriously said "Leticia of Sampson did a great, honourable thing for you, Virginia. Never forget it. She saved your life in return for her own."

"She's going to die?" asked Virginia fearfully, and Dracula chuckled before he kissed her forehead.

"No, sweet daughter. But remember. If it wasn't for her, you wouldn't be alive today and the many days months and years after."

Virginia nodded. "Yes Daddy."

Nancy brushed herself off, outraged. "How dare that vile woman steal your happiness! Why is she so against you being anywhere near Leticia of Sampson??"

"She will regret what she did today," Dracula said quietly as he stood, holding Virginia's little hand. "Virginia isn't going to school for the rest of the week. Call the school and let them know."

Nancy nodded. "Yes sir."

Dracula vanished with Virginia, and Jeiklee and Spirit were pulled to the hospital again. Westley was now awake, but still a little weak.

Leticia sat by his bed, face cold as ice as their parents sat opposite them. Curious, Westley looked at Leticia.

"What's wrong, Leticia?"

"Everything," she said icily, and he frowned at her, but before he could ask what she meant her mother said "Leticia is ready to marry you, Westley. We discussed it earlier. If you are feeling stronger, you could be wed by sunset. Leticia doesn't disagree."

Westley gaped. "Really?"

Leticia said nothing as her mother nodded, saying "Really. If you are feeling stronger, why wait?"

"I don't disagree! I'm ready to marry her," Westley said, smiling broadly, and his parents smiled back at him, Leticia's mother saying "Good! Everything has already been prepared. George has agreed to be your best man- what a lovely boy he is too, for a servant. All you need to do is get dressed and be at Severna's Chapel by six in the evening."

"I'll be there," Westley said, smile even broader. "I've been dreaming of this day for years!"

"Well now that dream has become a reality, my darling. I'll take Leticia now to get ready also."

"Great!"

"Come Leticia," her mother said firmly, and Leticia stood without saying a word and left the room. Westley frowned again, and he asked "What's wrong with Leticia?"

"It's a long story," started Sampson, and Leticia's mother cut across "You will hear it after the wedding, and only from Leticia. Come, Sampson."

Sampson glared at his wife. "Woman! Don't even *think* of trying to order me about. Do I look like I will waver?"

"We have a wedding to get ready for," Leticia's mother said through gritted teeth, "And Westley also needs to prepare. Ok??"

Sampson's glare intensified and he did a Leticia, leaving the room without answering her.

They were pulled to the Chapel, where practically the whole of Severna stood with smiles on their faces, Westley smiling broadly too as he watched Leticia walk down the aisle on her father's arm, looking ever so beautiful- but tears were trailing down her face as she walked towards him.

Westley's smile faded as she came to a stop beside him, and he asked "Why are you crying, Tish?"

"I... I-"

"They're tears of joy," her mother said abruptly. "Wipe your face, Leticia."

"Yes darling," Westley's mother added a little more gently. "This is your big day. Don't be upset."

Leticia swallowed before she whispered "I can't do this-"

"Yes, you can. Look, you've got my son worried. You don't want to displease him, do you? For no logical reason?"

"But-"

"Let's not waste anymore time," Leticia's mother said, turning to the registrar, and they nodded, everyone sitting down.

When Leticia and Westley were pronounced man and wife, cheers went up in the Chapel, horns blowing, people stamping and calling congrats delightedly, and while Westley beamed elatedly and called thank you, tears were still falling down Leticia's face.

"Poor Mum," said Jeiklee sadly, and Spirit hissed "It was for the best!"

"How can you say that?!" Jeiklee hissed back furiously, and Spirit said "You don't understand, Jeiklee-"

"No, *you* don't understand. The deal was marry my Dad or Virginia dies. That's the only reason she did it," Jeiklee said angrily. "I feel so bad for her! She wasn't happy about the wedding and she didn't want to marry him in the first place!"

"Well, that's how *you* see it," Spirit said just as angrily. "It was for the best, ok?!"

"Go to Hell, Spirit."

Spirit dropped his hand, just as mad as he was. "What is *wrong* with you??"

"This whole marriage is a sham, that's what's wrong with me! It wasn't what Mum wanted! She was forced into it!" Jeiklee said furiously. "And if you say 'it was for the best' *one* more time-"

"But it was! Dracula was corrupting her, probably had her under some crazy infatuation spell or something!" Spirit said, growing impatient with his attitude. "Try to understand where everyone was coming from, Jeiklee! She married Westley and she got away from that mess!"

"That *mess?!* She was happy, for God's sake! They stole her happiness just like they stole Dracula's happiness and she felt she couldn't do a thing about it because they could hurt Virginia again! Why don't *you* try to flipping understand!!" Jeiklee was livid now. "You're just like everyone else in Severna! Who the hell do you all think you are trying to play God with my mother's life?? When we get back I'm going to talk to her on my own- I don't want you there! Now can we just get back to the bloody present!!"

"We've got more to see, Jeiklee!"

"Just be quiet!"

* * *

Leticia frowned, holding her cup of tea. She looked at Westley, saying "Something has angered our son. I can feel his energy."
"Amazing. You truly are connected," Westley said admiringly. "As am I, but to sense how he feels when he is in a different time frame? You are brilliant, Leticia."
Leticia smiled at him. "Thank you, Westley."

* * *

Three hours had passed by since they got back to their clearing, and Jeiklee and Spirit hadn't spoken at all. Even Bari the tree was silent, unsure whether he'd be able to break the ice between the pair.
Jeiklee stared into the fire burning, still fuming. Spirit ate a sandwich, not saying anything. Jeiklee got up, then he said "Bari, can you give me a meal please? I'm real hungry now and I don't fancy searching for food."
"Yes sir. Of course. What would you like?"
"A kebab please. Lamb doner."
Jeiklee grabbed the food as soon as it appeared on Bari's branch, in a takeaway box.
"Thanks a lot." He sat down, then he started to glow bright yellow. "Oh, great! Flipping fabulous. Now I have to wait before I can eat."
Jeiklee and Spirit vanished before the tree could reply.
Westley was pacing the living area in their mansion, looking real troubled. Leticia's parents and his were there too.
"Westley, what have you called us here for?"
"It's been months since we married and Leticia hasn't smiled once," Westley said angrily. "She hardly talks. She won't sleep in the same suite as I, and she just about eats. Something may have happened to her!"
"Don't be silly, darling. Nothing happened," Westley's mother said gently. "She may just be coming to terms with married life. It was a lot to take in, after all."
"What are you talking about??" Westley stared at his mother, then he rounded on Leticia's. "You said Leticia wanted to marry me!"
"She did!"
"If she did then why is she acting this way??" Hurt, Westley stared at them all. "What did I do?"
"You didn't do anything," Leticia said quietly, and everyone whipped round.
"Leticia!"
She was standing at the door, in her cloak. Two servants stood with her, holding two medium sized suitcases.

"I'm leaving," she said, voice still quiet, and everyone leapt to their feet. "I need to be away from all of this. I did as was asked and I married Westley. There was nothing in the deal about doing what a wife is meant to do. So I shall do as I please, which is leaving this place. Alone. And I will curse whoever tries to stop me."

Westley took a step towards her, then he cautiously moved closer. "Leticia, please tell me what the matter is. We can talk about it- you don't have to leave-"

"If I stay I will only make you unhappy," Leticia said softly. "Because *I* am unhappy. I don't want to drag you down."

"You could never drag me down," Westley said, lifting a hand and caressing her cheek. "I'm your husband now. Your problems are my problems. My heart is yours Leticia, and you know that. Just tell me what's bothering you and we'll fix it, I promise we will."

Leticia shook her head, eyes filling over. "I can't tell you."

"Why not?"

"I just can't."

"But-"

"I'm not saying I won't return. But you have to let me go, Westley."

"How long for?" Defeated, Westley's shoulders fell. "Promise me you will come back to me and we'll fix the problem."

Leticia sighed. "Only one can fix this problem, and that is Count Dracula."

"Dracula?!" Westley grabbed her, outraged. "What did he do to you?! Has he threatened you? Is he making you leave? Leticia!"

Leticia said nothing, eyes on her mother, who was glaring at her.

"Everyone, allow me to speak with my daughter alone."

"I'm not leaving her," Westley said angrily, and Sampson said "She's just talking to her mother, son. Come on."

Westley was pulled from the room, his mother saying to Leticia's "Fix this. Now."

"I will," Leticia' mother replied, and everyone but she and Leticia left the room. Leticia's mother turned to her, furious. "What is wrong with you, Leticia?! Were you about to run away to Castle Dracula??"

"And what if I were?" snapped Leticia. "You got what you wanted. I married Westley. You never included anything else in the deal, which I deem quite stupid now that I think about it. You could have added whatever else you wanted, Mother. But you were so desperate for me to keep away from Count Dracula you hardly thought about what you were doing."

"Why are you being like this?! You have a husband who adores you!"

"I know," snapped Leticia. "I'm going to Castle Dracula and you cannot stop me. And if you try, I will curse you. I don't care if you're my mother. A mother wouldn't have done what you did to their daughter."

Westley burst back into the room, his parents behind.

"Westley!"

"You didn't want to marry me?" he asked, hurt as Leticia said "I don't regret marrying you, Westley."

"That's not what I asked you, Tish!"

"I have things to sort out. I will be back," she told him. "You've been kept in the dark about a lot and I'm sorry about that. But I can't explain why I have to go."

"Is Dracula forcing you to? Has he threatened you?"

Jeiklee scowled; why was everyone so idiotic about Count Dracula??

Leticia said calmly "No one has threatened me and no one is forcing me to do anything. Please let me go, Westley."

Westley stared at her, then he nodded. Leticia breathed out, relieved as she said "Thank you."

"Will you at least tell me where you're going?"

"No, because you will try and see me or bring me back. Be content, Westley Inferno, and be patient."

Westley sighed. "For you I'll be anything."

Leticia nodded, and she vanished in a flash of white light, gone. Westley looked around at everyone, then he said "I'm being kept in the dark about something and I don't appreciate it. Who knows why Leticia went? The real reason?"

No one spoke.

Westley scowled, and Sampson said "We're being truthful, Westley. It has been almost four months since your wedding day. Who knows why Leticia has decided to leave. There could be a ton of reasons."

Westley sighed and nodded. "Yes sir. I'm going to my suite."

Everyone nodded as well, and Westley vanished.

They were pulled to Castle Dracula, and it was now pouring down with rain. Leticia pounded the doors, hood thrown on as she cried "Dracula!"

Dracula appeared at once before his servants could get to the giant doors, and he pulled her into his arms and vanished.

Jeiklee and Spirit appeared in Dracula's study, Dracula lowering Leticia's hood, then he gently pulled her cloak of her body as he softly said "You're soaked to the bone, Leticia."

"I'm fine," she said, shivering, and Dracula smiled and snapped his fingers. Suddenly Leticia was warm and dry again, and she smiled at him.

"I could have done that myself, Dracula. But thank you."

"You're welcome." Dracula paused, then he said "Virginia asks after you all the time. She hasn't forgotten what you did."

Leticia smiled again. "I couldn't have done anything else."

Dracula took her hand. "What brings you back to me, Leticia? It has been pretty much four months."

"I could never keep away forever," Leticia said softly. "You know that."

Dracula smiled, touched. "Will you stay for a few hours then return to your husband?"

"No," Leticia replied quietly. "I had to leave, get away from them. I've been so miserable without you."

Dracula was surprised. "Where will you stay?"

Leticia shrugged. "Anywhere but there."

"Stay here then," Dracula said, smile growing. "You may have the chamber you slept in, it is now yours. Where are your belongings?"

"I will summon them," Leticia said, and Virginia burst into the room, Nancy behind her as she squealed "Miss Leticia of Sampson!"

Leticia knelt with her arms held out, and little Virginia ran and hugged her hard, Leticia sweeping her up as she hugged her back.

Dracula and Nancy smiled as Virginia gabbled "Are you staying for long this time, Miss Leticia? Did Daddy say you can stay for ages? Are you going to live with us?"

Dracula laughed as Leticia smiled and kissed the child on her forehead before setting her down.

"I will stay for a small while, Virginia, then I must return home."

"Oh," said Virginia, disappointed. "But will you play with me?"

"Of course I will," smiled Leticia, and Dracula said "Nancy, ready Virginia for bed please."

"Yes sir. Come, Virginia." Nancy smiled as Leticia set her down. "Say goodnight."

Virginia hugged Leticia again, then Dracula, saying "Goodnight Miss Leticia! Goodnight Daddy!"

"Goodnight," they said, smiling, and Nancy and Virginia left the study.

Dracula turned to Leticia. "Are you hungry? Would you like a hot beverage at all? Something to eat? We can dine in here if you wish."

"I'd be glad to," Leticia said a little shyly, and Dracula smiled and ordered his servants to alert the chef to make he and Leticia a special meal.

Not long later they were both enjoying their dinner, sat in front of the fireplace.

Dracula was looking at Leticia dreamily as she ate, and she smiled at him. "What is it, Dracula?"

"I love you, Leticia of Sampson. That's all. And I always will love you."

"I love you just as much, if not more. I married Westley because-"

"Because of Virginia. And we will always remember that," Dracula said softly, and he shifted closer to her. Leticia took a deep breath, her grey eyes seeming to darken a little in colour.

Dracula kissed her gently, Leticia's plate sliding off her lap as she pulled him to her, both of them sinking to the floor, Dracula on top of Leticia.

There was a knock on the door. "My Lord?"

Dracula cursed as he broke the kiss, and he snapped "What is it?"

"The chef would like to know if you and Miss Leticia of Sampson would like dessert. He has made a splendid Red Velvet cake for Miss Leticia especially as he once heard you say it is her favourite."

Dracula could help smiling at that, Leticia as well as she looked up at him, and she whispered "You never forgot."

"I never will forget anything about you," Dracula said softly, and she reached up and kissed him again.

"Sir?"

"Yes," said Dracula, annoyed as Leticia laughed. "Yes, set the cake on the table in the dining area. We will be down soon."

"Yes sir."

Leticia kissed Dracula gently before she stood. "I'm going to shower and change for bed. I'll see you in the dining area for that cake."

"Ok," Dracula said breathlessly, and she smiled and vanished.

Jeiklee was smiling; Spirit was fuming as they were pulled to the dining area.

Dracula and Leticia both were eating a large slice of Red Velvet each, talking happily.

"Leticia, if you'd like, you can spend your first night here in a while with me in my suite," Dracula said, as Leticia sipped from a mug of hot chocolate. "That is, if you'd like to." He paused, then admitted "I'd like you to."

Leticia smiled at him. "Then I will."

Dracula breathed out, relieved. "Thank you."

Jeiklee's smile grew, and Spirit looked at him furiously.

"You're loving this, aren't you?"

"They're so content, Spirit- what's not to love?" Jeiklee said, still smiling. "They're perfect for each other. Well they were, anyway."

"She's married to your father," Spirit snapped, "And she left to be with Count Dracula- does that make sense to you??"

"She was *forced* to marry my father," said Jeiklee, heat rising, "So yeah, it makes perfect sense. Mum and Count Dracula loved each other and I'd bet all I own they still do secretly. I have to talk to Mum about it, find out what she truly wants."

"Don't do that, Jeiklee! You're going to disrupt everything for Count *Dracula's* sake?!" Spirit couldn't believe what she just heard. "You don't even know him!"

"Well my mother knows him. And if she still loves him-"

"She doesn't! She's with your Dad- Westley! She loves *Westley*, ok? Even if she stayed with Dracula a few months after they married, she came to her senses eventually, don't you understand that??" Spirit was trying to get through to him, but Jeiklee was hardly listening as he watched his mother smile happily. "Jeiklee!"

"What?!"

"I know this seems romantic, but it's wrong, ok?" Spirit shook him exasperatedly. "It's wrong!"

"For flip's sake- Spirit, don't talk from now on," Jeiklee said, annoyed now. "Or I'm going to finish watching this alone!"

"You don't even know *how* to watch it alone," Spirit said angrily. "And I should watch it with you as I'm the only one seeing sense!"

"I get where you're coming from, ok? Mum's with Dad and they're perfect now. But she has a secret! And we're going to find out everything nobody else apart from Count Dracula knows, not even Dad!"

"So what are you going to do when we get back home?" demanded Spirit. "Break up your parent's marriage for something that happened in the past? It's not worth it, Jeiklee!"

"Alright," snapped Jeiklee. "I won't say anything to Mum or Dad-"

"Good!"

"But that doesn't mean I won't discuss it with Count Dracula."

"Dracula isn't the same man we're seeing here, Jeiklee! He kidnapped Leticia and all sorts!" said Spirit angrily. "He's friggin' evil! Don't go to Castle Dracula- please! I don't want anything to happen to you!"

Jeiklee was touched. "You care about me that much? Or are you tugging my heartstrings to keep me sweet?"

Spirit burst out laughing as Dracula and Leticia finished their hot drinks and cake, and they were pulled to Dracula's suite.

Leticia's head was on Dracula's chest, Dracula stroking her glossy hair.

"You have no heartbeat," whispered Leticia, and Dracula murmured "It will beat for you, Leticia... listen closely."

Leticia shifted and placed her ear directly over Dracula's heart, then she gasped amazedly.

"I don't believe it!"

"A vampire's heart will awaken when deeply in love," Dracula said softly, and she gazed up at him. "But it rarely happens. Most vampires don't have that luxury."

"You're deeply in love with me?" she asked quietly, and he smiled at her. "You know I am."

Leticia kissed him. "And I you."

Jeiklee's heart was pounding, that's how happy for them he was. Spirit noticed his big grin, and she sighed and shook her head.

Suddenly it was the next day.

Dracula woke up to Virginia pounding the door, saying "Daddy, wake up!"

"What is it, my daughter?" murmured Dracula, and Virginia said "Miss Leticia's taking me out and she wants to know if you want to come!"

Dracula snapped awake, glancing at his side.

Leticia wasn't there.

He leapt up. "How I didn't sense her waking or getting up is beyond me!"
Virginia giggled. "Are you coming, Daddy?"

"Yes, Princess. Tell Leticia to wait for me."

"Ok!"

Spirit was gaping. "So many secrets! I never had a clue about this and
neither did Westley!"

"Well I did say she has an ocean of secrets," smiled Jeiklee. "Something
like that anyway. But this is a good thing!"

"No it isn't, you flipping-"

They were pulled to the lakeside before Spirit could finish, where they saw
Virginia running around happily, Leticia and Dracula sitting on a picnic
blanket.

"Red Velvet, Leticia?" offered Dracula, and she smiled and accepted,
taking the plated cake slice from him.

"Daddy, look! Look at the fish!" said Virginia happily. "They're pink and
purple!"

Dracula smiled at his daughter. "Thank you for this, Leticia. She's so
happy."

Leticia smiled at Virginia as well. "You're welcome, Dracula. Virginia is
lovely."

"I left Nancy to do a lot," Dracula said thoughtfully. "I need to spend more
time with my daughter."

"Dracula, you spend a lot of time with Virginia. I know you do."

"But we've never had a family picnic before like today."

"I know." Leticia took his hand. "Today can be the start of many."

"Will you be there on the other picnics?" asked Dracula, looking hopeful,
and Leticia smiled at him.

"I'm not certain. But I'd love to be."

Dracula waited until Virginia peered down at the water before he kissed
Leticia. Virginia glanced at them anyway, about to point something else
out. She gasped at the sight of her Daddy kissing Miss Leticia of Sampson,
then she quickly peered back down at the water when they broke apart…
and she had a massive smile on her face.

"She's so glad," said Jeiklee, Spirit scowling at the little Virginia. "She
seems like any happy kid. It was when she started high school things went
bad, right Spirit?"

"She cursed a boy in primary school, did you forget?" Spirit said irritably,
and Jeiklee glared at her.

"I give up. Keep being sour about her."

"I will."

They were pulled back to Castle Dracula, this time in Virginia's room.
Leticia had just finished telling her a bedtime story, Dracula standing by
the door with a smile on his face as Virginia's eyes started to close, then

she mumbled "When I'm big, I want to have a coffin bed. Like the vampire in the story!"

"I'm sure your Daddy will let you have one, sweetie. Good night."

"Good night," mumbled Virginia; Leticia kissed her forehead before she joined Dracula, and they both left the room.

As they walked down the corridor, Dracula put an arm around Leticia.

"You are amazing."

"Thank you," Leticia said softly, and he kissed her.

Suddenly Jeiklee and Spirit were at their mansion, and they saw Westley pacing the living area, his and Leticia's parents there as an old man spoke nervously.

"You're certain that's what you saw," said Westley angrily; the old man nodded.

"I'm certain, sir."

"It has been two months since Leticia disappeared. Why come forward now?" demanded Westley. "If what you say is true and she was with Count Dracula and she's there now-"

"I don't know if she's there now, sir, but I know she was with him two months ago. At the lake with his little one. They were having a picnic, sir."

"You came forward for the reward," Leticia's mother said, glaring at him. "We don't want to know where she was two months ago. We want to know where she is *now.*"

"Well, I... I don't know where the Countess is now-"

"Seize him," spat Leticia's mother, and her guards grabbed the poor old man. "Before money clouds your vision make sure your story actually counts. Take him away."

"My grandmother is just... hard," said Jeiklee amazedly. "She really doesn't give a damn. Like, at all."

"Calm down, Westley," said Westley's mother gently. "You're hyperventilating."

"What if she's been at Castle Dracula this whole time??" Westley was agitated. "What if they're- they-"

"They are close friends, son." Sampson patted his shoulder. "Nothing more."

"But why leave in the first place??"

"She said she was unhappy, Westley. Take some deep breaths," Sampson said, and Westley obeyed. "What that man saw was two months ago. Leticia could be anywhere now. Remember, she told you she would return. All we have to do is wait."

"I'll go mad if I don't see or hear from her for another two months," Westley said angrily, and everyone saw his eyes had welled up. "I'm going to Castle Dracula for my wife!"

"Oh hell," said Jeiklee nervously, Spirit saying "Good!"

"Good??"

"Dracula has her in his clutches, Jeiklee, and she needs to get away before she does something totally nuts like fall crazily in love with him!"

"She's already crazily in love with him, dipstick! And he's just as in love with her," Jeiklee said angrily. "This isn't going to end well at all."

"It's dark out," Westley said, glaring out of the windows. "The creatures in the Forest of Fear will definitely defend Count Dracula if we attack. It's best we go in the day. I need to plan a strategy-"

"Westley, did you not hear what I said?" said Sampson exasperatedly. "It is best we wait for Leticia to return!"

"And that could take years, Sampson! I want her back and I want her back now!" Westley said angrily. "I'm going to Castle Dracula at dawn!"

"And what if she isn't even there?" demanded Sampson. "What if the last time she saw Dracula was when she had that picnic with him? Get your head screwed back on, and tight! If you want to do this, do it right! Or *I* will be the one making sure you don't see my daughter!"

"I don't have to listen to that. Leticia may be your daughter but she is also my wife. And I'm going to get her back!"

"Let him go," Leticia's mother said softly, when Sampson opened his mouth angrily. "He has to do this, Sampson. Let him be."

"This isn't going to end well," Sampson replied flatly, then he looked at his son-in-law. "Fine, Westley. Go for your wife. I will join you."

"Why?" asked Westley, still angry, and Sampson answered "Because if you attack Count Dracula and he almost kills you like the last time, or he *does* kill you, I will be there to stop my daughter from saving you."

Westley's jaw dropped. "How can you say that about me?!"

"Because you're not thinking straight," Sampson said flatly. "If what I just said reaches your brain at all, your mind will sort itself. You don't want to be killed by Count Dracula, do you?" Westley said no. "Then think properly."

"I'll think on the way to the castle. Let's go."

"What happened to waiting until dawn?" Westley's mother asked, and Westley snapped "I'm not waiting another minute! Men! Come!"

Westley's men joined him, weapons at the ready. Sampson shook his head as he joined him too, Westley saying "Mother, please stay indoors. You too, Ma'am," he added to Leticia's mother, who nodded.

Westley, Sampson and their men left the mansion.

The night air was cool.

The men marched on, Westley and Sampson on their own horses.

Jeiklee was nervous. So was Spirit, because she said "What do you think will happen, Jeiklee?"

"We'll see," Jeiklee replied, and she took his hand and squeezed it. Jeiklee squeezed back, both of them pulled back to Castle Dracula.

Leticia and Dracula were fast asleep in his suite, Leticia's head on Dracula's muscular torso, arms around him.

The uproar outside the castle could be heard faintly, and Jeiklee walked to the windows and looked down, his head slipping right through the glass.

"Spirit! Come see this!"

Spirit joined him, looking down too, then she gasped "A giant!"

Sampson drove his sword into a vampire's chest as Westley was knocked off his horse, slamming to the ground.

He rolled over just in time as a giant slammed his foot down, obviously trying to crush him.

"You will leave or die," roared the giant, and Westley unsteadily got to his feet, spitting blood out of his mouth.

Sampson was swung around by the same vampire he tried to kill, the vampire laughing as he pulled the sword out of his chest.

"You forget I am already dead, Lord Sampson!"

Sampson backed on his hands on knees, and Spirit and Jeiklee whipped round as there was frantic pounding on Dracula's suite doors.

"My Lord! My Lord, please wake up!!"

Dracula and Leticia snapped awake immediately, and they heard the roars from the giant again.

They both leapt up, running to the windows and looking down.

"Oh my-!! There's Westley and my father!" gasped Leticia, and suddenly Dracula was fully clothed as he said "Leticia, stay here."

"What??"

"Stay here!"

"I won't, Dracula! You are my everything and I won't let them kill you!"

"They could never kill me, sweetheart." Dracula kissed her. "They are here for you and they will be killed by my minions if they don't fall back. Unless they are willing to battle until dawn, that is, and it will have no effect as the trees block out most of the sunlight."

"Let me come with you," pleaded Leticia. "Please!"

"Will you go back to Westley?" asked Dracula, and Leticia said "I don't know but I won't let you go out there alone!"

"My minions will protect me, Leticia."

"Westley wants you dead, Dracula! He'll stop at nothing!" cried Leticia, and Dracula paused as he began to put on his cloak.

"How do you know?"

"I can feel his rage." Tears were falling down her face now. "He has something on him that will harm you! You have to let me come, to protect you!"

Dracula sighed and took her hand. "Nothing, whether it harms me or not, will kill me, Leticia of Sampson."

"But-"

"Stay here. His men aren't bold enough to penetrate the walls of my castle."

"I won't," said Leticia angrily. "No matter what you say, I'm coming!"

Dracula sighed before he kissed her. Leticia gripped his cloak as she responded, Dracula murmuring as he broke the kiss, "You are so stubborn." Leticia smiled. "So you will let me come?"

"Yes."

"We will do this together, do you promise me that?"

Dracula nodded. "I promise."

Jeiklee and Spirit were pulled to the grounds of the castle, where Westley was standing injured, Sampson as well as Westley gasped "Ignite your arrows and kill the giant!"

His archers obeyed; flamed arrows shot through the air and plunged deep into the giants chest- suddenly every soldier was thrown back in a blast of an orange spell and slammed to the ground, unconscious.

"Miss Leticia!" cried some vampires, and Sampson's jaw dropped as he saw his daughter, her body blazing with orange light as she walked beside Count Dracula, whose eyes were on Westley.

"Leticia, what are you *doing?!*" gasped Westley; Leticia didn't reply.

"What have you to harm me with, Westley Inferno?" Dracula asked icily, and Westley reached into his bag and pulled out a bottle of-

"Holy water?" smiled Dracula, and Spirit took Jeiklee's hand again, scared. "How cute."

"You will die when this holy water touches you!" spat Westley, and Dracula's smile grew. "Then I will take my wife!"

"Alright. Kill me with the holy water," smirked Dracula, and Westley stared at him. "You are so confident, Inferno, aren't you? Go ahead!"

Leticia looked at Dracula fearfully as Westley uncorked the bottle.

"Dracula, what are you-?"

"I'm letting him murder me, Leticia. Or should I say I'm letting him *believe* he will murder me."

The vampires and other creatures surrounding them sniggered as Westley uncorked the bottle and shouted "DIE!!"

"NO!!" screamed Leticia as he curled the contents directly at Dracula's face, and Dracula gasped, hands clapping to his face.

"Aaaargh!!"

"Vermin!" spat Westley as steam issued from behind Dracula's hands; Dracula stumbled as Leticia cried "Dracula!"

Westley grabbed Leticia's hand and half dragged her away from Dracula, saying "He's going to be dead in a few seconds and good riddance! Now come *on,* Leticia!"

Dracula's laughter boomed around the forest, making them whip round. Westley, Leticia and Sampson gasped fearfully: Dracula was standing upright, unscathed… smiling.

"Well that was refreshing, Inferno. What else do you have in that little bag of yours?"

Westley couldn't believe it, mouth hanging open. "You're alive?!"

"In the flesh."

Leticia was so relieved as she pulled away from Westley and ran to Dracula, tears trailing down her face as she whispered "Holy water has no effect on you??"

"I told you, sweetheart."

"Westley," said Sampson nervously. "We need to get away from here. Now. Count Dracula cannot be killed."

"What are you talking about?? Of course he can!"

"Of course he can," snickered a tree, and laughter erupted, Dracula smiling at Westley like a cat who just caught a mouse.

"Anything else in your little goodie bag, Inferno?"

"A silver cross!" spat Westley, and the vampires hissed and shrank backwards as he held the cross up and advanced on Dracula, who didn't waver.

At all.

Still smiling, Dracula said "What else do you want to try before you listen to your father-in-law?"

Westley dropped the cross in shock, backing away from him.

"What kind of monster *are* you?!"

"A monster that cannot be killed," shrugged Dracula, smirking now. "It would be wise to leave, Westley Inferno, before I lose my temper. Your wife has taken out all of your men. You stand alone with Sampson. What is your next move?"

"Leticia," said Westley desperately, and she looked at him. "Please- please come home with me. We're married- you didn't have to do this- just come home."

"You were going to kill Count Dracula," Leticia said quietly. "When you know- you *know* how much he means to me. Was banning me from seeing him not enough, Westley? You had to make sure he was dead?"

"But Leticia-!!"

"My father was against this and he is injured because of you," spat Leticia. "I will heal him, but I will not heal you. You deserve to be in pain, Westley Inferno. You deserve *everything you get!!*"

She walked towards her father, hands glowing purple as she placed her hands on both his cheeks.

Everyone said "Ooooh!" and "Aaaaah!" as the purple light swirled around Sampson, his wounds healing, his broken wrist mending. Moments later Sampson was in perfect condition, and he was smiling at his child.

"Thank you, my daughter."

"You're welcome, Father."

"When will you return home?"

"Soon. But not to him," Leticia said, glaring at Westley, who looked really hurt. "I'll return home to you and Mother. That is where I will stay. I will be back in a month, Father, is that ok with you?"

"Anything is ok with me," smiled Sampson. "Now… please remove the curse from these poor soldiers. They were only obeying Westley."

Leticia obeyed, snapping her fingers.

Green light shot out of every soldier's chest and vanished, and they snapped awake, gasping.

"What happened?!"

"Return to the mansion with my coward of a husband," said Leticia coldly. "And don't ever think of returning to Castle Dracula, no matter what orders he gives you."

"Yes Ma'am," they mumbled, getting up unsteadily, and Sampson pulled Leticia into a hug, kissing her forehead as he said "A month?"

"Yes Father. A month," Leticia said, hugging him back, then she turned and joined Dracula, who put an arm around her.

Westley eyes filled over as he said "Leticia! Please-"

"No," she spat. "Leave and do not come here again. Do not come to my parent's home to seek me after a month has passed. You crossed the line, Westley Inferno, and I want nothing to *do* with you!"

Westley took a step towards her, then he gasped at the pain in his left leg. A knife was embedded deep in his thigh.

"What?!"

"A thigh for a chest," smirked a vampire, the same vampire who Sampson stabbed, and Westley gasped "It wasn't even *me* who stabbed you in the chest!"

"Well you did throw holy water in my master's face, so it fits somehow."

"That makes no sense," said Westley angrily, then he realised Dracula and Leticia were gone. "Leticia?? Leticia!"

"Come on son, let's go," Sampson said gently, taking Westley's arm as he pulled the knife out of his leg. "We need to get you to the hospital. You have more than one wound, Westley."

Westley shook his head. "I need Leticia- I just need Leticia!"

"She's very angry with you," Sampson said soothingly. "Just give her time to calm down. Give her the space she needs."

"But-"

"Westley," said Sampson firmly. "For once listen to the orders you are given. Now come on. We're taking you to the hospital to be treated. Give Leticia some space."

Westley's eyes filled again as he stared up at Castle Dracula. Hurt was etched across his face.

"She chose him over me."

"Don't look at it like that, son." Sampson took his arm and led him away, Westley limping very badly. "You need a horse."

"My horse fled the scene when the giant arrived," muttered Westley, Sampson throwing his arm over his shoulder to support him. "I can do without it."

"Alright."

"Wow," said Jeiklee, Spirit shocked as well as they appeared back in their clearing. "Just… wow. That is a *lot*. Like… friggin' hell! That was crazy!" His stomach rumbled, and he looked about for Bari the Tree desperately. "Bari? Are you around?"

"I am, sir."

"Then give us a feast please. A *feast.*"

* * *

"Leticia?" said Westley anxiously, and she stopped by the giant doors of the mansion. "Where are you going?"

"Just for a walk, Westley." Leticia smiled at him. "I won't be longer than two hours."

"Our son is back today, Leticia- can it wait?"

Leticia hesitated; she was going to see Count Dracula. He was waiting for her, she could sense it. She couldn't be late.

"I'll be back before Jeiklee returns with Spirit. I promise," she said, but before Westley could protest she vanished.

Leticia reappeared at the entrance of the Forest of Fear, fastening her cloak as the wind blew.

She took a deep breath, then she entered.

The trees whispered her name as she walked deeper and deeper into the Forest, daylight slowly fading as the trees grew thicker.

Suddenly Virginia of Dracula appeared, startling her.

"Virginia!"

"Miss Leticia," said Virginia humbly, bowing a little, and Leticia asked "What are you doing in the Forest?"

"I was on my way into town," Virginia said honestly. "I walked with Father to both of your clearing, and I left him and continued my journey."

Leticia nodded, but Virginia didn't start walking again.

"Miss Leticia, please don't hurt him," she pleaded, surprising Leticia. "I'm begging you! He's been smiling more and singing around the castle, he's always in a great mood since he saw you and you did whatever you do to infatuate him-"

"What do you mean infatuate him?" Leticia asked, slightly amused. "You think I affect your father like this deliberately? And he I?"

"Well I don't know what you do to each other but if he's going to get hurt I'm not allowing it," Virginia said crossly, and Leticia laughed and pulled her into a hug. Virginia stiffened her body for a moment then hugged her back with a big smile, Leticia saying "Surely you haven't forgotten the fun we used to have, Virginia? I did love you so."

"I loved you too Miss Leticia. I still do," Virginia said shyly as Leticia let her go. "I know I angered you because of what I did to Spirit McKenzie."

Leticia nodded, and Virginia quickly said "But I won't trouble her anymore. I even told Professor Gene at Thrill I wouldn't. I'll be good from now on, I promise."

"You were always good, Virginia. You're just dangerous when angered," Leticia replied with a smile, and Virginia smiled back. "Now I really must head on to your father."

"Yes Miss."

"Don't get into any trouble in town," called Leticia as she walked away, and a beaming Virginia called back "I won't!"

Leticia entered her and Count Dracula's special clearing, where Dracula sat staring down at the ground, deep in thought.

"Dracula," she said softly, and he smiled and looked at her before he stood, saying "Leticia," just as softly.

"I just ran into Virginia," smiled Leticia, as he walked towards her. "She's on her way into town."

"Mmm. To friends, I believe. How have you been, Leticia?" Dracula took Leticia's hand and kissed it gently.

The feel of his lips on her skin made Leticia's legs almost turn to jelly, and she whispered "Let's sit down."

* * *

Jeiklee and Spirit vanished just as they were waking up.

"Hey!"

They reappeared at the gates of Dracula's castle, where they saw Dracula and Leticia standing lip locked at the castle doors, obviously saying their goodbyes.

The sound of horse hooves made them break apart and look around, and they saw Sampson emerge from the trees, some more men behind him.

"Count Dracula, my boy. My brilliant, brilliant boy," smiled Sampson, and Dracula smiled back.

"Hello sir."

"Look at that big smile on my daughter's face," said Sampson happily. "Going away has done her plenty of good. She was so *miserable!* And now she's happy. Thank you for having her these past months, Dracula."

"You're welcome, sir. I was happy having Leticia here also," smiled Dracula, and Spirit scowled and muttered "If only Sampson knew why. If only Westley and *everyone else* knew why!"

"Shut up," snapped Jeiklee, and she pouted at him. "I'm trying to listen."

Leticia hugged Dracula hard, whispering in his ear "I love you."

"I love you more," Dracula whispered back, and Leticia straightened up, clearly saying "Thank you for everything, Dracula. Farewell."

"Farewell," Dracula responded just as clearly, and Leticia walked towards her father and his men; one helped her onto a horse.

Dracula smiled dreamily as Leticia waved again, and he waved back as the party began to move, back into the Forest of Fear.

Little Virginia ran out of the doors, startling Dracula as she cried "Miss Leticia! Don't go!"

"I will be back, Virginia," Leticia called back, voice gentle as ever. "I will miss you ever so much."

"I'll miss you too!" Virginia called, and her eyes welled up. "Daddy?"

"She'll be back, sweetheart. Don't cry," said Dracula, kneeling beside his little girl as Leticia and her father disappeared into the trees with their men. "Shall we have some Red Velvet cake? You know that's Leticia's favourite. We can have some when we feel sad because she isn't with us anymore. But she will be back."

"I miss her already," wept Virginia, and Dracula sighed before he said "As do I. Come inside, Virginia."

"Yes Daddy."

"So sad," said Jeiklee, a bit upset. "Virginia loved my mother to pieces."

"Well I'm glad it's over with and she left," Spirit said flatly, but before Jeiklee could answer furiously they were pulled to Leticia's parent's home. Westley stood at the door, Leticia standing there with folded arms.

"It's been two months since you came back from Count Dracula's castle, Leticia."

"And your point is?"

"That we've been married almost a year and we've hardly spent that time together," said Westley desperately. "I miss you."

"Well I don't miss you. At all."

"If you just let me explain-"

"There's nothing to explain," snapped Leticia. "You didn't think of me when you threw holy water into Count Dracula's face, did you?"

"You were *all* I thought about!" said Westley, heat rising. "And Count Dracula can't be killed anyway!"

"You didn't know that," Leticia said angrily. "You expected him to die! You actually intended to murder, to take a life!"

"For you, Leticia- for *you!* There is nothing I wouldn't do for you," said Westley, and for a moment Leticia looked touched. "Nothing!"

Leticia's face grew stone cold again. "I don't care. Please leave, Westley."

"So this is it?" said Westley. "We're over?"

"We may as well be."

"I won't let you end our marriage over someone so minimal!"

"Wrong word," muttered Jeiklee, and Spirit shushed him, nervous.

"Minimal?" Leticia repeated furiously. "Count Dracula means more to me than you *ever* could! Now I see you for what you are, Westley Inferno- a cruel being who only thinks and acts for himself!"

"I'm not cruel!" said Westley angrily; Leticia's body lit scarlet.

"You say you were doing all of this for me. Did I not tell you to be patient? Did I not say I would return?"

Westley didn't answer, looking abashed.

Leticia nodded angrily. "All you had to do was wait until I pulled myself together. That was *all you had to do!* But you couldn't, could you? You didn't want to listen to your wife, the one you claim is your other half. Why should I be with someone who won't listen to me?!"

"I can change, Leticia- I swear I will change! I will be there for you, and I will listen to everything you have to say, I promise you," pleaded Westley. "Just come home with me. We'll work on our problems-"

"Our problems??" scowled Leticia, and Jeiklee nodded, feeling the same. Spirit pushed him angrily, and he nudged her back gently.

"My problems then!" said Westley desperately. "I can't lose you!"

Leticia didn't speak for a moment. "Why should I trust you?"

"Because I love you, Leticia." Westley was pleading harder than ever. "Please, just come home with me. I can change, I promise I will change. If you want to see Count Dracula, well… I-"

"You won't change your mind about that," Leticia said stonily. "Right?"

Westley opened his mouth to say he would, but he couldn't do it. He kicked a stone as they stood in awkward silence, then Sampson walked out of the mansion's giant doors behind Leticia.

"My sweet daughter. Your husband is begging you to forgive him."

"I don't think I can, Father."

"Maybe not now, but let time pass. Let him court you again at least."

"I don't want to be courted by him," Leticia said flatly. "When that finally reaches his brain-"

Sampson chuckled, and Leticia looked at him.

"What's funny, Father?"

"I have something to show you. Take my hand."

Leticia shook her head. "I don't want to jump through time, Father."

"Just take my hand, darling."

Leticia sighed and obeyed, then her eyes lit bright blue, startling Westley. "Leticia?"

Sampson shushed him, a mix of emotions showing on Leticia's expression as she saw whatever her father was showing her.

Westley stood nervously, Sampson murmuring "It will be alright, son."

Leticia gasped a minute later and pulled away from her father, eyes grey again as she looked at Westley. He stared back at her, and she quietly said "I didn't think my leaving had such an effect on you, Westley."

"What did you see?" asked Westley, and she replied "How you were when I was gone. You may have needed help with your mental health."

Westley pouted at her, and she smiled at him for the first time in months. Westley cautiously smiled back, then suddenly they were hugging each other hard, Westley stroking her hair as he whispered "I'm so sorry, Leticia. I didn't think."

"I know you didn't."

"Will you come home with me? We can get through this, I know we can."

Leticia looked at her father, who nodded. She sighed saying "If you mess up again, Westley Inferno-"

"I won't, I promise you."

"Ok," sighed Leticia. "I'll come home."

Sampson smiled broadly. "Good! Go now with your husband, Leticia. I will send some servants with your belongings later today."

Leticia nodded, Westley taking her hand a little nervously, then he breathed out when she didn't pull away.

They vanished, Sampson smiling even more broadly as his wife joined him.

"Where is Leticia? We need to convince her to go back to her husband and get that scoundrel Count Dracula out of her head."

"I've already done that, minus the Count Dracula part. She has gone to the mansion with Westley."

"What? How did you do it??"

"She had a vision."

"A vision you forced her to look at? Made by yourself?"

Sampson nodded. "Yes."

"Well finally you and I are on the same page," smiled Leticia's mother. "Now-"

Suddenly they heard the boom of drums faintly, Sampson frowning.

"Not the drums of war?" gasped Leticia's mother, and men thundered through the gates of their house.

"Dragons are upon us, Lord Sampson! Two adults from each family must take part in the war to defend our land, defend our children from destruction!"

"We will go," Leticia's mother said firmly. "Please leave my daughter out of this! Sampson and I will fight for Severna!"

Suddenly it was night time. Smoke was everywhere.

"Oh no," said Jeiklee sadly, when he saw his mother in tears, Westley holding her as the King of Severna cautiously walked towards them.

"Why so glum, Leticia of Sampson? The war is won! It did take eight days, but the dragons have retreated! We can move on!"

"Move on?" Leticia repeated, furious as she looked at him. "We have lost our parents! They were killed by those dragons and where were *you?* Sipping wine in your palace while everyone else fought for you? A King is supposed to lead his soldiers, not cower away behind closed doors while the dragons wreak havoc on our land! What kind of man are you?!"

"We can discuss this over dinner, my girl. Westley, I want you both at the palace in three days. I am terribly sorry for both of your loss."

Westley nodded. "Yes sir."

"No," said Leticia angrily, wiping her tears away. "I won't have stopped grieving in three days. If you want to go to dinner with the King then go ahead Westley, but I will not join you!"

She turned and walked indoors before Westley could reply, and the King sighed.

"I fear your wife will always hate me, my boy. Because of the law I passed about your little boy. You do understand why I didn't take part in the war, don't you?"

Westley started to say yes, then he shook his head. "No. I don't understand at all, sir. Leticia is right. A King is supposed to lead his soldiers."

He turned and walked indoors as well, and the King sighed and left.

Jeiklee felt emotional as they were pulled to another moment in time. It was daytime, and the air was full of dragons.

"Mum!" cried Spirit suddenly, as a woman dodged a blast of flame from a dragon's mouth, then she tumbled off the edge of a cliff, the dragon swooping after her. "Mum!! DAD!!"

A man ran after the dragon as a loud scream rang out, Leticia screaming

"Rachel!!"

Count Dracula suddenly appeared and grabbed her arm. "Leticia!"

"Dracula!"

"I'm getting you out of here right now!"

"No- my friend has just been killed!"

"And so has her husband, Leticia!" said Dracula angrily, as the dragon roared triumphantly before flying back into the sky. "I'm taking you!"

"No! Let go of me!"

"Count Dracula!" someone shrieked angrily. "Let go of her right now!"

Dracula ignored them, pulling Leticia to him and vanishing on the spot.

Westley ran to the spot they vanished, yelling "What happened?!"

"Count Dracula kidnapped your wife!" everyone shouted, and Westley dived out of the way as a dragon's tail flew out of nowhere. "Go for her, sir!"

"Two of my friends have just been killed!" said Westley angrily. "I can't abandon you all!"

Tears were trailing down Spirit's face as they were pulled to Castle Dracula, Jeiklee putting an arm around her.

"It's ok, Spirit. It'll be ok."

"I never saw how my Mum and Dad were killed," wept Spirit. "I know it was dragons who killed them, but I never actually saw it-"

"Dracula, have you gone mad?!" Leticia said angrily, glowing scarlet, and Dracula calmly replied "You are not fighting in that war, Leticia. When it's over, you may return to your home. Until then, you are staying here. Do I make myself clear?"

"But-"

"But nothing. I have my reasons for doing this. You have to trust me." Dracula took off his cloak, then he looked at her. "Do you trust me?"

Leticia glared at him, but she couldn't say no. "Fine. I will stay."

"You have no choice. I'm equally as powerful as you are and I have bound you to the castle."

"My friends are dead," Leticia said furiously. "I can't just sit around and do nothing, Dracula! I could have at least killed a dragon to avenge them, killed two or three even!"

"No. The people of Severna think I kidnapped you-"

"Well you kind of did!"

"I have my reasons for taking you like I said," Dracula said calmly. "I will share them with you once the war is over- the second war. I don't know why the King doesn't just give the dragons back their treasure. It is not his."

"Their treasure?" Leticia repeated curiously. "King Harlot has treasure that belongs to the dragons?"

"Yes. He journeyed to the mountains years ago, far beyond my castle, beyond the oceans to the part of the land where the dragons reside. He stole very powerful jewels from those caves while the dragons slept, years ago. Those jewels kept peace and harmony amongst the dragons. Now, they have awoken and are furious. They want their jewels back before it's too late."

"Too late?"

"Those dragons will keep coming back until they get what's theirs, Leticia. There is a second war now because King Harlot deceived them."

"How?" demanded Leticia, and Dracula sighed.

"In the first Dragon War, where your parents were killed, the King pretended to give the right jewels back. He gave them very similar looking jewels and the dragons went away, happy they had their jewels once more." Dracula nodded when Leticia's jaw dropped. "Yes. Now, the dragons have realised that the jewels are fake, and are beyond furious. More people will die, and the King will stay hidden in his palace like the coward he is."

"Dracula, I have to go back," Leticia said desperately. "Please let me go!"

Dracula shook his head. "No."

"But I can stop this war!"

"How can you do that, Leticia?"

"I'll go to the palace and get the jewels," Leticia said, pleading with Dracula now. "I'll give the jewels back to the dragons and there will be peace again! I'm sure there won't be another war if they have the right jewels!"

Dracula looked thoughtful for a moment. "You may be right."

"I *am* right! Please, you have to let me do this. Now that I know the reason behind the war-"

"You are staying here, Leticia." Leticia threw up her hands exasperatedly, and Dracula said *"I* will go."

"You??"

Dracula nodded. "Yes."

Leticia gaped. "Since when did you care for Severna??"

"I don't," shrugged Dracula, "But I care for *you* and this war will only continue if I don't do something. You are so fierce and brave, sweetheart. But this is one fight I won't let you take part in. I will not lose you, do you understand?" She didn't answer, Dracula moving closer to her before he softly said "You have to trust me."

Leticia opened her mouth, then she closed it and nodded. Dracula took her hand and kissed it, then he vanished.

Jeiklee and Spirit appeared in the Palace of Severna, where they saw the King pacing his hall worriedly.

Count Dracula appeared, sheathed in a black cloak with the hood thrown up, his face unseen as he walked towards King Harlot, who said "The dragons will no doubt attack more buildings including my Palace! And I will not have anything happen to these walls. Are the false jewels ready to present to the dragons yet?"

"Yes Your Highness."

"Then take them. Hopefully they are fooled for a few years like the last time."

"Stop," ordered Dracula, and everyone whipped round, startled.

"Who are you?" demanded the King, frightened as his soldiers picked up their weapons immediately, advancing on Dracula menacingly. "How did you get past my guards this far into the Palace?!"

Dracula didn't even step back. Cold as ever, he said "Lives, King Harlot. Many lives have been lost in this war with the dragons, twice now."

"And your point is??"

"You have left a little girl orphaned because of your greed. Leticia of Sampson has lost two close friends because of you!" Dracula's body was suddenly ablaze with scarlet light. "She is angry and distraught and she knows you have the magical jewels. I've told her everything."

"But how do *you* know of the magical jewels?! They were a heavily guarded secret!" said the King fearfully. "Who are you?! Speak before I order my men to kill you!"

"Well that would be a waste of time, because I am a being who cannot be killed," Dracula said flatly. "It was all over the news a while back. I look it, but I am hardly human. You may even go as far as to say I am a demon."

The soldiers dropped their weapons, backing away from him as they gasped "Count Dracula!"

"The very one," said Dracula amusedly, lowering his hood. "Now I am glad you lowered your weapons, men. Things could have gotten quite ugly if you tried to murder me."

The King was shaking with fear. "What do you want?!"

"I want the magical jewels."

"For yourself?!"

"To return to the dragons," spat Dracula, and King Harlot flinched as he said "You've caused enough damage to this land. I will make sure peace is restored or so help me, you will become my plaything for the rest of your miserable, greedy life."

The King swallowed, and so did his guards as he asked "Your plaything, Count Dracula?"

"The one I sink my fangs into when I need to feed. The one who will be on the receiving end of knives and red hot pokers. The one who will suffer like these poor people have suffered because of you. I think that should make up for the lives lost, don't you agree *Your Highness?"*

"I do not! Guards!"

The soldiers perked up immediately, but from a distance as they looked at Dracula fearfully.

"Please don't attack," muttered Jeiklee, Spirit holding his hand.

The King was glaring at Count Dracula, almost about to have him attacked; Dracula smiled at him, and everyone saw his fangs were unsheathed.

The King stumbled backwards in terror. "You will not turn me into a creature of the night!!"

"And who will stop me?" smirked Dracula. "Your pathetic soldiers? They seem to want to flee rather than protect you."

"What do you want?!"

"Give me the jewels," spat Dracula. "The real ones. I cannot be deceived and I sense deceit. Bring them to me. Now!"

The King jumped and whipped round. "You heard him! Bring the dragon's jewels this instant!"

The soldiers ran to it immediately, Dracula tapping his foot as he waited.

"I do love when I get my own way. Don't you King Harlot?"

The King glared at him, but didn't dare answer.

Moments later the solders returned with three giant chests, and they knelt and rested them at Dracula's feet.

"There you are Count Dracula sir."

"Thank you," Dracula said coldly. "And is that all of them?"

"Yes," spat the King before the soldier could reply. "You have my word! I promise that's all there is- now can you please leave!"

"And if I said no?" smiled Dracula. "What would you do?"

The King stared at him, Dracula repeating the question.

"Well?"

"I… I wouldn't do a thing," muttered King Harlot, and Dracula laughed.

"More like you *couldn't* do a thing. Farewell, King Harlot."

Dracula vanished with the treasure chests, and King cursed him to high heaven.

"My jewels! My precious, precious jewels- gone forever!"

"Gone back to their rightful owner," Dracula's voice boomed around the Palace coldly, and the King flinched.

"Go Dracula," said Jeiklee impressively, and Spirit scowled as they appeared outside.

The dragons screeched and flew about angrily, blasting the ground with fire, people screaming and running everywhere.

Count Dracula calmly walked through the chaos, the chests hovering in front of him. His hood was thrown up; nobody knew it was him as he held his hands up to the dragons, who stared down at him, flapping their gigantic wings.

"Dragons!" Dracula's voice boomed just like it did in the palace, magically magnified. "Rage no longer. I have what is rightfully yours, all of it! In these chests, are the jewels you have been seeking for years!"

"How do we know we can trust you?" snarled a dragon, one who was further in front than the rest. Jeiklee assumed he was the leader as it spat "We were fooled by the King years ago and we are now wiser!"

"See for yourself, oh mighty one," Dracula replied, and he snapped his fingers.

The chests burst open, everyone watching fearfully as the leader dragon swooped down, landing on it's clawed feet and walking closer, smoke unfurling from his mouth as it stared down at the glowing jewels.

Everyone held their breath as the dragon scoped each chest, then it looked at Count Dracula incredulously.

"How is this possible?!"

"I persuaded the King to return the jewels," Dracula replied, and the dragon said "Impossible. He wouldn't return them even when war was upon him. He is the cause of plenty of deaths! What is it about *you* that convinced him?? Speak!"

"His fear of me," Dracula replied truthfully. "Everyone fears me in this land, more than dragons, more than werewolves or giants."

"But why? What is it about one human that can make everyone fear him so?"

"Maybe the fact that though I look it, I am barely human," Dracula replied, and the dragon stared at him. Dracula sighed, then he lifted his hood a tiny bit so the dragon saw his face clearly- the dragon flew backwards in shock as Dracula dropped his hood.

"My Lord!! It was *you??"*

"Yes," said Dracula. "Do not reveal who I am to these people. Take the jewels you created war for, twice. There will be no reason to war again."

Jeiklee saw his father, bleeding as the dragons took up the treasure chests in their jaws and flapped their wings, ready for take off.

"This Lord," boomed the leader of the dragons, "This mighty man you see here, has ended the war. You think poorly of him! You loathe him! I would love to see the looks on all of your faces when you realise he is a hero, who has saved this land from destruction!"

"Who are you?" demanded Westley, and Dracula looked at him.

"Nobody special. The war is over! Care for those injured, mourn and see to the dead! It is done!"

Cheers went up as everyone ran towards Dracula to shake his hand, but he vanished.

Jeiklee and Spirit appeared in Dracula's study, where Leticia was pacing. She tried opening the door, but it wouldn't budge.

Dracula appeared behind her. "Leticia."

She whipped round. "Dracula!"

He removed his cloak, smiling at her. "It is over."

Relieved, Leticia ran and hugged him hard. Dracula held her as tears trailed down her face, and she whispered "Thank you. Thank you, thank you!"

"You are most welcome. You'd better get back to your husband, Leticia."
Leticia nodded, taking a deep breath as he let her go. They stared at each
other for a moment, Dracula moving closer, then he stopped himself.
"Goodbye Leticia. I hope to see you soon."
"Goodbye," Leticia said softly, and she vanished.
Dracula smiled, sitting down in his chair.
They were pulled to the town in Severna, where everyone was talking
excitedly about the stranger who had saved the land, stopped the war.
Leticia and Westley were holding hands as they spoke to reporters, some
angry people around them as they cursed Count Dracula angrily.
"He kidnapped her," Westley said, furious. "Leticia has great power. She
knocked out *three* dragons! She would have been useful if he never-"
"Even so, the land was saved without my help," Leticia cut across, camera
flashing. "We owe our gratitude towards the stranger who saved us all."
"Yes Leticia," the journalists said humbly. "And nobody saw his face?"
Everyone said no.
"The dragons called him their lord. He must be very important to those
creatures."
"More than likely," Leticia replied. "Now I must go. Come, Westley."
Westley excused himself and followed his wife.
"Leticia? Where are you going?"
"To the orphanage. They've taken Simon and Rachel's child there."
"Spirit??"
"Yes!"
Westley ran after her. "Not so fast, Leticia!"
Everything dissolved, and Spirit and Jeiklee were back in their clearing.
Jeiklee pouted. "What happened after that??"
"They took me to live with them," Spirit replied quietly, and Jeiklee looked
at her.
"You ok now?"
"Yeah. I'm fine." Spirit reached and picked up her bow and arrow. "I just…
I never saw what happened to my parents before now. It was painful. That's
why I cried. No big deal."
Jeiklee smiled at her. "You don't have to be tough all the time, you know.
I'm here for you."
Spirit smiled back. "Thanks, Jeiklee."
Jeiklee suddenly began to glow white. "What the-!!"
"It is time you returned to the present!" Bari the Tree said excitedly, as their
belongings glowed too. "Farewell to both of you!"
"Bye Bari!" Jeiklee called just as excitedly, Spirit calling "We won't forget
you!"
They vanished before Bari could reply, reappearing in their giant garden.
Jeiklee lost his balance and fell, Spirit as well.

Their belongings appeared on the grass beside them, and Jeiklee laughed with relief. He laid there laughing, Spirit laughing as well.

"I'm so glad to be back!"

Leticia and Westley ran outside, Antonio behind them.

"Mum! Dad!" Jeiklee scrambled to his feet and ran and hugged his mother hard. "I've missed you so much!"

Spirit hugged Westley as well, Jeiklee letting Leticia go and hugging his father as well as Leticia gave Spirit a happy kiss on the cheek.

"How was your adventure?" smiled Leticia, and Spirit said "It was amazing. But I'm *soooo* glad to be home! We were sleeping in a clearing on the dirt by a fire, I can't wait to have a hot soak in my bathtub and fall asleep in my own comfy bed with all my pillows-"

"Alright alright," Jeiklee said amusedly, and everyone laughed. "Mum, Dad, I perfected all of my spells. I think I'll be totally fine at Thrill. I've caught up with everything."

Leticia smiled and hugged her son again. "We know, Jeiklee. The Elder Samantha told us. I am so proud of both of you! Are you hungry?"

"Starving," said Spirit, and Westley said "Antonio, take their things inside."

"Yes sir.'

"Come and eat, the pair of you," smiled Westley, and Jeiklee and Spirit smiled back. "You're just in time for dinner."

"Awesome."

Element Four: Making Friends

* * *

Castle Dracula…

Virginia knocked on Dracula's study door. "Father? Are you there?"
"I am. Enter, my daughter."
Virginia obeyed. Dracula stood staring into the fireplace thoughtfully.
"What can I help you with?"
"I saw Miss Leticia on her way to you," Virginia said truthfully. "Earlier today when I left you at your clearing."
Dracula just nodded.
Virginia hesitated, then she said "I wanted to make sure she didn't hurt you."
Dracula looked at her sharply. "What did you say to her?"
"Nothing! Well, I just said not to hurt you and stuff-"
"And *stuff?*" repeated Dracula, glaring now. "Such as?"
"I don't want her to hurt you, Father! I remember how down you were and I don't want it to be like that again!"
"And do you remember how happy I was with Leticia in my life?!"
Virginia hesitated again, then she nodded. "Yes Father."
"So you remember how down I was and how happy I was, but you don't want either," said Dracula angrily. "Does that make sense, Virginia??"
"Please don't be mad Father! I just-"
"You just decided to interfere in things that don't concern you!"
Virginias eyes filled. "But… I was only-"
"Leave," spat Dracula. "Now!"
Virginia turned and ran out of the study, tears streaming down her face as she ran down many flights of stairs. She crashed into Nancy as she made for the giant doors, but she didn't stop.
Startled, Nancy said "Virginia! Where are you going after dark??"
Virginia didn't reply, pushing the doors open and running into the night.
Nancy ran up to Dracula's study, knocking. "My Lord?"
"Leave me be, Nancy. Make sure Virginia is in her coffin at a decent time."
"But sir-!!"
"Now, Nancy!"
"My Lord, I am trying to tell you-"
"Tell me when I have calmed down. That will be in at least an hour."
Nancy sighed. "Yes sir."

* * *

Virginia ran and ran, the wind and her tears almost blinding her, but she didn't stop. She ran through the Forest of Fear, startled creatures including vampires calling her concernedly.

"Princess of the Night! What is the matter??"

Virginia kept running. All the way through the forest towards the exit; the entrance into the town, where all the *normal* people lived.

* * *

Jeiklee jogged towards the Forest of Fear happily, wondering if he could find Bari the Tree. His parents had told him to be back by half nine: it was eight now.

"I'm sure I can find him. Whoa!"

Virginia ran straight into him, and they both tumbled to the ground, rolling entangled along the dust for a moment before they came to a stop.

Virginia pushed Jeiklee away and sat up, furious as she said "Watch where you're going!"

"Me!" said Jeiklee, annoyed. "It was you who ran into *me,* not the other way- hey." He stared at her filled green eyes, at the tears rolling down her face. Then he realised who she was when he noticed her glimmering red hair. "Virginia of Dracula?"

"What?" she spat, and Jeiklee hesitated before he said "I… are you ok?"

"I'm fine," she snapped, dusting her arms and standing. "Leave me be, Inferno!"

"Why are you crying?"

"It's none of your business! Do you want me to curse you for being so nosey?!"

"Why are you so defensive?" said Jeiklee, heat rising as he stood as well. "I don't mean any harm, ok? Stop acting like you don't give a damn about anything!"

"I don't!"

"If you didn't you wouldn't be crying!"

Virginia opened her mouth, then she closed it. "It doesn't matter."

"Look, I know you have this tough as nails reputation and a lot of people are scared of you," said Jeiklee, cautiously moving closer. "But I know you're not like that all the time. Just in front of people, right?"

Virginia didn't answer.

"I could be that friend you open up to," Jeiklee said gently, and she pouted at him.

"You're Spirit McKenzie's boyfriend. Why would I open up to *you?*"

"How do you-?" Then Jeiklee realised. "It was you who saw us kissing."

"Yes it was," shrugged Virginia, and Jeiklee frowned.

"I thought your presence couldn't be felt or sensed by magical beings?"

"It can't. But my emotions can sometimes," Virginia told him. "That's what Spirit McKenzie sensed. My emotions, not my presence. And I could have spread the word throughout the land about you two if I wasn't thinking of your mother."

"You love my mother, don't you Virginia?" smiled Jeiklee, and she glared at him as she replied "That's none of your business."

"Alright. How about we walk and talk?" suggested Jeiklee. "I have roughly an hour and a bit before I have to be home. Do you want to go back into the forest instead of being out in the open?"

"The forest isn't safe for you at night, Inferno. The creatures in there will have you for dinner."

Jeiklee grinned. "Well, you're the Princess of Darkness. Protect me."

Virginia smiled back. "I'm not my father. I can't stop anything from happening to you."

"The hell you can't. Come on, it'll be fun."

Virginia shook her head. "No, Inferno. If you really want to walk and talk with me then we'll go the river close to Thrill."

"Ok, let's go."

* * *

"It wasn't like I was threatening her," Virginia said, scowling down at the water. "I just pleaded with her not to hurt him. That's all. And Father flipped out."

"He had a good day and you kind of rained on his parade," Jeiklee said, shrugging a shoulder. "That's what I get from what you said, Virginia. Besides, Mum would never hurt Count Dracula. They meant everything to each other once."

"I know," sighed Virginia. "I was scared of Father when I saw how mad he got. I wish I didn't open my big mouth. He's angry with me."

"Nah." Jeiklee shook his head. "He was just annoyed you interfered, that's all. Don't worry about it. When you get back to the castle everything will be fine."

"He probably thinks I'm asleep in my coffin," shrugged Virginia. "I doubt he'd even bother looking for me if he knew I wasn't, don't you think Inferno?"

"I think you're still upset he wiled out and you don't mean that. Dracula would definitely look for you," Jeiklee told her. "And my name is Jeiklee, Virginia. I'm not someone formal. I'm your friend now. So call me Jeiklee."

Virginia opened her mouth, then she nodded with a smile. "Apologies…

Jeiklee."

* * *

Count Dracula found them not long later.

Nancy had banged on his study door exactly an hour later, telling him Virginia had ran out of the castle in tears. Dracula didn't panic, knowing his child was safe- but he still had to find her and bring her home.

Jeiklee and Virginia sat with their feet in the river, their shoes beside them as Jeiklee said to Virginia, "You know, you're not as bad as everyone makes out."

"Does Spirit McKenzie make me out to be very bad?"

Jeiklee nodded. "Yep. My Dad does too. But I don't think you are at all."

Virginia frowned at him. "Why not? I have a terrible reputation and I'm pure evil like my Father, according to the people of Severna."

"I did hear that from some. But I don't go by what everyone thinks or says. You're pretty cool, Virginia. And I'd like to know the real you."

Virginia looked away, at the river. "Nobody but my father and your mother know the real me. My friends don't either. Well, not much."

"Then they're not proper friends," said Jeiklee gently. "Hey. You ok?"

"I'm fine," sniffed Virginia, and Jeiklee teased "You're as soft as cotton, Virginia. Look at you getting all emotional!"

"Shut up," laughed Virginia, pushing him playfully. "You're just really nice and I'm not used to it at all. That's all. I'm not soft!"

Dracula smiled at them, not really wanting to disturb them, but it was late. "Virginia."

Jeiklee and Virginia whipped round, Virginia gasping "Father! What- you came to find me?"

"Of course I did. I didn't want to disturb you as it seems you are really enjoying Jeiklee's company, but it is gone ten at night."

"What??" Jeiklee scrambled to his feet. "I have to go!"

"Wait, Jeiklee!" said Virginia, as Jeiklee pulled on his trainers. Jeiklee looked at her, and Virginia blushed before she casually asked "Want to hang out at Thrill on Monday? It'll be your first day. I can show you around if you want, and we can have lunch and stuff. If you want to."

"Sure," smiled Jeiklee, and Virginia smiled back a little shyly. "I'd love to."

Leticia appeared, startling them.

"Mum!" said Jeiklee, looking at her disapproving face. "I'm really sorry- I was going to be back at half nine but I lost track of time talking to Virginia-"

"Jeiklee, please try to be home on time. It is your first night back," Leticia said gently. "I almost thought you jumped through time again. Your father is looking for you in the Forest of Fear."

"It was my fault, Miss Leticia," Virginia said humbly. "I was upset and Jeiklee wanted to make sure I was alright. Then we got talking."

Leticia's face softened. "Why were you upset, Virginia?"

"Oh- well…"

"You know better than to lie to me," said Leticia amusedly, and Dracula said "She was upset because of me. I got angry because she told me she warned you not to hurt me. I didn't want her to put you off us being friends again, Leticia. The thought of losing you again because of my daughter frightened me, and I overreacted."

Leticia nodded, and Virginia said "I'm sorry, Father. I shouldn't have involved myself in something that doesn't concern me."

"*I* am sorry, sweet daughter. I didn't mean to scare you and I definitely didn't mean to make you cry." Dracula pulled his daughter into a hug and kissed her forehead. "I apologise."

Leticia smiled as Virginia hugged him back, saying "We'd better get going. Come, Jeiklee."

"Bye Virginia. I'll see you at Thrill," Jeiklee said, and Virginia smiled and said bye. "Bye Count Dracula sir. It was nice meeting you."

"And you also after hearing so much about you, Jeiklee." Dracula smiled at him. "I am surprised and also pleased that you can make my daughter laugh, blush and smile. I know not of many of her so-called friends can do that."

Jeiklee was chuffed. "Thank you sir."

"Goodbye Leticia," Dracula said softly, and Leticia said "Goodbye Dracula," just as softly.

Virginia looked at both of them knowingly, then she said "Come on, Father. Let's go home."

Leticia took Jeiklee's arm and teleported with him, reappearing at the mansion.

Westley had just got back, placing his weapons down. "Son!"

"Sorry Dad," Jeiklee said apologetically. "I lost track of time."

"Well if you lose track of time again-"

"I won't, I promise," said Jeiklee quickly. "I ran into Virginia of Dracula and-"

"Virginia?" said Spirit disgustedly, joining everyone. "What did she want?"

"I ran into her," Jeiklee repeated. "And we talked for a while, then Mum found us."

"It's not like Count Dracula to allow his daughter to be out so late," Westley said with a frown, then he scowled. "Not that I care."

"Dracula came for Virginia, Westley," Leticia told him, "The same time I came for Jeiklee. He has taken Virginia back to the castle."

"Did he do anything to you?"

Jeiklee almost threw his hands up: seriously, *why* was everyone so stupid when it came to Count Dracula??

Leticia just said "No. Now let's all have a hot drink in about an hour, after we get ready for bed. We can watch a movie even; it is Friday night, after all."

"Great!" said Spirit happily, Jeiklee as well. "See you in a bit."

Jeiklee followed Spirit upstairs, Spirit saying "I had the longest bath ever. It felt great."

"I'm going to have a shower," Jeiklee responded. "I fell over and got my clothes a bit dirty."

"Leave them in your linen basket for a servant to collect tomorrow."

"I know, Spirit."

Spirit glanced at him as they walked. "You ok?"

"Hmm? Oh- yeah. I'm fine," smiled Jeiklee, and she smiled back. "I guess I can't give you a kiss before we watch the movie?"

"Shh! After lights out," Spirit whispered, and Jeiklee whispered back "Promise?"

"I promise. Go get your shower."

* * *

Castle Dracula...

Virginia climbed into her coffin, a smile on her face.

Nancy pulled a quilt over her as she laid on her back, saying "You did give me such a fright, Virginia. Don't ever run off again."

"I won't, Nancy. But it was kind of worth it."

Dracula listened at the door as Nancy said "Is that so?"

Virginia nodded, still smiling.

"And why was it worth it, Virginia of Dracula?"

Virginia closed her eyes, mumbling "Because of Jeiklee Inferno."

She blushed big time, then she said "Close the lid, Nancy. I want to be in total darkness."

Nancy nodded, saying "Alright, young one. Sleep tight. Dream of evil tonight."

"As always."

Nancy chuckled and closed the coffin lid, leaving the room. She closed Virginia's door, then she smiled at Dracula.

"I have never seen such a deep shade of pink on that girl's pale face, my Lord."

"Nor I," smiled Dracula. "I do believe Virginia has finally made a true friend."

"I doubt Westley Inferno will want his son to be a friend of your daughter's, sir."

"I doubt that also. But Leticia doesn't mind at all." Dracula smiled as he said Leticia's name. "So I do not care about what her husband thinks."

* * *

All the lights in the mansion were out.

Jeiklee crept along the corridor towards Spirit's room, gently knocking on her door when he reached.

Spirit opened her door quietly, then she pulled him inside. "Jeiklee-"

Jeiklee kissed her tenderly, and she threw her arms around his neck as she responded, Jeiklee pulling her closer as he deepened the kiss. He was pouring everything he wanted, felt and missed into her soul; Spirit felt it as a moan sounded deep in her throat, and the image of Bruce Finnegan flashed before her eyes suddenly. A little guiltily she kept kissing Jeiklee, then she pulled away with a gasp when she realised Jeiklee was glowing bright blue.

"Jeiklee!"

"I'm sorry," hissed Jeiklee, and Spirit whispered "I felt it- I felt what you felt and more! Did you feel what I felt too?"

"I saw Bruce Finnegan," Jeiklee said a little coldly, and Spirit opened her mouth, then closed it. Jeiklee hesitated, then asked "Are you playing me, Spirit? Do you still want Bruce after everything we've been through, everything he's done to you?"

"No! I don't know. Wait, Jeiklee!" Spirit ran after Jeiklee as he left her room without another word: her answer was enough. Spirit grabbed his hand and he pulled away as he headed for his room, Spirit whispering "Jeiklee, please come back!"

"I need to think, and I need to sleep. Goodnight, Spirit."

He entered his room and closed the door just like that, Spirit's eyes filling over as she stared at the door, then she turned and went back into her bedroom.

* * *

Jeiklee woke up at seven in the morning.

He hadn't slept well, tossing and turning as two girls invaded his thoughts, Spirit McKenzie and Virginia of Dracula. He was angry that he'd accidentally seen Spirit's thoughts, seen Bruce Finnegan- she clearly wasn't over him. And if she was, why had she imagined him when being kissed by another guy?

"Probably because she wished it was Bruce kissing her," Jeiklee muttered, and his thoughts went to Virginia, his new friend.

Virginia was pretty cool, and fun. He made her laugh, she made him care. Dracula himself was surprised at Virginia, Jeiklee thought with a smile.

His heart tugged when he saw those beautiful green eyes brimming with tears, how upset she was. He couldn't have left her.

Jeiklee wondered if his mother's heart tugged last night when she saw the love in Count Dracula's green eyes when he looked at her. He'd bet everything he had it did.

Jeiklee rolled out of bed and walked onto his balcony, staring down at the garden.

There was a knock on his door, and he frowned at it. Antonio wouldn't wake him before ten on a Saturday.

"Jeiklee?" said Spirit softly: he didn't answer. "Jeiklee, are you up?"

Jeiklee was still annoyed and upset with her. Spirit seemed to know that, as she whispered "Can we talk about this please? I know you're awake."

When Jeiklee still didn't answer, she got slightly annoyed.

"Jeiklee, me and you aren't together anyway so what's the big deal?"

"Are you serious?" said Jeiklee angrily as he strode up to his door. "You're all I had on my mind and I obviously wasn't the only guy on yours! You-"

"Good morning Leticia," said Spirit clearly and in a forced tone, obviously wanting him to shut up before his mother heard him. "Are you leaving with Westley for the day?"

"For half the day instead of the whole day, darling. What are you doing by Jeiklee's door at this time?"

"Oh- I woke up early and wanted to see if he was up."

"I see," said Leticia with a smile. "Well, he is. I can sense it. Good morning Jeiklee."

"Morning Mum," said Jeiklee, smiling. "What time are you leaving with Dad?"

"In half an hour."

Jeiklee opened his door and gave his mother a hug. Leticia hugged him back as he said "Have a good time Mum."

"I will darling. You have a good Saturday also and no jumping through time again," Leticia said as he let her go. "Even if it *was* an adventure the last time, do not attempt it without my being there."

"Yes Mum."

Leticia smiled and kissed Spirit. "Have a good day, both of you. I am going to meet Westley now."

"Tell him we said bye," said Spirit; Jeiklee nodded as well. "You'll be back in time for dinner right?"

"Right," smiled Leticia, and she dissolved into thin air, gone.

Spirit looked at Jeiklee. "Can we please sort this out?"

"There's nothing to sort," shrugged Jeiklee. "Like you said, we're not in a relationship. So what is the big deal really? If you can be that blunt about it why should I give a damn about you or anything?"

Spirit took a step back, hurt. "You don't mean that."

"I could have said that to you as well but I know you did mean it. I'm going out after breakfast and I don't want you coming with me."

"What? Where are you going?"

"That's none of your flipping business. You want to be friends then fine by me, let's just be friends. But when I get a girlfriend, don't catch feelings and don't get jealous." Jeiklee walked away from her. "And to think I thought me and you were going somewhere after everything."

"We were! Jeiklee, don't do this- please!"

Jeiklee turned to look at her. "You have Bruce Finnegan on your mind. I'm not going to be second best to him or anyone, ok?"

"We should talk about this, Jeiklee!" said Spirit desperately. "Don't walk out on me! Don't walk out on *us!"*

Jeiklee shook his head. "When your head is screwed on, talk to me. Until then-"

"What?" said Spirit, angry tears falling down her face now. "Keep my distance? *We live in the same mansion!!"*

"So?"

"Look, let's just talk about this now. My head *is* screwed on- I promise you. I don't want Bruce Finnegan!"

"Then why-"

"I don't know!" said Spirit agitatedly, and Jeiklee sighed and walked over to her, pulling her into his arms. Spirit's tears wet his shirt as she wept "I don't want Bruce. I want this. Me and you."

Jeiklee sighed again. "But you don't want us in a relationship. Because you're uncertain about what you really want."

"It's not that, I swear it. I've never been more certain about how I feel. But I just don't want to be in a relationship- not because of Bruce." Spirit held Jeiklee, and he stroked her hair as she quietly said "I just don't want one right now."

"But you want us to keep seeing each other?" Jeiklee asked her, and she nodded. "Well… that's good enough for me if that's what you want."

Spirit looked up at him. "Really?"

Jeiklee gave her a gentle kiss. "Yes."

Spirit smiled, and he wiped her tears away as she said "So... shall we have breakfast then?"

Jeiklee smiled back. "Sure. I'm sorry I reacted like that, Spirit."

"You had every right to." Spirit took his hand as they began walking. "I hate when we fall out."

"So do I."

"Will you still leave for the day?" asked Spirit, and Jeiklee said "Nah. I only would have been fuming."

"Master Inferno!"

Spirit dropped Jeiklee's hand immediately as they saw a servant coming up the stairs. He was smiling broadly.

"Yes?" said Jeiklee curiously, and Spirit said "Morning George."

"Good morning Miss McKenzie," smiled George, Jeiklee smiling as well now as he said "You're Dad's best friend! You grew up together!"

"Oh, has your father told you about me?" smiled George, and Spirit trod on Jeiklee's foot as she lied "I told him, George. Jeiklee wanted to know who Westley's close friends were and I said you right away."

George laughed. "Much appreciated. Now the table is being set for breakfast as Leticia let Chef know you are both up. So make sure you grab the food while it's hot."

"Yes George."

"Good. I'll be on my way now. And Master Inferno, it was good meeting you."

"You too," Jeiklee responded, and George continued his way up the stairs.

"He seems nice."

"He's very nice," smiled Spirit. "Always there to listen to anyone's problems. Leticia rarely speaks to him though."

"Well he's Dad's best friend, not Mum's. Mum had her own best friend."

Spirit sighed. "You mean Count Dracula?"

Jeiklee nodded. "Yep."

"Well she had my Mum too. And everyone around here loves her to death," Spirit said, and Jeiklee said "Maybe, but they don't know her the way George knows Dad, the way Dracula knows her. Dracula probably knows more about Mum than Dad ever will."

Spirit sighed again, then she smiled at the smell of hot food. "Mmm. I want sausages, bacon, eggs-"

"I want everything." Jeiklee smiled at her, a true smile, and Spirit kissed him on the cheek before she quickly walked into the dining area.

* * *

Castle Dracula…

Dracula sat in his armchair, brooding.

He knew Leticia was away with Westley as she was every Saturday. He wondered what it was they got up to together when they practically vanished off the face of Severna.

Then he scowled, muttering "I do not want to know."

There was a knock on the door. "My Lord?"

"Yes Nancy," said Dracula, and Nancy said "You have a visitor, sir."

Dracula frowned. "A visitor?"

"Yes my Lord."

"Who is it?"

"Who indeed," said Nancy amusedly, and Dracula said irritably as he walked to the door, "Nancy, do not play games with me. I asked you a simple question and I want a simple answer, like a *name.*"

"Open the door sir."

Dracula sighed and obeyed, pulling open the door- his jaw dropped. "Leticia!"

"Hello Dracula," said Leticia amusedly, and he bit his lip stupidly, gasping in pain as his fangs pierced them. "You've hurt yourself."

Virginia was smiling broadly as she stood in her dressing gown next to Nancy as Dracula spluttered "What- I was thinking of you, and you- you're here?? I cannot make sense of this!"

"Well I wasn't reading your mind, silly. I just thought I'd pay you a visit, spend time with you for a while." Leticia's smile grew as he stared at her, his face growing a little hot. "You're blushing, Dracula."

"You look like a tomato, Father," said Virginia amusedly, and Dracula glared at her as he retorted "You looked worse when talking about Jeiklee Inferno."

Virginia scowled, and Dracula smirked at her before she said "I'm going into the Forest today. Will both of you go too, Miss Leticia?"

"It's up to Dracula," Leticia replied, and Dracula said "I'm not sure. We can stay here also. But I was thinking of going to the lake later."

"Then you can do that," said Virginia happily. "Stay here then go to the lake-"

"We will decide for ourselves, thank you," Dracula said amusedly, and she pouted. "Run along and get dressed."

Virginia smiled and jogged away, Nancy leaving them as well.

"Leticia, come in," Dracula said breathlessly, and Leticia smiled and entered his study, Dracula closing the door before he turned to her with a smile. "So what would you like to do?"

"Anything. We can talk or sit in silence," Leticia said softly. "I had an overwhelming urge to see you." Dracula stared at her. "Don't ask me why, because I... Dracula?"

He'd moved closer to her. Leticia didn't back away, heart racing as he lifted a hand and caressed her cheek.

"You came because your feelings for me are still there," Dracula said softly. "The memories are still fresh in your mind as if it all happened only yesterday. Us seeing each other again has awakened those dormant feelings. Am I right?"

"Dracula, don't," Leticia whispered, but he ignored her as he murmured "We can be like that again, Leticia. All you have to do..."

She closed her eyes as he brought his mouth to his ear, and he whispered "Is trust how you feel."

Leticia shuddered, and he lowered his mouth to hers... she tilted her head to accept the kiss... then they both nearly jumped out of their skin when Virginia banged her fist on the door.

"Father!"

"What!" exploded Dracula, and Virginia laughed out loud.

"Was I interrupting something?"

"You-!!" Dracula practically tore the door off it's hinges as she laughed her head off. "You did that on purpose!"

"Well I thought it was too quiet so I decided to add some noise," Virginia said mischievously, and Leticia laughed as Dracula began to glow scarlet.

"Miss Leticia, I got the chef to whip up a Red Velvet cake just for you. It's on the dining table with hot chocolate for you and Father."

"Thank you, Virginia. That sounds lovely." Leticia was still laughing. "Come on Dracula, let's go and have some Red Velvet."

Dracula took a deep breath, then he exhaled and nodded. They began walking, Dracula saying to his daughter "Go and find something to do, Virginia."

"Aww." Virginia mock pouted at him. "Can't I stay with you two?"

"No you cannot." Dracula scowled at her. "The castle is gigantic, my daughter- busy yourself with some kind of activity."

"Alright, fine. I'll be back to make sure Miss Leticia is ok in two hours." Virginia jogged away before he could answer irritably, laughing.

"Virginia is a pleasure, Dracula," said Leticia lovingly. "Don't be annoyed at her. She's just having fun."

"I know, I know."

* * *

Spirit and Jeiklee sat by the pool in the garden, on their stomachs as they gazed down at the water contentedly.

"I hope Leticia and Westley are having a good time," said Spirit, and Jeiklee said "Yeah. It's nice that they get to spend some alone time together sometimes."

"When I was younger I used to hate them going," Spirit admitted. "I was only comfortable and happiest around them. I used to just watch the hours tick by. Then Leticia said I should go for walks, meet with friends and stuff. I hardly ever did until I was around fifteen."

Jeiklee nodded, listening to her.

Spirit sighed, then she said "I'm a bit of a loner at times. You may have noticed."

"Well... I am too, to be fair. All I had was my adopted parents and two mates. Everyone, like literally *everyone* I was ever around thought there was something creepy about me. Even when I got a job. My colleagues thought I was different. They avoided me pretty much all the time."

"They felt your energy, your power. And it scared them," said Spirit, looking at him. "Mortals have gut feelings too. They knew something was different about you. I'm glad we got you out of that world before something bad happened."

"Something bad did happen, Spirit. My friend ended up in hospital because-"

"Because he was flirting with your ex. That wasn't cool," said Spirit, shaking her head. "At all. Anyway, you didn't expect your punch to knock him into the motorway. That's when Leticia said she's not waiting anymore. That anything else could happen, and it was time for you to come home. Westley agreed. He had words with King Harlot too, and Leticia said you're coming back to Severna whether the King allows it or not. She didn't give a damn what he thought, still doesn't. She never did like him- and with all the stuff she knows about him, I don't blame her."

"Mum really is fire," said Jeiklee admiringly. "The King was the cause of those wars with the dragons. My grandparents on both sides were killed because of him."

"And so were my parents," said Spirit, glaring down at the water now. "King Harlot is more than an idiot. He's cruel. And that's why Leticia can't stand him. He only thought about himself when those wars happened. He didn't care how about many people would die because of his greed. He didn't care about anything but those jewels."

"Good thing Count Dracula saved the day," Jeiklee replied with a smile, and Spirit scowled and didn't answer. Jeiklee sighed. "Come on Spirit, you know you agree deep down. Those dragons worship Dracula-"

"Because he's evil and so are they."
"And he stopped the war," Jeiklee said, ignoring her. "With Mum's help."
"He kidnapped her, Jeiklee!"
"Really, Spirit?" Jeiklee scowled at her. "Stop being so-"
The horn for lunch went off before he could finish, and Spirit got up.
"Come on, let's go."

* * *

Castle Dracula…

Dracula smiled at Leticia, and she smiled back before she sipped her hot chocolate.
"Leticia?"
"Mmm?"
"Would you like to go to our clearing or would you rather go to the lake?" asked Dracula, and Leticia replied "It's totally up to you, Dracula. I don't mind where we go, as long as…"
She trailed off, and Dracula quietly finished her sentence.
"As long as we're together."
Leticia didn't say anything, looking down at her hot chocolate. Dracula didn't know whether that was confirmation to what he said or not, and he didn't want to ask.
"It's going rain, I can sense it," Dracula said after a few minutes of silence. "We can stay right here."
Leticia nodded.
"What's bothering you, Leticia? You seem a little withdrawn," Dracula said concernedly. "You were smiling a moment ago."
"We almost kissed in your study, Dracula," Leticia said softly. "And you were right. The feelings I have for you were dormant… and are back. Now I feel everything I felt every time I used to see you."
"That's not a bad thing, Leticia."
"It is when I have a doting husband and son at home. I shouldn't have-"
"Even if you feel you shouldn't have gotten back into contact with me, you would have eventually," Dracula said quietly. "We are like magnets, drawn to each other. We always have been and we can't help it."
"And do you think that's a good thing?" asked Leticia, looking at him seriously. "The way we always find each other no matter what happens or how long it's been? That our feelings for each other never fade?"
Dracula nodded. "I think it's an amazing thing."
Leticia looked away, then she softly admitted "As do I."
Dracula's heart broke as he breathed out, relieved and sad at the same time as they looked at each other.
Leticia's eyes filled over. "If only-"
"Nobody has to know," Dracula said softly. "Well… Virginia has always known since she was a tiny girl and so does Nancy, but that's it. Nobody else knows about the love we have for one another. The people of Severna and your husband just believe it was just a very, *very* unhealthy friendship. They think you haven't even seen me at will for years, that our friendship was just a phase you were going through, and you will never see me again."

"They thought wrong," said Leticia softly, and Dracula said "Let them continue to think it," just as softly.

"I don't want anyone hurt, Dracula."

"Nobody has to know," Dracula repeated. "Nobody *did* know, not even your father. Does your husband know where you are?"

Leticia shook her head and said no. "I told him I'd rather be alone with my thoughts. He accepted that without question and went on his way."

Dracula smiled. "Then that's a start."

Leticia smiled back, but she looked a little uncertain of what she was doing. "Are you sure you want this, Leticia?" Dracula asked her gently, and she stood slowly. "If you're uncertain, then we should remain as we are."

"As we are?" Leticia repeated quietly. "Dracula, what exactly is *'as we are'*? Friends?"

Dracula nodded. "Yes."

"We haven't been just friends since we became teenagers," Leticia said, shaking her head. "I love you and you love me."

"So what do you want to do, Leticia?"

"I-"

"Father, I'm going to meet some friends in town," Virginia said, popping her head around the door. "I'll be back this evening."

Dracula just nodded, eyes on Leticia.

Virginia looked at them both. "Is everything ok?"

"Everything is fine, my daughter." Dracula spoke quietly. "Go on out."

Virginia looked at Leticia uncertainly. Leticia nodded, so Virginia shrugged and left.

Dracula stood as Leticia ran a hand through her hair. "Leticia."

"Don't, Dracula. You know I don't like being uncertain of things and I don't want you to convince me to be just friends when all I want-"

"Is me." Dracula finished her sentence, and her eyes filled over. He walked towards her, softly saying "All you want is me."

Leticia swallowed, tears trailing down her face as she said "The last time this happened, Westley tried to kill you even when he had no clue we were seeing each other. When he and everyone else thought we were just friends, he still tried to take your life."

Dracula nodded. "I know."

"Promise me nobody will get hurt if we do this again." Leticia looked at him. "Promise me, Dracula."

"I cannot promise that, Leticia." Dracula took her hand. "But I *can* promise I will protect you from anyone and anything if the people of Severna and your loved ones find out about us."

"I suppose that is good enough," sighed Leticia, and Dracula moved closer and kissed her tenderly. Leticia's knees gave way and he caught her quickly, holding her to him. He felt his heart come to life as she responded to the kiss, beating fiercely with love.

Reluctantly breaking the kiss almost five minutes later, Dracula murmured "Let's go to my suite, Leticia."

She looked up at him through hazy eyes, and he said "We don't have to do anything you don't want to do. But I want to lay with you in my arms."

Leticia nodded, and he teleported with her to his suite.

* * *

"Let's go for a walk," suggested Jeiklee. "We've got ages before Mum and Dad get back."

"Ok," smiled Spirit. "Let me get my satchel."

Jeiklee frowned at her. "What are you getting your satchel for?"

"To pack food," smiled Spirit. "I'll get Chef to make me some sandwiches. I have a craving for sandwiches since we stayed in the Forest of Fear."

Jeiklee smiled at that. "Get some sandwiches for me as well."

"Alright. I'll be ten minutes."

"Ok."

* * *

"Your heart is beating," whispered Leticia, head on Dracula's chest. "So steadily."

Dracula kissed her forehead. "It only beats for you."

Leticia smiled at that. "Don't lie, Dracula."

"I am not lying. It doesn't even beat for my daughter, though I love her very much." Dracula stroked her hair. "It has never beat for anyone but you."

Leticia opened her mouth, then she paused before quietly asking "It didn't even beat for Malinda of Brubeck?"

Dracula looked down at her. Leticia looked back up at him, and then she said "I'm sorry. I shouldn't have asked you something so personal."

"You can ask me anything, Leticia. No matter how personal," Dracula said gently. "And no. My heart never beat for Malinda. Ever."

"Oh," said Leticia softly, and Dracula pulled his duvet up over their bodies, Leticia snuggling down next to him.

They listened to the rain falling outside, and Dracula sighed happily.

"This feels so nice."

Leticia smiled, eyes closed as she murmured "I wish I could stay here like this. With you... forever."

"I wish so too, sweetheart. Go to sleep," Dracula said softly. "I won't go anywhere."

Leticia sighed happily, and she did just that.

* * *

"Flipping rain," said Spirit angrily, as they trudged back home. "I don't even know *why* we left the bloody mansion. We can't even eat our sandwiches! And my hair is ruined. So are my shoes!"

"Stop complaining, Spirit." Jeiklee smiled at her. "It's not bad."

"Yeah, well-"

Jeiklee stopped walking when he saw something bright and red in the distance, coming towards them.

He wiped his face and peered harder, then he smiled broadly. "Virginia!"

"Hey Jeiklee," Virginia called. "What are you doing out in the rain with... oh." She walked up to them, then she took a deep breath before she forced the words out. "Hello Spirit McKenzie."

"Go to Hell," spat Spirit, and Virginia rolled her eyes.

"Really? I'm being civil here. All I said was hello and you're telling me to go to Hell? Nice."

"Shut up," snapped Spirit, and Virginia couldn't help smirking. "Come on Jeiklee, let's go home."

"What are you doing out in the rain, Virginia?" asked Jeiklee curiously, and Virginia sighed.

"I was hanging with some mates in town. Then it started pouring down so I left them. I don't want to get sick-"

"You're *already* sick," Spirit said angrily. "Sick in the head!"

Thunder boomed overhead as Virginia said "Jeiklee, sort out your friend with benefits. I promised I wouldn't hurt her again but she's pushing my buttons. And I don't want to get into trouble."

Jeiklee nodded, saying "Spirit, stop insulting her. Virginia hasn't said one bad thing to you. It's you being offensive, not the other way round."

Spirit's jaw dropped. "You're taking *her* side?!"

"Well... yeah," said Jeiklee a little apologetically. "She hasn't done a thing, but you have."

"I can't believe you," Spirit said angrily. "Why the hell are you even *talking* to a creep like Virginia of Dracula?!"

"I'm the creep?" said Virginia, raising an eyebrow. "Says the girl who everyone hardly interacts with and sits alone at lunch when we're at Thrill? Who everyone pretty much avoids and talks about behind your back? And your only real supporters are the professors? I have a ton of friends and admirers, McKenzie, but *I'm* the creep? You need to look in the mirror you have at home. The mirror always shows the true creep when you look in it." Virginia smirked at her. "Get it?"

"Ricato!!"

BANG!!

Virginia vanished before the spell could hit her, reappearing behind them.

"Not nice."

Jeiklee and Spirit whirled round, Spirit crying *"Mordzmorda!!"*

"Spirit, stop!" yelled Jeiklee- BAAANG!!!

Virginia ducked, the curse whooshing over her head.

"Don't make me retaliate, Spirit McKenzie!" Virginia said angrily; people came running, Bruce Finnegan at the front.

"What the hell's going on here??" he demanded, and Virginia spat "Spirit McKenzie has flipping issues is what the hell's going on!"

"Drop dead, Virginia!" snarled Spirit, hand lighting up, and Virginia icily said "Try and hex me a third time and I swear, it will be *you* who drops dead."

Everyone went *"Ooooh!!"*; Spirit wavered for a moment as Virginia said "You think I'm joking? Try me."

"Play nice, Virginia," said Bruce amusedly, and Virginia pouted at him.

"Bruce, I was just talking to Jeiklee. Miss *I Have To Keep Him To Myself* here obviously has a problem with that."

"I don't want to keep Jeiklee to myself!" said Spirit furiously, and everyone rolled their eyes, Clarissa saying "Sure you don't. You couldn't stand me being near him either!"

"Shut up, Clarissa!" spat Spirit, glaring at her. "You don't even have a place in all of this- you just want to suck up to Virginia like you always do!"

"Virginia's my best friend so I *do* have a place in all of this," Clarissa said coldly, and Bruce said "I have heard that, Spirit. Why don't you want Inferno to mix with us? We're all in the same age group. There's no harm in it."

"I don't care about you lot being around Jeiklee, it's *her* I can't stand!" Spirit said, glaring at Virginia, and Virginia replied "Likewise. But I'm being the bigger person and not retaliating to your pettiness. Grow up, Spirit McKenzie!"

Everyone nodded, some staring at Spirit incredulously, some glaring at her. Spirit looked around at everyone's faces, and never felt more embarrassed. She turned and stormed away, Jeiklee calling after her. "Spirit, wait!"

She ignored him, the rain thinning a little as she became smaller and smaller in the distance.

Jeiklee sighed, and Bruce said "Don't worry Jeiklee. She'll calm down."

Forgetting that he'd decided he didn't like Bruce Finnegan, Jeiklee nodded. Then he said "She really hates Virginia."

"Bad history," shrugged Bruce. "Look, I know you might not like me and I was a bit of a prick to you before. But it would be great if we could get along. What do you say?"

He held out a hand.

Jeiklee stared at it for a moment, everyone waiting with bated breath. Jeiklee noticed Julius Charter in the crowd, Spirit's friend.

He nodded, and Jeiklee took that as a "Bruce isn't really a bad guy."

Bruce was still holding out a hand as he said "It's cool if you don't want to be mates."

"No, I'm good." Jeiklee shook his hand. "Just er… don't be mean to Spirit anymore, ok? Virginia stopped because she's being the bigger person. I think you should as well, Bruce."

Bruce sighed as they let go. "I don't want to be mean to her like I did when you first met me. You saw me try to get Spirit back that night in your garden, didn't you. She's not interested."

"Yeah, but it doesn't mean you have to be a prick about it."

Bruce nodded. "Alright, Jeiklee. Mates?"

Jeiklee nodded. "Mates."

Julius grinned, saying "Great! We can all hang out at Thrill on Monday when Jeiklee starts. That ok, Jeiklee?"

"Not ok," said Virginia, folding her arms. "I already asked Jeiklee to hang with me. So no. We can't all hang out because he's exclusively getting Virginia of Dracula."

She smiled at them, and everyone saw her fangs, her eyes glowing scarlet. Everyone drew back fearfully as she sweetly asked "Who has a problem with that?"

No one spoke.

Virginia smirked, her fangs sheathed and her eyes normal again as she said "Good."

"Bully," said Jeiklee amusedly, and she laughed. "Alright, I'll be with Virginia on Monday but we can all hang out on Tuesday."

Everyone smiled broadly, Julius saying "Great!"

"We need to get out of this rain before we're all *ill* by Tuesday," Bruce said, wiping water from his face. "I was on my way home, but then I saw the hexes from Spirit in the distance."

"We all did," said Clarissa, scowling. "If she hurt you, Virginia-"

"I can handle myself, Clarissa," Virginia said flatly. "Thanks, though."

Clarissa blushed, and she nodded.

"I'm going to get out of this rain," Virginia said. "I'll see you guys at Thrill on Monday."

"Bye Virginia," everyone said admiringly, and Virginia nodded and vanished.

Virginia is so *cool!* Jeiklee couldn't help thinking just as admiringly, and he said "I'm going to go and find Spirit. She must be real upset."

Everyone nodded, Julius saying "Tell her I'll see her at Thrill."

"I will," Jeiklee replied, and everyone said goodbye with broad smiles as he turned and walked away.

Jeiklee was smiling too as he walked home. He wasn't even bothered about being soaked to the bone.

For the first time ever, he'd just made a bunch of new friends.

* * *

Castle Dracula…

Leticia woke up glowing pure brilliant white.

She sat up and lifted a glowing hand, staring at it. "What…?"

"You're at peace, Leticia."

She looked and saw Count Dracula sitting in his armchair, watching her with a thoughtful look on his face.

"What do you mean?" she asked a little nervously, and Dracula stood.

"You've never been more happy, comfortable, relaxed. You finally have your son home, and you have me back after such a long time. You've had thoughts about Jeiklee and I rushing around your brain for so long and you have us both now. You're happier than you've been in years, and you feel amazing. I watched you glow all sorts of colours as you slept, and pure brilliant white was the colour I was hoping for," he said softly. "I too glowed as I held you. A heavy weight has been lifted from both of our shoulders because we have each other again."

Leticia's eyes filled over and she smiled in spite of her tears trailing down her face as she said "You are right, Dracula. You are definitely right. I feel amazing."

Dracula smiled back. "As do I. It's dark out, Leticia- and almost six in the evening. The rain has stopped."

Leticia quickly got out of bed and summoned her shoes and cloak as she said "I must return home, Dracula. I told Jeiklee and Spirit I'd be back in time for dinner."

"That's fine. Will I see you again soon?"

Leticia paused as she was putting her cloak on, and she walked up to him and kissed him tenderly.

Dracula inhaled sharply when she broke the kiss, murmuring "Definitely."

She vanished before he could say anything else, and Dracula smiled and sat back in his armchair.

He started to glow white again, and he softly said "We are both at peace."

* * *

Jeiklee hesitated, then he entered the lounge.

Spirit was sitting cross legged at the far end of the massive room, her back to him as she stared out of the giant windows.

"Spirit?" said Jeiklee cautiously; she didn't reply. "Are you ok?"

"Now you're bothered if I'm ok or not?" was her reply, and Jeiklee said "I've been combing the mansion for over three hours, Spirit- I was outside your door talking for forty minutes and waiting for you to open it before I realised you weren't in there."

Spirit didn't answer him.

"I guess I should have come to the lounge first," Jeiklee said, rubbing his neck. "I was really worried about you."

She said nothing still, and Jeiklee walked towards her, sitting next to her on the crème carpet.

"Hey."

She looked at him, and he saw her face was wet with tears.

"Aww, Spirit. Don't be so upset about today."

"I'm not upset," sniffed Spirit, and he gently wiped her tears away. "Virginia always makes a fool of me. And Bruce saw with Jules and everyone else from Thrill. They're not going to forget it."

"Well you kind of did snap, Spirit," Jeiklee said reasonably. "Virginia was being real civil to you and I know that was hard for her. You could have done the same even though it would have been hard for you too."

"She really gets under my skin," said Spirit angrily. "Nothing you say will make me stop loathing her, Jeiklee- nothing."

"Alright, I won't press the subject." Jeiklee kissed her gently just as they heard Westley call them from the large corridor, Leticia as well.

"Spirit? Jeiklee? We're back," called Leticia. "Are you home?"

Spirit scrambled to her feet, Jeiklee getting up slowly as she wiped her mouth, calling "We're in the lounge!"

Leticia and Westley entered holding hands, smiling at them.

"How was your day, both of you?" asked Westley, and Jeiklee said "It was great!"

"For you it was," Spirit said, scowling at him, and Westley asked "But not for you, Spirit?" She said no. "What happened?"

"Virginia of Dracula happened."

Westley glared. "What did she do?"

"She didn't do anything," Jeiklee said before Spirit could answer angrily. "Virginia was actually being real nice to Spirit, but Spirit flipped out and started firing hexes-"

"And everyone saw," Spirit said furiously. "As usual, I'm a laughing stock at Thrill."

"Don't worry about it," said Leticia soothingly. "Virginia has promised she won't cause any more trouble with you, Spirit. Professor Gene told me so and Virginia did also."

"Well she can still wind me up," Spirit said, still furious about the whole incident. "Now I have to keep my cool like she did or *I'll* look like the bully when it's really her."

Deciding not to answer that, Leticia said "Let's go and have dinner."

* * *

"So tomorrow I'm going to prepare for Thrill," Jeiklee said at the dinner table happily. "I'll practise everything I know-"

"There's more to do than just practising and casting spells, son." Westley smiled at him. "Everything won't be practical at Thrill."

"What? How come?"

"Just how it is," said Spirit as she cut her pork chops, and Jeiklee frowned at her, a little bewildered.

"You'll be doing a fair amount of written work also," Leticia explained gently, and Jeiklee pouted. "Aside from practical work. It won't be spell casting all the time every day, Jeiklee."

"Oh, ok." Jeiklee looked put out for a moment, then he smiled. "I'm still looking forward to going. I made some new friends after the incident with Spirit and Virginia today."

"That's good, son." Westley's smile grew. "You're already popular, and you know that. Don't let it get to your head."

"I won't, Dad." Jeiklee smiled back at his father and leant back in his seat, feeling elated. "I'll work hard."

"Sure you will," said Spirit dryly, and he scowled at her.

"I will! I always have when it came to my education."

"Yeah, in the mortal world." Spirit forked a roast potato. "Things are different here in Severna."

Jeiklee glared at her. "Are you trying to put me off or something?"

"I'm just saying-"

"Saying what?"

"That Virginia and her crowd will lead you astray if you're not careful," Spirit said flatly. "If you're serious about your education-"

"It's not all work and no fun," Jeiklee said, heat rising. "No school or college is ever like that. You just don't want me near Virginia."

"That's not what I said!" said Spirit angrily, and Jeiklee snapped "You implied it!"

"She's *evil*, Jeiklee!"

"No she isn't!"

"You don't even *know* her!"

"Neither do you!" said Jeiklee angrily, putting his fork down. "All you've done is talk trash about her when you hardly know her either!"

"I know more than you!" said Spirit, livid. "I've been her target for years! You got here practically yesterday and you think just because you found out a few things you *know her??* You know nothing, Jeiklee Inferno!"

Westley was gaping at them, Leticia surprised as well as she said "Spirit, what's troubling you like this? Why are you so upset?"

"Virginia's evil," Spirit said, looking at her and Westley furiously. "She's a wolf in sheep's clothing-"

"No she isn't," said Jeiklee flatly. "You're just being a stick in the mud. If you're jealous that me and her clicked so well-"

"I'm not jealous!" spat Spirit, and Jeiklee snapped "Well what are you? I mean I know you're upset about today but that's no reason to flip out over Virginia of Dracula! She said she wouldn't hurt you again and I believe her. Stop being so hateful!"

Spirit stared at him, hurt. Then she stood without another word and left the dining room.

Frustrated, Jeiklee said "I don't get her! All the time it's *"Virginia is evil"*, she's this that and the other!"

"But she is," Westley started, and Jeiklee shook his head.

"She isn't, Dad. I know you don't like her or her father Count Dracula. When I ran into Virginia the other night, she was in tears," Jeiklee told him. "Evil has no emotion but rage and hate. I saw something in Virginia that night and before. She's not evil. I know she isn't."

Westley sighed. "I don't want to argue with you, Jeiklee. But I'm telling you. Count Dracula and his daughter are both cruel, evil beings." Jeiklee saw anger flash across his mother's face as his father continued "I can see why Spirit doesn't want you near Virginia, and to be honest I don't either."

"But-!!"

"That's all I have to say," Westley said, standing. "I'm going to check on Spirit."

Jeiklee was twice as frustrated now as Westley left the room as well. Then Jeiklee looked at his mother.

"Mum, I know you don't feel the same."

"I don't, Jeiklee. You and I both know Virginia isn't evil."

"Trust me Mum, I know a lot. And I've learnt a lot too. I know Count Dracula isn't evil either."

"You've only seen him in the flesh once, Jeiklee." Leticia looked at him curiously. "What do you think you know about Count Dracula?"

"Well... I..." Jeiklee trailed off, then he shook his head. "Nothing."

"Jeiklee," said Leticia, not taking that for an answer. "Is there something you're not telling me?"

"I just know he's not a bad guy."

Leticia frowned at him. "Who did you hear say otherwise?"

"Well... nobody-"

"Then how would you know Dracula isn't evil and cruel like the entire world thinks he and his daughter is, Jeiklee?"

"I just know," Jeiklee said seriously. "And I know you know too. I know you know things about Count Dracula, Mum- good things. *Great* things. And..." he took a deep breath, pondering if he was mad, then he said "I do too."

Leticia stared at him. Then her jaw dropped when she realised her son actually *did* know great things about Count Dracula. She could see it in his eyes, his serious eyes. She knew he wasn't bluffing.

Leticia drew a deep breath, Jeiklee as well. Then she said "This adventure you were on, Jeiklee. Did you learn about Count Dracula then? During your time in the past?"

Jeiklee hesitated.

"You can tell me, Jeiklee. I won't tell your father a thing. This is between me and you," Leticia said reassuringly. Jeiklee believed her.

"Yes Mum. I learnt a lot about Count Dracula while I was away."

"Ok," said Leticia curiously. "What do you know about him?"

"I know that you and Count Dracula-" Jeiklee stopped as her eyes widened in shock, and he quickly decided not to tell all. Sighing, he said "I know you and Count Dracula were best friends when you were kids."

Relieved, Leticia said "Oh. Well- yes we were. We grew up together."

"I saw how close you were," Jeiklee said, and her eyes filled over. "They shouldn't have tried to split you up like that. Dracula was nothing but good to you. You were so close."

"I know," sighed Leticia. "I can sense you know more than you're letting on, Jeiklee. Yes, we were close. And..."

She stopped, and Jeiklee said "And you're back in contact with him, aren't you Mum?" Leticia hesitated, and he added "This is between me and you. Like you said."

"Yes," said Leticia after pausing to think about what she was doing. "Yes we are in contact."

"Mum, why don't you just... go to Count Dracula? Be with him?"

Leticia stared at him. "What?"

"I just... I know you two are meant to be together," said Jeiklee, trying to express how much he felt about his mother's happiness. "And I know that Count Dracula's the one your heart truly belongs to. Right?"

"Jeiklee, I can't discuss that with you. Just know that I love your father."

"Not as much as you love Dracula," Jeiklee said, looking at her knowingly. "I don't think like everyone else here; I know he's not evil. You deserve to be happy, Mum. I want you to be happy."

Two tears fell from Leticia's eyes, and she wiped them away quickly before she said "You really are special, sweetie."

"Thanks Mum. I think Count Dracula's special too." Jeiklee smiled at her. "He'd do anything for you."

"So much time has passed," said Leticia quietly, and Jeiklee said "That doesn't mean a thing. You're used to Dad and your life with him, but that doesn't mean *anything*. If you go to Dracula, you'd still be a Countess."

"Jeiklee, how can you think this way after a simple five days?" Leticia was very surprised. "Just how much do you know exactly?"

Jeiklee paused, then he admitted "Everything."

Leticia stared at him. "Everything?"

"Yes. The Elder Samantha- it was some sort of test. Spirit didn't care about your happiness or the fact you loved Dracula, she said it was for the best you married Dad and Dracula probably had you under some kind of love spell."

Anger flashed across Leticia's face like before. "That's not true."

"Yeah, I told her so," Jeiklee said with a small smile. "I'm Count Dracula's defender. Like you, Mum."

Leticia smiled at her son. "You don't think like the people of Severna do about Count Dracula. You truly have my heart."

"Yep. And I think you should just do what you feel is right deep down," Jeiklee told his mother. "Dracula's right."

"Right about what, honey?"

"You've worried about what the people of Severna and Dad will think for far too long, Mum." Jeiklee looked at her seriously. "You was forced to marry my Dad. If you didn't, Virginia would be dead."

Leticia's jaw dropped. "You know it all."

"Yes I do. You was so brave, Mum!" Jeiklee felt his own eyes about to well up as his mother looked at him. "I saw those tears when you married Dad. You was distraught and you felt helpless. That's why you left and went to Dracula after pretty much four months."

"Jeiklee, you can't repeat any of this to anyone," Leticia said quietly. "Nobody knows the truth about why I agreed to marry Westley and why I stayed married."

"They can know now, Mum. You don't have to hide anymore," Jeiklee said earnestly. "Be true to your heart. I promise you, I won't be angry whatever you decide to do."

Leticia stared at him again, then she said "I-"

"Spirit's quite upset," Westley said, coming in out of nowhere, and Leticia looked at her husband- the husband she was forced to marry, Jeiklee thought to himself ruefully, and Leticia said "Jeiklee, maybe you should go and patch things up with her. After all, you and Spirit are close. You don't want to start Thrill upset with her, do you?"

Jeiklee sighed. "No Mum. I'll go and talk to her."

He stood and walked to the doors, then he looked back at his mother. "Think about what I said, Mum."

"I will." Leticia spoke softly. "I promise you."

Jeiklee smiled at her and left the room.

Westley looked at his wife curiously. "Think about what he said? What were you both talking about, Tish?"

"Nothing, it doesn't matter." Leticia smiled and stood. "I'm going to my Chamber of Serenity. I have a lot of thinking to do, contemplating. When I come to a conclusion, I will come out."

"Will you be in there for the rest of the night?" asked Westley, and she replied "Maybe. Keep Jeiklee and Spirit in check please."

"I will."

* * *

Jeiklee knocked on Spirit's door. "Spirit?"

"Go away."

Jeiklee sighed. "Come on Spirit, don't be a grouch. Can you come out?"

"No," said Spirit flatly, and Jeiklee grew annoyed.

"You're going to stay mad at me all night?"

"Probably for a week and two more after."

"Fine. Be like that." Jeiklee wasn't in the mood to grovel. "I'm going to my room."

"Go ahead," Spirit said as flatly as before, and Jeiklee scowled and left.

Westley appeared in front of his door, startling him as he said "Dad!"

"Go back and make things right," Westley said firmly, and Jeiklee pouted but didn't dare disobey, turning back around and walking back to Spirit's room.

He rapped on the door. "Spirit!"

"What??"

"Uh… Fancy some ice cream in the garden?" Jeiklee suggested. "We can chill by the pool."

Spirit thought about it. Jeiklee waited, then she said "Fine. As long as you don't bring up Virginia of Dracula for the rest of the night."

Jeiklee opened his mouth to retort, then decided against it. "Ok."

* * *

"I've been thinking about what we saw in the past," Spirit said quietly, and Jeiklee looked at her as she spooned some ice cream.

"And?"

"And I think we should just forget about it. All of it." Spirit looked at him as he gaped at her disbelievingly. "It's all in the past and over with. Everything is great how it is, you know? Leticia's happy with her husband Westley, and they're both amazing parents to both of us. We shouldn't disturb that. Let's just forget it all."

Jeiklee knew Spirit meant it, but he totally disagreed. Still, he said "Yeah, alright. We'll forget about it."

Spirit smiled at him, relieved. "Good. I almost thought you were going to put up a huge fight about it."

"Nah. You're right. You should forget about it, Spirit." His hand was glowing behind her, but she didn't see. "You should forget everything."

He placed a hand on her head gently, and her eyes grew heavier and heavier before she slumped back on the grass, in a deep sleep.

Leticia appeared by his side, startled. "Jeiklee? What did you just do?"

"Mum, please help me," said Jeiklee pleadingly. "I need you to wipe

Spirit's memory of everything she found out with me about you and Count Dracula. Every memory in those five days away gone. Can you do that?"

Leticia hesitated, and Jeiklee said "Please, Mum. I don't want Spirit to say anything about it or let anything slip. And anyway, it should just be between me and you," Jeiklee added, and Leticia smiled a little. "Plus Spirit wants to forget it anyway! I'm just making sure she really does."

Leticia sighed and nodded, hand glowing white, and she knelt and touched Spirit's forehead gently. The light seeped into her head, Leticia murmuring *"Tegrof..."*

Spirit's body was aglow for a moment, then she seemed to go back to normal, eyes flicking open uncertainly before she seemed to focus.

"Leticia?"

"Hello sweetie." Leticia smiled at her. "Are you alright?"

"I… what happened?" said Spirit, confused as she sat up, and Jeiklee said "You blacked out for a moment. I was saying we should forget the argument about Virginia and just be cool."

"Oh," said Spirit, nonplussed. "Yeah, I agree."

"I'll leave you both alone," smiled Leticia, and Spirit and Jeiklee smiled back as she walked back into the mansion, Jeiklee handing Spirit her bowl of ice cream.

"You ok?"

"I'm fine," smiled Spirit. "Well… I'm really glad you'll be starting Thrill. I won't be a loner now and again."

"I'll hang with you, you know I will." Jeiklee put an arm around her, relieved as she rested his head on his shoulder. Spirit didn't even remember the conversation they were really having!

His mother was *awesome.*

* * *

Castle Dracula…

"Leticia," said Dracula, surprised as Nancy brought her to his study. "It's three in the morning- what brings you to see me at this time?"

"I…" Leticia stopped, Nancy leaving them alone quickly. Dracula took Leticia's hand and drew her inside his study, closing his door.

"What is it, sweetheart?"

"It's Jeiklee. He knows everything about you and I," Leticia said quietly, and Dracula gaped.

"You… you told-?"

"No, of course not. He discovered it through the powers of the Elders."

Dracula sighed. "So your son hates me too."

"No," said Leticia, eyes shining. "No. Jeiklee likes you and thinks you're great. He even called himself your defender. Isn't that cute?"

"Very cute," said Dracula. "So what happens now? Will he tell his father?"

"No," Leticia repeated, smiling. "He… he seems to like the idea of you and I being… together."

Dracula stared at her. "You're joking."

"I'm not."

"Does he care not for his father??"

"Of course he does," Leticia said reassuringly. "But Jeiklee cares for my happiness and what *I* truly want more. He knows I was forced to marry his father and he hates it. He… he just wants me to be happy." She paused, then softly said "Happy with you."

"That is amazing," admitted Dracula. He sat in his armchair, stunned. "Truly amazing."

There was an "I agree Father!" from outside the door, and Dracula glared. "Virginia, what are you doing up?!"

Virginia tiptoed into the study, then she ran and hugged Leticia hard.

"So Inferno Junior doesn't mind about you and my Father's friendship, Miss Leticia? He won't be hateful to him like everyone?" gushed Virginia, and they could tell she was delighted. "That really *is* amazing!"

"Go back to bed," scolded Dracula. "And do not listen at my study door again."

"Don't be mean, Dracula," said Leticia amusedly, and Dracula smiled at her. "She's happy for you."

Dracula rubbed his chin, then he grudgingly said "Alright, I won't be mean. But you must go back to bed, Virginia."

"Yes Father." Smiling broadly, Virginia left the study. Dracula smiled at Leticia.

"So when will you properly introduce me to Jeiklee, Leticia? I would love to hear what he thinks and knows about me."

"Hmm… I'm not sure." Leticia looked thoughtful for a moment. "He starts Thrill soon, so it would have to be on a weekend. How about I ask Jeiklee if he would like to come with me when I visit you next? I doubt he will say no. After all, he is your defender."

Dracula chuckled. "I find that very cute."

"Spirit McKenzie thought everything that happened to me was for the best," said Leticia with a pout, Dracula startled.

"Spirit McKenzie knows too??"

"Not anymore. I wiped her memory," shrugged Leticia. "Now she knows as little about us as she did before Jeiklee came to Severna."

Dracula relaxed. "Good. I know Spirit McKenzie is loyal to your husband."

"And Jeiklee is loyal to me. All he wants is for me to be happy."

"That is brilliant, Leticia. I'm so pleased for you."

"And I am also pleased for you, Dracula." Leticia stood on tiptoe and kissed the handsome Count gently on the mouth. "My son didn't judge you without knowing you like Spirit did, even after she saw everything. I used the power of the Force and went to see Jeiklee and Spirit's adventure for myself. Jeiklee really is on your side. I'm so glad."

Dracula hugged her. He couldn't help it. "I love you. And I love the sound of Jeiklee. I can't wait to meet my defender."

Element Five: Freedom

* * *

Antonio woke Jeiklee up with the horn.
Startled, Jeiklee tumbled out of bed. "Antonio! What was that for?!"
"Master Inferno, your parents asked me to wake you. It is soon time for you to go to college."
Jeiklee gaped at him, then he leapt up excitedly, heart pounding.
"This is it!"
"Your bag is packed, sir." Antonio smiled at him. "All you have to do is be ready for breakfast in an hour and leave for Thrill in another hour."
"Wait- what? What time is it?" said Jeiklee confusedly, and Antonio replied "It's half seven in the morning, sir. Thrill's doors open at ten on the dot. You need to be at the school half an hour before, your father said, to acquaint yourselves with your schoolmates."
"Awesome. I'll be down for breakfast in an hour, Antonio. Thank you."
Antonio bowed and left the room, Jeiklee smiling broadly.
"I can't wait to start."

* * *

Spirit smiled at Jeiklee, sipping her cup of tea. "Are you nervous?"
"Excited," said Jeiklee, heart still pounding as Spirit smiled at him. "I hope I don't embarrass myself. I've studied everything that was taught and I mastered all the spells taught in class too."
"That was just the Hovering and Lowering charms, Jeiklee. You only missed a few weeks. Don't worry." Spirit smiled at him. "We're going to be tested before we learn the next spells in a week."
"I'm ready," said Jeiklee determinedly, then he frowned. "So I didn't need to learn all those other spells and hexes?"
"Oh, you definitely needed to, silly. You need to be able to defend yourself with those spells and hexes," Spirit told him amusedly, "And the spells are handy. Every kid knew a spell or two growing up. We knew hexes too, before we started Thrill. It was a necessity growing up in Severna."
"Oh," said Jeiklee, pausing. "Well, I'm ready like I said. But I don't really want to play-duel. I'm a lover, not a fighter."
Spirit laughed as Leticia entered the dining hall in her dressing gown, Westley behind her as he said "Are you ready, son?"
"I'm ready Dad."
"Have you eaten already? Breakfast is the most important meal of the day, Jeiklee." Westley smiled at his son. "And you're definitely going to need your fuel for your first day at Thrill and all the days after."
"Yes Dad. I'm going to eat something now."
Leticia took her seat, reaching for the jug of ice cold water which was set

on the table.

"I'm sure you'll have a great first day, Jeiklee."

"I will Mum. No matter what," smiled Jeiklee, eyes shining as he looked at her happily. He had a feeling she'd done a lot of thinking about what they'd discussed, and hoped she wouldn't brush things under the carpet. "Will you be home when we get back?"

"Of course," smiled Leticia. "I want to hear all about how your first day went."

Jeiklee smiled back, heart pounding with love for his mother. How could he ever have said he didn't want to know her?

"Mum?"

"Mmm?"

"I... well... I love you loads," blurted Jeiklee, and Westley and Spirit gaped at him. "Like, I really love you to death. I wish I had you all my life instead of when I came of age in the mortal world."

"I love you too, Jeiklee." Leticia was glowing pink, and they all knew it was true. Pink light was a sign of love. "I never once felt anything aside from love. You are my son, my special boy. I love you just as much if not even more."

Westley smiled. "Where did that come from, Jeiklee?"

"I love you too Dad," Jeiklee said amusedly, and Westley laughed out loud. "I love you both. I've wanted to say it for ages but I thought it might be too soon."

"It's never too soon, son. We love you too."

"Soppy Inferno," Spirit said amusedly to Jeiklee. "I thought you were tough as nails, Jeiklee?"

"Not when it comes to my Mum."

"Mama's Boy."

"Daddy's Girl," Jeiklee retorted amusedly, and Spirit beamed at Westley. "Yes I am."

* * *

Jeiklee was almost jumping up and down as he and Spirit bade his parents goodbye and left the mansion.

"Spirit?"

"Yes?"

"You'll look out for me, right?" asked Jeiklee, and Spirit smiled at him.

"Sure. We can spend the whole day together today."

"Oh. Well… we can't."

"Why not?" asked Spirit curiously, and Jeiklee hesitated. "Jeiklee?"

"Because I'm spending the day with Virginia." Jeiklee waited for the bomb to explode, but Spirit just coolly said "Fine."

"We can spend tomorrow together if you-"

"No. Stick to your precious Virginia of Dracula."

Jeiklee grabbed her arm as she made to storm away, and she snapped "Let go of me!"

"No! Spirit, don't be like this. We can hang out all week if you want-"

"I said *let go of me!*"

Her free hand sparked with bright blue electricity, and he let her go sharpish before she could sizzle the life out of him.

"You know what? I'm done. From now on we're through, Jeiklee! We can just be friends from now on, and if you keep seeing that omen, friends is all we will ever be!"

"Fine," said Jeiklee angrily as they neared Thrill. "You're acting like a spoilt, jealous, bitter little-"

"Lover's tiff?" said an amused voice, and they whipped round, startled. Virginia of Dracula was walking behind them, highly amused as she said "Ready to hang out for the day, Jeiklee?"

"Yeah," said Jeiklee, calming down a little. Virginia seemed to have that effect on him. "Sure I am."

"Well, I sit at the back of the class," Virginia told him. "Is that ok? Nobody really sits at the front aside from Spirit McKenzie."

"Don't say my name," spat Spirit, and Virginia rolled her eyes.

"It's illegal to say your name now?"

Spirit looked like she was about to explode. "Jeiklee, you want to hang with trash then fine. But don't expect me to hang out with you if you do."

"That's blackmail," said Virginia, tutting. "Why are you putting pressure on Jeiklee, McKenzie? Your problem is with me, not him. Grow up!"

"If you tell me to grow up *one* more time-"

"Grow. The hell. Up." Virginia smirked at her. "What are you going to do about it?"

Before Spirit could retort angrily Jeiklee realised they were at the massive building.

"We're here!"

"Jeiklee Inferno!" called a few voices excitedly, and Jeiklee waved and called hi. "Welcome to Thrill, Jeiklee!"

"Thank you," Jeiklee called back, then he saw Bruce Finnegan with his group of friends, including Clarissa.

"Jeiklee," smiled Bruce, and Jeiklee smiled back as he said "Hey Bruce."

"Ready to kick butt here at Thrill?" grinned Bruce, as he held a hand up, and Jeiklee slapped it in a high-five as he said "Of course!"

Spirit couldn't believe it. "You're friends with Bruce now??"

"Yeah, we patched things up in the rain," said Bruce, and Spirit gaped at him as he said "After you was being childish and shooting hexes all over the place and you stormed off, me and Jeiklee sorted our differences."

"You know what? I don't care. Just keep away from me," spat Spirit. "All of you keep away from me!"

"We always do anyway," Virginia said amusedly, and a lot of people sniggered. "It won't be anything new."

The bell went before Spirit could answer, and everyone started to go in.

Jeiklee felt like he would burst with different emotions as Spirit walked away from them. Virginia linked arms with him, asking "You ok, Jeiklee?"

"Yeah," he said breathlessly. "I'm hanging out with you like I said I would."

"Great. I'll show you around and make sure you don't get lost."

* * *

"Take notes please," Professor Levart drawled as he wrote on the white board, and everyone picked up their pens. "The Hovering and Lowering Charms have been used over the years for everyday use, assistance when danger occurs, in wars, and in many other circumstances. Although they are simple spells, they are important because…"

Jeiklee glanced across the classroom at Spirit, who was on the other side of the room, pretty much as far away from him and Virginia as she could get. She was writing furiously, not looking in his direction once.

"She's butt-hurt," whispered Virginia, and he looked at her. "Best to let her cool down before you try going up to her."

"She ended it," Jeiklee whispered back as he started taking notes. "Just because I'm hanging out with you today."

"She'll never want you around me." Virginia shrugged as she took notes as well. "If you want to forget hanging out-"

"Even if I did, I'd never stop wanting to be your close friend."

Virginia blushed big time, and Professor Levart looked at her amazedly.

"Virginia?"

"Yes Professor?"

"Why is your face so red?"

Everyone turned to look at Virginia in surprise, and Virginia said "Er… no reason, Professor. I… well…"

"Looks like Jeiklee has a way with the ladies," grinned Bruce, and the class laughed, but in a good way. Virginia smiled as well before she said "Quiet, Finnegan. Apologies Professor."

"No reason to apologise, Virginia. Now settle down everyone and carry on taking notes. You will need to study these notes at home every day to prepare you for the monthly Spell Exam."

"Monthly Spell Exam?" Jeiklee repeated amazedly, and Professor Levart said "Yes, Mr Inferno. At the end of each month, there is an exam for the spells you learnt in that time. Your results determine your end of year grade."

"Oh- so there's no final exam at the end of the year?" asked Jeiklee, and Virginia smiled amusedly as she said "This isn't the mortal world, Jeiklee. Things are done differently here in Severna."

Jeiklee nudged her amusedly. "I don't know anything, remember?"

"I'll teach you everything," smiled Virginia, and he smiled back at her.

Spirit's eyes filled over, and she stood. "May I be excused, Professor? I need to use the bathroom."

"To have a little cry?" smirked Clarissa, and the class sniggered as Professor Levart said "You're excused, Spirit. Be back in ten minutes."

Spirit quickly left before the tears rolled down her face.

"Now, Mr Inferno- may I call you Jeiklee?"

"Yes sir."

"Jeiklee," said Professor Levart with a gentle smile, "We had the induction before September, explaining how things are run here at Thrill. If you'd like, I can organise one with you after Thrill closes for the day? It will only take half an hour."

"I'd appreciate that, Professor. Thank you," smiled Jeiklee, and Professor Levart said "You're most welcome."

Jeiklee smiled and picked up his pencil, staring to take his notes again.

Spirit came back in the class ten minutes later, eyes red. Virginia rolled her eyes, and Spirit snapped "What, Virginia?"

"What do you mean what?"

"Why are you rolling your eyes?"

"How about you focus on the task set for the class instead of me, Spirit McKenzie," said Virginia lazily. "You act like you hate me yet you observe every little thing I do. Are you sure you're not a fan of mine?"

The class burst out laughing, Bruce Finnegan saying "Snap!"

"One of these days you'll get what's coming to you, Virginia." Spirit sat down. "And when you do, I will be the first one to spit on your grave!"

"Aww. My heart bleeds," said Virginia amusedly. "Are you saying you want me dead, Spirit McKenzie? That's a bit dark, even for you."

"Yeah it is," said Jeiklee, a bit surprised at Spirit. "Spirit, calm down."

"Just shut up, Jeiklee."

The class said "Ooooh!" and looked at Jeiklee, who said "You know what? Fine. I'm done defending you. I can see why you're not that well thought of and not taken seriously, Spirit. You really *do* act like a kid."

"Snap," said Bruce Finnegan again amusedly, and the class laughed. "Spirit, even Jeiklee thinks you should grow up. Why not try it?"

"Settle down," scolded Professor Levart before Spirit could retort furiously. "When break comes, continue your discussion. Until then, take notes please."

Everyone said "Yes Professor" and continued writing.

* * *

Jeiklee and Virginia sat by the river at lunch, talking happily.

"Yep, my Mum loves Red Velvet cake. I do too," Jeiklee told Virginia with a smile. "But I haven't had any in maybe three years."

"Well, how about you come to mine and we have some?" suggested Virginia. "And end that three year absence of Miss Leticia's favourite cake."

"You mean… come to Castle Dracula?" said Jeiklee amazedly, and Virginia nodded.

"Sure. Father won't mind me bringing a friend home."

"But have you brought friends home before?" asked Jeiklee, and she replied "No. I usually see my friends away from the castle. They're terrified of coming. I'm used to it though."

"Well I'm not terrified," smiled Jeiklee. "I really like your father, Virginia."

"So I've heard," said Virginia knowingly, and he looked at her.

"Heard? From who?"

"From Miss Leticia," Virginia said, smiling at him. "She told my father that you know everything about him and you don't hate him nor have you judged him."

"It's true," said Jeiklee, and her smile grew. "I think Count Dracula is awesome."

"Well, I heard Miss Leticia say you know everything about him. Yet you still think he's awesome?" Jeiklee said yes. "Well, I'm glad. I think Miss Leticia's awesome too."

"She definitely is," said Jeiklee happily. "I'm going to ask her if I can come with her to Castle Dracula. I don't want to turn up there on my own and Count Dracula asks me what I'm doing at his castle."

"He won't, Jeiklee."

"I'll come with Mum just in case. I don't like going to places unannounced."

"I get that," said Virginia understandingly. "How about I ask him when I get home if he minds you coming? Then I can tell you tomorrow what he says."

"Yes please. Thanks, Virginia." Jeiklee shot her a dazzling smile, and she smiled back and picked up her sandwich.

Spirit watched them from a distance, upset as she stood with Julius.

"I feel like I'm losing him to her!"

"Don't be silly, Spirit. You're not losing him," Julius reassured her. "Just try not to flip out again today. Apologise to Jeiklee for being rude to him in class and patch things up when you get home."

"Why should *I* apologise?? It's him sticking to Virginia like glue when it should be me he hangs with on his first day here," said Spirit angrily. "What are they even talking about?? They look so happy, smiling and laughing together. It had better not be me they're laughing at!"

"Spirit, calm down," Julius said firmly. "You're winding yourself up for no reason."

"Am I??"

"Yes. Now can we please stop watching Jeiklee and Virginia of Dracula? Let's go into the cafeteria and eat before the hour's up."

"I just want to make things right. Before Virginia wormed her way into Jeiklee's life, me and Jeiklee were just... great. And now we're not. I don't know if-"

"You can keep him to yourself?" snickered a voice, and they whipped round and saw Clarissa standing with a group of people behind them. "Why do you always play the victim, Spirit McKenzie?"

"Get lost, Clarissa." Spirit wasn't even bothered with the likes of Virginia's side-kick. "You don't faze me at all. And you don't faze Jeiklee either. Oh, and for the record, that whole 'keep him to yourself' thing is getting old. So try and update your brainwaves."

"Ricato!!"

BANG!!

Spirit was blasted off her feet, tumbling onto the grass.

"Spirit!" yelled Julius, Jeiklee and Virginia standing with frowns on their faces. "Spirit, are you alright??"

Spirit spat grass out of her mouth and stood, furious. *"Elementasin!!"*

WHOOSH!!

Clarissa was pulled into the air by an unknown force, screaming in pain as she began to glow acid green.

Everyone screamed as well as they realised what spell Spirit used, Bruce Finnegan shouting "What the hell, Spirit! The Horror Curse?! *You're insane!!"*

Spirit ignored him, holding her glowing green hands up.

"You want to try and give me a Burn Hex, Clarissa?! Well now your whole body will burn- with horrors out of this world!"

"Spirit, stop!" shouted Jeiklee as he ran over with Virginia, Clarissa spinning in a circle sobbing "I'm sorry, I'm sorry! Make it stop!"

There was an ear splitting shriek as a gigantic cloaked figure appeared, and everyone screamed again, backing away.

"The Sin!!"

The figure swooped down, everyone ducking fearfully, before it flew back into the air, their skeletal hands reaching for Clarissa hungrily. Clarissa screamed in fear again.

"Don't let it take me!!"

The hovering cloaked figure turned to look down at Spirit, rasping *"Is this the soul you desire I take?"*

"What the hell!" said Jeiklee in shock, everyone pulling him back quickly. "Spirit, what the hell are you doing?!"

"Mordzmorda!!" cried Virginia before Spirit could give the monster an order- BAANNNNG!!!

Spirit slammed into a tree with the impact of the spell and collapsed, lifeless. Her spell and the monster she conjured vanished, Clarissa falling to the grass crying her eyes out.

"She's evil," gasped Clarissa, tears streaming as Bruce and Virginia helped her up. *"She's evil!!"*

"Calm down, Clarissa. Spirit wouldn't have let the Sin take you," Virginia said reassuringly. "She just wanted to scare you."

"The Sin?" Jeiklee repeated as the professors ran outside. "What-"

"Thrill is closed for the day!" shouted Professor Gene, as teachers and paramedics ran to Spirit's body. "Everybody grab your belongings and go home!"

"Clarissa, come with us," another Professor said firmly. "You too Mr Inferno and Virginia. Everyone else leave!"

The buzz of annoyed and excited chatter broke out as the students obeyed, Jeiklee following the Professors inside with Virginia and Clarissa.

"Will Spirit be ok?" he asked, a bit scared as he watched Spirit get carried away on a stretcher, still out cold.

"Her body went into shock," Professor Gene said grimly. "Virginia, couldn't you have hit her with a weaker spell? Your levels with hexes are super extraordinary, just like your father's and Jeiklee Inferno's mother's!"

"I didn't think Professor, I just reacted when I saw the Sin appear," Virginia replied, unsympathetic. "Spirit McKenzie took it too far. And Clarissa was begging her to stop. I had to do something."

"Yes, I agree *something* had to be done. Now why did Spirit use the Horror Curse to begin with?" asked Professor Gene curiously. "Surely she knew how dangerous it was to unleash the Sin??"

"She must have known," said Jeiklee, and Clarissa angrily said "But she didn't care. I think she wanted me to get sucked into the Underworld. That's what she wanted, Professor! She wanted me to die!"

"Why did Spirit use the Horror Curse?" repeated Professor Gene, just not asked to deal with Clarissa's dramatics. "It definitely *is* out of character. Clarissa, what did you say to her? We saw you exchanging words before she lost her temper."

"I... I heard her talking to Julius about Jeiklee and Virginia. She was really upset," Clarissa said grudgingly, "And I kind of made it worse by winding her up. She flipped out. I'm sorry, Professor."

"You know better that to pick on people Clarissa, especially Spirit McKenzie," said Professor Gene, shaking her head. "Virginia stopped and you started. Why would you do that?"

"It won't happen again Professor."

"I'm glad. Now are you in any pain at all? Do you need checking over?"

"No Professor."

"Fine. You may leave," Professor Gene said, and Clarissa obeyed quickly. "Now Virginia. I'm sorry, but I have to alert your father of what happened today and your actions."

"But Professor-!!"

"No buts. A Stun Hex would have been better than a Fire Bone Hex, young lady. Spirit McKenzie has gone into shock and may remain unconscious for the rest of the day."

"But- but-"

"I will call your parents also, Jeiklee." Professor Gene smiled at him, and Jeiklee nervously asked "Am I in trouble like Virginia?"

"No, of course not. But I'd rather your parents collect you. Also, they are Spirit's guardians also and they must be informed that she has been taken to the hospital."

"Oh," said Jeiklee. "Ok."

Almost an hour later, Count Dracula, Westley and Leticia were walking towards them. Virginia kept her head down, and Jeiklee could see why: her father looked furious.

"Please, come into my office," Professor Gene said quickly and nervously as Dracula opened his mouth angrily, and Dracula closed it, taking a deep breath as he said "Very well."

"This sucks," muttered Virginia, as Westley shot her a piercing glare before entering the office with Dracula and Leticia. "I didn't know what else to do and now I'm going to be punished!"

"Don't worry. I'll back you up," Jeiklee said reassuringly, and she smiled at him.

"Thanks Jeiklee."

When Dracula left the office, he was glowing scarlet. Virginia stood quickly, saying "Father, it's not what you think. I didn't randomly attack Spirit McKenzie like I used to, I was trying to stop her from having Clarissa sucked to the Underworld!"

"So you hit her with a Fire Bone Hex which sent her into shock?!" Dracula was furious. "Of all the spells and hexes you could have used-"

"I know, and I'm sorry! But I had to stop her, Father! I didn't think about what spell to use, I just had to save Clarissa!"

"I know you did," Dracula said grudgingly, calming down a little. "You were trying to save your friend, I understand. But next time, please use a less dangerous spell!"

"There won't be a next time," spat Westley. "If your Spawn of Satan ever goes near Spirit again- or Jeiklee, in fact- I will take action, Dracula!"

"That's not fair!" said Jeiklee and Virginia at the same time, outraged. "Dad, me and Virginia are friends!"

"I don't care," said Westley roughly. "Your *friend* put Spirit in the hospital, Jeiklee- and was her bully for years! I forbid you from going near her, talking to her, visiting her- everything to do with Virginia of Dracula and Count Dracula is forbidden, do you understand me?!"

"No I don't understand! And I won't stop seeing Virginia," Jeiklee said angrily. "I like her, she's really cool. And she's not evil!"

Westley took a deep breath, then said as calmly as he could "I told you already Jeiklee, that Count Dracula and his daughter are cruel, evil beings. I don't want you near either of them!"

"Well we don't want to be near *you*, Westley," Dracula said flatly, and Virginia nodded angrily. "So the feeling is sort of mutual. I have nothing against your son of course. It is *you* who is the stick in the mud."

"You think I won't use the Horror Curse on you, Dracula?" spat Westley. "Don't push my buttons! I'd unleash the Sin on you in a heartbeat!"

"The Sin would bow to me, you foolish man." Dracula smirked at him. "Have you forgotten I am the master of pretty much any demon or monster no matter who they are meant to obey? The Sin would be under my control. And if you don't believe me, summon it and see for yourself."

Westley looked like he was going to let rip. Looking at Jeiklee, he said "Now do you see what I was trying to tell you, Jeiklee? Count Dracula is evil and so is his daughter, and I don't want you anywhere near *either* of them!"

"Well what you want and what I want are two different things, Dad!"

"We're going home," Westley said flatly, not answering what his son just said. "Come on, Leticia and Jeiklee. We're leaving."

Virginia looked really hurt. Dracula looked like he wanted to knock the living daylights out of Westley, and Leticia looked very annoyed at her husband as well. Jeiklee was angry, and as his father walked away, he whispered to Virginia "Meet you at seven this evening at the entrance to the Forest of Fear."

"What?" she hissed back. "But your father just said-"

"I don't care," whispered Jeiklee. "See you then."

"Jeiklee!" called Westley sharply, and Jeiklee jogged away. Leticia shook her head, quietly saying "Apologies for Westley's behaviour, Dracula."

"I will see you soon Leticia," Dracula replied softly as he took Virginia's arm, and they both vanished.

Leticia shook her head as she walked to catch up with her son and husband.

* * *

Castle Dracula…

"Father, Jeiklee wants to meet me at seven. Can I go?" asked Virginia, as they walked through the giant doors. Dracula was very annoyed as he walked towards the giant staircase, Virginia following him. "Please?"
"Of course you can go, my daughter. Just be back by nine," Dracula replied, and Virginia beamed at him.
"Great! Thank you!"
"You're welcome."
Dracula entered his study and sat down, wondering what Leticia was doing and if she was attempting to calm her husband down. Dracula doubted it, actually. Leticia's heart belonged to him. He had a feeling he would see her after sundown.

* * *

Jeiklee stared at Spirit, who was still unconscious in a hospital bed. They had gone to see her an hour after going home, and Jeiklee hadn't said a word to his father in that time.
"Will she be ok, Mum?" asked Jeiklee, and Leticia replied "Yes, sweetie. She'll be fine. Her body is in shock, so it's unwise for me to tamper with it, but once she is back to normal, I will heal her of any injuries."
Jeiklee breathed out, relieved. "Thanks Mum."
"So you see now what I was trying to say, Jeiklee?" scowled Westley. "Your new friend did this to Spirit. Are you not upset even a little?"
"No I'm not," Jeiklee said flatly. "Virginia had to act quickly before that monster harmed Clarissa, and this was the quickest thing she thought of. Nobody knew Spirit would go into shock like that. So no, I'm not upset and I don't blame Virginia either. It was an accident."
Westley looked furious as he began to glow scarlet. "And what do you think of Count Dracula, Jeiklee?"
"He seems pretty cool," shrugged Jeiklee, and Westley spat "Cool?! He is our enemy!"
"He's *your* enemy." Jeiklee glared at him. "I have nothing to do with why you hate Dracula so much. I wasn't around. So don't try and force me to think of Count Dracula and Virginia the way you do!"
"You… you're… stupid," muttered Spirit, and everyone whipped round, startled as Spirit opened her eyes uncertainly.
"Spirit, sweetheart. Are you alright?" asked Leticia gently, and Westley said "I'll get a doctor."
"What happened to me?" Spirit asked weakly as Westley left the room.

"I… I can't feel my legs."

"One was broken, darling. Virginia's hex hit you pretty hard," Leticia said, as Spirit winced. "Also three of your ribs were broken."

"But not anymore?"

Leticia smiled at her, hands glowing bright yellow as she walked to the bed and placed her hands on Spirit's body. Jeiklee wowed as the light swirled around her, Spirit aglow as well as she took deep breaths, and Leticia stepped back a minute later after the lights faded, saying "Not anymore."

"Wow," said Jeiklee amazedly, Spirit saying "I love you Leticia. Thanks a lot!"

"You're welcome. Spirit, we need to talk about what you did today," Leticia said seriously, and Spirit bit her lip. "You could have put that girl in serious danger using the Horror Curse. You know that is a very dangerous curse, Spirit- I've told you many times. If Virginia didn't stop you, that demon would have snatched her friend and taken her to the Underworld. And I know you wouldn't have been up for rescuing her from there in twenty four hours. You know that is how long the Sin will allow a form of rescue before devouring it's victim."

"I know. I'm sorry, Leticia. She got under my skin," said Spirit, avoiding Leticia's eyes as she spoke, and Leticia said "A lot seems to be getting under your skin lately. Maybe you should try and think rationally before acting, Spirit. I don't want anyone else in or out of Thrill in danger because of your temper."

"Yes Leticia." Spirit looked ashamed now. "I'm really sorry."

"And so you should be. I'm going to see where Westley's got to. Would you like a drink, Spirit? I advise you to have some cool water."

Spirit nodded. "Yes please Leticia. Water's great."

Leticia smiled and nodded, leaving the room.

Spirit avoided Jeiklee's eye as he looked at her, and she didn't say a word.

"You know what you did was wrong, right?" Jeiklee said flatly. "Spirit. Casting that curse on Clarissa was bang out of order."

"I know," muttered Spirit. "I was going to stop-"

"It didn't look like it." Jeiklee scowled at her. "You could have stopped after she was in a bit of pain, but you held out until that demon appeared. Anything could have happened! You don't know how to control that monster-"

"I've read books about it," said Spirit, embarrassed. "It obeys the one who calls it."

"Yeah, and what if it didn't obey?" demanded Jeiklee. "Just because you've read books-"

"I'm not in the mood for a lecture, ok? I already said I'm sorry." Spirit rolled onto her side, staring at the wall as her eyes filled over. Jeiklee walked around the bed so he could see her face.

"Because of you, my Dad doesn't want me anywhere near Virginia." Jeiklee didn't want to sound angry, but he was. "If you just controlled your temper-"

"Well maybe it's best you keep away from Virginia," Spirit said flatly. "She's evil just like her father. Westley's right about her and Dracula and you're too stupid to see it."

"I give up," said Jeiklee angrily. "Think what you want, Spirit. And you know what? I'm glad you ended it with me. Because now, I see you for what you are!"

"Which is what?" said Spirit just as angrily. "Go on!"

"Jealous, spoilt and bitter like I said before! I'm going to remain friends with Virginia no matter what anyone says," Jeiklee told her heatedly. "So get used to it!"

Spirit opened her mouth, then closed it. "You don't think I'm evil like everybody else?"

"In case you forgot, I'm not like everybody else," Jeiklee said roughly. "No, I don't think you're evil. But you can't stop me from speaking to who I want to speak to, ok? Because everyone will think you really *do* want to keep me to yourself. And you don't, do you?"

"Of course not," said Spirit indignantly. "But I do want us to be cool like we were before."

"We'll always be cool really." Jeiklee smiled at her, and she smiled back.

"I've been a real cow to you, haven't I?"

"Nah. Well... a bit. But forget it," smiled Jeiklee. "I'm fine."

"Can I have a hug?" asked Spirit a little shyly. "I know I don't deserve one."

Jeiklee hugged her and kissed her forehead. "You're a nutcase."

Leticia and Westley entered the room as he let her go, Westley looking concerned as he asked "How are you feeling, Spirit?"

"Not bad. I just want a shower really," Spirit replied, and Westley nodded. "Am I going to get in trouble with the law?"

"No, of course not. Clarissa was not taken by the Sin, so everything will be ok. But Spirit, you must never let your temper get the better of you," Westley said seriously. "Anything could have happened to that poor girl had you continued using the Horror Curse."

"Which basically means Virginia did the right thing in knocking you out," Jeiklee said, annoyed, and Westley said "I did not say that, Jeiklee."

"But that's what you meant! You just don't want to give Virginia credit," Jeiklee said to his father angrily. "Virginia did the right thing and you know it, you'd just rather not admit it!"

"Can we go home please Leticia?" said Spirit, when Westley opened his mouth just as angrily. "I feel fine."

"The doctor wants to give you a final check, Spirit." Leticia spoke calmly.

"He is aware that I healed you so there is no need to keep you here for much longer."

"Ok," said Spirit, Jeiklee glaring at his father. "I'll just have some water while I wait."

Half an hour later, Spirit was free to go home.

Jeiklee stepped into the waiting chariot, fuming. He looked at his watch; it was only four. He had three hours to chill before he would see Virginia.

The chariot flew up into the air, Jeiklee smiling a little at the feel of the wind on his face. Spirit looked at him, and she smiled.

"We're ok now?"

"Yeah," said Jeiklee, looking down at the town as they flew by. "We're ok. But lay off about me seeing Virginia and we'll stay ok."

"Don't mention her to me then. At all," replied Spirit, and he scowled at her. "I don't want to hear a thing about her, no matter what it is."

"Fine, if that's what you want." Jeiklee released a frustrated sigh. "I can't wait to have dinner."

Spirit didn't reply, but she smiled.

* * *

Castle Dracula…

Dracula stood at his study window, staring out thoughtfully.

"Father?" said Virginia curiously. "What's the matter?"

"Something is coming, my daughter. Something I cannot make head nor tail of." Dracula's green eyes were glowing, Virginia asking "Is it a storm, Father? We haven't had a thunderstorm in a while."

"No. It's something that will come into play very soon."

"Shall we warn the people of Severna?"

"No," Dracula repeated. "It is I who will be affected by whatever it is. Not the land or it's people."

"Oh," said Virginia. "I… will Westley Inferno try to kill you again?" Dracula glanced at her, surprised. "I have no idea."

"But what if he does?" Virginia looked scared. "What will happen?"

"I'm not sure," admitted Dracula, as Nancy knocked on the door.

"My Lord?"

"Yes Nancy."

"Leticia of Sampson is here."

Dracula ran to the door and pulled it open immediately, breathing "Leticia." Leticia smiled at him before she hugged him, Dracula holding her close as he murmured "What brings you to see me?"

"My husband," Leticia replied quietly, and Virginia gasped "I knew it! He's going to try and kill you, Father!"

Dracula looked at Leticia. "Is that true, Leticia?"

"The way he acted towards you today reminded me of the Westley who tried to murder you years ago," Leticia said softly. "He is fuming about you just like he used to. And it doesn't help that Jeiklee is determined to keep Virginia as a friend despite Westley banning him from seeing her."

"He is a fool," Dracula said flatly. "He and both your families banned you from seeing me and he almost lost you that way. Does he want to lose his son too?"

"I fear he will do something drastic, Dracula." Leticia took his hand. "Something is going to happen. I can feel it."

"As can I," Dracula replied softly. "We truly are connected."

Virginia smiled, saying "I'll leave you both alone, Father. I have to meet Jeiklee in an hour."

Dracula just nodded, eyes on Leticia's. Virginia shook her head and left the study, pulling the door closed behind her.

* * *

"Where's Leticia?" asked Spirit, entering the dining area, and Jeiklee replied "She's gone for a walk."

"Oh," said Spirit, Westley entering the dining area as well. "Did she say when she'll be back? She's going to miss dinner."

"Chef can whip her up a meal when she gets back, Spirit. It's no big deal if Mum misses dinner."

"She's gone?" said Westley sharply. "Where did she say she was going?"

"On a walk," said Jeiklee coldly. "Like I said."

Westley looked furious. "Jeiklee, you will not disrespect me just because I've laid down a few laws."

"You're not the King of Severna. You haven't laid down *any* laws as far as I'm concerned. And you're not the boss of me either." Jeiklee glared at him as Antonio entered, announcing "Dinner is served!"

"Great," said Spirit nervously, looking from Westley to Jeiklee and back. "Uh... Jeiklee, don't you think you're being a little... out of order?"

"No, I don't. It's my father who's being out of order." Jeiklee sat at the table, Spirit and Westley sitting down as well. "All the time, it's him calling the shots. He did it with my mother and now's he's trying to do it to me-"

"What are you talking about?" demanded Westley. "I'm doing what's best for you, Jeiklee! I stand by what I said- you are not to see Virginia of Dracula or her evil father!"

"Well you'd better think back to when you said pretty much the same to my mother!" spat Jeiklee, and Westley froze.

"What did you say?!"

"You heard me! You tried banning her from seeing who she wanted and what happened, Dad? She went *straight to them!* And speaking of going straight to them, I'm meeting Virginia at seven. Stuff what you think!"

"This is getting out of control!" said Spirit desperately, Westley glowing scarlet. "Jeiklee, calm down- Westley, calm down as well! And Jeiklee, what are you talking about? Westley didn't ban Leticia from seeing who she wanted-"

"Like hell he didn't! Ask him!" said Jeiklee angrily. "He just wanted her to himself-"

"I don't know what you think you know, Jeiklee, but you're wrong!" spat Westley. "I banned Leticia from seeing Count Dracula because it was the right thing to do, not because I wanted her to myself! He was leading her astray!"

"Everyone knows that," said Spirit reasonably. "Jeiklee, you've got your wires crossed. We all know Leticia and Count Dracula used to be friends. That's over now, and everyone is better for it! Leticia's happy, I'm happy, Westley's happy. Now can we please forget this incident and have dinner?

Please!"

Jeiklee scowled as he remembered Spirit didn't know any better, not anymore. "Fine, but I'm going to see Virginia at seven whether he likes it or not!"

"No you are not, Jeiklee!" said Westley angrily, and Spirit said "Just let him go, Westley, so I can eat my dinner in peace!"

"Spirit, you know what that girl and her father are like!" Westley said, livid. "I don't want you or my son anywhere near them!"

Leticia entered the dining area, pulling her cloak off before Jeiklee or Spirit could reply.

"Enough."

Everyone whipped round, Spirit gasping "Leticia!"

"I thought you was on a walk, Mum?" said Jeiklee confusedly, and Leticia replied "I could hear the altercation with your father in my head and it was annoying me, so I returned. Now sit down all of you, and eat your dinner before it gets cold. Jeiklee, you may see Virginia if you please-"

"Great!"

"But do not disrespect your father in any way again," Leticia said calmly as she sat at the table, Westley sitting as well. "He's trying to do what's best for you, although I disagree that keeping you away from Virginia is what's best."

"What?" Westley's jaw dropped. "Leticia-"

"Not another word." Leticia looked at her husband. "Jeiklee had a point. I won't allow you to do to him what you did to me. He may see who he pleases, no matter what the consequences are."

"And if he is put in danger?" Westley said angrily. "What then?"

"You really think Virginia will put him in danger?" said Leticia, glaring at him now, and Westley said "Judging by the way she's hurt Spirit physically countless times, yes!"

"That is different."

"How is it different?!"

Leticia took a deep breath, looking like she wanted to hex her husband. Spirit and Jeiklee looked at her nervously before she quietly said "I am allowing Jeiklee to see Virginia, and you will not get in the way of that, Westley Inferno. You will not tell our son who he can and can't see again." She picked up her fork and helped herself to the food set without another word, Spirit and Jeiklee looking at each other nervously before doing the same.

Westley couldn't believe it. "So my say doesn't matter to you, Leticia?"

"Fortunately, it does not."

"Fine. It is now *my* turn to go on a walk," said Westley angrily. "I will see you tonight."

Westley stormed out of the dining area, and Leticia forked some food and

popped it in her mouth, not even acknowledging the fact he left.
Jeiklee and Spirit ate too, Jeiklee smiling to himself.
His mother was *way* too cool.

* * *

Virginia walked through the Forest of Fear quite comfortably, hands in her pockets.
"Princess of the Night," called a voice she was used to but got annoyed when hearing, and she stopped and sighed.
"Go away, Bartley."
"Now come on, little girl- I just want a word with your father." The middle aged vampire stepped out of the trees, and Virginia said "My father will never have your daughter to be his Bride. Please get used to that fact, and stop harassing me. Because I will call upon his loyal servants to deal with you."
"Ooh, tough girl. They're *his* servants, not yours. Even if you *are* his daughter, I doubt Count Dracula's minions would obey your commands." Bartley smirked at her. "And it's not good to threaten an elder, Princess."
"Just leave me alone," said Virginia huffily, and she turned and walked away.
"Count Dracula needs a Bride," Bartley called after her. "He will have my daughter as his first!"
"In your dreams," Virginia called back, and she kept walking.

* * *

Jeiklee walked to the giant doors of the mansion, glancing at his watch. It was twenty to seven in the evening.

"Jeiklee."

He whipped round, then he breathed out, relieved. "Hey Spirit."

"I... look," she said, coming up to him. "I don't know what's going to happen between you and Westley if you keep seeing Virginia. And what will happen between Westley and Leticia either. Don't you think you should just... back down and keep away from her? It would be better for all of us."

Before Jeiklee could reply his mother appeared in a cloak by the doors, hood thrown up as she made to leave.

"Leticia?" said Spirit curiously, and Leticia turned. "Are you going somewhere?"

"I'm going for a walk, Spirit."

"At this time?" said Spirit, even more curious. "You hardly ever go out after sunset unless it's urgent or-"

"Spirit, I can leave the mansion whenever I like. I'm not a prisoner," said Leticia with a smile, and Spirit smiled back.

"Yes Leticia. Sorry."

"Are you still to meet Virginia, Jeiklee?" asked Leticia, and Jeiklee nodded, saying "Yes Mum."

"Then we can leave together," smiled Leticia, and Jeiklee smiled back.

"Ok. Spirit, see you later."

"See you," said Spirit, still looking curious at Leticia leaving the mansion, but she seemed to think nothing more of it as Jeiklee left with her.

"Be home for nine, Jeiklee," Leticia said, looking at her son from under her hood, and Jeiklee said "Yes Mum. I... can I ask where you're-"

"No, sweetie. I'll be back soon."

"Yes Mum."

Leticia sped up, and Jeiklee stopped to watch her go. His mother dissolved into thin air after a few more steps, and he gasped.

"Whoa."

* * *

"You're late," pouted Virginia when she saw Jeiklee, and Jeiklee smiled at her.

"Only five minutes late. I'll make it up to you."

Virginia smiled back. "Want to go back to the river near Thrill? That can be our spot."

"Yeah, ok. Uh…" Jeiklee hesitated, and she looked at him curiously.

"What's up?"

"Do you want to go get some ice cream from Moo-Moos?" Jeiklee blurted the words out. "Or frozen yoghurt- or just yoghurt or-"

"Sure," shrugged Virginia. "Do you want to sit inside? I don't mind but I'm going to get a lot of dirty looks from all over."

"Nah, we can just get what we want and go to our spot." Jeiklee smiled at her, overcoming his shyness and awe of her. "Unless you want to sit inside?"

"Nope. Let's go. I really fancy some ice cream now."

The staff at the popular ice cream café were startled when Virginia entered with Jeiklee.

"Virginia of Dracula! And… Jeiklee Inferno?? What- this is an unlikely er… friendship-"

"Yeah, we know. Our fathers hate each other and whatever," said Virginia lazily, and Jeiklee smiled at her. She was so cool. "We're not going to stick around for you to gape and whisper before advising Jeiklee to steer clear of me, we just want some ice cream."

Everyone staring looked really embarrassed at her words, the manager saying "Take their orders and don't be rude to the daughter of Count Dracula. The last thing I want is this store blasted to smithereens if the Count is angered."

Virginia rolled her eyes, Jeiklee saying to her "You get this all the time?"

"All the time," shrugged Virginia, and he scowled. "Uh… can I have four scoops of ice cream, flavours bubble-gum, mango, strawberry and mint chocolate flavour please. In a bowl, not on a cone."

"Yes Virginia," the man behind the counter said nervously. "And you, Mr Inferno? What would you like?"

"The same as Virginia please," Jeiklee replied, and he nodded. "So… was your Dad real ticked off at my Dad, Virginia?"

"Yeah, he was. But he brushed it off, no bother. Father doesn't fume for long unless whatever he's fuming about *really* ticked him off. He has bigger things to worry about anyway," Virginia replied, and Jeiklee frowned at her.

"Like what?"

"I'll tell you when we're alone. The press are always looking for a story and when it comes to my Father, they'll publish any little thing to discredit him further."

"Yeah, I know."

Virginia glanced at him, surprised. "You know? How?"

"Well... I'll tell you when we're alone," smiled Jeiklee, and she smiled back.

* * *

"So *that's* how you know everything," smiled Virginia, and Jeiklee nodded. "I knew Miss Leticia wouldn't have told you about her and my Father. Nobody ever knew- not even Miss Leticia's close friends or family. But *you* know. Thanks to the Elders. And you still think my Father's great?"

"Of course!" Jeiklee popped a spoonful of mint ice cream into his mouth. "I'm not like everybody else, Virginia. I think you're both amazing."

Virginia blushed big time, and she ate some strawberry ice cream quickly to try and stop her face from turning as red as her hair.

"Jeiklee?"

"Yeah?"

"I... you won't let you father get to you about seeing me, will you?"

"No, of course not. I promise you." Jeiklee put an arm around her, and she rested her head on his shoulder as she looked up at the sky.

"It's such a beautiful night," she said happily. "So many stars."

"Did you ever wish on the biggest star?" asked Jeiklee, and Virginia said "I used to when I was a little kid. But now, I don't know what to wish for."

"Oh," said Jeiklee. "What did you wish for when you were little?"

Virginia opened her mouth, then closed it. "You'll laugh at me."

"No I won't, I promise."

Virginia sighed. "I used to wish your mother and my father would finally be together, and everyone would just accept it and leave them alone. All they wanted was to be together, and if it wasn't for your grandmother, they would be. She blackmailed Miss Leticia and-"

"And forced her to marry my Dad. Yeah, I know," said Jeiklee. "I know. If that didn't happen, I'm certain they'd be together right now."

"Oh, they definitely would be together."

Westley appeared not far off, looking around. Spotting him, he walked towards his son as Virginia said "Miss Leticia's with my father right now. You know that, right?"

Jeiklee nodded. "I don't know for sure but I have a feeling she is."

"Jeiklee!" said Westley angrily, and Jeiklee whipped round.

"Dad!"

"Why didn't you tell me your mother went to Castle Dracula?!"

"Why should I have told you?" said Jeiklee, heat rising. "And anyway, I don't know she's there anyway!"

"That vile creature next to you just said she was!"

"Vile creature?" repeated Virginia angrily, Jeiklee as well, but before Westley could say something that would make things ten times worse Count Dracula appeared behind her, Leticia morphing next to Jeiklee.

"Repeat what you called my daughter, Inferno, if you dare," Dracula said, glowing scarlet. "It will be the last thing you do, I promise you that."

"Were you with my wife?" spat Westley, and Leticia angrily said "Westley, what is the *matter* with you?? You're acting like the man I started to despise years ago when it came to Count Dracula!"

"Well maybe that man has resurfaced," snapped Westley. "Everything I have said and done of late was for you and our son. You alter my orders, Leticia, and you're back in contact with Count Dracula-"

"Who said I was back in contact with Count Dracula??"

"She did!" said Westley, glaring at Virginia, and Virginia said "I was just messing around, ok?"

"No you was not! I *know* you wasn't," said Westley, furious. "Leticia, I'm going to ask you one time and you'd better not lie to me. Were you with Count Dracula?!"

"I'm not going to speak to you when you're acting like this," Leticia said flatly, and Dracula said "You need to calm down, Inferno. And I can answer your question. No Leticia was not with me. I haven't seen her alone for an excruciatingly long time. Now stop acting like a spoilt child and go home." The fact that Count Dracula was being quite civil to him seemed to anger Westley even more.

"Just keep away from my wife, do you understand me?! Because if you don't, I'll-"

"You'll what?" said Dracula, raising an eyebrow. "Throw a tantrum?"

Jeiklee couldn't help smirking, Virginia as well as Westley spat "Leticia, we're going home- now! Jeiklee, say goodbye to that evil monstrosity and let's go!"

"You know what? I've had it up to *here* with you and your insults towards me, Westley Inferno," said Virginia, heat rising. "You'd better pipe down and go home!"

"You dare speak to me like I am a child?! *I am not your age!* " said Westley furiously, and Virginia said "Well you're acting like it! Now I see where Spirit McKenzie gets her childish flare from!"

Westley looked like he wanted to strangle Virginia. Leticia glared at him, saying "I agree with Virginia. You're acting very immature, Westley. Throwing insults and threats around isn't going to solve anything. I think you need to cool off in my Chamber of Serenity."

Westley glared at her, repeating himself. "We're going home."

"Fine," said Leticia flatly. "You ruined our son's evening, I hope you know that. And you've ruined mine also. I will sleep in my second suite tonight, away from you. Until you get your act together, I don't want to be around you."

Westley's jaw dropped as she walked away. "Leticia! I-"

"Save it, Westley." Leticia didn't even look back. "Jeiklee, come."

"See you later Virginia," said Jeiklee, and Virginia said "See you Jeiklee." Jeiklee jogged after his mother, Dracula taking Virginia's arm and dissolving into thin air with her. Westley was left standing alone, and that's how he felt.

Alone.

* * *

The atmosphere was tense in the mansion.

Everyone was sat in the lounge, just hanging out together before bed. Jeiklee sipped some hot chocolate, Spirit as well. Westley was looking at Leticia angrily, and Leticia was reading a book. She didn't look at her husband at all.

"Um… is everything alright?" Spirit asked uncertainly. "Has something happened, Leticia? I'm picking up on some negative energy."

"Yes Spirit, something has happened," Leticia said calmly, looking up from her book. "My husband seems to think it's ok to act like a bully and try to control everything that goes on in my life. He is under the impression that I've been in contact with Count Dracula."

Spirit burst out laughing. "What?? Westley, everyone knows Dracula and Leticia haven't been in contact in years! Leticia never goes near him!"

"Well he goes near *her,* that I know," said Westley angrily. "I saw the way he looked at you tonight, Leticia. He's probably missing the way you both used to be; very close friends! If you're not in contact with him, you will be soon!"

"And if I will be?" said Leticia, glaring at him. "What will you do about it? You don't have a say in who I do and do not see, Westley!"

"I'm your husband, so I *do* have a say!"

"And what makes you believe something so ridiculous?" demanded Leticia, her body picking up a faint scarlet glow. "You think you can control me and keep me tied down? Is that what you want, Westley?"

"I don't want you anywhere near Count Dracula, Leticia." Westley glared at his wife. "I forbid it!"

"Go to Hell, Westley Inferno." Leticia looked back down at her book. "If I want to see Count Dracula I will see him, and there is nothing you can do about it."

"It feels like everything is going to crumble," said Spirit nervously, and Westley said "You're right, Spirit- history is repeating itself! Leticia will most likely want to rekindle her friendship with that vile demon, but this time it won't be like it was years ago. Because I won't let it happen!"

"You're not the boss of her!" said Jeiklee, furious. "She can see who she likes!"

"This isn't your fight, Jeiklee!" said Westley angrily. "You don't know anything about your mother and Count Dracula or the history-"

"I know more than you think, Dad! If you keep on like this, you're going to lose your wife for good! Think about what you're doing and how unhappy you're going to make her," pleaded Jeiklee, and Westley and Spirit stared at him. "Do you really want Mum unhappy being here and with you? It's not going to be cool, Dad! Things will only get worse!"

"You speak as if you know a lot, Jeiklee. But you know nothing. I'm doing what's best for all of us." Westley seemed to calm down as he started pacing. "Leticia, you're going to hate me for this. But you'll thank me later when you realise it's for your own good."

Leticia stared at him. "What are you going to do?"

"I'm going to go to the King and have him instate a law about you seeing Count Dracula, and forbid it," said Westley coldly. "King Harlot will do what needs to be done. You don't want to be on the wrong side of the law, do you?"

Everyone stared at him, Jeiklee and Spirit gaping as Leticia spat "You're a monster."

"I'm less of a monster than Count Dracula is," said Westley flatly. "I'm sure you don't want to be imprisoned on Dragon Island, am I right Leticia? Not when we've just got our son back."

"And just like that it got worse," muttered Jeiklee as Leticia stared at her husband. She was beyond furious, they could tell from the look on her face. Hesitating, Spirit said "Westley, you're upset right now- think about what you're doing-"

"I have thought, Spirit. And I should have done this as soon as Leticia became my wife," Westley said flatly. "I'm going to make sure she stays far from Count Dracula no matter what it takes."

* * *

A week later…

Spirit and Jeiklee walked home from Thrill, Spirit saying "Leticia is never going to forgive Westley for the new law. I mean, what was he *thinking??* It's been all over the news and the press have been mad with excitement about the whole thing!"
"Yeah, I know. And Mum hasn't really come out of her Chamber," Jeiklee replied. "Only to eat something."
"He went too far," said Spirit. "Leticia wasn't in contact with Count Dracula anyway! Westley saw him near her and he just… went *nuts.* It definitely isn't ok! Leticia probably hates him right now."
"So… how does this law work?" asked Jeiklee curiously. "I mean, nobody can *really* stop my mother from seeing who she wants. Plus even if she did go and see Dracula, who'd have the guts to go his castle and get her?"
"The soldiers would," Spirit replied. "They'd be terrified but it's the law. And if it's broken, Leticia goes to prison on Dragon Island. King Harlot is a jerk."
"So is my Dad," said Jeiklee, shaking his head. "I don't rate him for this at all."

* * *

Leticia walked towards the exit of the mansion as Jeiklee and Spirit were walking in.
"Mum," said Jeiklee, relieved that she still looked as stunning as ever. "Are you alright? I haven't spoken to you properly in a week!"
"I will talk with you soon, Jeiklee- but I need to get some air."
"Leticia," a voice said, and everyone turned and saw Westley standing there. "Where are you going?"
"I'm going for a walk," Leticia said icily. "Or is that illegal now also?"
Westley looked pained as he said "If you'd like I can join you-"
"I'd hate, actually." Leticia glared at him. "The farther I am away from you, the happier I am. So just keep away from me."
Before Westley could reply she vanished into thin air, gone. Westley sighed, and Spirit looked sorry for him as she said "This is it, isn't it Westley? Everything's over. Nothing will be the same ever again because of what you did. Leticia isn't going to forgive you anytime soon-"
"She's not going to forgive you at all," Jeiklee cut across flatly. "And I don't blame her, Dad. You brought this on yourself. Just know if my mother leaves this place for good, and she leaves you too, I'm going with her no matter where she goes."

Westley's jaw dropped. "You don't mean that, Jeiklee."

"I mean every word," Jeiklee said coldly. "Now I'm going to my room to study for our end of month exam-"

"Shouldn't you have had that already??"

"It was delayed," said Jeiklee coldly. "And I'm not coming down until dinner."

Westley sighed. "Alright. And Spirit? What are you doing?"

"I may as well study as well," shrugged Spirit. "My room is the only place where everything feels normal. Everything here has changed because of you, Westley, and I hate it."

She walked up the stairs, and Jeiklee followed suit.

Westley ran a hand over his head and sighed, going into the lounge.

* * *

Leticia walked through the Forest of Fear, wondering whether to go back at all. Then she thought of Jeiklee and Spirit, and she knew she would.

She walked into her and Count Dracula's special clearing and dropped to her knees, gripping her hair.

"How do I get out of this mess?" she whispered, and a voice replied "Come to my castle and be free from it all, Leticia."

She whipped round, gasping "Dracula! How did you-"

"I could sense your agitation a mile away." Dracula walked towards her as she stared up at him, and he gently pulled her to her feet. "I'm sorry, but your husband is even crueller than he makes me out to be."

"I know," said Leticia, eyes filling over. "I don't think he would even care if I went to prison. As long as it kept you and I apart, he'd be fine with it."

Dracula gently wiped her tears away as they fell from her eyes.

"Don't cry, Leticia. Everything will be ok."

"What am I going to do? I can't stay there, not after what he's done to me," she wept, and Dracula replied "You could go back to your own mansion if you'd rather not come to my castle."

Leticia looked up at him. "What?"

"Your own mansion," Dracula repeated. "The house of Sampson. It's still there, being tended to by workers and maids. All it needs is it's rightful owner back."

"If I go back to my mansion, I won't look back," whispered Leticia, and Dracula said "Then what are you waiting for? Get away from Westley and find yourself. Everything will be fine."

"But I can't be seen with you or I'll go to prison," Leticia reminded him, and Dracula laughed.

"You really think I'd let you go to prison, Leticia? You can be seen with me, I promise you. I'll make sure nothing happens to you."

"Something could happen to me when you're not there," Leticia pointed out, and Dracula kissed her forehead.

"I will always be with you, Leticia. And I will always know if you are in danger."

"If I go to my mansion, I'm definitely going to take my son with me. But Spirit may not want to come," Leticia told him, Dracula holding her in his arms as she said "She is, as Jeiklee called her, a Daddy's Girl."

"Well it was you who signed the adoption papers as her jurisdictional parent, Leticia. It is you who is responsible for Spirit."

"But what if she doesn't want to come?"

"You can't force her. Just let her know she has a choice." Dracula's eyes fell to Leticia's lush mouth as he spoke. "And that it's totally up to her."

"Will you visit me there?" whispered Leticia, as he lifted a hand to caress her cheek. "Like you used to when we were children?"

"Of course. Your mother isn't around to turn me away like she often did." Leticia smiled, arms around him. "We would play for hours."

"Yes we would." Dracula stroked Leticia's hair as they brooded. "We should sit down."

Leticia smiled and let him go reluctantly, and they both sat down.

"How is Virginia?" asked Leticia, and Dracula replied "She is studying hard for her end of month exam. She's a very hard worker although everyone thinks she is quite-"

"Cool?" smiled Leticia. "Jeiklee thinks Virginia is *extremely* cool."

Dracula smiled at her. "She thinks the same about Jeiklee. I believe our children will become great friends, Leticia."

"As do I." Leticia smiled at him. "So… when do you think the best time to move to my mansion is?"

"Whenever you want to." Dracula smiled back, and she said "I want to go as soon as possible. I can't stand being near my husband or looking at his face. I just want to get as far away from him as possible."

"Well then go. Westley can't stop you, although he will definitely try."

"I will. And… if I invite you to stay over, like you do I… would you come?" asked Leticia shyly, and Dracula said "Of course I would. Would you mind me bringing Virginia?"

"Of course not."

Dracula smiled and gave her a gentle kiss.

They sat in peaceful silence, Dracula's arm around Leticia. She rested her head on his shoulder, and he cuddled her close.

* * *

"Dad, can you just calm down?" said Jeiklee, Westley pacing the lounge agitatedly. "She'll be back soon."

"Jeiklee. It has been three hours and she hasn't returned. She has missed dinner-"

Antonio hurried into the lounge, saying "Apologies my Lord, but you must come to the entrance of the mansion at once."

"Why?" said Westley curiously. "What's going on?"

"It's My Lady, sir- she has ordered for everything of hers to be brought outside- everything," Antonio said nervously. "Including her Chamber of Serenity."

"What!"

Westley and Jeiklee ran to the entrance of the mansion, Spirit already at the doors gaping in disbelief as people grabbed Leticia's packed belongings (boxes, suitcases and more), and carried them away.

"My Lady, I will compress your Chamber and put it back in it's rightful place in your home," a tall muscly man said to her gruffly, and Leticia said "Thank you Marcus. It is wonderful to see you all again."

"And you, My Lady." The man called Marcus held his hands up to a big ball of glowing blue light, saying "Pocket size until we get to the mansion. Do you mind?"

"Of course not."

"What the hell is going on here?!" shouted Westley as he ran forwards, but he was ignored. "Stop taking her things- stop! I order you to stop!"

"They are not your servants, Westley. They're mine," said Leticia coldly. "Your orders have no effect on my workers. I suggest you let them do what they are doing, or things could get very ugly."

"Why are they taking your things, Leticia? Where are you going?!"

"I'm going to my mansion," Leticia said flatly, and Spirit and Westley's jaw dropped, Spirit asking "The house of Sampson??"

"Yes. It is my house, Spirit, and I am going there to live. I can't stay here and I don't want to be near Westley at all. Every time I look at him, I want to kill him," Leticia said icily, glaring at Westley, who stepped back a little. "So I'm leaving before I do something worthy of spending the rest of my life in prison."

"Good for you Mum," said Jeiklee impressively, and Westley whipped round to glare at his son furiously.

"How is this good, Jeiklee?! Explain how any of this is good!"

"I said this would happen, didn't I?" shrugged Jeiklee. "And I said if Mum leaves, I'm going with her."

"What? Jeiklee, you can't-"

"Mum, can your servants get my stuff too?" asked Jeiklee, and Leticia nodded, snapping her fingers.

Four well built men walked into the mansion, brushing past Antonio.

"Leticia, please think about what you're doing," pleaded Westley, and Leticia replied "I've thought about it for a long time. It's the right thing to do. So what are you going to do, Westley? Go running to King Harlot and make him announce a law that states I cannot leave here?"

Westley opened his mouth, then closed it. "You would hate me if I did that."

"I already hate you," snapped Leticia, glaring at him. "You made a law against your *wife,* the person you claim to love so much- a law that could make me spend years in prison. You are vile, toxic- poison. And I want nothing to *do* with you!"

"So this is it?" said Westley angrily. "You're leaving me?"

"I already have left you," Leticia said coldly. "I'm just leaving this place I don't think of as home anymore. I left you the moment you went to the King of Severna and made him instate a law against me!"

"All of the boy's belongings are here, My Lady," a voice said, and everyone turned and saw Leticia's loyal subjects leaving the mansion with suitcases and a few boxes. "Is there anything else you would like us to do before we teleport?"

"No thank you. Please, be on your way to the mansion. I will be there soon," Leticia replied, and the men nodded and vanished along with the other servants, all of Leticia and Jeiklee's things gone.

Westley shook his head in disbelief as Jeiklee joined his mother's side. "This can't be happening! You can't leave, Leticia!"

"This *is* happening and I can do what I want," Leticia said icily. "I'm going to pay the King a visit and give him a piece of my mind after I settle in my home."

"But-"

Cameras flashed, the paparazzi watching excitedly as a reporter said to a camera, "Leticia is leaving the Severna mansion to return to her own! Could this be the end of her marriage to Westley Inferno?"

Leticia shook her head as they crowded and bombarded her with questions, saying "I don't want to discuss everything in too much detail, thank you. I am disgusted with my husband's actions against me and yes, I will be ending my marriage to him as soon as I see fit. He has hurt me like no one else ever has. I hate him. You can put that in the news if you want, I'm past caring." Westley gaped at her, everyone looking at him as Leticia continued "Westley Inferno only thinks about himself. He claims to love me, yet he created a law against me that would make me spend years imprisoned if I broke it. I want nothing more to do with him and please, do not come to my home looking for a story. I have said all I have had to say."

She turned and walked away, the journalists calling after her as they scribbled excitedly on their notepads.

"She's going to divorce her husband!"

Tears were streaming down Spirit's face as she cried "Leticia, wait! What am I supposed to *do??* I can't live without you, Leticia!"

"Then come, Spirit." Leticia stopped and looked back, and everyone saw the tears in her eyes. "I leave the choice up to you of course, but if you need me as much as you say you do-"

"I'm coming!" said Spirit determinedly, running after Leticia, and Jeiklee said "Mum, someone has to get Spirit's things!"

"I'll send Marcus back, Jeiklee." Leticia smiled a little sadly as Spirit hugged her hard. "You don't think I'm wrong for leaving?"

"No, of course not," said Jeiklee firmly. "I think you're amazing!"

"Fine!" said Westley furiously. "Go! But I'm telling you now, you'll be sorry you did this, Leticia! I gave you everything!"

"And I gave you everything also, Westley." Leticia looked at him coldly. "Everything but my heart."

Westley stopped dead, shocked. "You- what? *You don't mean that!!*"

"I mean every word."

"Well why did you marry me if your heart was never mine?!"

"Because I was forced to!" spat Leticia, and his jaw dropped in disbelief. "You may as well know now that I'm going to divorce you. Your parents and mine forced me by threatening the life of an innocent child. They said if I didn't marry you, the child would die!"

The press were filming and scribbling excitedly, obviously thinking they struck gold.

"The tears I cried on our wedding day were not tears of joy, they were tears of sadness and regret," Leticia said angrily. "I even told your mother I couldn't go through with it! I wasn't going to marry you at all, Westley! If I wasn't threatened, I wouldn't have. Even if we *did* have a son!"

"So why stay with me?!" Westley was really hurt, everyone could tell. "After our parents died, the threat against you wouldn't have stood! Why didn't you leave me after the first Dragon War?!"

"Because we were mourning and you needed me!" spat Leticia. "Why would I turn my back on you, Westley? I'm not heartless like *you* obviously are!"

"Leticia, wait! We can fix this- fix everything!"

"You can fix a broken mirror, but you will always see the cracks," Leticia replied coldly. "I want nothing to do with you like I said. I will file for divorce as soon as possible. It was a long time coming and now that you've shown your true colours, nobody will think I'm wrong for ending our marriage."

"Good for you Leticia!" someone shouted, and cheers went up, Westley turning and gaping at the crowd that gathered in disbelief.

"How can you be on her side?! Our marriage was pretty much a charade!"

"A charade?" Spirit repeated, heat rising. "She saved a kid's life! She could have said no, Westley, and the kid would have been murdered! But she didn't! That's why she married you- Leticia's a hero! And I think she's right about you!" she added angrily. "You only think about yourself and what's best for *you!* Did you even stop to think about how hard it must have been for Leticia, being forced into marriage?! You just assumed she was crying that day because she was happy to be your wife! You're selfish, and cruel! I can see why she hates you for everything you've done- and she never did a *thing* to hurt you! Why don't you wake up and realise where *you* went wrong, not Leticia! I don't blame her for divorcing you and moving out at all! I will back her *always!"*

Cheers went up again as Westley gaped at her disbelievingly, Bruce Finnegan calling "You go, Spirit!"

"Shut up Bruce," snapped Spirit, and he grinned at her. "Come on Leticia and Jeiklee, let's go. I know you want to get away from the cameras and paparazzi, Leticia."

Leticia nodded as they began walking. "Thank you for what you said just now, Spirit. I never thought you'd be on my side, or understand."

"Now I do." Spirit smiled at her. "I'm so glad I woke up and saw everything for what it was. And Leticia, if... if you want to get back in contact with Count Dracula and stuff, and see him... I won't have a problem with it. I promise."

"Praise the Lord," said Jeiklee amusedly, and Leticia laughed. "Finally! I hope you won't have a problem with Virginia either, Spirit."

"If she's civil, I'll be civil too," shrugged Spirit. "I'm just glad you're finally free, Leticia. Don't you feel like a massive weight has been lifted off your shoulders?"

"I do," smiled Leticia. "And I am glad also, Spirit. Now let's go to our new home."

Element Six: Malinda

* * *

Two weeks later…

Count Dracula walked through town, everyone gasping when they saw him, his black cape billowing in the wind. He was smiling as he walked, deep in thought.

He had heard, read and watched everything about what happened two weeks ago with Leticia and her ex-husband. Dracula didn't think she was really going to divorce Westley, but when Virginia burst into the castle a week ago shouting for him excitedly, he knew he loved Leticia even more than he already did.

"Good to see you, Count Dracula sir," a man said nervously as Dracula passed him, and Dracula nodded as everyone on his side of the pavement crossed to the other side quickly. "It's always er… nice when you come to town."

Dracula stopped and looked back at him. "Nice?"

Everyone drew back fearfully, the man dropping to his knees as he gasped "Always a pleasure, then!"

Dracula's eyes flashed. "A *pleasure?*"

"I… I don't know what you want me to say, sir!"

"How about you drop the pretences and say what you really want to say, which is: 'what are you doing in town, Count Dracula? There's nothing for you here and you are not wanted'," Dracula said flatly, and the man gushed "Oh no sir, that's not what I was really thinking-"

"Do not lie to me," Dracula cut across, and he cried "Apologies! I didn't mean-"

"To offend me? You are far from it," said Dracula, amused now. "Get to your feet at once." The man scrambled to his feet, scared. "I am far from the terrifying, vile monster you all believe me to be. If I were, do you think Leticia of Sampson would have invited me to her mansion? She never would have if I were what you all believe I am."

"Apologies sir," the man said quickly again. "I… so you are back in contact with Leticia of Sampson?"

"Yes," Dracula said flatly, and he glanced at the people watching from a distance. "Surely nobody has a problem with that? Leticia is not a little girl anymore and can choose who she speaks to herself."

"Good thing the King revoked the law her ex-husband made against her," the man said nervously, and Dracula smiled at him. The man gaped, then cautiously smiled back. "I bet you're super glad to have your best friend back, sir."

"Yes, I am. And I'm also super glad I have just had a conversation with you, a stranger in town, without you running a mile," Dracula told him, and the man blushed big time. "What is your name?"

"Lazarus, sir. But everyone calls me Larry."

"Nice to meet you, Larry."

"And you sir," said Larry, amazed. "You... you're not a terrifying monster at all! I expected you to-"

"To curse you for no reason or cause some kind of plague?" smiled Dracula, and Larry smiled back embarrassedly, everyone shocked as they watched and listened. "Would you like a piece of advice, Larry?"

"Yes sir."

"Never judge someone without getting to know them," said Dracula, and he continued walking, Larry calling "Never again, sir! I promise!"

Cameras flashed after Dracula as talk broke out, and Dracula smiled to himself.

Maybe, after so long, things would finally get better.

* * *

Jeiklee's stomach somersaulted as Spirit came into the dining area in a pretty dress, her hair and nails done.

"Spirit?"

She looked at him. "Yes?"

Jeiklee opened his mouth, but the words didn't come out.

"Yes Jeiklee?"

"I… you…"

"You look amazing," Virginia said amusedly. "That's what he wanted to say."

"Oh. Thanks," said Spirit, trying her best to be as nice to Virginia of Dracula as she was being to her. "When will your father arrive, then?"

"In about fifteen minutes," Virginia replied, looking down at herself. "Um…"

"You look fine, Virginia," Jeiklee said reassuringly. "It's just dinner with my Mum and your Dad."

"Yeah, but Spirit McKenzie's all glammed up. I'm just in-"

"I want to make a good impression on Count Dracula and apologise too," blurted Spirit, and they looked at her, surprised as she said "I was wrong about him. And maybe I was wrong about you too, Virginia- maybe. I don't know about you yet."

Virginia couldn't help smirking at that. "You'll figure it out."

"Anyway- me and Leticia had a long talk late last night, and… I understand her and Count Dracula so much more," Spirit said contentedly, and Jeiklee gaped at her.

"What time was this? Why wasn't I included??"

"Because you already know and understand and I needed to as well," shrugged Spirit. "Um, Virginia, maybe you should put on a-"

"Why?" said Virginia, scowling. "Father always sees me in a blouse and trousers. I don't wear dresses, Spirit McKenzie."

"Yeah, about how you call me. You don't have to be icy and formal, you can call me Spirit," Spirit told her. "There's no harm in that, right?"

Virginia thought about it, then she smiled. "Right."

"So come to my room," Spirit said, smiling back. "Me and you are the same size, I'm sure we can fix you up properly before Leticia comes out of her suite and your father gets here. And Jeiklee, your tie is too short."

Jeiklee scrabbled at his neck and ran to the mirror in the lounge quickly, then he scowled. His tie was fine.

"You're out of order, Spirit!"

Spirit and Virginia giggled as they went back up the stairs, and Jeiklee smiled.

* * *

Leticia entered her dining hall, content. She gaped at the three teenagers sat talking happily at the table, and she smiled.

"You all look beautiful. Are you ready to eat? Count Dracula will be here any second."

"Yes Mum, we're ready," said Jeiklee, smiling back. "You look amazing! Like a Queen fit for a King."

The doorbell chimed through the mansion, and they heard Leticia's butler Washington answer the door.

"Good to see you Count Dracula sir. Do come in."

"This is it," said Jeiklee excitedly, and everyone smiled at him. "I'm going to meet Count Dracula properly!"

"My Lady, Count Dracula has arrived," Washington said calmly as he entered the dining room, Dracula behind him. "Sir, may I take your cloak?"

"Of course," Dracula replied, removing his black cloak and revealing a black suit with a red shirt inside. Leticia averted her gaze quickly before her jaw could drop, and Virginia said "You look great, Father. Really handsome."

"Thank you, Virginia." Dracula smiled at his daughter, Washington leaving the room with Dracula's cloak. "Hello, Jeiklee and Spirit."

"Hello Count Dracula," Spirit said politely, and Dracula smiled at her. Spirit hesitated, then she smiled back as she said "I think you look great too."

"Thank you," said Dracula, slightly amused, and Leticia said "Take a seat, Dracula. Dinner is being prepared."

A maid entered the room, saying "May I offer you all a beverage before dinner is served? Is that ok, My Lady?"

"Of course it is," smiled Leticia. "I will have a glass of red wine, thank you."

"I'll have a glass of Coke with ice please," said Virginia, and Jeiklee said "Me too. I'll have what Virginia's having thanks."

"I'll have a glass of Sprite, no ice please," smiled Spirit as she looked at Jeiklee amusedly, and Dracula said "And I will have a Hurricane cocktail thank you. You do still make those, don't you?"

"Yes sir, we do," smiled the maid, and she left the room after jotting down their orders.

Leticia smiled at Dracula. "My mother went mad when she caught us having a Hurricane cocktail in the back garden."

Dracula chuckled. "I remember. She half dragged you into the house shouting about the dangers of alcohol and she will not have a drunk for a daughter."

Everyone laughed, Jeiklee asking "What happened next, sir?"

"Leticia was grounded for two weeks," smiled Dracula. "I had to keep away in that time. I missed her terribly."

"I would miss Virginia terribly if I was grounded for two weeks," said Jeiklee, and Virginia blushed, face turning red as a tomato. "I bet you didn't know what to do with yourself, sir."

"Oh, that is definitely correct," smiled Dracula, and Jeiklee smiled back. "I tried distracting myself with books and activities about my castle, and going on walks. But everything seemed to remind me of your mother."

"That's really sweet," said Spirit, touched. "I think it was wrong you were always deemed bad for Leticia, Dracula sir. Now I do, anyway, because I know the full story. You're not bad at all. And... I'm really sorry for judging you the way I did. I didn't know any better."

Everyone smiled at Spirit, Virginia saying "Top marks for that admission, Spirit."

Spirit smiled at her, and Virginia smiled back as Dracula said "It's no problem at all, Spirit. I'm very used to being judged without being known."

Spirit smiled at him. "You're nothing like I was told you were."

"I'm glad to hear it."

* * *

Her boat washed ashore of the Severna lake, and she climbed out, eyes glowing scarlet as she looked around. She hadn't been back to this part of Severna for eighteen years.

The beautiful vampire lowered her hood, her bright red hair tumbling down her back as she took a step forward.

Malinda of Brubeck sighed, whispering his name. *"Count Dracula…"*

* * *

"Dessert is served," Washington announced, and Jeiklee said "Great! I'm hungry for some cheesecake."

Everyone laughed, Leticia so happy that her children really hit it off with Count Dracula.

Spirit had asked Dracula a ton of questions about life as a vampire and his history, really intrigued, and Dracula answered them all without feeling uncomfortable, telling her that she had a lot in common with Virginia.

Spirit felt pretty happy about that, warming up to Virginia as well. Jeiklee asked Dracula a lot too, mainly about the things he used to get up to with his mother, and Dracula told many stories with a big smile on his face, relieved that Leticia's son seemed to really like him.

"I wish tonight didn't have to end," said Virginia happily, and everyone smiled at her, Dracula saying "As do I."

"Well, how about we arrange a weekend together?" smiled Leticia. "After your exams, the three of you. There's plenty of room for you and your father to stay, Virginia. Would you like that?"

"Yes I would Miss Leticia," said Virginia shyly. "Thank you!"

"Thank you," Dracula repeated softly, and Leticia smiled at him as the maids set plenty of dessert dishes on the table.

"You're welcome. I leave the date up to you, Dracula." Leticia reached for the Red Velvet cake, and everyone smiled at her knowingly. She paused, saying "What is it?"

"We are just all aware of how much you love Red Velvet cake," smiled Dracula, and Spirit, Jeiklee and Virginia nodded.

"Father, can Jeiklee come and see the castle one day? I did invite him but he didn't want to come without being invited by you yourself."

"Of course you can come, Jeiklee," smiled Dracula, and Jeiklee smiled back, forking some cheesecake. "Spirit, you are welcome to come also."

"Oh, I'll definitely come sir. But not yet. Maybe if me and Virginia become good friends, then I'll come. I'm not as close to her as Jeiklee is."

Dracula nodded, and he said "Virginia, you owe Spirit an apology for the years of torment she went through because of you."

Virginia sighed. "Yes Father. Spirit, I'm really sorry. You're not so bad after all," she added with a smile, and Spirit couldn't help smiling back.

"Neither are you."

* * *

Malinda walked through the Forest of Fear, running her hands along the trees, waking them from their slumber as she went past them.

"Who- what-"

"Silence," she commanded softly, and the trees stopped talking. "Tell me, where is Count Dracula's castle? I do not remember the way."

"You should never take directions from a tree," a voice cackled, and Malinda whipped round.

"Who's there?" Silence. "Show yourself!"

Two vampires, one male one female, emerged from the shadows into the moonlight.

"Malinda of Brubeck," spat the male vampire named Terrence, eyes glowing scarlet as he recognised her. "How dare you show your face in this part of the land after what you did to our beloved Master?"

"I know what I did was wrong," Malinda said, stepping back as more vampires and creatures emerged from the trees.

"Wrong?" said Terrence icily. "Wrong is too weak a word. It was all over the news and Count Dracula was furious! I could kill you right now."

"I have come to make peace with Count Dracula," Malinda said, sounding nervous, but really she was anything but. "Please, let me be on my way. I just want to find his castle."

"You won't be going anywhere, not tonight," said Terrence coldly, Malinda reaching into her pocket. "You will go with the werewolves, Malinda- to their cave, and stay there until dusk tomorrow. Then, you will return to your home in the middle of the ocean where you belong."

"And if I don't obey?" asked Malinda, and Terrence said "Don't make this harder than it has to be, you loathsome beast. I will spread the word of your return and make sure you don't go anywhere near Castle Dracula!"

Malinda suddenly uncorked a bottle and flung the contents into Terrence's face, Terrence falling to the ground with a scream.

"AAAAARRGH!!"

"Holy water!" cried another vampire as Terrence's body convulsed on the ground violently before he dissolved into nothing- he was dead. "She has *HOLY WATER!!"*

"Murderer!" screamed another vampire, and Malinda smiled at the crowd. "You are all very loyal to Count Dracula, and I understand that. But I will not be insulted nor do I want him to know I have returned to this part of the land. Nobody here will speak of it. And if I find anyone has told him, they will go the same way as poor Terrence." Malinda's eyes were glowing scarlet. "I know one of you will disobey and tell him. The Tongue-Tie curse on all of you seems to be a good idea until I have done what I need to do." Her hands were glowing bright orange. The crowd turned and tried to run, but not before the curse hit them all in a bright orange blast.

* * *

"Best night ever!" said Virginia happily as she walked through the Forest of Fear with her father, full of beans. "I think Spirit McKenzie is starting to like me a lot, Father. And I really like Jeiklee too!"

"Yes, I know you are very fond of Jeiklee, Virginia." Dracula smiled at his daughter as she beamed at him. "I am glad he and I got on so well at dinner."

"Miss Leticia was really glad too, I could tell. Jeiklee is nothing like his father," said Virginia, striding ahead. "Do you think the people of Severna will accept you being in a relationship with Miss Leticia?"

"Who said I was in a relationship with Leticia?" said Dracula amusedly, and Virginia looked back happily. "Neither of us have told you we are together in that way."

"You couldn't take your eyes off her, Father."

"Well she looked stunning. No man in his right mind would take his eyes off her," Dracula pointed out, and Virginia said "I guess so, but with you it's much deeper that that. You don't have to keep your feelings for Miss Leticia a secret anymore, Father."

Dracula sighed. "I know. But I'd rather the world didn't know my business. I like things the way they are. If Leticia and I ever do enter an exclusive relationship-"

"You definitely will." Virginia jogged back and linked arms with her father. "I know you will, Father."

"Then I leave the decision up to her about the privacy of it."

Virginia stopped walking suddenly. "Father? Something's wrong."

Dracula stopped too as he saw a bright light in the distance. "What on earth is that?"

They peered harder, then they both realised what it was.

"Fire," gasped Virginia, and she started sprinting the direction of the light, Dracula shouting "Virginia!" Before he dashed after his daughter.

Virginia stopped when she reached the flames, coughing as she yelled "Bari! Are you alright?! You're on fire!!"

"It is too late for me," rasped the tree, smoke everywhere. "Run, girl! Go to your castle, quickly!"

"No- we can save you! Father, help me!"

"What happened here?!" yelled Dracula, the crowd of vampires trying to indicate frantically, but without saying a word. "Speak!"

The vampires tapped their throats agitatedly, the fire spreading as Dracula said "You can't talk??" They shook their heads. "Why on earth not?!"

"We need to put out the fire," coughed Virginia, smoke swirling around them, and Dracula raised his hands, water shooting from his palms onto the flames, but it had no effect.

"What?" said Dracula disbelievingly, then he realised. "It's cursed fire!"

"Sir," croaked Bari. "It is done. I... thank you for all of our conversations and-"

"You're not dying, Bari!" said Dracula angrily, and Virginia dropped to her knees, coughing. "Virginia!"

"My... my chest is tight," gasped Virginia, and Dracula lifted her into his arms. "There's poison in the smoke, Father!"

"Sir... please... run," rasped Bari as two of his branches fell. "She will not... stop... until she has what she came for-"

"Who won't?" said Dracula desperately. "Who is doing this?!"

Another branch fell directly in front of Dracula, and two vampires grabbed him and pulled him away, fearfully but silent as the grave, and Dracula almost fell backwards holding his child as they tugged him away.

"Let go of me at once!!"

They released him quickly, and Dracula knew only his true love could help him.

"LETICIA!!"

Bari's trunk began to break as Leticia appeared, shocked.

"What's going on?? Virginia!"

Virginia was very drowsy in her father's arms as she stared hazily into the trees at a figure standing there.

"Father... Miss Leticia... they- they're in... the trees..."

Dracula and Leticia looked immediately, Leticia's eyes locking onto the figure as Dracula said "Who are you?!"

The figure turned away, and Dracula caught a glimpse of something bright red before they vanished.

Dracula looked at Leticia. "That wasn't their eyes, Leticia."

"I know," said Leticia, unnerved. "Whoever they were-"

Virginia coughed, slowly slipping into unconsciousness as Leticia raised her hands and commanded *"Wind."*

The wind blew harshly at once, nature obeying her as the smoke was blown away, the flames growing smaller and smaller as the wind overpowered it... and soon all that surrounded them was ashes, clean air, and heavy breathing.

Amazed, Dracula took a deep breath. "You are brilliant, Leticia."

"Thank you," Leticia said quietly as she turned to the vampires surrounding them, but before she could ask them what the hell happened Dracula said "They can't talk, Leticia- so they can't answer your questions or even say why."

Leticia frowned at him. "They can't talk?"

"No."

Leticia's frown deepened, then she pointed to a vampire. "You. Step forward at once."

The vampire shuffled forwards nervously, and Leticia examined them, hands glowing as she held them over their head, torso, arms, legs, and finally their feet.

Stumped, she looked at Count Dracula. "They are in perfect health. I can't sense an illness of some sort. Even vampires can fall ill, Dracula."

Dracula nodded. "I know, Leticia. You can't sense any kind of illness or spell at all?"

"No spells," said Leticia softly, then she realised. "It could be a curse."

"Who would curse my minions?!" Dracula was outraged as Leticia turned back to the nervous vampire, and she gently said "Open your mouth."

The vampire obeyed, Leticia ignoring their fangs as she stared amazedly, then she softly said "Of course. The Tongue-Tie Curse."

Dracula gaped at her. "The Tongue-Tie Curse??"

Leticia said yes, her hands glowing bright orange. "I will remove the curse from them. We need answers and Virginia is in a bad way."

"Whoever did this wanted to get my attention," said Dracula quietly, and the vampires nodded quickly, Leticia placing her hands on their throats one by one.

"You will be able to speak again by dawn, although for you all the time will be nightfall, which is when you awaken from your deep sleep. Please come to Castle Dracula tomorrow night so we can get some answers."

The vampires nodded and bowed to Leticia, one daring to clasp her hand in gratitude, before they all jogged away.

Dracula looked down at Virginia, who was still in his arms. She could just about manage to stay conscious, Leticia conjuring a goblet and waving her hand over it. Blue steam flew up into the air as a liquid the same colour appeared, Leticia saying "Virginia? Please, drink this."

Virginia lifted a hand weakly, and Leticia gently handed her the goblet.

With each sip of the blue liquid Virginia began to feel stronger and stronger, and she gently climbed down from her father's arms and stood moments later, taking a deep breath before she smiled.

"I feel much better. Thank you Miss Leticia."

"You're welcome. Virginia, I am very sorry, but Bari the tree, he… burned out," she said quietly, and Virginia whipped round to stare at the broken branches and tree stump.

"No," she said sadly. "Bari was my friend!"

"I know, sweetie. He was my friend also, and Jeiklee's too, when they met in the past. Bari will be missed but never forgotten," Leticia said, and Virginia ran and hugged her, eyes shut tight in an attempt to stop the tears.

"Whoever did this is evil," she whispered, and Leticia stroked her hair.

"Your father and I will get to the bottom of it, Virginia. I promise you. Now, you must go home and rest. The antidote will keep working while you are asleep," Leticia said gently as she released her, and Virginia nodded. "And

Dracula, don't worry. The vampires will be able to tell us real soon what exactly happened."

Dracula nodded, staring at the burnt tree and the ashes on the ground. "Why did they want to silence Bari?"

Virginia and Leticia looked at him, Leticia asking "Silence Bari?"

"Yes. They wanted to silence Bari just like they wanted to silence the vampires." Dracula started pacing. "This is the big something that I sensed was coming. It's here, Leticia. And it's going to affect me."

"I sensed it too," Leticia said softly. "But the big something for me, which was the whole Westley fiasco and everything finally being over, has already passed. Now, it seems it's your turn."

Dracula nodded, Virginia asking "Will I be affected, Miss Leticia?"

"You will need to be very careful when out after dark," Leticia said gently. "I don't think you will be affected, but I do believe a vampire was behind this. A vampire who wants your father's attention."

Dracula frowned. "But... all the vampires I am in contact with are my minions. None of them would-"

"Bartley!" exclaimed Virginia, and they looked at her.

"What?"

"Bartley the vampire," gushed Virginia, Dracula saying "That middle aged bloodsucker? Why would he want to get to me?"

"He wants his daughter to be your Bride, a Bride of Dracula," Virginia explained, heart racing. "He said you will have her as your first!"

Dracula gaped at her. "When was this??"

"He's always badgering me about it," Virginia said, "Wanting to arrange some kind of meeting with you about making her your Bride. But I told him there was no chance and-"

"And you think he acted out of spite?" asked Leticia, and Virginia nodded. "Virginia, are you sure this man is capable of doing such a thing?"

"I don't know, but he's the only person that springs to mind," Virginia replied, rubbing her cheek as Dracula fumed. "No other vampire would betray my father. They were all trying to protect him from the cursed fire, even though they couldn't talk."

"Alright. Now just say you're correct and it was Bartley behind this, Virginia," Leticia said, thinking hard. "Don't you think harming fellow vampires and setting fire to a beloved tree isn't the right way to get Count Dracula's attention? I'm sure he'd be sucking up to Dracula, not attacking his minions, if he wanted his daughter to become a Bride."

Virginia opened her mouth, then closed it. "That's true."

"However I think just to be certain we should pay him a visit," Leticia said as she looked at Dracula, and he nodded, Virginia saying "Let's go!"

"No, Virginia." Leticia shook her head. "You must rest in Castle Dracula, and get your energy back. I know you feel well, but please sweetheart, you

need to recuperate. I will check on you before I go home. My guards are keeping an eye on Jeiklee and Spirit, and Nancy will keep an eye on you."
Virginia sighed. "Ok."
They began walking, Leticia very alert as she put an arm around Virginia.
Dracula was fuming. "If Bartley was behind this I will have his head."

* * *

Dracula grabbed Bartley by the collar and slammed him into the wall, Bartley crying out in fright.

"What did I do, sir?!"

"Were you behind the evil events that happened tonight?!" Eyes glowing scarlet along with his body, Dracula was livid. "Tell the truth before I snap you like a twig!"

"I- I was not behind it!" gasped Bartley, Dracula pinning him by the throat now. "I only heard from the werewolves that there was a vampire from the past back in this part of the land- I know not who they are or what they did, sir!"

"He's telling the truth," Leticia said softly. "Let him go, Dracula."

Furious, Dracula obeyed. "Where is your daughter?"

"I- I have three daughters, sir-"

"The one you want me to have as my first Bride," Dracula said angrily. "Bring her to me at once!"

Bartley stared at him amazedly, then he shouted "Michelle! Come!"

Bartley's daughter Michelle, a brunette with bright blue eyes, ran into the living area where everyone stood.

"Count Dracula," she said, bowing, but before she could get another word out Dracula flatly said "Never going to happen. Even if she was the last female in Severna. Thank you for your information, Bartley."

"But sir-!!"

"But what?" snapped Dracula, and Michelle and Bartley flinched. "All I wanted was to look upon the woman you kept harassing my daughter over. And I'm telling you now, Bartley, not to approach Virginia about me again. If I so much as *sense* you have-"

"You won't sir, I promise!"

"Good. I'm going back to my castle," Dracula said coldly, and Leticia warmly added "Thank you for your help, Bartley."

Bartley nodded, rubbing his throat. "You're welcome Ma'am."

Dracula glared at him before he stormed out of Bartley's home, cloak flying behind him. Once outside in the cool night air, he inhaled deeply.

"Leticia, what if more incidents arise? I am worried for Virginia."

"It's not Virginia's attention the vampire wants, Dracula. It's yours," Leticia said softly. "Would you like me to stay with you?"

"Yes please."

Malinda watched them walk and talk, hidden deep in the trees. Dracula shook his head.

"If only I had a clue... a sign. Then I would know which vampire it was for sure, Leticia."

Malinda smiled at that, before she whistled softly. Dracula and Leticia whipped round, and Malinda vanished before they could get a good look at her.

Leticia looked at Dracula. "They are playing mind games."

"Well mind games aren't going to work on me," Dracula said, shaking his head. "Leticia, it is not safe you being around me. They could make you a target to get to me."

"Nobody in their right mind would try and attack me," shrugged Leticia. "I would easily go back in time and take away the day they were born, making them cease to exist."

Dracula stared at her, then he smiled. "I would have said that was extremely arrogant if I didn't know you meant every word."

Leticia smiled at that, and Dracula put an arm around her as they walked. "I wish we could go to the lake."

Leticia looked up at him. "The lake?"

"Yes. The lake at night is so beautiful. The water glows turquoise when the moonlight shines on it, and glows red when there is evil present. It's amazing," admitted Dracula. "Also, the sea creatures are a sight."

"Then let us go," smiled Leticia. "Just for an hour."

Dracula checked the time. "It is just past midnight, Leticia."

"We're adults, Dracula. We have no curfew." Leticia smiled at him. "I want to see the lake at night. And there's a full moon out too. It will be perfect."

* * *

"Jeiklee." Jeiklee mumbled in his sleep and rolled over, Spirit whispering "Jeiklee!"

"What…"

"Leticia's not here," whispered Spirit, and Jeiklee pulled his duvet over his head. "Where do you think she is?"

"Probably just gone for a walk." Jeiklee's voice was muffled under his duvet. "Don't start acting like Dad, Spirit. You're not Mum's keeper."

"I never said I was!"

"She's a grown woman," yawned Jeiklee as he sat up, more awake now. "And she's probably with Count Dracula."

"Why would she- because they're best friends?" said Spirit, confused, and Jeiklee sighed.

"Because they mean everything to each other."

"Oh," said Spirit, trying to understand, then she decided not to in case she got a headache. "As long as he keeps her safe it's fine."

"He will. Go back to bed."

* * *

"So beautiful," sighed Leticia, the lake glowing turquoise just like Dracula said it did. They were sat on the bank, Dracula's arm around Leticia. "Beautiful."

"It is lovely," smiled Dracula. "I have always wanted to experience the lake at night with you, Leticia."

Leticia smiled and pulled him down onto the grass with her, so they laid flat on their backs, gazing up at the twinkling stars.

"We should definitely do this again," said Dracula, Leticia snuggling up to him, and he put an arm around her. "Look, a whale has surfaced."

Leticia lifted her head to look at the whale, and she smiled. Dracula sighed, saying "I can't stop thinking about the events of tonight."

"Don't worry about it, Dracula. Nightfall will come sooner than you think." Leticia turned on her side to look at him, Dracula doing likewise. "Unless something else happens before then, we will get some answers."

Dracula smiled at that. "Leticia, I don't know what I'd do without you. Thank you for helping me tonight."

"I will always help you," Leticia replied quietly, and he kissed her forehead. "Dracula… would you like to…"

Dracula looked at her, his handsome face intent in the moonlight. "To what, sweetheart?"

Leticia's eyes roamed over him before she quietly said "To swim."

Dracula smiled at that. "We shouldn't disturb the creatures in the water at this time."

"Ok," she said, voice still quiet, and Dracula knew she wasn't really asking him for a swim. "Well… maybe we should-"

Dracula kissed her before she could finish, and Leticia's arms went around him urgently as she pulled him on top of her, both of them kissing passionately.

"We should get back," panted Leticia when they broke apart, and Dracula said "Not yet, Leticia- please. Five more minutes…"

He kissed her neck, and Leticia almost melted as she gripped his shoulders. "Dracula…"

"Shh…"

Leticia closed her eyes as sensations rocked through her, and she whispered "Bite me, Dracula…"

Dracula lifted his head to look at her. "What?"

"Bite me," murmured Leticia. "I want to feel everything I'm feeling now, times ten."

"Do you want me to be hunted with pitchforks and torches, Leticia? I cannot do that to you. I will never be forgiven if-"

"You don't have to drink my blood, Dracula."

"I won't bite you," he said, shaking his head. "I always promised myself I never would, no matter how tempting it may be."

Leticia pouted at him, and he laughed. "Why do you want me to bite you, Leticia?"

"I heard a vampire's bite of lust gives you intense pleasure," Leticia replied, and Dracula said "You don't need a vampire's bite to feel intense pleasure, Leticia. I can give that to you without piercing your flesh."

Leticia locked eyes with him, the glowing water from the lake illuminating their faces.

"Really?"

Dracula nodded. "Yes."

Leticia smiled, and she softly said "Then give it to me. Right now."

Dracula kissed her again, hands trailing up her body before he began to unbutton her blouse, Leticia's breathing growing heavier and heavier as he gently removed it from her body, mouth still on hers.

Leticia kicked off her shoes and trousers, Dracula on top of her again, and she whispered "Take your clothes off, Dracula."

Dracula looked at her. "If this isn't what you desire-"

"It is, you know it is," said Leticia softly. "It's been so long. I want this more than ever. I want *you.*"

Touched, Dracula breathed out and removed his shirt and trousers. Exhaling, Leticia ran her hands over his smooth hard chest before he pulled her on top of him, Leticia wrapping her legs around his waist.

Dracula shifted under her, Leticia positioning herself, and she gasped when she felt him- *all of him,* inside her body. Leticia's eyes closed as she bit her lip and began to move slowly, Dracula's hands on her waist.

"Leticia, I want us to be together- properly." He gritted his teeth as sensations rocked through him, but he needed to get his point across before their lovemaking reached it's peak. "I don't want this to be a regret either."

"It won't be." Leticia half moaned the words, and his heart beat faster. "I have always wanted to be with you and you know that-" She gasped harshly, then she managed "Nothing can stop us now. I love you."

"I love you too."

Leticia leant down and kissed him, Dracula gently turning so that she was the one underneath him.

The lake seemed to glow even brighter as Dracula asserted dominance, taking control.

Their heavy breathing was all that could be heard, until a scream of pleasure from Leticia rang through the air, followed by Dracula's harsh gasp, both of them satisfied as he fell on top of her, panting.

It was a dream come true, the beginning of something amazing. They both knew it, Leticia taking a deep breath before she whispered "Dracula?"

"Mmm?"

"Are you alright?"

"I've never been better," he admitted. "I needed this and I needed you."

"Well you have me," Leticia said softly. "We are together."

Dracula looked at her. "You promise?"

Leticia kissed him. "I promise."

* * *

Dawn was breaking when Dracula and Leticia said their goodbyes.

He had walked her back to her mansion, and Leticia looked around for any sign of the paparazzi. Seeing none, she kissed him tenderly.

"See you tonight."

"Tonight?" Dracula repeated, surprised. "You want us to meet again so soon?"

"We need to talk to the vampires tonight because they will have their voices back," Leticia reminded him softly, and he gaped at her.

"That totally slipped my mind. Being with you cancelled my worries."

Leticia smiled at that. "Get some rest, Dracula. I will be at the castle at eight in the evening on the dot."

"Alright. See you tonight, Leticia."

Leticia smiled and walked towards the giant doors of her mansion, guards opening it immediately. Dracula watched her walk in, the doors closing behind her.

He sighed happily, then he turned and walked away, heart pounding. He rubbed his chest when he realised his heart had come alive because of the love he felt for his new partner, and his face broke into a smile as he murmured "What a night."

* * *

Jeiklee woke up in good spirits.

He was super glad about the dinner Leticia arranged with Count Dracula and Virginia, and was surprised at how much Spirit seemed to like the handsome Count. Things really seemed to be looking up.

Jeiklee went into his bathroom and washed his face, then brushed his teeth. "It's Saturday! No college until Monday."

After he was dressed, he jogged down the flights of stairs into the dining area.

"Morning Spirit," he said with a smile, and Spirit smiled back at him.

"Morning."

"Any plans for today?"

"Nope. None," she said, shaking her head, and Leticia entered the dining room in her dressing gown, sighing "Good morning to you both."

"Morning Mum," Jeiklee said happily, Spirit saying "Morning Leticia. You look very worn out!"

"Oh, I am. I am going back to bed, but I'm also making sure you are both alright and contented."

"We are," said Spirit reassuringly. "I woke up and saw you were gone, Leticia. I was a little worried."

"I was fine, Spirit." Leticia smiled at her. "I was spending a little more time with-"

The doorbell rang, and Washington went to answer it.

"Yes, Mr Inferno?"

"I want to see my family," a slurred voice said angrily, and Washington said "Sir, I cannot allow you to come in."

"Why… why not!"

"Because you are drunk, sir, that is one reason," Washington said calmly, "And another reason is because the lady of the house has told us you are not allowed on the premises. Must I call the guards to escort you off them?"

"Stop being such- such a… a fool," said Westley, doing his best to get his words out clearly, and Washington said, oozing calmness and ultimate perfection to Jeiklee, "If I were a fool I would let you in, sir. Please go home."

"Look, I just want to see my- my wife!"

"She is not your wife anymore sir, and through fault of your own. Now for the final time before I call the guards, please leave the house of Leticia."

"Fine," spat Westley. "I will- I… I will be back!"

Washington signalled the close of the giant doors and came into the dining area, shaking his head as he said "My Lady, your ex-husband wanted to see you."

"Well I did not want to see him, especially in that state." Leticia took a seat at the table before she asked "How drunk is he?"

"Very drunk, Ma'am, and reeking of alcohol. He could just about walk."

Leticia sighed. "The paparazzi are out there. He's going to look ridiculous and it will reach the news that he turned up drunk and desperate."

Jeiklee nodded, and Spirit said "Westley's reputation is pretty much ruined. You know that, right Leticia?"

"I know, Spirit." Leticia took a seat at the table. "Washington, please inform the chef that we are all awake and waiting for breakfast."

"Yes My Lady." Washington bowed and left the room.

Jeiklee was wondering what Virginia was up to. "Mum?"

"Mmm?"

"Are you going to Castle Dracula anytime soon?" asked Jeiklee, and Leticia replied "I'm going tonight, reaching there for eight on the dot. Something bad happened in the Forest of Fear last night and Count Dracula and I are going to get to the bottom of it."

"What happened, Mum? Is Virginia ok? What-"

"I made sure Virginia was perfectly fine, sweetie. But Bari the tree… wasn't so lucky," said Leticia sadly. "He was set alight by an evil vampire, and he burned out."

"Oh no," said Spirit, eyes filling, and Jeiklee sadly said "Bari was awesome!"

"Yes he was. Which is why I'm determined to find out who was behind it all. It is not safe right now, Jeiklee and Spirit, to wander in the Forest of Fear after dark. I told Virginia pretty much the same," Leticia told them seriously, and they nodded. "I still want you both home by nine, is that understood?"

"Yes Mum," said Jeiklee, and Spirit said "Yes Leticia."

"Good. Now, I'm going into my Chamber of Serenity to rest until later today. Don't get up to any mischief," she added amusedly, and they smiled at her. "And Jeiklee, no using the power of the Force."

"I won't Mum. I promise."

Leticia smiled and left the dining area as Washington walked in, announcing "Breakfast will be ready in half an hour. My Lady, are you not going to eat?

"I'll be back for lunch, Washington. Thank you," smiled Leticia, and Washington bowed as she walked away.

Jeiklee looked at Spirit. "So there's a bad vampire on the loose in the Forest of Fear. Why would he kill Bari?"

"Who says it's a he?" retorted Spirit. "Females can be just as devious when it comes to getting what they want."

"So you think they want something?"

"Of course they do," said Spirit, shrugging. "They're not just going to start murdering for no reason. Something in their mind is behind it. Whatever they're after, or whoever- I just hope they're safe."

* * *

Castle Dracula...

Dracula sighed happily, Virginia and Nancy smiling at him.
"Did you have a nice night with Leticia of Sampson, sir?" asked Nancy, and Dracula said "Nice?? It was an *amazing* night. Dinner with her family went very well, and our time alone together was just… perfect. Even after the cruel events that took place."
"Yes, Virginia told me about that," said Nancy, concerned. "Who do you think this vampire is, sir?"
"I have no idea," admitted Dracula. "But I do know they want my attention, and they have it. I just need to speak to my minions when they come at nightfall. I have to keep my people safe from this vampire."

* * *

The doorbell rang.

Washington strode up to the door as Leticia entered the lounge, yawning.

"Hey Mum," said Jeiklee brightly, Spirit as well. "Are you feeling better? You was exhausted this morning."

"I was very tired, Jeiklee, thank you." Leticia smiled at her son and Spirit. "Are you both alright? Have you eaten your dinner? It is getting late."

"Yes Leticia," said Spirit, smiling. "The maids said the chef will make you a fresh meal when you wake up."

Leticia nodded, then she called "Washington, who is at the door?"

"It's your ex-husband again, My Lady," Washington called back, slightly annoyed, and Leticia sighed.

"I'll come in a moment, Washington."

"Yes My Lady."

Jeiklee and Spirit got up too, Jeiklee saying "We'll come too, Mum."

"We've got your back," Spirit added, and Leticia smiled at them.

"I couldn't ask for children sweeter than the pair of you."

They went out to the entrance of the mansion, where Westley stood angrily. He seemed to be sober this time, but he looked terrible.

His clothes were crumpled, he hadn't shaved, and his hair was a mess. He looked like he hadn't had a wink of sleep, dark circles under his eyes.

"What on earth happened to you, Westley?" said Leticia, staring at him. "You look like you've been sleeping rough for weeks!"

"Leticia, I need to talk to you," he said desperately. "About us."

"There is no 'us' anymore, hasn't that fact sunk into that thick skull of yours yet?" said Leticia, scowling at him, and he said "I know you're mad at me, and you've every right to be. But don't you think divorcing me was going a bit too far? I didn't deserve-"

"You deserved everything you got and more," snapped Leticia. "Like I said, I want nothing to do with you. Now please leave, Westley."

"I'm not going anywhere until you agree to have me back!"

"I don't *want* you back."

Westley opened his mouth, then closed it. "You don't mean that."

"I mean every word," said Leticia icily. "Like you said, our marriage was a charade. You couldn't care less about what I went through-"

"I've had a while to think about it!" said Westley desperately, and Spirit said "Westley, you're not making things any easier. Leticia's trying to get her life back on track and you need to keep away from her for a while."

Westley looked back at the paparazzi and watching crowd that had gathered at the gates, and he quietly said "Leticia, I need you."

"Well I don't need *you,* Westley. Not after everything you've done to me, just because you're insecure about Count Dracula."

"Count Dracula is a monster," spat Westley, and Spirit said "No he isn't, Westley! He's really kind, and caring! He came for dinner and-"

"He came for dinner?" Westley repeated, glaring. "When was this?"

"I- um… never mind," said Spirit meekly, and Leticia said "It was last night. I invited Count Dracula and Virginia for dinner with Jeiklee, Spirit and I, and it went very well. Spirit warmed up to Dracula and was even getting along with Virginia."

"And what about Jeiklee?" said Westley angrily, and Jeiklee said "Count Dracula's a cool guy, Dad. If you just-"

"Just what! Get to know him? I already know him!" said Westley furiously. "He's a vile demon! Leticia, you will not see him again- ever!"

"You can't tell her what to do!" said Spirit, outraged, Jeiklee as well. "She can see who she wants! And I think Count Dracula isn't bad at all!"

"Spirit, you've been brainwashed," said Westley angrily. "Jeiklee, you have too! I don't know what kind of spell Count Dracula has you all under, but it won't turn out great for any of you!"

"Ok, I think you should leave, Westley. Now," said Leticia flatly. "You're just looking very, very stupid in front of your children and the press."

Westley turned to look at the public and paparazzi filming them, and he turned back to Leticia.

"I don't care if I look stupid. I just… I want you back," said Westley sadly, and Leticia's expression changed as she stared over his shoulder at an approaching figure. "Leticia? What-"

"Leticia," said Count Dracula softly, and Westley whipped round. "You!"

"Apologies Dracula," said Leticia, and anyone looking at her could tell just how much she cared for the Count. Love was etched across her face as she said "I was exhausted. I overslept, and when I woke up it was eight. I was going to come as soon as possible, I promise you."

"That's alright, sweetheart. I just had to make sure you were ok."

Leticia smiled at him. Dracula smiled back.

Westley looked from Leticia to Dracula, then he gaped.

"Don't tell me you're both… together?!"

"No," said Leticia, irritated. "We are close friends and always have been."

"Do you have a problem with that?" Dracula added with a raised eyebrow, and Westley spat "I have a problem with you making googly eyes at my wife!"

"But she's not your wife." Dracula smirked at him. "Is she?"

"I will knock the living *daylights* out of you, Dracula!"

"If you touch him, I will hurt you," Leticia said flatly, and everyone gasped. "Make a decision and I will make one also, Westley."

Everyone looked from Westley to Leticia and back as they glared at each other, amazed as a journalist said to the camera "It looks like even friendship isn't on the cards for Westley Inferno and Leticia of Sampson! As long as Count Dracula is in the mix, there will always be a feud between the two!"

Westley took a deep breath, then he said "I won't fight you, Leticia. But I *will* duel with Count Dracula!"

"And I will hurt you," Leticia said, shrugging. "So if you want that, make your move. I'm waiting."

"I didn't come here for a duel," Dracula said, eyebrow raised as Westley removed his jacket and tossed it to the ground. "You really want a fight, Westley?"

"I want you out of Leticia's life for good!"

"Well that's not going to happen," said Leticia coldly. "Pick up your jacket and leave my premises, Westley."

"No!"

"No?" Leticia repeated dangerously, body erupting in a scarlet glow, and everyone drew back fearfully, Dracula joining her side. "If you don't leave I will make you!"

"I said I don't want to fight you, Leticia! It's Count Dracula who is the problem, not-"

"Dracula isn't the problem, you stupid boy in a man's body!" Leticia was livid. "If you knew the half of what he has done for Severna-"

"He has done nothing!" spat Westley, "And he is pretty much a pimple on the face of this land! Unloved, unwanted, unneeded!"

Dracula laughed, eyes aglow. "Anything else, Inferno?"

"I want *you,*" said Westley angrily, "To keep away from my family! Leticia will always belong to me, do you understand that?!"

"Westley, have you gone insane?" demanded Leticia, Dracula saying "Leticia is her own person and belongs to no one. Stop trying to control her, Inferno. She divorced you. She does not want you anymore, or need you. And I don't think she even *loves* you."

"Elementasin!!"

"Dad, no!" yelled Jeiklee, as a burst of green light rushed at Dracula, but the Horror Curse did not pull him into the air like it did Clarissa.

Dracula sighed as everyone screamed, the deadly cloaked figure known as the Sin appearing.

"Take him!" yelled Westley as everyone ducked, the Sin's skeletal hands outstretched as it swooped over everyone hungrily. *"Take Count Dracula!!"*

"Dad, didn't you listen to what Count Dracula told you?!" Jeiklee shouted angrily. "He's the master of the Sin!"

The Sin turned to look down at Westley, who shouted "Do as I say and take Count Dracula to the Underworld!"

The press were filming from their knees, afraid but still looking for a story, and the Sin turned to Count Dracula.

"What to do with this man, Master?"

Dracula shrugged a shoulder before he replied "Take him."

Everyone gasped disbelievingly, Spirit screaming as the Sin swooped down and grabbed Westley before flying up into the air with him, Westley shouting "No!! *HELP ME!!"*

The ground trembled, everyone screaming as a large whirlpool appeared, and the Sin, still holding Westley tightly, dived into the whirlpool with him and was gone.

The whirlpool vanished, everyone gaping down at the grass disbelievingly as they nervously got to their feet.

Shaking, the reporter said to the camera "Westley- Westley Inferno was… he was taken by the Sin. You… you saw it here first. Following it's master Count Dracula's orders, the Sin has taken Westley Inferno to the Underworld."

Dracula took a deep breath, Leticia looking at him.

"Are you ok, Dracula?"

"I'm fine, sweetheart."

"What will happen to my Dad, sir?" asked Jeiklee nervously, and Dracula smiled at him.

"Do not worry, Jeiklee. I will have your father brought back in twenty four hours. I just wanted to frighten him," he said warmly, and Jeiklee relaxed.

"I believe he deserves a small dose of fright and punishment."

Spirit nodded. "He does. I agree he does, Dracula sir."

Everyone relaxed, a journalist nervously asking "So you don't intend for Westley Inferno to die, Count Dracula?"

"No, of course not. He will be terribly shaken up when he returns, but he will be fine," Dracula said reassuringly. "I'm just teaching him a lesson."

"I believe that is enough excitement for one day," Leticia added, as talk broke out excitedly. "It is nine at night. My children must now go inside, and I am leaving with Count Dracula. If you want to see when Westley is brought back from the Underworld, and I know you all do, then return in twenty four hours. Until then, please keep away. Thank you and good night."

Everyone called "Goodnight Leticia, and "Goodnight Count Dracula sir!"

Jeiklee and Spirit waved as people called goodnight to them too, and they entered the mansion behind Leticia and Count Dracula.

"Where are the vampires, Dracula?" asked Leticia, looking at him. "They could be harmed again if left outside your castle."

"They are all waiting inside the castle, Leticia." Dracula smiled at her. "I thought exactly the same. I made them all enter the castle and I told them to wait for me to return with you."

"Then let us go," Leticia said, summoning her cloak, and Dracula said

"Very well. Jeiklee, Spirit- please do not leave the mansion."
"We won't sir," Jeiklee said reassuringly. "Mum's rule is we have to be in by nine."
"Like Virginia also," smiled Dracula. "The same rule applies to her."
"Now both of you go to bed at a decent time," Leticia said to Jeiklee and Spirit, and they nodded. "I don't know how long I will be, but if it is past three in the morning, I expect you both to be in bed when I am back."
"Yes Mum," said Jeiklee, and Spirit smiled and said to him "We can hang out until three in the morning. Movies and popcorn?"
"Sure!" said Jeiklee happily, and Leticia smiled and left them, Dracula at her side as he said "We will find out who the evil vampire is. I can't wait."
"Nor I."

* * *

Jeiklee and Spirit sat in the lounge, talking happily.
"I think Count Dracula is super cool," Jeiklee said, still astounded at the events that happened that evening, and so quickly. "Dad needed to be brought down. I mean I know he's my Dad, but he was totally asking for a bit of punishment."
"The Sin didn't even hear what Westley said, it looked like," said Spirit, shaking her head. "It was nuts! I didn't think the whole Count Dracula being the master of everything was true, but it really is. The Sin even *called* him master. Remind me not to do anything to Dracula's daughter again, Jeiklee. Because I definitely am *not* looking for punishment."
Jeiklee burst out laughing. "Dracula wouldn't set the Sin on you, nutcase. Dad had it coming, trust me. How dare he say Mum *belongs* to him?? I bet King Harlot was the one who put that rubbish in his head!"
"Well it definitely didn't come out of nowhere," scowled Spirit. "King Harlot probably did tell him that. And if he did, then Westley is a fool for believing what he said would work on Leticia!"
"The way Dracula defended Mum though," said Jeiklee admiringly. "He didn't even say 'No Westley, Leticia belongs to me'. He said she belongs to *no one.* Top marks for that comment!"
Spirit laughed. "So what movies do you want to watch?"
"Anything," smiled Jeiklee. "Um... Spirit?"
"Yes?"
"Now that everything is... well, alright again- can we pick up where we left off before we fell out over Virginia?" Jeiklee asked shyly. "I've missed you."
Spirit looked down at her knees, then she softly admitted "I've missed you too. I didn't really want to break up."
"I know. You was angry."

"Do you think Virginia will be upset if we start… you know. Being involved with each other?" Spirit asked a little uncertainly, and Jeiklee said "Nah. Well, I don't think so anyway. You think she might be jealous?"

"I don't know," admitted Spirit. "She didn't like me being with Bruce Finnegan. That's how it all started, you know that already."

"Yeah, but she knew we kissed and were seeing each other and she was fine about it," shrugged Jeiklee. "I think she'll be fine. Besides, we wasn't officially together, Spirit. That was your choice."

"Leticia calls us her children. She sees us as siblings," Spirit said quietly, and Jeiklee said "If we do see each other officially, she'll be the first to know. I promise. I won't hide our relationship from her."

"Well…" Spirit took a deep breath. "We *should* be together officially."
Jeiklee stared at her. "What did you say?"

"We should be together officially," Spirit repeated softly. "In a relationship. A proper one."

"What changed your mind? You were against it before," Jeiklee said, a little perplexed, and Spirit said "Does it matter what changed my mind? I don't want to run from my feelings anymore."

"Well… do you want me to ask you properly?" smiled Jeiklee, and Spirit smiled back.

"Yes. I'd like that."

"Spirit McKenzie," said Jeiklee softly, and she shivered as he asked "Will you go out with me?"

Spirit got up from her seat and hugged him hard, then she kissed him. When they broke apart, she whispered "Yes."

* * *

Castle Dracula…

"Malinda of Brubeck?" Leticia said disbelievingly, and the vampires said yes angrily. "Why has she returned to this part of Severna?"

"She wants to see Count Dracula, Ma'am, but we don't know why," a female vampire named Sarah replied angrily. "She murdered our good friend Terrence-"

"Terrence!" said Dracula, outraged. "She killed one of my closest men?!"

"Yes sir, she threw holy water at his face," Sarah said solemnly. "Terrence was furious with her and told her to leave, and she got angry and killed him. After she used the Tongue-Tie Curse on us, she warned the trees not to speak of the incidents or of her arrival. Poor Bari stood up to her, saying he will tell all, and she got angry and used cursed fire on him- cursed fire to the highest degree."

"Water had no effect on that fire. I couldn't put it out," said Dracula grudgingly, and another vampire said "Neither could we, sir. If Leticia of Sampson hadn't arrived when she did, a lot of the Forest could have been damaged because of Malinda."

"But what does she want?" demanded Dracula. "Why is she here? And why hasn't she shown herself to me yet? What on earth is she waiting for??"

"We don't know, sir."

"You won't know until you see her, Dracula," Leticia said softly, and Dracula scowled. "She may continue to do things until she is bored of playing games."

Dracula nodded, then he said to his minions "You may leave."

The vampires sauntered out of the room, one of them crashing into-

"Virginia! Do forgive me," the vampire said humbly, and Dracula stood.

Virginia looked furious as she entered the study. "Malinda of Brubeck, Father? She's back?"

Dracula nodded. "It seems so, my daughter."

"What does she want??"

"We don't have a clue," Leticia said gently. "It could be you, Virginia."

Virginia stared at her. "Me??"

"Yes," said Leticia, as gently as before. "Remember, she is your mother."

"That woman is nothing to me," spat Virginia, Nancy entering the room quickly when she sensed growing agitation in Virginia. "She dumped me when I was a baby and she didn't look back for eighteen years! She killed Bari and Terrence, and she cursed my father's servants!"

"I know, sweetie. But aren't you even curious about Malinda? You don't know your mother."

"Nancy is my mother," Virginia said angrily. "And you are too, Miss

Leticia. Whatever Malinda is back for, it's not me. I know it isn't! She wants something from my Father, and I'm telling you *right now* Father! Don't give it to her."

"I won't," said Dracula, amused and touched at the same time. "What if Malinda wants contact with you, Virginia?"

"She can take her wants and choke on them," said Virginia flatly. "She had eighteen years to try and make contact, and I had eighteen great years without her. I'm going to bed!"

"But it's not late," said Nancy, surprised at her. "Normally on a weekend you stay up for a long time-"

"I'm upset and angry, ok Nancy? I just want to lay in my coffin and read a book," Virginia said, and everyone nodded. "Goodnight Father, Miss Leticia."

"Goodnight," Dracula and Leticia said gently, and Virginia left the study. Leticia looked at Dracula. "She's very upset."

"I know," said Dracula, sighing. "And I agree with her whole heartedly. Malinda probably has not returned for our daughter. She wants something else. But what, I have no idea."

* * *

Spirit laid her head on Jeiklee's shoulder. "We'll tell Leticia soon, right?" Jeiklee nodded. "Right. Are you still worried about what she'll think? You was worried even when we wasn't officially dating."

"I am, but… I'm not going to run from it. We'll tell her tomorrow."

* * *

Leticia smiled, her head on Dracula's chest. Dracula stroked her hair lovingly as they laid deep in thought, and Leticia murmured "I always had a feeling that Spirit was attracted to Jeiklee. I noticed the way she looked at him and got upset over tiny things… tiny things about him."

"Are they dating?" Dracula murmured back, and she said "Yes. They're going to tell me tomorrow. But Spirit seems to think I will disapprove." Dracula glanced at her. "And will you?"

"No, of course not. Spirit is a lovely girl, and Jeiklee is an amazing young man." Leticia smiled again. "They are a perfect match in my eyes."

Dracula smiled too. "What will Westley say?"

"He has no say," Leticia said, shrugging a shoulder. "I have no problem with it, and neither should he."

Dracula nodded. "It's almost three in the morning, sweetheart. Would you like to stay the night?"

"I wish I could." Leticia kissed him and sat up. "I have to go."

"Alright. I'll walk you home," Dracula said, getting up as well. "I don't want you walking through the Forest of Fear alone at this time."
Leticia smiled at him. "Thank you, Dracula."
"It feels so nice knowing we are together finally," Dracula said lovingly, Leticia putting on her cloak and stepping into her shoes. "I've wanted this for so long."
"As have I," Leticia said quietly, and he looked at her. "Always."
Dracula pulled her into his arms and kissed her tenderly, Leticia's arms curving around him and pulling him as close as possible.
"Let us go," Dracula said breathlessly, when she broke the kiss moments later, but she removed her cloak. "Leticia?"
"We can go soon, Dracula," Leticia said quietly, and he looked at her eyes, which looked hazy from their kiss. "Let us stay together a while longer."
Dracula removed his cloak and kissed her again, both of them falling back onto his bed.
"Why… why don't you have a coffin?" panted Leticia as she gazed up at him from Dracula's pillows, and Dracula smiled down at her.
"I'm not your typical vampire, Leticia. And I don't follow all the ways of a vampire."
"I'm glad. I don't know how it would feel to make love in a coffin, though. There isn't a lot of space and it most likely has a hard feel."
Dracula stared at her, then he burst out laughing. Leticia laughed as well, and he kissed her again.

* * *

Jeiklee and Spirit woke up in the lounge.

"What… did we fall asleep here?" yawned Jeiklee, then he noticed the sun shining brightly outside. He checked the time, then gaped. "It's midday!"

"Well we'd better get fixed up and then come back down for lunch," Spirit said, rubbing her eyes. "I thought Washington would have woken us up. He usually does."

"I told him you were not to be disturbed," a voice replied amusedly, and they whipped round.

"Mum!" said Jeiklee, relieved. "I- what time did you get back?"

"At around five in the morning, or six," smiled Leticia. "Good afternoon to both of you."

"Good afternoon," Spirit and Jeiklee said as they smiled back, then Spirit said "Leticia? I… We have to tell you something."

"I know you are dating each other," Leticia replied, and their jaws practically hit the floor as she continued "And I know you have strong feelings for Jeiklee, Spirit. In fact, I always knew. I had a feeling, and my feelings are normally accurate. You felt threatened by Virginia becoming friends with Jeiklee and you thought you would lose him. And Jeiklee, I noticed the way you look at Spirit when you think nobody is watching. You both really like each other and I will not get in the way of that. I couldn't think of anyone more perfect for you both. I'm glad."

Spirit ran and hugged Leticia, Jeiklee touched as well as Spirit said "I was so scared you would hate it- you said that I'm your daughter- one of your children-"

"I will always see you as my daughter, Spirit." Leticia hugged her back. "But that doesn't mean I don't want you to be with my son."

Tears fell from Spirits eyes as she nodded and let go, and Leticia smiled at her.

"Both of you, please come down for lunch in an hour. And after you eat, study for Thrill. Your exam is tomorrow and will commence all day. So whatever you think you know about the Hovering and Lowering Charms, go over it with each other. Studying in a group is sometimes much better than studying alone."

"Wish Virginia could study with us," said Jeiklee with a sigh, and Leticia said "That's a great idea, Jeiklee. I will contact Count Dracula, and he can come over with Virginia. We will be seeing him tonight anyway."

"How come?" asked Jeiklee, and Leticia replied "He is having your father brought back from the Underworld. The press will be here and so will the public."

"We saw on the news when Westley got snatched by the Sin," said Spirit, shivering. "I mean I know we saw it right before our eyes but having to watch it again scared me. The Sin is scary! I'm never going to use the Horror Curse on anyone *again.*"

* * *

"Come on Father, walk up!" called Virginia happily, and Dracula obeyed.
"Virginia, have you realised we have seen Leticia of Sampson for the whole weekend? From Friday until today, we have been around her."
Virginia nodded. "Yes Father, I know. What's worrying you?"
"I don't want her to get fed up of me," Dracula admitted, and Virginia stopped and looked back at him. Dracula sighed, and she said "Father, don't think like that. You'll wind yourself up and then you'll try and keep away and that will drive you nuts. Miss Leticia will wonder what's up and think that you have got fed up of *her.* This is a good thing, ok? Just relax."
Dracula let her words sink in, and he did relax. "I don't know what I'd do without you, Virginia. Now, did you pack your bag for Thrill? And do you have a change of clothes? Leticia was very kind to suggest you stay over and go to Thrill with Jeiklee and Spirit in the morning."
"Yes Father, I have everything I need." Virginia smiled at him. "Are you going to stay over too?"
"Well... I... I'm not sure," admitted Dracula. "Leticia did not ask me."
"Should I ask her if you can stay?"
"No," said Dracula quickly, and she pouted at him.
"Why not, Father?"
"I don't want you asking questions for me, Virginia," Dracula said as they continued walking. "I will see what happens after I bring Westley back from the Underworld."

* * *

Washington opened the door to Virginia and Dracula, and he smiled.
"Good to see you again, Count Dracula."
"Not too soon I hope?" said Dracula amusedly as Washington let them into the mansion, and Washington laughed.
"Of course not. Greetings, Virginia."
"Greetings," Virginia replied with a small smile, and Washington led them into the lounge, where Jeiklee and Spirit sat talking happily, Leticia reading a book with a smile.
"My Lady, Count Dracula and his daughter Virginia have arrived," Washington said humbly, and Leticia looked up.
Spirit noticed the look on her face when her eyes fell on Count Dracula, and she said "Leticia?"
"Mmm?"

"I… are you- never mind," Spirit said quickly, and Leticia smiled at her. "Washington, please show Virginia to her room so she can put her things away."

"Yes Ma'am. Right this way, Virginia," Washington said warmly, and Virginia followed him out of the lounge.

"So," said Dracula, smiling at Leticia. "I am back again."

"And I'm glad," said Leticia as she smiled back. "Would you like to join us for a late lunch, Dracula? Jeiklee didn't want us to eat without you and Virginia."

"In that case I have no choice," said Dracula amusedly as he looked at Jeiklee, and Jeiklee smiled back. "Would you like me to leave afterwards until the press arrive, Leticia? I don't want to get under your feet."

"You could never get under my feet, silly. Stay," smiled Leticia, and he smiled back. "Let's have some lunch."

* * *

It was dark.

It was cold.

There were whispers.

Ghostly figures.

Walking skeletons.

Demons.

Monsters.

Westley hung from a beam by his arms, shaking and sweating as the Sin flew around under him.

"Please- let me go!" he cried. "I don't belong in this world- set me free! I promise, I will never call you to harm Count Dracula again!"

The Sin laughed. *"You will not leave here, Westley Inferno. Your twenty four hours of remaining alive are almost up. Soon, you will belong to the Underworld. You will never see the land of Severna again!"*

"But- but what if I'm rescued?" gasped Westley. "That's what the books said- when taken by the Sin, the victim has twenty four hours to be rescued! The book said it!"

"It is true," rasped the Sin, *"But who is brave enough to rescue you? Who will come to the Underworld to battle me for your soul, you silly man? It won't be Leticia of Sampson. Her heart belongs to my Master!"*

"That's a lie!" spat Westley, and the Sin laughed. "She's just angry with me, she didn't mean a word she said! I will win her back no matter what it takes!"

"Fairy tales are for children, Westley Inferno." The Sin flew around him, then started to fly away. *"It is time you wake up and see everything for what it really is."*

"Wait! Where are you going?!" yelled Westley, head spinning. "Stay with me!"

"I will be back in time to devour your soul," the Sin replied coldly, then it vanished in a burst of green light.

Ghosts swirled around Westley as he struggled, then he realised if he fell from the height he was at, he would surely be killed.

"Westley Inferno," a spooky voice whispered, and Westley lifted his head… *to stare into the ghostly face of his mother.*

He screamed like a child who had his bike stolen, then he fainted.

* * *

"And we are back! Live, at the house of Leticia," a journalist said happily, the large crowd babbling excitedly. "Will Count Dracula keep his world and have Westley Inferno brought back from the Underworld?"

"Obviously he will," scowled Virginia, arms folded as Jeiklee and Spirit stood on the grounds with her. "Anything to exaggerate the story!"

Jeiklee laughed. "It's their job, Virginia. They have to make it look good."

Leticia left the house with Count Dracula at her side, and cameras flashed immediately, people shouting "Leticia! It is time!"

Dracula looked at Leticia, who checked the time. She nodded, looking at Dracula.

"You only have ten minutes before Westley's soul is taken and he is trapped in the Underworld for eternity. Do it now, Dracula."

Dracula sighed and raised his hands, saying *"Elementasin!!"*

Everyone drew back, Dracula's hands glowing bright green. There was a screech and the Sin appeared, rasping *"Yes Master!"*

"Bring Westley Inferno back to the land of the living," Dracula said grudgingly. "His twenty four hours are almost up."

The Sin was a little confused. *"You did not intend for him to die, Master?"*

"No I did not," said Dracula, scowling a little, and everyone could tell he was seriously pondering the idea of letting Westley remain in the Underworld forever. "Bring him back, and hurry. I know there is no way to help him when twenty four hours are over."

The Sin bowed. *"Yes Master."*

It vanished, and excited talk broke out again. Leticia looked at Dracula, saying "Thank you."

"I didn't do it for him, Leticia. I did it for you," Dracula said softly, and Spirit looked from him to her curiously, but before she could ask something the Sin reappeared with Westley in it's skeletal arms, flying around regretfully before it placed Westley on the grass.

"A soul I missed out on by three minutes," it said sadly and irritably, and Dracula replied "Thank you. Your work is done."

"You are most welcome Master."

The Sin vanished, and everyone cheered, Westley out cold on the grass.

Leticia stepped down from the entrance to her mansion and walked towards him, kneeling down as she stared at his face.

Silence fell.

Jeiklee glanced at Dracula, and so did Spirit and Virginia. He was watching Leticia, expression unreadable.

Leticia took a deep breath, then she looked at the crowd. "Westley needs the hospital."

"Won't you heal him, Leticia?" a journalist said disbelievingly, and she replied "I have healed Westley of almost everything he has ever had in the years I was married to him. And after the way he treated me, I can tell he hasn't even a scrap of gratitude for all I have done for him. So no. I'm not going to heal him this time. He doesn't deserve a shred of help from me."

Dracula breathed out, relieved. Virginia was too, and so was Jeiklee. Spirit hesitated, then she said "Can you at least wake him, Leticia? Please?"

Leticia sighed. "Fine. Someone call an ambulance also."

"You heard her!" someone shouted. "Call an ambulance!"

Leticia's right hand started to glow bright purple, and she gently placed it on Westley's forehead.

"Wake up Westley," she said quietly, everyone waiting with bated breath as he stirred, then opened his eyes uncertainly.

"Le… Leticia??"

"Yes," she said stonily, and he gasped "I- I saw- in the Underworld, it was- I saw horrifying things! I saw… I saw the ghost of my mother!"

Leticia didn't even blink at what he just said. "Ok."

"Ok?" Westley repeated amazedly, but he let it go. "Thank you so much for rescuing me-"

"I didn't rescue you," Leticia said coldly, and he stared at her. "Count Dracula ordered the Sin to bring you back alive. That is all."

"You… you didn't rescue me?"

"No. Count Dracula did."

"But- but Leticia-" Westley stopped when an owl hooted, looking around wildly, then he relaxed, whispering "I'm not there anymore. I'm ok."

Leticia stood, unfazed. "Don't move, Westley. You're in shock, and traumatised. Whatever horrors you saw in the Underworld, it has you shaken up. You're trembling like a leaf on a breezy day."

Westley was very cold. "I'm freezing."

Leticia sighed, conjuring a blanket and handing it to him. "Here."

Westley wrapped it around himself as sirens sounded in the distance and laid there in a ball, eyes closed as he bit his lip.

Leticia looked at Count Dracula, who shrugged a shoulder. "Punishment enough, Leticia?"

"Yes," Leticia said softly, and she looked down at Westley. "Me and you are over, Westley Inferno. If it wasn't for Count Dracula, you would be dead right now. I wasn't going to rescue you, do you understand me?"

Westley just nodded, holding himself as the ambulance pulled up outside the giant gates.

"I want no more visits from you or demands for me to have you back. We are finished. If you want to visit our children, you are welcome to come. But do not try to communicate with me," Leticia said flatly, everyone stunned at her words. "Moving on from me would be better for both of us. Now I'm going to tell you this *one* time, and one time only. Leave Count Dracula *alone.* Do not try to duel with him again. If you do, he is not going to be as lenient as he was before."

"Dracula has brainwashed you," gasped Westley as the paramedics ran over. "You need to be with *me,* Leticia! I- I…"

He passed out before he could finish talking, and Leticia said to the paramedics "He has been through a very traumatic experience and needs a lot of care. Take him please."

"Yes Leticia," the paramedics said humbly, and more talk broke out, the cameramen filming Leticia as she walked back up the steps of the mansion entrance, a journalist calling "Leticia, what now?"

"Now?" repeated Leticia, slightly amused. "Nothing. I'm going indoors and the children will do the same. They have an exam tomorrow and must rest. For now, there will be no more big stories. Leave me in peace please."

"After being shocked and left in the horrors of the Underworld only to escape death by an inch, Westley Inferno is now being taken to the hospital," a journalist said to the camera, the press unable to believe their luck at having such a great story. "We will keep everybody updated and will stay informed about his recovery! Count Dracula saved him this time, but like Leticia said, he won't be as lenient if crossed by Westley again!"

"Spirit!" shouted Bruce Finnegan, and Spirit turned.

"Bruce? What do you want??"

"I- well… I was just wondering if you wanted to-"

Jeiklee pulled Spirit into his arms and kissed her hard on the mouth, gasps going up and cameras flashing as Spirit's arms went around him.

Virginia was smirking as Jeiklee ended the kiss moments later, and he looked at Bruce with a hard glint in his eyes.

"She doesn't want or need to do *anything* with you."

Cheers went up again from the students at Thrill and some other people who had gathered, and the journalist quickly said "On a side note, Jeiklee Inferno and Spirit McKenzie are a couple!"

"No they aren't!" said Bruce angrily, and Spirit said "Yes we are, Bruce. I already told you to leave me alone. Jeiklee is my boyfriend and I'd appreciate it if you stopped trying to get me back. I'm done with you."

Smiling broadly, Jeiklee put an arm around Spirit and they went inside, the crowd leaving slowly, talking excitedly.

Virginia smiled and went inside as well, Bruce calling "Virginia, wait!"

"I'm no one's second best, Bruce," Virginia called back, and cheers went up again, Dracula and Leticia smiling as the doors closed behind her.

"I'm very proud of you, Virginia. I know you had a crush on Bruce Finnegan for a while," smiled Leticia, and Virginia said "In high school I did, when he was dating Spirit. But now I know he's an arrogant jerk."

Everyone smiled at her, Jeiklee holding Spirit's hand as Virginia added "I'm still friends with him though. He's not a bad guy deep down."

Jeiklee nodded, Leticia saying "You all have your exams tomorrow. Ready yourselves for bed and be back down for a hot drink please. Then be in bed by ten, thank you."

"Yes Mum," said Jeiklee, Spirit and Virginia saying likewise, and he added "You're the best."

Leticia smiled at her son as he jogged up the stairs with Spirit and Virginia, and Dracula smiled at her.

"He loves you so much, Leticia. All three of them do."

Leticia stood on tiptoe and kissed him. "I love them too."

* * *

Malinda of Brubeck looked through the window at Westley Inferno, who was shaking and shivering in bed. He had refused to be left alone, and so the staff were doing a bed watch, changing workers every three hours.

Malinda entered the room, smiling at him. "Good night, Count Inferno."

Westley stared at her disbelievingly. "Malinda of Brubeck??"

"Yes."

"What- what are you doing- back in… this part of Severna?" managed Westley, and her smile grew.

"I have come to rekindle my relationship with Count Dracula." Her eyes glowed scarlet as she looked at the intimidated nurse seated by Westley's bed. "May you leave us alone for ten minutes?"

"Count Inferno insisted he cannot be alone," the nurse said nervously, and Malinda rolled her eyes.

"Are you foolish? He won't *be* alone. I am in the room with him, am I not?"

"Well… yes, but-"

"So leave," Malinda said coldly. "Now."

The nurse hesitated, not knowing whether to obey or stay with his patient.

"It's ok," Westley said weakly. "Wait outside."

The nurse nodded and left the room, Malinda running a hand through her bright red hair. Westley waited curiously, shaking with cold.

"What do you… want from- from me?"

"I want you to get Leticia of Sampson to back off."

"Back… off?" repeated Westley. "From- from what?"

"From seeing Count Dracula," Malinda replied stonily. "Every time I look at a television, I see them together. Every time I am in the Forest of Fear, I see them together. Even when I go near Castle Dracula, I can sense they are in there together! What is going on between the two?"

"I don't know," said Westley weakly. "I know as much as you do. Leticia warned me away from Count Dracula tonight. She really cares for him, but everyone knows he is no good for her, no good for anyone."

"Everyone is changing their mind about Dracula," Malinda told him flatly. "I want you to charm Leticia back into your life. Make her see that she was wrong to leave you, make her realise she still loves you."

Westley shook his head sadly. "She doesn't love me anymore, Malinda."

"Look," said Malinda, growing impatient, "If you have to use a Love Charm, then do it. Or a Love Potion, the strongest kind! Just get her away from Count Dracula so I can-"

"So you can what?" a cold voice said, and Malinda whipped round.

"Leticia of Sampson?!" Leticia was right behind her. "How much did you hear?!"

"Oh, I heard everything from when you asked Westley what was going on between me and Count Dracula."

"And?" Malinda said angrily. "What is exactly is going on between you both?"

"Why are you here?" Leticia replied coldly, and Malinda snapped "Why are *you* here? The last time I checked, you wanted nothing to do with Westley Inferno. So what exactly are *you* doing here??"

"I came to make sure Westley would be ok." Leticia glared at Malinda, who glared right back before she snapped "He'll be fine. He's just still traumatised by the ordeal he went through in the Underworld."

"Yes, and it will take a while for him to get back to normal." Leticia's tone was ice cold, but Malinda didn't care.

"Were you going to heal me, Leticia?" Westley asked hopefully before Malinda could snap something, and Leticia flatly said "No. I was just going to talk to the staff."

"Oh," said Westley, put out. "Well… Malinda, thank you for coming. Can you leave so I can speak with Leticia alone please?"

Malinda's jaw dropped. "You're ending our discussion for Leticia of Sampson?!"

"She's my wife," said Westley apologetically, and Malinda and Leticia both snapped "Ex-wife!"

"I don't know what you want from me, Malinda," Westley said, seeming stronger now that Leticia was there. "I can't force her to take me back."

"And why do you want me back with him?" Leticia said stonily, looking at

Malinda with immense dislike. "Why did you even come back to this part of the land?"

"That is none of your business," Malinda said icily. "Fine. I will leave, Westley. But think about what I said. Do you really like things the way they are at present?"

She left the room before Westley could answer, then she vanished. Westley breathed out, Leticia saying "Keep away from that vampire, Westley. She's evil."

"Why act like you care whether I keep away from her or not when you don't?" said Westley bitterly, arms folded now. "All you really care about is your precious Count Dracula."

"Are you going to argue with me for no reason?" Leticia said, an eyebrow raised. "I'm trying to warn you about Malinda of Brubeck-"

"Well I can look after myself."

"Fine," shrugged Leticia. "If she harms you, I won't bat an eyelid. She has murdered already since she returned, and will most likely do it again."

"What??"

"You heard me," Leticia said flatly as she turned to leave. "Oh, and by the way, even if you *did* make a Love Potion and somehow managed to get me to drink it, it wouldn't have an effect on me. I am too powerful to be fazed by something so minimal."

"And a Love Charm?" demanded Westley, scowling. "Are you going to tell me that won't have an effect on you either?"

"That would be telling," smirked Leticia. "Just know this. If you ever, and I mean *ever*- attempt to force me to love you or take you back using a spell or potion, it will be the last thing you ever do. I will make sure you are paralysed from the shoulders down. I will blast your home to smithereens with the workers inside and make sure the King does not let you stay in the Palace. I will make sure you lose it all whilst being a vegetable. When I am done with you, you will never want to cast a spell or make a potion again. Well, you would think it," she added thoughtfully, "Because you wouldn't be able to do anything ever again, whether you wanted to or not."

Westley's mouth was hanging open. "When did you become so *dark??*"

"I have always had a dark side and you know that. You knew it from the moment you attempted to murder Count Dracula years ago and I blasted all of your men unconscious. So don't act surprised," Leticia said flatly. "Whatever Malinda wants you to do to me so she can get to Count Dracula, you'd better not do it."

"I would never do a thing to hurt you," Westley told her, weakly now. He was starting to shiver again. "I promise you."

"Your promise is void. You've already done plenty to hurt me."

She turned to leave, and Westley managed "Leticia, wait."

Leticia sighed and turned back around. "What?"

"When you said… that your heart was never mine." Westley looked hurt as if she'd said it just now for the first time. "Did you-"

"Mean it? Yes," Leticia said flatly. "I'm not saying the feelings were one sided. I did have feelings for you and I wanted it to work. And it did. I was happy, Westley. I was completely fine."

"Until- until Count Dracula came back… back into your life," Westley said bitterly, and she glared at him.

"Until *you* began acting like a madman. And your son and Spirit find your behaviour and actions appalling, Westley. Oh," she said, remembering. "Before you hear it from the news or the Severna newspaper, you should know that Jeiklee and Spirit are dating now."

"Dating?" said Westley, frowning, then he glared. "Dating who? Don't tell me our son is with Virginia of Dracula?! Because I won't allow it!"

"Westley-"

"No!" spat Westley. "I won't have it, Leticia! Jeiklee will not be with that mini monster, do you understand?! And who is Spirit seeing??"

"They are dating each other," snapped Leticia, and his jaw dropped. "Jeiklee isn't dating Virginia of Dracula, he's dating Spirit McKenzie!"

"Our Spirit McKenzie?" said Westley disbelievingly, and Leticia said "Well how many other Spirit McKenzies do you know??"

"They're dating each other." Westley leant back against his pillows. "I… are you serious, Leticia?"

"Yes. Now don't even think of blowing a fuse about it," Leticia said flatly. "I don't have a problem with it and I always knew Spirit felt something for Jeiklee."

"Well why didn't you tell me?" said Westley, hurt again. "You started pulling away from me for no reason!"

"I started pulling away from you because-"

There was a knock on the door. "Miss Leticia of Sampson?"

"Yes," Leticia said, turning to the doctor, and the doctor said "Visiting hours are over, Ma'am. Apologies."

"Please let her stay," pleaded Westley. "I was having a conversation with my wife-"

"Ex-wife," Leticia said flatly, and Westley scowled at her.

"Can you please stop that?"

"No I cannot. Now I've filled you in on the latest to do with Jeiklee and I've warned you not to get involved with Malinda or try and do anything to me," Leticia said stonily. "So I'm leaving."

Westley slumped back against his pillows, defeated. "Fine."

Leticia turned and left without another word, and Westley's eyes filled over. The doctor stared at him amazedly.

"Sir?"

"What?"

"Are you *crying?"*
"No," said Westley angrily, wiping his eyes before the tears could fall.
"Can you please have my one on one nurse return to my bedside."
"Yes sir."

* * *

Dracula checked on Virginia, Leticia at his side.
"Have a good night, Virginia."
"Thank you Father. You too," smiled Virginia, and Dracula smiled back.
"You are comfortable, aren't you? Being away from the castle?"
"I finally get to stay with Miss Leticia at her mansion," said Virginia happily. "And with Jeiklee too, and Spirit. I'm very comfortable, Father."
"Good."
"Do you like your room, Virginia?" Leticia asked warmly, and Virginia smiled back at her from her bed, snuggled under the covers.
"Yes Miss Leticia. I love it!"
Leticia's smile grew. "I'm glad. Sweet Dreams, darling."
"Goodnight," smiled Virginia, and Leticia closed the door.
Spirit and Jeiklee were both fast asleep. Leticia remembered that Virginia was a young vampire, so she would find it a little more difficult than Jeiklee and Spirit to nod off at night.
"I got her into the habit of sleeping at night from a young age," Dracula said softly, hearing her thoughts, and Leticia turned to him with a smile.
"Just like your father did with you."
"Yes he did. So," Dracula said, jamming his thumbs in his pockets. "I guess I'd better go home."
"What? Why?" Leticia was surprised. "Aren't you going to stay?"
"I wasn't sure if you wanted me to," admitted Dracula, a little embarrassed. "You invited Virginia to stay overnight, not me."
"Oh," said Leticia, still surprised. "I didn't think I had to ask, Dracula."
"I didn't want to outstay my welcome and I wouldn't stay without an invitation." Dracula lifted a hand and caressed her cheek, Leticia's eyes closing at his touch. Lifting her hand to his, she whispered "Please stay."
Dracula kissed her gently, and her legs suddenly felt like jelly. Leticia wrapped her arms around him and stood on tiptoe as she deepened the kiss, taking control before she unfastened Dracula's black cape, letting it billow to the floor.
There was a cough, and they broke apart and turned to see Washington.
"Yes Washington," Leticia said embarrassedly, and he said "Apologies for disturbing you, My Lady. I came to ask if you'd like a hot drink and cake, toast or biscuits before bed, as I always do each night."
Leticia looked at Dracula. "Would you like to spend a bit of time in the

lounge with me, Dracula?"

"Of course," smiled Dracula, and Leticia said "Can two large mugs of hot chocolate and two large slices of chocolate cake be brought to the lounge for us please Washington."

"Yes My Lady." Washington bowed and went on his way.

Leticia took a deep breath, trying to steady her pounding heart. Dracula knelt and picked up his cape, then he smiled up at her.

"We'd better get dressed for bed, Leticia. Which of the guest rooms am I to sleep in?"

"That question is poison to my ears," smiled Leticia, and he laughed. "You can stay with me in my suite. You don't need a guest room, Dracula."

"I figured as much, but let me have one anyway," smiled Dracula. "I would like a room to call my own here."

"Ok. You can have the guest room on my floor."

"Your floor?" repeated Dracula amazedly. "You have your own floor?"

"Of course. It's on the next level up," smiled Leticia. "I'll show you."

Dracula nodded, and he followed her back down the corridor up another flight of stairs.

When they reached the next floor up, Leticia smiled at Dracula.

"Welcome to Leticia's floor in the house of Sampson."

"Newly dubbed the house of Leticia," smiled Dracula, and she laughed.

"Do you see that glowing blue door at the end of the corridor, Dracula?"

Dracula looked, then nodded. "I see it. What is that?"

"That's my Chamber of Serenity."

Dracula gaped. "It looks as if it has always been there."

"Well, it was there when I created it, exactly where it is now," Leticia told him. "I had to place it under Westley's mansion when I moved there. In one of the many basements. I'm glad it's back where it belongs."

"And your suite?" asked Dracula, and she took his hand and led him down the corridor.

"My suite is opposite the guest room that will become yours," she told him softly. "There is also a spa on this floor, with a Jacuzzi in it and also a swimming pool."

"Only for you?" smiled Dracula, and Leticia smiled back.

"Only for me." She kissed him lightly on the mouth. "I'm going to change for bed. I'll meet you in the lounge."

"Ok," smiled Dracula, and they walked down the corridor together, Leticia showing Dracula where his room was. "Leticia?"

"Mmm?"

"Can I knock on your door if I get lonely while changing?" smiled Dracula, and she laughed.

"Naughty vampire. I'll meet you downstairs."

She entered her suite and smiled at him before she closed the door, and

Dracula chuckled before he entered the suite opposite.

* * *

Westley tossed and turned, trying to get some sleep, but the memories of everything he'd witnessed in the Underworld were still fresh. He had shouted out in his sleep and woken five times already.
Westley shivered as he remembered it all, and was suddenly ice cold again.
"I… I'm freezing. It's the Horror Curse affecting me."
"I'll bring you another hot drink, Count Inferno," his nurse said warmly as he stood, and Westley said "Thank you" gratefully.
Moments later he was sipping hot chocolate from a large mug, under three blankets.
"I saw the ghost of my mother," he said, and his nurse looked at him. "I don't know if I will ever forget it. I never should have tried to challenge Count Dracula, Nurse. I didn't expect him to have me snatched by the Sin and taken to the Underworld. Those twenty four hours were the worst of my life. So many things flashed before my eyes, so many horrors I saw. I wish Leticia healed me like she always used to. But she refused to do it."
"Sir, it's two in the morning. Try not to dwell on the memories of the Underworld," his nurse said gently. "If you do, you will be up all night. Keep calm and drink your hot chocolate."
"Alright."
Doing his best to obey, Westley took deep breaths and began to drink his hot chocolate. After he'd finished, he fell back asleep.

* * *

Leticia and Dracula laid together in her massive bed, Dracula's arms around Leticia.

"If only we could stay like this forever," Leticia murmured, and Dracula smiled. "I'm going to miss you so much when you leave tomorrow."

"I will miss you too, sweetheart." Dracula kissed her forehead. "I will leave at lunchtime instead of in the morning."

Leticia sighed. "Ok. I'm looking forward to hearing how it was for Jeiklee and Spirit, taking their first monthly exam at Thrill."

"Do you remember when it was our first exam there?" smiled Dracula. "You was so nervous."

"I was indeed. But after that I was totally fine." Leticia took his hand and kissed it. "Besides, I had you to calm me."

"Yes, and you had Westley when our contact with each other ceased."

Leticia looked at him. "You're upset? It's in the past, Dracula. We have each other now, and we are together. That's all that matters. It was what we wanted for so long and we finally have it."

Dracula nodded. "I know. But the memories-"

"Forget the bad memories," Leticia said softly. "Focus on the good ones and revel in the new ones made. I love you, Dracula."

Dracula kissed her. "I love you too Leticia. I'm looking forward to making new and brilliant memories with you."

* * *

"Malinda of Brubeck?" Spirit said disbelievingly the next morning as they walked to Thrill, and Virginia nodded.

"Yes. She's back and she's killed twice. She set fire to Bari the tree and she killed my father's wingman Terrence."

Jeiklee was frowning. "What does she want? Why is she murdering?"

"Well she doesn't want me, that's for sure," scowled Virginia. "She's evil."

"She's still your mother, Virginia," Jeiklee said reasonably, and Virginia and Spirit both scowled at him. "What? It's true!"

"Did you not hear her, Jeiklee? Malinda may be Virginia's mother but she's evil," Spirit told him. "And she's after something!"

"How do you know?" asked Jeiklee curiously, and Virginia said "She wants something that involves my father. I know she does. Malinda was gone for eighteen years without a care in the world, and now she's back- but only because she wants something that doesn't involve me. If she wanted contact with me she wouldn't have ignored my existence for eighteen years. Malinda doesn't care about me, Jeiklee, whether she's my mother or not. I had Nancy and Miss Leticia growing up; *they* were my mother figures. Not Malinda of Brubeck."

Jeiklee understood. "Sorry Virginia. I was trying to be reasonable."

"It's alright, Jeiklee. But Malinda of Brubeck and *'reasonable'* go together like water and oil," Virginia told him, and he nodded. "If she was a reasonable vampire she wouldn't have dumped me as a baby. She wouldn't have killed Bari and Terrence; she would have just gone straight to my father for whatever it is she wants. But she wants to have a cruel form of fun first."

Spirit was scowling. "You're better off without her, Virginia."

"I agree," Virginia said, smiling a little, and Spirit smiled back as they heard the bell ring in the distance, sounding the start of Thrill.

The three of them walked faster, not wanting to be late. When they reached the building, Virginia said "Want to sit with me and Jeiklee, Spirit?"

"Wha- you mean that?" said Spirit amazedly, and Virginia nodded.

"You've been sitting away from everyone since you tried to curse Clarissa."

"Everyone's been sitting away from *me,*" Spirit corrected, and Virginia said "So sit with us. If they see I don't have a problem with you anymore, they might relax."

"Wait. I wanted to ask you something, Virginia." Spirit stopped, and Virginia and Jeiklee stopped too. "Are you ok with me and Jeiklee being together?"

"If I wasn't, you wouldn't even have to ask that question. You would know," Virginia said amusedly, and Spirit smiled back. "I don't have a problem with it at all."

"Told you," Jeiklee said, and they laughed as they entered the building. "Exam time!"

* * *

"I wish you didn't have to go," Leticia said a little sadly, and Dracula smiled at her.

"I will be back soon, you know I will. Our children have their exams today and will want to tell us all about it. I think I should spend some time with Virginia, Leticia. She doesn't mind, but we've been in your presence for pretty much four days in a row." Dracula hesitated, then he added "I don't want you to get fed up of me."

"I have never gotten fed up with you in all the years I've known you," Leticia told him, and she stood on tiptoe and kissed his jaw gently. "And I never will. Oh- Dracula? There's something I need to tell you."

Dracula looked at her serious face, then he took her hand and led her into her lounge.

"What is it, Leticia?" Leticia hesitated, and he said "I won't be angry with you, sweetheart. I promise."

"I saw Malinda of Brubeck." Leticia waited for the blow, but Dracula just stared at her. She took a deep breath, then continued "Malinda was at the hospital, paying Westley a visit. She wanted him to persuade me to go back to him, and to keep me away from you. She even told Westley to use a Love Charm or Love Potion on me. It made my skin crawl."

"So Virginia was right," Dracula said, taking what she said in thoughtfully. "Malinda wants me for something. We should go to the hospital, Leticia, so Westley can tell us exactly what she said to him."

Leticia nodded. "You aren't mad I didn't tell you sooner?"

"Of course not." Dracula took her hand and kissed it. "Better late than never."

* * *

It was afternoon break.

Jeiklee and Virginia had gone to the cafeteria to get drinks, and Spirit waited for them outside, sat by the tree near the river. It was Jeiklee and Virginia's spot, and they invited her to sit with them too.

"Well if it isn't the weirdo who thinks it's ok to set the Sin on people," sneered a voice, and Spirit looked up sharply.

"Clarissa! What the hell do you want?!"

"I want an apology. Or else," Clarissa added menacingly, and Spirit stood, her body starting to glow scarlet.

"Or else what, you cow? What are you going to do?"

Clarissa glared at Spirit, her bright blue eyes sparkling as a crowd started to gather, Jules saying "What's going on?"

"This idiot won't give me an apology for setting the Sin on me," Clarissa said as she tossed her blonde hair over her shoulder, and Spirit said "I'm not going to apologise. Get lost, Clarissa."

"Why should I? You owe me a lot for what you did to me."

"It was over two weeks ago," Spirit said irritably. "Are you bored or something? Or are you trying to pick up where Virginia left off? Because I'll hex you just like I did her and you'll regret trying to mouth off!"

"Oh yeah? Well I'll hex *you* right now!"

"Do it then!" spat Spirit, and Clarissa raised her hand, crying *"Ricato!"*

"Glasora!" another voice cried, and a shiny glass wall appeared in front of Spirit just before the spell hit her; Clarissa's spell shattered the protection spell, dissolving into nothing.

Everyone whipped round to see Virginia standing there, her arm outstretched, Jeiklee at her side holding three Slushies from the canteen.

Surprised, Clarissa said "Virginia, what are you doing?! Why did you block the hex??"

"Leave Spirit alone," Virginia said dangerously, glowing scarlet, and some people backed away nervously as Clarissa said "Spirit McKenzie needs to stop with that attitude! Someone needs to sort her out, Virginia!"

"You mean she still needs to be bullied?" said Virginia angrily, and Clarissa said "Well…. I guess so, yes!"

"If you think I'm going to let you pick on her you're insane," spat Virginia. "You want to hex someone, Clarissa? Hex me! You want to be a bully? *Bully me!!"*

Clarissa backed away from Virginia as her scarlet glow spread and deepened in colour.

"I- I don't want to fight you, Virginia!"

"Why? Because you know I'll probably kill you?" spat Virginia. "But it's ok to bully Spirit McKenzie like I did before? You're not me, Clarissa, and you never will be!"

Clarissa's face turned bright red as everyone looked at her, most of their faces disapproving. Bruce Finnegan shrugged a shoulder, saying "It was funny when it was Virginia doing it, but you just look like a twat, Clarissa." Clarissa's eyes filled over as everyone nodded, someone else saying "Leave Spirit alone, Clarissa! She doesn't have to apologise to you anyway because it was you who approached her to begin with!"

Angry and embarrassed, Clarissa said "Virginia, we're best friends! How can you choose Spirit McKenzie over me?!"

"Spirit isn't half bad once you get to know her," Virginia said angrily. "Bruce knows that, he'll tell you himself! And I'm going to tell you again- leave Spirit alone! Anyone else who dares trouble her will have me to answer to, and it won't be pretty! Am I understood?!"

Spirit's mouth hung open in shock as everyone quickly said "Yes Virginia", and so did Jeiklee's and the mouths of the college professors that had come to see what was going on.

"Good," Virginia said heatedly. "Now leave us alone!"

The crowd departed quickly, buzzing excitedly.

"Virginia of Dracula isn't enemies with Spirit McKenzie anymore!"

Virginia took a Slushie from Jeiklee and handed it to Spirit. "Here, Spirit."

"Thank you," said Spirit, still shocked, but touched. "I mean it- thank you so much. You didn't have to-"

"To get you a Slushie? I know," Virginia said as she sat on the grass, and Jeiklee and Spirit smiled at her, knowing she didn't like people getting mushy over her. Still, Spirit pressed "You didn't have to defend me like that or protect me from Clarissa's hex, Virginia."

"I know, I know." Virginia looked embarrassed. "I guess I saw myself in Clarissa and it made me mad. You're my friend now, Spirit. I would never just watch a friend get hurt without doing anything. And I won't let anyone hurt you or Jeiklee."

* * *

"I don't have to tell you a thing, Dracula," spat Westley. "You ruined me! You took away everything I had and loved, everything and everyone that was important to me! And when I'm one hundred percent healthy, I'm going to come after you-"

"Well if you want a second trip to the Underworld, go ahead and come after me," snapped Dracula. "Tell me what Malinda said to you!"

"No!"

"You-!!"

"Malinda is up to something and we need to know what it is," Leticia said firmly. "Tell us what she said before I arrived, Westley. Please."

"I'll tell you what she said if you promise to keep away from Count Dracula."

"This again?" Leticia almost lost her temper. "You can't control who I do and don't see, Westley! Your opinion may have mattered when we were together, but I am not your wife anymore! Just tell us what Malinda said!"

"As long as you stay in contact with Dracula I am keeping my mouth shut tighter than King Harlot's safe," Westley said flatly. "So make your choice!"

"Things are going to get real ugly real quickly," Dracula said, glowing scarlet now, and Leticia said "Westley, I didn't want to have to do this. But you leave me no choice."

Westley stared at her as her body began to glow bright purple. "Leticia? What are you-"

"I'm going to use the power of the Force and go back in time. I will see what Malinda said for myself."

Dracula glanced at her amazedly. "I completely forgot how powerful you are, Leticia."

"You can't do that!" spat Westley, and Leticia tossed back "I can do what the hell I want."

"Fine!" spat Westley. "Do it! But I'm telling you Leticia, if you continue seeing Count Dracula-"

"You'll continue to sulk and curse to high Heaven? I know that already," Leticia said flatly. "Dracula, let us go. Westley can be bitter alone and in peace. I will go back in time tonight, and with you."

Dracula smiled at her. "Thank you."

Westley swore as Leticia turned and left the room without saying another word to him. Dracula turned to leave as well, then he turned back.

"Tell me something, Inferno. What was it like seeing the ghost of your mother?"

Westley stared at him, visibly beginning to shake with cold that instantly came back the moment the words left Count Dracula's mouth.

"Get- get out, Dracula!"

Smirking, Dracula replied "I'm going. Oh, you may need a hot drink, Westley. You're in for another rough night."

Westley pulled his covers up to his shoulders, shivering again as Dracula left the room, jogging to catch up with Leticia.

Malinda of Brubeck appeared, tutting. "Why don't you do something about him, Westley Inferno? Clearly you hate each other."

"If I do anything to him Leticia will hurt me," Westley said weakly. "Besides, I know not how to kill Count Dracula. If I did, he would have been dead for at least ten years."

"My father killed *his* father," Malinda told him. "He knows how to kill Count Dracula. I could ask him of course, but that would be doing something for you with nothing in return."

"Please tell me," pleaded Westley. "I want Dracula gone for good!"

"I will give you what you need, in exchange for you giving me what *I* need also," Malinda told him, and Westley stared at her.

"What do you want?"

"I want Leticia of Sampson far away from Count Dracula."

"But if he'll be dead, why would she need to be far away from him?" asked Westley, perplexed. "That doesn't make sense, Malinda."

Malinda hesitated, and then Westley realised.

"You're trying to trick me."

Malinda sighed. "My love for Count Dracula never faded. Surely you can understand that?"

"You were going to give me false information while I got Leticia far away from him?! That's deceptiveness at the highest level!" spat Westley, and Malinda quickly said "Keep your voice down, Westley!"

"Get out," Westley said angrily. "Now!"

"But if you just listen to me!"

"I've done enough of listening to you and your rubbish," snarled Westley.

"I thought we were pretty much on the same page!"

"Well I've only spoken to you once before today," Malinda snapped back.

"How can we be on the same page?? We don't know each other!"

"Get out," spat Westley again. "And don't ever approach me again!"

"Fine," Malinda said angrily. "I will get Leticia of Sampson away from Dracula without your help!"

"Good luck!" Westley said furiously, and she stormed out of his room.

* * *

Jeiklee, Virginia and Spirit left Thrill, talking happily.

"Bye Spirit!" some people shouted happily, surprising Spirit, and she called bye back. People called goodbye to Jeiklee and Virginia too, and Jeiklee called bye while Virginia simply waved without stopping.

Spirit shook her head. "Virginia, they're being nice to me because of how popular you are."

"And how scary you are," Jeiklee added amusedly, and they laughed.

"I wish I could come back to yours," Virginia said wistfully. "But my father is really anxious about Miss Leticia."

"What? Why is Count Dracula anxious about Leticia?" asked Spirit curiously, and Virginia sighed "He doesn't want her to get sick of him. Even though she never has and probably never will. He's super scared."

"Aww! He doesn't have to be," Spirit said reassuringly, and Virginia replied "I know, I've told him so. But he really cares for Miss Leticia and he doesn't want to screw things up."

"That's really sweet," Spirit said, and she meant it too. "Can you tell him from me there's no need to worry? Make sure you tell him I said that!"

"Looks like *you* don't want to screw things up either," Jeiklee said amusedly as he put an arm around her, and Spirit smiled back, leaning into him as they walked.

"I really don't. Plus Leticia would never forgive me if I did a Westley and started wiling out. I like Count Dracula, Jeiklee. I was a cow about him before, but now-"

"Now you want to get to know him and be in his good books," Virginia said lazily. "We know."

"Now I know he's not what everyone made him out to be," Spirit corrected amusedly, and Jeiklee and Virginia smiled. "I never knew he was so kind and caring."

"Well, he has built a wall of defence up that's hard to break down," shrugged Virginia. "People are changing their mind about my father, but that doesn't mean he's just going to accept their new found kindness and fondness of him after years and years of hatred and insults just like that."

"I wouldn't accept it just like that either," Jeiklee said, and Spirit nodded. "My dad is a great example of how ignorant the people of Severna are when it comes to Count Dracula."

"We should visit him," Spirit said, and they looked at her. "I know Leticia wants nothing to do with him, but he's your dad, Jeiklee. And the closest to a father I've had since I lost mine."

Jeiklee sighed. "Fine. Let's go to the hospital."

"I'll go home," Virginia said, and they nodded. "I'll see you at Thrill tomorrow."

Jeiklee and Spirit bade her goodbye, Spirit taking Jeiklee's hand.

"We should tell Leticia we're going to visit him, so she doesn't worry."

"Mum's psychic, Spirit. She probably will wonder and then instantly know where we are, just like she knew we were dating," Jeiklee said a little admiringly. "She's just awesome."

Spirit nodded. "She definitely is."

* * *

"Count Inferno?"

Westley snapped awake. "Yes?"

"Your son and Spirit McKenzie have come to see you."

Westley sat up instantly, but slowly and weakly as Jeiklee and Spirit entered his hospital room.

"Dad," said Jeiklee, a little stonily, and Spirit said "Westley, how are you?"

"I… I'm fine, Spirit." Westley's throat had gone a little dry as he noticed a glimmer of something bright red through the blinds of his bedroom window. "Um… I don't want to sound rude, both of you, but this really isn't a good time to visit."

"You're kidding." Jeiklee scowled at him. "We just paid twelve Vernons for a Luma Carriage to bring us here!"

Malinda of Brubeck was watching them, invisible now, but Westley knew she was somewhere in the room.

"I'm sorry, but you have to go. Unless you're here to tell me Leticia isn't having anything more to do with Count Dracula, I don't want to be disturbed."

"We're your kids, Westley!" Spirit said angrily. "Leticia dumping you isn't the cause of the world coming to the end, you know! And it was all *your* fault anyway! Are you still affected by the Horror Curse? Is that why you're saying this? Don't you care about me and Jeiklee anymore??"

"You know I do. But the two of you aren't at the top of my priority list right now," Westley said, and they gaped at him. "I just need my wife back. No matter what it takes, Leticia will be mine again. And Count Dracula will die at my hands!"

"Westley, you've gone nuts over this Count Dracula thing! Please come back to your senses," pleaded Spirit, and Jeiklee said "We're wasting our time, Spirit. Let's go."

"Wait," said Spirit firmly, and she turned back to Westley. "So because Leticia's back in contact with Count Dracula, you'll ruin your life and disrupt the lives of the ones you love? That's ridiculous, Westley!"

"You don't understand. I won't let Count Dracula ruin our marriage-"

"You ruined your marriage yourself!" spat Jeiklee. "You're the one who freaked out and went nuts, not Mum! You didn't even know for certain she was back in contact with him, and you made a law against her anyway! How could you do that to her, Dad?! She gave you everything like she said!"

"Everything but her heart! She said that too!"

"Well I don't bloody blame her!" said Jeiklee irately. "You're just a-"

"A what!"

Jeiklee took a deep breath, then he said more calmly "Mum told me not to disrespect you so I'm going to try my best not to. But this obsession with her isn't cool, ok? She doesn't want anything to do with you, Dad. Just accept that and leave her alone."

"Never! We were solid," Westley said angrily, and he felt someone standing by his side. Knowing it was Malinda of Brubeck, he added "I will get her back no matter what she wants or how I do it. Now leave, both of you. I want to be alone."

Spirit shook her head, saying "Come on Jeiklee. We're wasting our time."

"There was a time when you cared about your kids," Jeiklee said to his father angrily. "When you cared about *me*. So you're saying you don't care about us anymore? All you care about is Mum?"

"Look," said Westley impatiently, "I'm not in the mood for this. I'm expecting a visitor and both of you yapping in my ear about how I went wrong is not helping. I'm not in a good place right now, and I need both of you to keep away."

"But why?"

"Because I need to figure out a way to win Leticia's heart."

Jeiklee and Spirit both scowled at him, Spirit saying "Fine. Just know this isn't cool and it's not like you. Whatever you meant by 'I will get her back no matter what she wants or how I do it', it doesn't sound good at all. If you're planning something crazy-"

"Spirit, just go. Take Jeiklee and go." Westley leant back against his pillows and closed his eyes. "What I'm planning- *if* I'm planning anything, should I say, isn't you or Jeiklee's concern."

"You know what? I'm done," said Jeiklee. "When you're ready to stop obsessing over Mum and Count Dracula and be a proper father again, by all means contact me. Until then, I'm keeping away! Come on Spirit, let's go."

Jeiklee walked out of Westley's room without another word, and Spirit looked at Westley sadly.

"Just know that all of this happened because of you," she said quietly, and she left the room before Westley could reply.

Malinda of Brubeck appeared, looking amused. "What sweet children."

"I thought I told you to keep away?" Westley replied, and Malinda said "I thought about what you said. I won't lie to you anymore, Westley, because I realised we actually *are* on the same page. I have a Love Potion," she added, when he opened his mouth to interrupt, "And I'm going to use it on Count Dracula. Leticia of Sampson may be too powerful to be deceived with something like this, but I'm sure Count Dracula isn't. If we can get him to drink it-"

"No. I want Leticia to drink it. You can win Count Dracula back easily but it's not the same for me and Leticia," Westley told her. "And I don't want her hurting. I want him to hurt when he sees Leticia has chosen me over him. He will most likely fall into a deep depression. Then, I take his life."

"You still want to take his life?" Malinda said exasperatedly. "This potion is very strong and lasts a month with each dose. All you have to do is take this bottle and add a drop to whatever she drinks. One drop, do you understand me?" Westley nodded. "Good. I was lucky to find the potion in my father's secret lab. He is very good with potions, as everyone knows."

"So what's the plan?" asked Westley. "We get Leticia to drink the potion?"

"Yes. And also you must keep her away from Count Dracula until I win him back."

"Well… why don't you use the potion on Dracula too?" asked Westley curiously. "He won't take you back after everything."

"I believe he might after he sees that Leticia is back with you. But if he doesn't," she said thoughtfully, "Then I will definitely use the potion too. I can go back to my father's lab and take another bottle for myself."

"This is wrong," Westley said, more to himself than to Malinda, and she rolled her eyes. "If they find out I've done this, I will lose my family forever-"

"And that is why they will never find out. Keep your mouth shut, Westley Inferno."

"Fine," sighed Westley. "Are we done?"

"Yes. When will you be discharged from the hospital?"

"In four days."

"Ok," Malinda said. "I will meet you in the Forest of Fear by the stump of what was Bari the Tree, in seven days exactly, after sunset. Don't be late."

"I won't."

Malinda vanished, and Westley sighed.

"All of this just to be with the ones we love."

* * *

Jeiklee was annoyed as he picked at his dinner.

Leticia looked at him. "Jeiklee? What's wrong? Did something happen at Thrill?"

"No Mum. Something happened after Thrill."

"We went to see Westley, Leticia, and he was being a jerk," Spirit said, shaking her head. "He said we're not at the top of his priority list."

"What?" Leticia said disbelievingly. "You're our children!"

"Well all he cares about is killing Dracula and getting you back," Jeiklee said angrily. "Mum, something changed in him. He's not the same guy I was in awe of and had total respect for. He's obsessed with you and Dracula, and I'm staring to dislike him a lot."

Leticia was frowning. "Malinda of Brubeck was in contact with him."

"What?" said Spirit disbelievingly. "Why would she visit Westley??"

"She tried to convince him to use a love spell or potion on me," Leticia said, "But I curbed Westley's thoughts about that by telling him what I would do if he ever tried."

"So… what now, Leticia?" asked Spirit. "Do you think Malinda will visit him again?"

"I'm not sure, sweetheart. But I sense trouble. Count Dracula did too."

"What should we do, Mum?" asked Jeiklee. "Is there anything we can do to help?"

"No, sweetie. Just focus on your studies, have fun with your friends, and enjoy life. I don't want you worrying. Either of you," Leticia added, and Jeiklee and Spirit nodded. "I don't believe Westley is stupid enough to let Malinda convince him to get me in that way."

"But what if he is?" said Spirit worriedly. "The state he was in, it seemed like he'd try just about *anything* to get you back."

"If he is, he will feel my wrath times ten. I will be beyond furious," Leticia said, and they swallowed. "But I don't think he is that stupid, both of you. Eat up."

Jeiklee and Spirit obeyed.

* * *

One week later…

Virginia invited Jeiklee and Spirit to Castle Dracula after Thrill. Jeiklee asked her to come home quickly with him first so he could ask his mother, and Virginia said ok. Spirit declined, saying she wanted to have a quiet evening after she went on a walk, and they said ok to that as well.

When they got home, Leticia said it was perfectly fine for Jeiklee to go to Castle Dracula, as long as he wasn't home late. Excited, Jeiklee and Virginia left.

"I asked Father if you could come today, as I was going to invite you. He said it's perfectly fine," Virginia said happily as they walked. "You're the first friend of mine ever to come home with me."

"That's great. It makes it extra special," smiled Jeiklee, and she smiled back. "Could Count Dracula show me around? It is his castle, after all. I bet he has secret exits and allsorts."

"You could ask him," smiled Virginia. "I doubt he'll say no."

"Jeiklee."

Jeiklee and Virginia whipped round, startled. Westley Inferno was right behind them.

"Dad!"

"Where are you going with Virginia of Dracula?" Westley asked, in a voice of deadly calm, and Jeiklee replied "Er… she's going to introduce me to some of the trees that are alive. Deep in the forest."

"And your mother knows about this?"

"Yes," said Jeiklee flatly. "Unlike you, she's cool about me hanging out with Virginia."

"Fine," said Westley, and Virginia said "Let's go, Jeiklee."

Jeiklee nodded, both of them turning to walk away, and Westley said "Jeiklee."

"Yes??"

"I… tell your mother I will pass by on Sunday."

"Ok, fine. See you later," Jeiklee said flatly, and he and Virginia walked away. Westley sighed, and he made his way in the opposite direction.

"What is he doing in the Forest of Fear?" Virginia said curiously ten minutes later, and Jeiklee replied "I have no idea. He's not hunting. He would have his men with him if he were."

"Oh," said Virginia. "Should we stick around and find out what he's up to?"

"Nah. I want to see Count Dracula's castle."

* * *

Malinda smiled at Westley. "Tonight is the night I go to Castle Dracula."

"I saw my son with your daughter," Westley told her, and she replied "I care not for that child of mine. I just want Count Dracula."

"But if you rekindle your relationship with him, you will have to come into contact with her at some point," Westley said reasonably. "They come as a package."

"They come as no such thing. And when I have Count Dracula under my control, the first thing I will do is throw her out."

A gasp went up and they whipped round, Malinda snapping "Who's there?" Spirit stayed hidden, scared. She didn't say anything, trying to keep as still as possible. Malinda's eyes roamed the trees, but she didn't have super vision or senses like Leticia.

Shrugging, Westley said "It could have been the wind or a tree. Don't worry, Malinda."

"I am not worrying at all. Now here. Take this," she said, handing him a box with an envelope. "If all fails, post this letter."

"What is in it?"

"A spell," she told him. "But like I said, don't use it right away. Try your other methods first. Inside this box is a bottle of what we discussed at the hospital, and a cake. If all fails, hand them the letter. Make sure it doesn't fall into the wrong hands."

Spirit frowned, wondering what they were talking about. She kept listening as Westley asked "You're sure this will work, Malinda?"

"I'm certain. Now you have a cake, that bottle, and the letter. Meaning you have three attempts, Westley Inferno, so you'd better not mess this up. I have to go."

Malinda turned and walked away, her bright red hair glimmering. Westley hesitated, then he called "Malinda!"

She looked back, eyes glowing scarlet. "Yes?"

"I… thank you," Westley said, and she nodded and vanished.

Westley smiled a little before he turned and walked in the opposite direction, past Spirit, who had a hand to her mouth. She didn't dare move again until Westley was just a dot in the distance, then she breathed out.

She didn't know what the hell that was about, but she was going straight home to Leticia so she could tell her what she saw.

* * *

"And this is the ballroom," smiled Dracula, Jeiklee exclaiming "It's huge! When do you have balls, sir?"

"Normally every six months. All of the villains, minions, monsters etcetera come to the ball from all across the land. The Monster's Ball is quite something," smiled Dracula, "And one is due at the end of the month. I leave the organising to Nancy and my minions, of course. All I have to do is make sure everything is in order before the event."

"Wow," said Jeiklee amazedly. "Can I come, sir?"

"It's not something I'd give permission to without consulting your parents, Jeiklee."

"Mum would say yes," said Jeiklee quickly. "Especially if you invited her too!"

"Leticia of Sampson has never come to Count Dracula's Ball. Any of them," a voice said, and they turned and saw Nancy, who was smiling at Jeiklee. "She often said as a teenager and adult she would love to come to one. Do you remember, sir? She said her mother would have her head if she ever attended one."

Dracula burst out laughing, Jeiklee smiling as he said "Yes, I remember. She got busted big time when she snuck out to come to one."

"I love hearing these stories about my mother," said Jeiklee happily, as they heard a bell chime through the castle. "What's that??"

"It's time for dinner," smiled Dracula. "I hope the chef has made something special for our guest. You did tell him we had a guest, Nancy?"

"I did sir."

"Come along Virginia and Jeiklee," said Dracula, and they obeyed, following him down the corridor. "Dinner is waiting."

"It smells delicious," smiled Jeiklee, and Virginia said "It definitely is. I just *love* frog tongue and snake eye soup."

Jeiklee stopped dead. "What??"

Dracula and Nancy burst out laughing, Virginia as well.

"She's joking, Jeiklee. Don't look so frightened," laughed Dracula, and Jeiklee laughed as well, relieved. "And Virginia, don't scare him away. I would like Jeiklee to come again."

"You would sir?" said Jeiklee, touched. "Thank you!"

"You're welcome."

* * *

"Leticia!" cried Spirit, running through the doors. *"Leticia!"*
Leticia appeared, startled. "Spirit? What's wrong?"
"Malinda of Brubeck and Westley," gasped Spirit. "They were in the Forest of Fear and she gave him a box!"
"A box?" repeated Leticia. "She hit Westley?"
"No, she-" Spirit paused, wanting to laugh when she realised how that must have sounded, but this was serious. "A cardboard box!"
"A cardboard box containing what?"
"I don't know what was inside, but she said- she said-"
"What did she say?" frowned Leticia, looking like she was thinking hard already. "Talk to me, Spirit."
"She said he had three attempts at something," panted Spirit. "They heard me, I was so scared! I stayed still and silent- I think they're planning to do something, Leticia! What if she wants to kill the King?"
Leticia blinked. "Kill the King? Did they mention that, Spirit? Or is your imagination running away with you?"
"I don't know, they didn't say it. But whatever it is, it's dodgy! Since when was Westley pals with Malinda of Brubeck?? She's evil!"
"I know she is. And I don't want you worrying about this, Spirit. Calm down and have a drink, then have dinner. You're very shaken up!"
Spirit nodded, holding her side. "I have a stitch. I ran all the way here! It was so scary seeing her, Leticia- I felt her dark energy! She's bad news and she might put Westley in danger!"
"Westley is a grown man, Spirit. Don't worry about him too much," Leticia told her, as reassuringly as she could. "As long as it has nothing to do with you or Jeiklee, it doesn't matter what they are planning."
Spirit nodded, taking deep breaths. "Are you sure?"
"I'm sure," smiled Leticia. "Now let's have some food."
Spirit nodded, seeming to calm down when she saw Leticia wasn't worried. Leticia put an arm around her as they walked to the dining area, her mind whirring.
As Spirit sat down to eat, Leticia's eyes began to glow.

* * *

Jeiklee and Virginia sat on the floor of Count Dracula's study, by the fire. Jeiklee didn't want to be away from Count Dracula, and so he invited the young man into his study to talk some more. Virginia stayed as well, listening to her father tell Jeiklee about the many adventures he got up to with Miss Leticia.

It was eight at night now, and dark out. Glancing at the time, Dracula said "Jeiklee, I will walk you back home. It is night time now in the Forest of Fear, and many creatures have arisen from their slumber. You will be fine if with me, but I cannot guarantee your safety if you want to go home alone."

"That's fine sir. I'll walk with you," smiled Jeiklee. "Thank you."

Just then they heard a bell sound throughout the castle, and Virginia frowned.

"Who would be visiting at this time?"

"Maybe my minions," Dracula replied curiously, and they jumped as Nancy pounded his study door frantically five minutes later.

"My Lord!!"

"Yes Nancy? What's the matter?"

"It's her, sir- she's here!"

"Who is?" frowned Dracula, standing up. "Who's here? Enter!"

Nancy obeyed, entering the study with the being who arrived, and Jeiklee gasped "Malinda of Brubeck!"

Dracula's jaw dropped as Virginia leapt up, screaming *"Ricato!"*

BANG!!

Malinda lazily blocked the hex with a smirk, saying "Try again, little girl." *"Mordzmorda!!"*

That wiped the smile off Malinda's face as the spell rushed for her; she vanished quickly, reappearing by the fireplace as it blasted the wall.

"If I retaliate you will get hurt badly!" she spat, and Jeiklee grabbed Virginia as she was about to fire a third hex at her mother.

"Virginia, stop!"

"Get off me, Jeiklee!"

"Just calm down!" said Jeiklee desperately, restraining her as she struggled, then she screamed *"Get off me!!"*

"No!"

Malinda of Brubeck looked amused at how agitated her daughter was getting, turning to Count Dracula instead as he stared at her disbelievingly.

"Count Dracula. How have you been?"

"How has he *been?!*" said Virginia furiously. "He's been great without *you!*"

Dracula was just as furious; Malinda chose not to answer Virginia as he spat "You turn up after eighteen years and you ask how I have been as if you were away for a month?!"

"I can explain!"

"I don't think you can!"

"At least hear me out, Dracula!"

"No!"

"Get out! Now!!" screamed Virginia, and Leticia appeared, shocked. "What on earth is going on??"

"Leticia," breathed Dracula, and Malinda looked at him curiously, noticing the look on his face and his tone of voice as he looked at Leticia. "What brings you here?"

"I was coming to collect Jeiklee," Leticia replied. "Night has fallen and he has to walk through the Forest of Fear to get back home. I wasn't going to allow him to walk through there on his own after nightfall."

"I would have escorted him," Dracula started, and Leticia said "You have your hands full at the moment, Dracula. But thank you all the same."

Dracula nodded, remembering Malinda. "May you take Virginia also, Leticia? I have a lot to deal with and I don't want any more hexes fired. She needs to calm down, and the sight of Malinda is aggravating her."

Virginia was still struggling in Jeiklee's arms.

"I wouldn't ask if I wasn't desperate," Dracula added a little pleadingly. "Please, Leticia. For me?"

Leticia nodded. "Of course."

"Good," Malinda said icily. "Take the beast. I won't be so lenient the next time she tries to attack me."

"How dare you," snarled Dracula, eyes lighting scarlet. "You haven't seen your daughter in eighteen years and that is how you speak of her?"

"I call it how I see it," snapped Malinda, glaring back at him. "I thought she was a nasty little beast when she was born and I think the same now."

"Virginia is not a beast," Leticia said quietly, and Malinda looked at her.

"No? Then tell me what you think she is, Leticia of Sampson."

"She is a troubled girl who grew up without a mother's love or attention," Leticia said calmly. "All Virginia had was her father, and he did an amazing job raising her on his own with Nancy to help. She loves Dracula to death. Virginia fell off the steady track when she was fifteen, but she is doing ok now. All she wanted was motherly love, and you haven't been there. She told me in private when she stayed at my home she had no idea how it felt to have a real mother and after eighteen years she may as well not have one."

"I don't need a mother," spat Virginia as she glared at Malinda, and Malinda coldly replied "That suits me fine because I don't need a daughter.

Another eighteen years without a brat like you in my life will suit me just fine."

"How can you say that?" Leticia said amazedly, Dracula beyond furious. "I missed eighteen years of being with my son and the pain of losing him never went away. It was terrible. I lost my child and I was powerless to get him back until now. And you stand there bold as anything and imply you don't care about your child? At all? Something must be terribly wrong with you, Malinda of Brubeck, to feel this way about your daughter."

"I am a vampire. What do you expect," shrugged Malinda, and Leticia said icily "That is a very poor excuse. Many vampires love their children and would do anything for them. Count Dracula is King of all Evil yet he loves his daughter with all his heart."

"And I love my father," hissed Virginia, glowing scarlet now. "Count Dracula is worth more than a billion of you!"

"My heart bleeds," Malinda said coldly. "I came to see your father, little girl. Go with Leticia of Sampson and her son before I lose my cool. You are starting to irritate me."

"Go now, Virginia," Dracula said gently, Virginia looking like she was about to explode. "I will collect you tomorrow."

"Come with me," Leticia said just as gently. "Release her, Jeiklee."

Jeiklee obeyed, Leticia holding an arm out. Virginia gladly fell into her embrace, taking a shaky breath as her eyes filled over.

"I will contact you soon, Leticia," Dracula said softly, and Leticia said ok. "If you need anything before then-"

"I will be fine," Leticia said just as softly, and Malinda raised a curious eyebrow as she looked at Dracula's face. "Come, Jeiklee."

She led Virginia out of the room, Jeiklee following after saying goodbye to Dracula. He said nothing to Malinda, closing the study door behind him. Malinda glanced at Dracula before she said "I see your feelings for Leticia of Sampson have not wavered or changed over the years."

"That is not your concern," Dracula replied coldly. "What do you want if nothing to do with Virginia?"

"I have come to ask your forgiveness."

"For what? Abandoning our child?" Dracula said dryly, but Malinda said no.

"For leaving you. I was to become a Bride of Dracula, have you forgotten?" Malinda sighed, Dracula glaring at her. "My father wouldn't allow me to be with you. He said he didn't want his daughter to be second best to anyone."

"What point are you trying to make, Malinda?" Dracula said roughly. "I have better things to do than listen to your tales of woe."

"I have been pleading with my father for the past three years to let me come to you," Malinda told him quietly, and he said "What is your point? Where are you going with this?"

"Dracula-"

"Just skip to the point, Malinda, and make it quick."

Malinda took a deep breath, then she quietly said "I humbly request to become your Bride."

Dracula stared at her. "I'm sorry?"

"You want me to repeat it?" asked Malinda, then she stepped back as Dracula's body erupted in a burst of scarlet light. "What's wrong??"

"Please tell me this is a joke," spat Dracula as he started pacing his study, his body so hot with rage the floor was hissing and steaming under his feet. "You turn up after eighteen years and hardly look at the daughter you abandoned, and you tell me you want to become a Bride of Dracula?!"

"Well wasn't I to become one?" demanded Malinda, heat rising. "If it wasn't for our fathers falling out I would have been a Bride- don't deny it! But you didn't love me to begin with, did you Count Dracula?"

"What are you talking about now?!"

"I'm talking about Leticia of Sampson," spat Malinda, and he stared at her. "My father told me everything after he got rid of yours. You never would have loved me and if you did, never as strongly as you love her."

"So why are you pining to become my Bride if you feel that way?" Dracula snapped back. "And also if you have no interest whatsoever in our daughter?"

"Because becoming a Bride of Dracula will make me a Queen of Evil as you are King," Malinda said flatly. "I would receive powers I have only dreamt of having. We would rule the Darkness together, Dracula, as we should have all along." She stepped closer to him despite the fury she saw etched across his face. "Wouldn't you enjoy having a Bride at last?"

"You make me sick," Dracula replied coldly. "Leave my castle at once, Malinda, and don't you dare return."

"But-"

"But what!"

"Can we at least have a drink together?" asked Malinda innocently as she reached into her pocket, and he laughed derisively.

"So you can drug me with the Love Potion you took from your father's lab?"

"I- what?" her eyes widened in shock before turning scarlet with rage. "How do you know of my plans?!"

"I rule the Darkness like you said, Malinda." Dracula smiled at her before he dissolved into nothing, Malinda looking around wildly, but she couldn't see him anywhere. *Even the wind* can give me information just like it can Leticia of Sampson. I know you and Westley have been making plans to get Leticia and I away from each other. *We both know.* I have told her everything I found out today, telepathically, and Leticia did the same vice versa. She knows it all, as do I. Now do the honorable thing and leave my castle. And never show your face here again."

Malinda was in a state of shock. "You- you-"

"Leticia and I are a powerful team when put together, Malinda." Dracula's voice swirled around her in an ice cold breeze, her red hair ruffling a little as he spoke. "There is no plan against us you could ever put together without us knowing. Leticia suspected you from the moment you visited Westley at the hospital for the first time. She even went back in time today to witness your little meeting together in the Forest. She went to Westley's mansion invisible and vanquished the cake, potion and letter. So I suggest you give up. I do not want you back and I will not stop seeing Leticia. Leticia does not want Westley back and she will not stop seeing me. Now are we done?"

"I- we are done." Malinda was frightened now. "I had no clue Leticia of Sampson was able to do such magic!"

"She has the power of the Force, yes. You didn't know?" Dracula was smirking now, still invisible. "If I wanted, I could easily convince her to get rid of you."

"Leticia of Sampson has no dark side. She doesn't have it in her!" spat Malinda as she felt in her pocket for the bottle- it was gone. "What??"

"Ah, Leticia must have vanquished your potion too. Just now," Dracula added amusedly. "Actually Malinda, Leticia *does* have a dark side. And once unleashed, whoever crosses her will pay the price. And the price is *very* expensive."

"I'm getting out of here." Very frightened now, Malinda turned and ran to the study door, but it slammed shut and locked itself. "Dracula! Let me out!"

"I will let you out on one condition. You return to wherever you have been residing for the past eighteen years," Dracula said icily. "You do not ever come back to this part of the land again- ever. I want nothing to do with you, and you want nothing to do with our daughter. So there is no reason to return. You will never become my Bride. Do you understand?"

"Yes," Malinda said eyes filling. "I won't come back. I'll never come back."

"Good. Now leave," Dracula said coldly, and Malinda turned to leave, tears falling as the feel of total rejection hit her hard. Nancy was shocked to see Malinda of Brubeck crying like a little girl whose puppy was put down.

"I- sir? Is everything ok?"

Dracula reappeared, saying "Everything is fine, Nancy. See Malinda out."

"Yes sir."

Malinda turned to look at him, face wet with tears, and she spat "You are *nothing* like the Count Draculas before you! The first Count Dracula was practically the Devil himself! Totally evil!"

"Well I am Count Dracula the Fifteenth, Malinda. And I don't think my ancestors would have a problem with the way I am." Dracula sat down in his chair. "Now leave."

Malinda stormed away, Nancy closing Dracula's study door before she jogged after her.

Dracula smiled. "It is now over."

* * *

Leticia smiled, and Jeiklee, Spirit and Virginia looked at her.

"Mum? What is it?" asked Jeiklee, and Leticia replied "Malinda has gone. She won't be returning to this part of Severna again. Count Dracula and I made sure of it."

"But you were right here with us," Spirit said, amazed and confused. "What did you do, Leticia?"

"What did I and *Count Dracula* do, Spirit. We fixed everything. There is nothing to worry about anymore. Malinda has gone and she won't be meeting with Westley again. I vanquished the box she gave him and also the items she had on her."

"What were they, Miss Leticia?" asked Virginia curiously, and Leticia opened her mouth, then closed it.

"Maybe it's better you don't know. I don't want you angry, the three of you."

"Come on, Mum! Tell us," pleaded Jeiklee. "Please?"

Leticia sighed her ok. "Malinda and Westley had a plan to give me a Love Potion so I would get back with him, and she would get back with Count Dracula. Westley doubted the potion would work on me so she also gave him a drugged cake and powerful spell contained in an envelope if the cake and potion failed."

Jeiklee, Spirit and Virginia's mouths hung open. Leticia sighed, and she continued "Westley told Malinda to use the potion on Count Dracula also, because he probably wouldn't take her back after everything. They both seemed to think it was a great plan, and didn't count on us finding out before they could put it into action. Well we did find out, and it shocked Malinda. She never knew I had the power of the Force and that made her very afraid. She left without much of a fuss and will not return. I will make sure of it. Now that it's all over, there's still the matter of what to do about Westley."

"Punish him," said Spirit angrily. "How could he plan something so evil?!"

"I agree with Spirit," Jeiklee said just as angrily. "He's cruel!"

"If my mother forced my father to be with her, she never would have let me remain in his life," Virginia said angrily, and Spirit said "She said she would throw you out once he was hers, Virginia."

"What!"

"When I saw them," Spirit said, shaking her head. "She said that to Westley."

"I could kill her!"

"No you couldn't, Virginia," Leticia said soothingly. "Don't let darkness overrule you. Your father and I have dealt with Malinda. You don't have anything to be angry over now that she's gone and won't return."

Virginia released a deep breath. "Yes Miss Leticia."

Leticia smiled at the three teenagers, loving them all so much. Standing, she said "All of you get ready for bed. You have college tomorrow."

"Yes Mum," Jeiklee said, standing. "Spirit, Virginia, meet you back here in half an hour for a hot drink."

"Ok," they said with a smile, and Leticia smiled too as she watched them go up the stairs, thinking that they were a great trio.

* * *

"Malinda!" hissed Westley, and she turned. "Where are you going?!"

"I'm leaving."

They were at the lake, Malinda about to step into the boat she arrived in.

"Leaving?" Westley repeated, and she said yes. "Why? Didn't the plan work? I thought you were going to give Dracula the potion?"

"I failed miserably. And all because of *you,*" Malinda said angrily, eyes filling up, Westley startled.

"What did *I* do??"

"You withheld information about Leticia of Sampson's power!"

Westley was confused.

Leticia and Count Dracula watched them, invisible as he demanded "What do you mean?"

"Leticia of Sampson is all powerful!" spat Malinda, and he said "Everybody knows that, Malinda! She's the most powerful being in Severna after her father!"

"And you didn't think to tell me she was the most powerful being in Severna?" Malinda said furiously. "That information could have been very useful had you told me when we were plotting against her, Westley Inferno!"

"What happened?"

"She and Count Dracula knew of our plans!" Malinda nearly screamed the words, Westley startled. "She knew all along and she informed Dracula of everything! They were talking telepathically and she went back in time, and she took Count Dracula with her! They knew it all, Westley, and Dracula laughed me away! Never have I been so scared and embarrassed in all my life! Now get out of my way!"

Westley stepped away, defeated as the boat began to move. Then he called "You were my last hope, Malinda!"

"Well keep hoping," snapped Malinda, the lake water turning red, recognising an evil presence. "I was eventually honest with you about everything and you were not honest with me! You-"

A whale burst out of the water suddenly, making her scream as it came crashing down on her, and her boat splintered into many pieces.

"Malinda!" yelled Westley, but there was no answer. *"Malinda!!"*

The glowing red water turned turquoise again, and Westley gasped.

"No."

"Wow," said Dracula amazedly, and Leticia whispered "Is she… dead?"

"I believe she is," Dracula said quietly. "The water would have remained red as a living evil being was in it. Death is the only reason it would have changed. The evil being is there no longer."

"Oh my God. What are we going to tell Virginia?"

Dracula glanced at her, touched. "We?"

"Yes, silly. We," smiled Leticia. "We're a team. Lovers, partners, best friends. You don't have to go through anything alone anymore."

Dracula kissed her, slipping his arms around her and pulling her to him. Westley, shocked at what happened to Malinda, quickly turned and ran into the trees.

"I have to inform the police!"

"Should we inform them also?" murmured Leticia, Dracula running his hands through her hair seductively. "Because we... we did... witness..."

Dracula kissed her again, both of them tumbling to the ground. Unbuttoning Leticia's blouse, Dracula murmured "We will, but not now."

* * *

Leticia's hair was tousled.

She laid on the bank of the lake with Dracula, eyes closed. They were both breathing heavily, Leticia's head on Dracula's chest.

"I can't seem to get enough of you, Dracula."

"And I will never get enough of you, Leticia." Dracula dropped a kiss on her forehead. "We need to get dressed. The police will be here soon, and so will the press. We have to tell them what we saw also."

Leticia sighed. "Ok."

* * *

By midday the next day, the news of the death of Malinda of Brubeck was swirling around everyone, and nobody could stop talking about it at Thrill. "It was a freak accident," Spirit was saying to Jeiklee and Virginia, and they nodded. "I would say sorry for your loss, Virginia, but I know you don't care."

"I don't. At all," shrugged Virginia. "Malinda was nothing to me. I saw her for the first time for pretty much a split second and I felt nothing. She felt nothing too and she even called me a beast. I'm glad she's dead."

"My Mum and your Dad backed my Dad's story about the whale," Jeiklee said, sighing. "I was kind of hoping they would press charges against him about what he was planning with Malinda."

"Oh, he's not out of the fire yet," said Spirit flatly. "Leticia's going to get him about that. I know she is. Whatever she does to him, he deserves it! I can't believe Westley would be so cruel and stupid rolled into one."

* * *

Count Dracula sat with Leticia at her mansion, in her Chamber of Serenity. Sheets of blue and purple light swirled around them, Dracula saying "It is truly beautiful, Leticia. I could sleep in here for days."
"As could I," smiled Leticia. "I have done many times."
"And the air is very cool in here," smiled Dracula. "It's like we are underwater. Thank you for sharing the delights of your chamber with me, Leticia."
"You're welcome," smiled Leticia, and he kissed her.

* * *

It was night time.
Jeiklee, Virginia and Spirit sat in the lounge at Leticia's mansion with Count Dracula and Leticia, watching the news on the television. Brubeck the vampire, Malinda's father, was very agitated as he spoke with many mikes to his mouth.
"This is all because of Count Dracula," he said angrily, eyes glistening with angry tears. "I warned Malinda to stay away from him! I warned her! And now she's dead! My only blood relative, gone!"
"What about your granddaughter, sir? Virginia of Dracula?"
"I want nothing to do with that girl. She is nothing to me," spat Brubeck, and Virginia glared at the television. "I will have my revenge!"
"On who, sir?"
"They know who," said Virginia, annoyed. "Anything to liven the story!"
"On Count Dracula," spat Brubeck, and a voice shouted "Count Dracula is the wrong person to enact revenge on, Brubeck!"
Camera swirled around, Brubeck as well as he snapped "Who said that?"
"I did," a man said, stepping forwards, and Dracula said "It's Larry!"
"Who?" frowned Virginia, and Dracula said "I met him on the way here for dinner that first time after everything. He was very nice to me."
"Looks like he's defending you too," smiled Jeiklee, as Larry said "Count Dracula has done nothing wrong, Brubeck! If you want to get revenge, it should be on Westley Inferno!"
"Westley Inferno?" Brubeck repeated, livid. "What role does *he* play in all of this?!"
"He convinced Malinda to go to Count Dracula," the reporter said, an eyebrow raised. "Did you not listen to our backstory on the death of your daughter, sir?"
"I listened a little," scowled Brubeck. "I was mad with grief! Tell me again."

By the time the reporter and Larry stopped speaking, Brubeck was mad with rage as well as grief.

"Show me the way to Westley Inferno's mansion! I will have his head!!"

"And Larry has just opened a can of worms," sighed Dracula. "Leticia, what shall we do?"

"Nothing," shrugged Leticia, and they gaped at her. "I was going to have my own revenge on Westley but it seems more fitting to let Brubeck do what he has to do. As long as he doesn't kill him, I'm not involving myself. Westley deserves everything that vampire throws at him."

* * *

Brubeck stormed towards the entrance of Westley's mansion, the press running after him excitedly, filming away.

"WESTLEY INFERNO!!" bellowed Brubeck. "COME OUT AND FACE ME!!"

"George, tell him I'm not here," hissed Westley, and George said "You want me to go out and face *that??* No way!"

"George, you serve me. Take the order without a fuss!"

"I'm also your best friend and I'm not dying for you," George retorted, as Brubeck roared for Westley again. "Go and face him! Explain what happened and-"

"If you do not come out, I will come in!" shouted Brubeck, eyes glowing scarlet, and Westley called "I'll be out in a minute! George, please- he doesn't know what I look like. He knows Leticia and Count Dracula, not me- just pretend you're me and go to him!"

"Are you that much of a coward?" George said angrily. "This is *your* mess!"

Westley grabbed George's arm and propelled him towards the exit of the mansion, saying "I may be a coward but I'm a smart coward! Now go!"

He pushed George out of the doors before George could say anything else, George tumbling onto the grass.

* * *

"It's George!" said Spirit in shock, and Count Dracula said "Westley Inferno is the biggest coward in Severna. He's making George pretend to be him!"

"What??" said Virginia amazedly. "Doesn't Brubeck know that-"

"Brubeck knows of myself and Leticia, but not Leticia's partner," Dracula said, shaking his head. "Westley knows that and he's using that fact to his advantage."

"Ex-partner," Leticia corrected softly, and Dracula smiled at her. Leticia smiled back, and Spirit said "You know what, Leticia? I'm just going to come right out and ask if-"

"Shh!" said Jeiklee, when George unsteadily got to his feet. "I want to see what George is going to do!"

"Are you Westley Inferno?" spat Brubeck, and he vanished and reappeared in front of George, startling him as he grabbed poor George by the collar. "Are you?!"

"I- I-" George swallowed, looking back at something or someone. Jeiklee peered at the screen, then he said "Dad's watching! I can see him!"

"Well?" said Brubeck angrily. "Speak now before I rip your tongue out!"

George took a deep breath, then he clearly said "I am Westley Inferno."

Gasps went up, on screen and in the lounge, and Spirit said "I don't believe it! Westley really *is* a coward! Brubeck's going to kill George!"

"We have to help him," Leticia said, looking at Dracula, but before Dracula could reply Brubeck yelled *"Mordzmorda!!"*

BANG!!

George slammed onto the grass, sliding through the flowers and stopping just before he crashed into the walls of the mansion.

"Oh my God," gasped Spirit. "Leticia, he won't be able to move much! Brubeck hit him with a Fire Bone Hex-"

"Ricato!!"

BANG!!

"And a Burn Hex," Jeiklee said amazedly, George's skin erupting in bright red patches all over as he gasped "Please- you don't understand-"

"I understand my daughter is dead!!" roared Brubeck, storming towards him in heavy black boots, and George tried to back on his hands and knees, but he was too weak. Brubeck placed a foot on his chest and pressed down hard, George gasping "It wasn't Westley's- er, my fault! It was an accident-"

"Paralisia!!"

George's body went limp, Jeiklee gasping "What spell did he just use??"

"He paralysed George," Dracula said quietly, and Brubeck conjured an axe. "What the-!!"

"Now, I take your head!" shouted Brubeck as he raised the axe- Spirit screamed and so did the crowd; Jeiklee and Virginia gasped as Brubeck brought the axe down, and Leticia appeared in front of George, crying *"Stop!"*

Brubeck gasped and froze just as the axe was about to collide with Leticia's forehead, Dracula looking around disbelievingly.

"When did Leticia leave??"

"No idea," said Jeiklee amazedly, eyes on the screen, and Dracula stood, saying "I have to go to her!"

"Go to her if she needs you, Father!" said Virginia. "That man knows how to kill you!"

"Leticia of Sampson," Brubeck said angrily. "Get out of my way! There's no need to protect this filth whether you are together or not!"

"Brubeck, I know you're hurting," said Leticia desperately. "But it was an accident!"

"It was no accident! Malinda has crossed the lake plenty of times and nothing out of the ordinary has ever happened! This poisonous man put stupid ideas into her head, ideas that were dark! That animal was defending the lake from evil! That's what happened," Brubeck said angrily. "It was *him-"*

He spat at George's feet, George unconscious now.

"He filled her head with hopes and dreams of getting back with Count Dracula in a ghastly way! My daughter never stole from me, ever! She stole two bottles of a very strong Love Potion from my lab! Malinda would *never* have done that had it not been for your husband here, Leticia!" Brubeck backed two steps, holding his axe angrily. "I want his head on my wall!"

Leticia took a deep breath, saying "Ex-husband to be precise. And you attacked the wrong man, Brubeck. This man laying almost dead, George, is Westley's friend and servant. He was never my husband."

Gasps went up, Brubeck gaping at her. "This is not Westley Inferno?!"

"No."

Cameras clicked as Brubeck turned to the crowd furiously. "None of you could have called that out when this man lied and said he was Westley?! You all just *watched??* What kind of people are you?!"

"Call an ambulance please," Leticia added when everyone hesitated fearfully, and talk broke out, Brubeck shouting "Westley Inferno!! I know you can hear me, you weak man! You are nothing but a *coward!! Come out and face me!"*

"No!"

"WHAT!!"

"I won't face you!" shouted Westley from somewhere, and Brubeck looked around angrily. "Malinda dying wasn't my fault! She was *always* evil! She murdered before she even came to me for the first time, Brubeck! She was far from the angel you think she was!"

"Come out and fight like a man, you overgrown weasel!!"

"Brubeck, please calm down," said Leticia, pleading with him now as paramedics rushed towards George's limp body. "This isn't going to solve anything and it won't bring Malinda back."

"It may not bring Malinda back but I will avenge her!" spat Brubeck, and Westley suddenly bolted, startling them as he rushed for the Magenta Birds's paddock.

"Ricato!!" yelled Brubeck- BANG!!

He missed Westley by a few inches, Westley running as fast as his legs could carry him.

"Mordzmorda!!"

BANG!!

Westley dived for the ground and rolled, the hex whooshing over his head. "He's a fast coward," commented Dracula, everyone watching the screen amazedly, and Jeiklee said "He's heading for the chariot!"

The Magenta Birds screeched as Westley ran towards them, Brubeck right behind him.

"It's me, it's your owner," said Westley desperately as he climbed into the chariot, when the giant birds stared down at him fiercely. "Please, fly! As high as possible and far away from here!"

The birds did nothing, Westley repeating himself. "Fly!!"

"They won't obey him," Spirit said, shaking her head. "Westley never bonded with the Magenta Birds. Leticia loved them and they love her."

"Step down from that chariot before I blow it to smithereens!" shouted Brubeck, Leticia calmly walking behind him.

"Leticia, please- stop him!" said Westley desperately. "Please! For me! If you ever felt anything for me, you'd help me!"

"You can go to Hell for all I care," Leticia said flatly, and his jaw dropped in shock. "Those are *my* birds and they won't obey you, Westley. Get out of the chariot."

"I won't! They just need coaxing, that's all-" Westley was super desperate and frightened now. "Fly, you stupid fire birds! Obey your master!"

One of the birds pecked at the ground lazily, and Westley conjured a whip.

"Don't you dare hurt my birds, Westley!" said Leticia angrily, but Westley ignored her as he raised the whip.

"I *said,* FLY!!"

CRACK!!

The Magenta Birds screeched angrily and suddenly took flight, zooming high into the air, Westley yelling "Yes! Now take me as far away as possible!"

"You won't get away with this!" yelled Brubeck, and Westley shouted "I just have!"

Brubeck turned to Leticia. "Please, bring him back to me."

"I will if you promise you won't murder him."

"Oh, I won't. I promise you that Leticia," Brubeck said furiously. "Death is the easy option. There are fates so much worse!"

Leticia raised her hands and stepped forwards, voice magically magnified as she commanded *"Crash dive!!"*

The birds did a U-turn and suddenly dived, everyone screaming from the ground. Leticia simply watched, Brubeck's mouth hanging open as they shot towards the ground like arrows, the chariot smashing to the ground.

"Oh my God," said Spirit, stunned. "They heard her voice and obeyed her!"

"Leticia is all powerful," said Dracula admiringly, and he stood up again. "I really have to go to her."

"No," the three teenagers said firmly, Spirit saying "You might make Brubeck furious again, sir. Leticia is completely fine and we don't want anything to happen to you. Please stay here. We can watch everything that's happening right here."

Westley rolled out of the rubble, his face scratched and his clothes singed. The Magenta Birds walked towards Leticia happily, and she said "Good birds. Mummy loves you! Go back to the paddock, there you go. What good birds you are!"

Pleased, the Magenta Birds walked back into their enclosure, bodies blazing as Leticia turned to glare at down at Westley.

"If you ever harm my birds again by abusing them with a whip, I will order them to eat you!"

Gasping for breath, Westley said "Leticia, why would you *do* that?! I was going to get away until this all blows over and I... I think my leg- I think it's broken!"

Leticia didn't answer him, looking at Brubeck. "Do what you must."

Grinning an evil grin, Brubeck walked towards Westley, whose leg was bent at an odd angle.

"One leg broken," said Brubeck icily. "Let's make it two."

He snapped his fingers and there was a loud crack. Jeiklee and Spirit flinched, Virginia amazed at her grandfather as Westley screamed in pain, Leticia looking totally unfazed.

"Let's Tongue-Tie you also." Brubeck snapped his fingers again, and Westley's mouth dropped open, his tongue stretching and tying itself into a knot before shrinking and slipping back in his mouth again. "Pain and silence for six months. I think that is fine for now, Westley Inferno. If I ever come back to this part of the land, it will be to punish you again. So I suggest you always sleep with one eye open from now on. I will never forgive you for what happened to my poor, sweet Malinda."

Virginia rolled her eyes. "Sweet? *Please!* Was she a Daddy's Girl, Father?"
"Yes she was," Dracula said grudgingly. "Malinda was always sweet as sugar and good as gold around her father. He hardly knows about her as an evil vampire, but he was the one who taught her everything she knows. Just not chemistry," he added, watching as paramedics grabbed a completely silent Westley and lifted him onto a stretcher. "He never trusted Malinda enough to teach her how to concoct poisons and potions."
"Well that doesn't surprise me. She probably would have poisoned me at birth if she could," Virginia said flatly, and Dracula replied "It's not nice to say but I do agree with you."
"Three cheers for Leticia!" a voice shouted on screen, and cheers went up, Brubeck turning and clasping her hand.
"Your power has always intrigued and amazed me, Leticia of Sampson. I wish you all the best and I hope you find someone worthy of you. Because Westley Inferno was *never* worthy."
Leticia nodded, looking touched. "Thank you, Brubeck."
"Thank *you.* I never would have got him without you."
"Aww," said Virginia amusedly. "Granddad has a soft side."
Jeiklee and Spirit laughed, Dracula amused at his daughter as well.
"The three of you need to go to bed. You have to go to Thrill tomorrow."
"You just want Miss Leticia to yourself, Father." Virginia smirked at him. "It's not happening."
Dracula laughed, Jeiklee and Spirit laughing too as he said "Fine. At least get ready for bed, then. Leticia won't be impressed if I haven't kept the three of you in order. She expects you to be in bed at ten and it's nine now. So get ready for bed please, and be back down for a hot drink in half an hour."
"Yes sir," said Jeiklee and Spirit, and Virginia sighed and got up as well. "Ok Father."
Dracula turned the television off, not wanting to see anymore, knowing Leticia was ok and Brubeck had his revenge thanks to her.
Dracula glanced up, sensing and noticing Spirit had come back down. "Spirit? Are you ok?"
"Yes sir, I am. I just… well… I notice the way you and Leticia look at each other, and I saw how scared you looked when she first appeared in front of Brubeck. You were scared for her. I just…" Spirit hesitated, and Dracula asked "What's bothering you?"
"Well… I just wanted to know if… if you're in love with her."
"Oh," said Dracula, and he hesitated. "What you should know about that is-"
"My Lady, you're back!" they heard Washington exclaim with relief, and Leticia said "Yes, I'm back Washington. And very tired."

"Never mind, sir. I'm going to get ready for bed," Spirit said, and she went upstairs, Dracula exhaling as Leticia entered the lounge.

She ran and hugged him, Dracula holding her to him as he said "You were amazing, sweetheart. I love you."

"I love you too," whispered Leticia, and he kissed her. "Mmm. Dracula, stop... I need to get a shower," she murmured against his mouth. "The Magenta Birds, they... they slightly singed my... Dracula..."

Jeiklee jogged down the stairs, then turned and jogged back up quickly as Dracula ran his hands down Leticia's back, kissing her again.

"Hot drinks not ready for another ten minutes," he said quickly, and Spirit and Virginia frowned at him. "Let's go to the chill out room."

"No," Virginia said flatly, and Spirit laughed. "Out of the way, Inferno."

"But-"

"Move it," Virginia said, and he saw her fangs were unsheathed. "I'm thirsty."

Jeiklee quickly moved out of her way, and Spirit laughed as Virginia smirked, saying "You know how to get your way, Virginia."

"I really am thirsty, Spirit." Virginia laughed as well. "I'm looking forward to hot chocolate and muffins, and reading for a few hours in bed in my room here."

"A few hours?" Spirit said interestedly. "Why so long? Don't you sleep much, Virginia?"

"I'm a vampire, Spirit. It's not as easy to sleep at night as it is for you and Jeiklee," Virginia explained, smiling at her. "But my Father stamped not sleeping at night at all right out of me, from a tiny age. When I was a baby and toddler, he'd cuddle me and play music until I nodded off. It was great. I love Father so much."

"Are you sure we shouldn't go in the chill out room?" Jeiklee said anxiously, and Virginia frowned at him. "Just for a bit?"

"What's the reason?" Virginia asked curiously, and Spirit looked at him as well. "I mean, if the hot drinks aren't ready we can still wait in the lounge with Father and Miss Leticia."

"Where are the children?" they heard Leticia ask curiously. "Their hot drinks are waiting for them."

"They are most likely talking in the corridor," Dracula replied amusedly, and Virginia and Spirit scowled at Jeiklee.

"Stop messing about, Jeiklee!"

"Sorry," he said meekly, and they went downstairs.

Dracula and Leticia sat talking at the table happily, Virginia smiling as she joined them, eyes glowing when she saw her tasty hot chocolate.

"With mint cream and sprinkles?" she said happily, and Leticia said "I added that just for you, Virginia."

"Thank you Miss Leticia," Virginia said happily, and Leticia said "You're welcome. Jeiklee and Spirit, both of you have marshmallows and cream added to your hot chocolate. And each of you have your favourite muffins. Virginia, you have chocolate chip, Spirit has blueberry, and Jeiklee, you have strawberry and white chocolate."

"Thanks Mum," said Jeiklee happily, Spirit as well. "Can you have some with us, you and Count Dracula? I wanted to talk about what we saw on the news."

"Ah. That reminds me," said Dracula, looking at his daughter. "Virginia. Would you like to er… meet your grandfather Brubeck? You're his flesh and blood."

Virginia opened her mouth, then closed it. "I don't think I want to, Father. Brubeck hates me. And Malinda did too. She called me a nasty little beast and Brubeck wants nothing to do with me. So no. I don't."

"Well I said so," Dracula said, looking at Leticia. "Leticia suggested I ask you, Virginia."

"I don't want to meet Brubeck," Virginia said, but she looked uncertain. "I mean, he can do some cool stuff. But he didn't want me and probably didn't even *think* of me before Malinda died."

Leticia looked at Dracula, then she softly said "Virginia, if I talk to Brubeck- get him to realise he isn't alone and we care for him, would you consider meeting him?"

"We care for him?" Dracula repeated, and Leticia said "Well I do. And I'm going to visit him."

"He said if he came back this this part of the land, it will only be for Westley," Spirit said uncertainly, and Leticia looked at her.

"I heard him, Spirit. But I believe I can change his mind."

"Why do you care so much, Leticia?" Dracula asked quietly, and she looked at him.

"Because he's all alone. Just as you felt when I left your life for a while, Dracula. You have me back, but Brubeck won't get Malinda back. I just want to help him."

Virginia was very touched, and so was Dracula as he said "The good in you always overrules the dark, Leticia. Would you like me to visit Brubeck with you?"

"No. It is best I go alone as feelings and hurt within Brubeck are high. I will go tomorrow while the children are at Thrill."

"I will wait for you at the shore of the lake," Dracula said softly, and Leticia replied just as softly "I don't know how long I'll be, Dracula."

"I will wait for you anyway."

Spirit noticed the affection between the two. "Leticia?"

"Yes Spirit?"

"I… well… it's just that… nothing," she said, and Leticia frowned at her.

"Say what's on your mind, Spirit."

"Ok," said Spirit, then she took a deep breath. "I… I've noticed the way you look at Count Dracula and the way he looks at you. And I can see and feel the affection, warmth and love. And don't tell me it's because you're best friends, either of you. I think it's more than that. *Way* more. So I'm just going to ask," she said, Virginia and Jeiklee staring at her amazedly. "Are you in love with each other?"

Leticia and Dracula looked at each other, and Spirit gasped before they could think of what to say.

"You are!"

"The cat's out the bag," Virginia said lazily, and Spirit looked at her.

"You knew, Virginia?"

"Well… yeah. And so did Jeiklee," Virginia said, dubbing him in. "So if you get annoyed with me you have to get annoyed with him too. It's fair." Spirit turned to look at Leticia for conformation. "Leticia?"

Leticia opened her mouth, then she took a deep breath before she replied "Yes, Spirit. We are a couple. I'm deeply in love with Count Dracula-"

"And I am deeply in love with Leticia," Dracula added, smiling at Spirit as he took Leticia's hand. "We have always loved each other."

Spirit's jaw practically hit the floor. "Oh my God! That… that's *brilliant!*"

"Brilliant?" everyone said at the same time amazedly, and Spirit said "Of course it is! You make Leticia really happy, sir! I love the positive energy that issues from her, the warmth! She hasn't been unhappy at all since she left Westley, and I know it's down to you! I'm really glad for you," she said happily. "I'm glad for *both* of you! You deserve each other!"

Leticia could have passed out with relief. "Thank the gods you aren't angry with me."

"I could never be angry with you, Leticia." Spirit got up and hugged her tight. "I couldn't think of anyone better for you."

Leticia hugged her back, Spirit asking "Will you announce the news, Leticia? That you and Count Dracula are together?"

"Not yet, Spirit."

"I think you should announce it as soon as possible," Spirit told her, and Dracula smiled at her before he asked "Why, Spirit?"

"Because you will be fully accepted by the people of Severna and you won't have to sneak around," Spirit said happily. "This practically makes us family! Well… you know what I mean. It's great!"

Everyone laughed, Jeiklee saying amusedly "You're really choked up about this, aren't you?"

"Of course I am," said Spirit happily. "I couldn't be happier."

* * *

Spirit hugged Leticia goodnight, and she turned to Count Dracula, expecting nothing more than a goodnight, but Dracula pulled her into a warm hug as he said "Goodnight Spirit."

"Goodnight!" she said happily, and she went upstairs with a big smile on her face as Virginia hugged her father and Leticia goodnight too, and Jeiklee hugged Leticia.

"No hug, Jeiklee?" said Dracula amusedly, and Jeiklee said "Well I wasn't sure if you… ok!"

Everyone laughed as Jeiklee eagerly hugged Count Dracula and said "Night sir, night Mum."

"Jeiklee, I won't be up to see you all off tomorrow," Leticia told him regretfully. "I am just exhausted. I'll be asleep, sweetie. I hope you don't mind?"

"No, of course not. I'll tell Spirit tomorrow."

"Washington will wake you up as usual. Goodnight both of you," smiled Leticia, and Jeiklee and Virginia smiled back and went upstairs. Leticia turned to Dracula with a happy sigh. "No more secrets."

"In the household, yes. But what about the people of Severna?" asked Dracula. "Do you want to announce our relationship, Leticia? I've been extremely comfortable with everyone thinking we were just close friends all my life. But it's totally up to you."

"I don't think we need to tell anyone just yet. I like it as we are, Dracula."

"But we will tell everyone eventually. Right?" said Dracula uncertainly. "I don't want to be a secret forever."

"What changed your mind?" asked Leticia, looking at him through smouldering eyes. "There was a time when you cared not what the people of Severna thought of you."

"I still don't, sweetheart. But I do care about you. I want you to be free without limitations, Leticia. I don't want to hold you back or-"

"Shh." Leticia placed a finger on his mouth. "We'll tell them in a month. We haven't been together for that long and I want to experience our love, being yours, some more. I want it to blossom like a beautiful flower, without being ogled by the press. Ok?"

"Ok," smiled Dracula. "So what shall we do now? You said you were very tired. Shall we go to bed?"

"Yes, I'd like that." Leticia stood on tiptoe and kissed him. "After I have a shower."

* * *

Jeiklee laid in bed, smiling broadly.

Things were going great. Spirit knew about Leticia and Dracula's love for each other and didn't have a problem with it. Jeiklee supposed that her knowing way back when they first found out after going back in time, wasn't a good thing. She was loyal to Westley then and wouldn't have understood. It was a good thing that her memory was wiped. Now she knew once more, and she adored the idea of Leticia being Count Dracula's partner. It was definitely great.

It was midnight.

Jeiklee got up and wondered if Spirit was awake. He hadn't given her a kiss in a while, being so wrapped up in other things. He didn't want her to think he stopped caring about her.

Jeiklee opened his door, and his jaw dropped when he saw Spirit standing there, a fist raised, about to knock on his door.

"Great minds think alike," he said amusedly, and she smiled back and entered his room. Jeiklee pulled her into his arms and gave her a tender kiss.

"Doesn't everything seem perfect?" Spirit whispered happily when they broke apart, and Jeiklee said "Yep it does. We're all a tight unit and it's great. Dad isn't going to like hearing that Mum and Count Dracula are together, though."

"Well he can't speak for six months anyway," shrugged Spirit. "Leticia might even be married by the time he gets his voice back."

"Married?" repeated Jeiklee, and his eyes lit up with happiness. "If that happened I'd have to praise God. I'd believe in miracles!"

Spirit laughed. "Me too!"

There was a knock on Jeiklee's door, and they whipped around as it opened, Washington striding in.

"Miss McKenzie, do return to your room. It is late. My Lady has stated this would be acceptable if you had no college tomorrow, but you *do* have college, and you need to concentrate in class. Also she firmly stated that you won't be able to concentrate if you haven't slept properly. So say goodnight to Master Inferno and be on your way please. I don't want to go and tell her you refused her order."

"Like that would happen," Jeiklee said, grinning. "Spirit won't refuse Mum's order."

Washington smiled too. "Miss McKenzie?"

"Goodnight Jeiklee," said Spirit amusedly, and Jeiklee laughed. "Night."

* * *

Dracula stroked Leticia's hair as she slept, her head on his shoulder.

He was daydreaming about life in Severna a year from now. He was hopeful that he and Leticia would be the same as they were now; in love, affectionate, passionate, and best friends as well as partners.

It was eight in the morning.

Washington would be waking the teens now. Dracula wondered whether to get up and say goodbye, but then he decided not to in case Leticia woke up. She was very tired.

Dracula held her to him, thinking of Westley Inferno and Brubeck. Leticia didn't want Brubeck to be alone, and that was very sweet of her, but Dracula didn't forgive him or Malinda for the way they turned Virginia away and wanted nothing to do with her all her life. Dracula made up his mind to go with Leticia to Brubeck's castle.

"No," murmured Leticia, and Dracula glanced down at her, startled.

"You were awake??"

"I was snoozing. And I could hear your thoughts," Leticia said softly, snuggling up to him. "I will go to Brubeck today alone, Dracula. If he decides he wants to see Virginia and vice versa, you should definitely go with her. But I need to go alone, ok?"

"Fine. But I am going to wait on the shore of the lake for you like I said," he told her, and Leticia said "That's fine. We can have a picnic there after I see him if you'd like. Or we can go to your castle."

"Either way suits me." Dracula gave her a gentle kiss. "Go back to sleep."

* * *

Spirit was in great spirits all day.

"What's got you smiling so much?" Bruce Finnegan asked curiously as she sat under the tree by the river with Jeiklee and Virginia, and Spirit totally forgot she didn't want anything to do with him as she happily replied "Life, Bruce. Life is great."

"Because Virginia's your bodyguard now?" said Bruce, and his gang sniggered. "It's a bit weird. She's your bully."

"Virginia's my friend, not my bully. Not anymore. She's one of the closest friends I have and I love her like a sister."

"Aww," said Virginia amusedly, and Jeiklee smiled too. "I love you like a sister too, Spirit. Miss Leticia is going to be so glad you said that. So will my Father."

"Yeah, um, we all saw everything on the news, Jeiklee. Is your dad ok?" asked Bruce, and Jeiklee knew he was trying to break the ice between them. "Brubeck was pretty mad at him."

"I haven't gone to see him yet," Jeiklee replied truthfully. "I was going to wait for a week to pass or so. He must be in pain and shock."

"Yeah, so don't you want to make sure he's ok? Why wait?" said Bruce, his group nodding behind him, and Jeiklee said "Because I think he deserved what he got and I don't sympathise. If you knew-"

"Knew what? Tell me," Bruce said curiously. "We're mates, right?"

Jeiklee sighed. "Right."

"So what's up?" Jeiklee looked at the crowd behind him meaningfully, and Bruce got the gist. Turning to them, he said "See you at last break."

"Aww," the said, but they didn't disobey the silent order to get lost. "See you in a bit."

Bruce sat down, Virginia reaching for a sandwich. "Do you mind if I sit?"

"Nah," said Jeiklee. "Me and Virginia are cool with you. Spirit's in a good mood so I doubt she minds. You ok, Spirit?"

"Sure," shrugged Spirit, and Bruce said "So why don't you want to see your dad?"

"You haven't heard?"

"Nope."

Jeiklee raised an eyebrow. "You didn't listen to the backstory on the news about Malinda of Brubeck's death?"

"No. Honestly," Bruce added, when Jeiklee looked cynical. "I just heard she was killed at the lake but I didn't look into it. So what went down? Why won't you see your dad?"

"He was planning to drug my mother," Jeiklee said flatly, "And force her to get back with him using that drug. If he succeeded, we'd be back with him and he'd have my mother under his control."

'Whoa," said Bruce, frowning now. "That's messed up."

"Yep."

"King Harlot is mad at Brubeck for what he did to your dad, and mad at Leticia of Sampson too for allowing it to happen," Bruce told Jeiklee, and Spirit said "What?? King Harlot is an idiot!"

"It was on the news this morning," Bruce said. "He's going to the hospital this afternoon to see Westley Inferno and then he's going to see your mother and plead with her to heal him. Everyone knows King Harlot loves your dad like a son."

"Yeah, we know. But my mother isn't going to heal him," Jeiklee said, shrugging. "She's perfectly within her rights not to."

"Miss Leticia's been through a lot because of Westley Inferno," Virginia added, and Bruce looked at her. "She doesn't have to do a thing."

"I guess so. But it would be cool if things were normal again. Everything has been weird on the news, dark. I just want things to get better," Bruce said, standing as the bell went for afternoon lessons, and Spirit said "Things will definitely get better. It won't be the same as before all of this happened, but I'm telling you Bruce, things will be great soon."

Bruce couldn't help smiling at her. "Ok Spirit. See you in class, you three."

"We have five minutes to get there," pouted Virginia. "I'm finishing my sandwich."

Jeiklee and Spirit laughed, Jeiklee saying "I'll wait with you, Virginia."

"Me too," smiled Spirit, and Virginia smiled back.

* * *

Leticia stepped into the boat and waved her hand.

It began to move away from the shore, Dracula anxious as he called "Be careful, Leticia!"

"I will be," she called back, and he sighed.

"Nothing can make you change your mind about this?"

"No," she called amusedly. "I won't be longer than an hour, Dracula!"

"Alright. Just take care of yourself!"

"I will," Leticia called before she sat down, and she began to magically manoeuvre the boat further and further away, until she became a dot in the distance.

Dracula sighed and sat down, checking the time. "If she's not back in an hour I'm going to that castle to find her."

* * *

"Leticia of Sampson??"

"Hello Brubeck," Leticia said warmly, and he stared at her. "Can I come in?"

"Of course," he said gruffly, standing aside to let her pass. "What brings you here?"

"I was coming to make sure that you are alright after everything," Leticia said truthfully, and Brubeck said "I'm not alright, but I will be fine. Time will heal me and I may even love again."

"Ok," Leticia said, and Brubeck said "Follow me."

She obeyed, walking down the dimly lit corridor of his castle, noticing large damp patches on the walls as she passed.

"I suppose living in the middle of the ocean has its disadvantages."

"Hmm? Oh, the walls. Yes," he said, glancing around briefly. "When there are storms water often manages to penetrate the walls. Malinda and I were used to it. There are good days and bad days here at the castle."

"And the good days? How are they?" asked Leticia, and Brubeck replied "Very good. It's warm and toasty and Malinda often had a helping hand. We have no servants here like you and Count Dracula have," he added, stopping outside a door. "We catered to the castle ourselves."

"That's nice, but it sounds like very hard work."

"It was," smiled Brubeck, "But it was something we enjoyed because we bonded. Malinda often complained about not spending enough time together when I spent hours in the lab making potions, poisons and antidotes. In here, Leticia."

Leticia went through the door he held open. "This is your lounge?"

"More my brooding room," Brubeck said. "I know the furniture isn't up to date or anything, but we liked it how it is."

"We?" asked Leticia, and Brubeck said "Me and Malinda."

"Of course. Apologies."

Brubeck sat down in a worn out armchair. "I'm guessing you're here because of the news also."

"The news?" repeated Leticia, nonplussed. "I didn't watch the news today."

"King Harlot is upset about his special boy Westley Inferno," Brubeck told her, and she scowled. "He is going to plead with you to heal him, possibly tonight. He was almost in tears when he spoke to the press. He said he couldn't believe you would let something like that happen to your husband."

"He's my ex-husband," Leticia said, annoyed. "And I will not heal him."

"Good. Because I would have to damage him again," chuckled Brubeck, and she couldn't help smiling. "Would you like a drink, Leticia?"

"No thank you. I can't stay for too long."

"Oh," said Brubeck, disappointed. "Never mind. So what would you like to talk about?"

"Well… I would also like to talk about your grandchild. Virginia."

Brubeck's pupils dilated. "What about her?"

"I was wondering if you'd like to meet her someday," Leticia said, holding her gaze. "I know you loved Malinda dearly and I'm not suggesting you replace her. But Virginia is a sweet girl and I know if you just let her in, you would love her as much as you loved Malinda."

Brubeck rubbed his chin. "That was a nice pitch, Leticia. But I don't want to see or know that girl. I have no feelings for her nor do I feel curious. It's been eighteen years since I sent her away in that basket. I never wanted to see her again and I still don't."

"Any reason?" asked Leticia, sighing as she stood. "Or are you being loyal to your daughter's memory?"

"That girl is the child of Count Dracula. Count Dracula is the reason Malinda went back to your part of the land. I warned her not to," Brubeck said, eyes welling up. "I told her she will find nothing but trouble going back. And I was right. When I sent that baby away, I cut all ties to Count Dracula. I don't want those ties reattached."

"Virginia never had a mother, but she could have a grandfather, Brubeck."

"You were the next best thing to her. I've seen it with my own eyes," Brubeck said gruffly. "Virginia of Dracula loves you. You were a better mother to her than Malinda ever could have been."

"Thank you, Brubeck. So that is your final word?" asked Leticia. "You want no contact with Virginia at all?"

"No."

"Then it is done. I will inform her father and we can all move on," Leticia said, sighing again. "Will you come to our part of the land anytime soon?"

"No," Brubeck repeated. "Not for six months. I want to see how Westley will feel when he has his voice back. Elated maybe. But I will punish him again in a different way. I know not what way," he added when Leticia opened her mouth, "Not yet. But I have six months to come up with something."

Leticia nodded. "I will leave now, Brubeck. I hope you find peace."

"Oh, I will Leticia. Thank you for coming to check on me. I will be fine." Brubeck led her back down the damp corridor towards the front doors. "Count Dracula needn't worry either. I won't disrupt his or his child's lives. We can all move on and be content."

"I am glad we are on the same page," smiled Leticia. "Goodbye, Brubeck."

"Goodbye Leticia. Maybe we will meet again someday."

"Someday. Definitely," Leticia said as she stepped into her boat, and Brubeck raised a hand as it started moving away. Leticia raised a hand in return, then she turned to manoeuvre the boat again.

She sat down and leant back, eyes closed. "I can't wait to get home."

* * *

Dracula stood immediately when the boat reached the shore, and he walked forwards, offering his hand. Leticia took it, and he kissed it before helping her out of the boat.

"How did it go?"

"It went pretty well. But he wants nothing to do with Virginia."

"Good," said Dracula flatly. "Now we can all move on."

"That's exactly what I said," Leticia said amusedly, standing on tiptoe and kissing the handsome Count gently on the lips. "Let's go home."

"Home?" Dracula repeated, touched. "To yours or to mine?"

"Either. I see them both as home," Leticia replied, and Dracula laughed as they joined hands and began walking.

"I feel exactly the same. I am one hundred percent comfortable in either."

* * *

When Jeiklee and Spirit arrived home with Virginia, they saw that the press were on the grounds again, as were the public, soldiers, and King Harlot's carriage.

"Great. Would it hurt to get some peace?" Virginia said, annoyed as they made their way towards Leticia, King Harlot and Count Dracula.

"You will heal Westley Inferno, Leticia of Sampson, or else!" King Harlot said angrily, and Leticia said "Or else what? Westley Inferno is not my problem."

"You are the only Healer in Severna!"

Leticia shrugged. "And your point is?"

"You can't just *abandon* him, Leticia!"

"I think I already have, King Harlot."

King Harlot realised that shouting at Leticia wasn't working, so he tried a different approach. Calming his tone, he said "Come now, Leticia. Don't be unreasonable. We were friends once upon a time, were we not?"

Leticia's jaw nearly dropped. "You have a lot of nerve!"

"Well we were!"

"You and I were never friends," spat Leticia. "I simply tolerated you because you were good friends with my parents and ex-husband. If I had a choice, I would never have attended any of your ridiculous dinner parties. I *loathe* you, King Harlot, for everything you have done!"

"All I did to you," the King said angrily, "Was stop you from getting your son until he was the right age. And he's back where he belongs now so what exactly is the problem?!"

Leticia was glowing scarlet as she calmly said "If I were you I'd leave, King Harlot. I am not going to heal Westley and the problem I have with you is *way* more than you stopping me from getting my son."

"Way more?" King Harlot said, perplexed. "I have done nothing more *to* you! And why are you back in contact with Count Dracula, Leticia?! Do you want the memory of your dear mother tarnished?? She hated him!"

Leticia's eyes began to glow scarlet, everyone backing away fearfully as she icily said "Leave. Before I do something I've wanted to do to you for a very long time."

"I am not going anywhere before you explain just what exactly is going on between you and this scoundrel. I feel that I should step in," King Harlot said pompously, "Because clearly you are not on the right track!"

"What!"

"You're hanging around with *vermin* for one thing, Leticia, and its offspring! You don't want to crush the family name, do you??"

"I'm going to count to ten," Leticia said quietly, "And if you are not off my property, I swear to you. I will slaughter you like I am a hunter and I won't bat an eyelid. One."

"You can't send me away!" King Harlot was outraged. "I am the King!"

"Two," Leticia said flatly, and everyone gasped "She's not bluffing!"

"Now see here Leticia!" King Harlot was scared, but het up as well. "I will not be forced to leave just because you have a bad temper! You wouldn't really-"

"Three."

"My Lord, just come along!" a soldier shouted, Leticia's eyes still scarlet. "It's not worth it, sir! Westley Inferno had it coming and Leticia won't heal him! Just accept it and we'll go!"

"Listen to your soldier, King Harlot," Dracula said quietly, as Leticia said "Four."

"I should get popcorn," Virginia said with a sly smile, and Dracula said "This isn't funny, Virginia."

"It *is* funny if King Harlot doubts that Miss Leticia will kill him, Father. Her parents aren't here to talk her out of it," shrugged Virginia. "Miss Leticia doesn't like being forced. King Harlot should know that as *he's* the one who gave her mother and Westley Inferno's parents the idea of forcing her to marry him."

Leticia froze as gasps went up, her scarlet eyes turning back to normal, grey and beautiful as Virginia's words hit her brain. Leticia turned to look at Virginia, stunned.

"What did you say?"

Virginia realised what she just said. "Um... I..."

"Ok Virginia, Spirit and Jeiklee. Go inside," Dracula said firmly, Leticia staring at King Harlot in shock and disbelief. "Now!"

Jeiklee and the girls obeyed immediately, Dracula snapping his fingers. The giant doors closed, Dracula ignoring their protests.

"Don't listen to what that girl said, Leticia. She and her father are vile," King Harlot said hastily. "She would say anything for a little fame-"

"Don't you *dare* lie on my daughter!" spat Dracula, and King Harlot quickly said "Fine! Apologies, Count Dracula! Don't turn me into a rat! And Leticia, this can all be explained if you calm down-"

"It was you all along." Leticia took steady breaths. "It was you!"

King Harlot was backing away now as he gushed "I will do as you asked, Leticia: I will leave!"

"Stay where you are!!"

Inside Jeiklee, Spirit and Virginia flinched, Jeiklee hissing "She's going to kill him, Virginia! Why couldn't you hold your tongue??"

"It just slipped out!" Virginia hissed back. "I'm sorry, ok?!"

"We can watch on the television," Spirit said quickly. "Everything's live anyway. Come on!"

They ran into the lounge, Virginia saying "Popcorn or not?"

"This isn't a joke, Virginia!" Jeiklee said angrily. "If my Mum kills the King-"

"Severna would be better off without him," Virginia said flatly. "He's a horrible fat toad. It's better that she knows the whole truth!"

On the screen, they watched fearfully as Leticia spat *"Paralisia!!"*

Everyone gasped as King Harlot's body wobbled like jelly, then he crumpled to the ground in a heap.

"Too much," gasped Leticia, tears falling now, and she screamed *"You have done too much!!"*

"I can make it right," gasped King Harlot from the ground; he was unable to move from the shoulders down, but he could still talk. "Tell me what you want me to do, Leticia! I will make it up to you, I promise you!"

"What have you got against me, Your Highness?! Why do you keep hurting me?!"

"Your mother and Westley's parents were worried about your relationship with Count Dracula and they came to me for help! It was all I could think of at the time!" King Harlot said desperately. "I knew you loved that little girl so I made sure she was used against you! If I could change what happened, I would! I see now that-"

"You see nothing now," spat Leticia, glowing scarlet as the tears cascaded down her face. "You're just trying to save yourself from my wrath!"

"Fine! Punish me some more if you will- I deserve it! You don't have to heal Westley, but please- don't hurt me anymore. I am paralysed!"

Everyone could sense Leticia's fury. Larry suddenly shouted "Apologise to her!" And cheers went up, King Harlot gasping "What good will it do?! She hates me!"

"Apologise or I will gut you like a fish!" spat Leticia, and King Harlot gasped "I'm sorry! I am so, *so* sorry! Please lift the paralysis, Leticia!"

"No." Leticia took a deep breath and wiped her eyes, calmer now. "You will remain paralysed until I feel like removing the curse. No counter curse, hex or antidote will heal you. You will stay in the hospital of Severna next to your precious Westley Inferno until they think you are ready to go home. I will set no time on when I will remove the curse from you. I will do it when I'm ready."

Everyone clapped, looking at each other, not knowing if that was a good thing or a bad thing, but they knew King Harlot deserved it.

"Everyone, please leave," Leticia called, and the crowd obeyed immediately. "I wish to be left alone."

Leticia turned to enter her home without even looking at Count Dracula, and he grabbed her arm.

"Leticia. I didn't tell you because-"

"You promised me there would be no secrets." Leticia yanked her arm out of his grip. "You told me there was nothing you were keeping from me, that everything was perfect!"

"Leticia, if you let me explain-"

"There's nothing to explain," she said, eyes welling up again, and he saw the hurt in her eyes. "I had to hear something so crucial from the mouth of your daughter rather than from *you.* And it wasn't even a private talk, it just slipped out! How could you tell your child something like that?!"

"I didn't tell her, Leticia!" Dracula stepped closer, but Leticia stepped away from him. That hurt, but she had to understand. "After your mother made that deal with you outside my castle years ago and threatened Virginia, I settled Virginia and went to the house of Sampson, invisible! Your mother was celebrating because she won, with Westley's parents! I heard their conversation, Leticia! They were all toasting King Harlot because his idea to use Virginia worked!"

"Why didn't you tell me?!"

"It all happened so fast." Dracula shook his head. "I got back home and told Terrence and Nancy in my castle. Virginia couldn't sleep, and she came to find me. She heard everything and I couldn't help that! I told her to forget it, to never repeat it!"

"Well she did repeat it." Leticia took a deep, shaky breath before she quietly said "I think you should go, Dracula."

"What?"

"Go!" she said angrily, tears falling. "I don't want to see you, to hear from you- just go! You deceived me!"

"Leticia, please don't do this!" Dracula was as agitated as she was. "You can't possibly want me out of your life-"

"That is *exactly* what I want! Go and get Virginia and return to your caste! Just leave me *alone!"*

She stormed into her mansion, sobbing. Jeiklee, Spirit and Virginia were startled as she rushed past them; Dracula ran after her, shouting "Leticia, *wait!"*

Leticia stopped, taking a deep breath. Then she vanished into thin air before anyone could call her again.

"She's gone to her Chamber of Serenity," Spirit said quietly, Dracula looking hurt and helpless.

Virginia looked very guilty. "Father, I... I'm really sorry-"

Dracula looked at his daughter, and his eyes darkened. Normally a bright green, they were almost black. Virginia recoiled, scared. Then she said "Maybe if I go and talk to Miss Leticia, we can-"

"Get your things, Virginia." Dracula spoke coldly. "We're going home."

"But-"

"But nothing. Say goodbye to Jeiklee and Spirit and let's go."
Virginia was shaking like a leaf as she obeyed. Jeiklee and Spirit muttered
"Bye" as she walked past them with her shoulder bag, and the massive
doors closed behind them, Count Dracula not looking back.
Spirit looked at Jeiklee sadly. "Do you think Leticia will forgive him?"
"I don't know," Jeiklee said just as sadly. "I do know she's going to be
upset and angry with him for a while.

* * *

One month later…

Leticia sobbed and sobbed, hands covering her face. She had been crying every time she was alone, feeling that she could trust nobody. It hurt. It hurt so much! And she missed Count Dracula more than anyone in the whole world of Severna.

He hadn't returned after she told him to leave a month ago, probably because he wasn't as weak as Westley to turn up and constantly beg to see her. Count Dracula had his pride. She couldn't help hoping that he wasn't angry with Virginia, that she was ok. She hadn't seen Virginia in a month either, and she missed the fiery teenager.

"Why am I always getting hurt by the ones who claim to love me?" she wept as she lowered her hands. "The pain is still so raw!"

Leticia hadn't seen much of Jeiklee and Spirit either. They knew she wanted to be alone, so they didn't disturb her. At all. She didn't know how they were getting on at Thrill or how their second exam went, as she was always in her Chamber of Serenity.

She'd been avoiding everyone and everything for a month. The press had repeatedly turned up at the mansion for a story, but nobody gave them any information other than Leticia of Sampson wanted to be left alone.

Leticia heard a voice call her from outside the chamber, and she gasped "Please go away!"

"My Lady, it's Washington. Can you please come out and talk to me?"

"No," she wept. "I want to be left alone!"

"Please, My Lady. I can see you're very depressed after everything," Washington said gently. "Come out? I won't be longer than ten minutes."

Leticia sighed and got up. "Ok. Ten minutes, and then I'm returning to my Chamber to weep some more."

She slipped right through the glowing blue door and stood, face wet.

"How can I help you, Washington?"

Washington looked at her sadly. "You look terrible, My Lady. Here."

He conjured a tissue out of thin air, and he gently mopped her face.

"That's better. Now tell me what's ailing you."

"You *know* what is-"

"I heard, but I don't know. I haven't heard it from your mouth, just backstories on the news. I want you to tell me how you feel and why you're so down."

Jeiklee and Spirit walked down the corridor towards them, praying that Washington would save the day. Jeiklee had his fingers crossed in his pockets as Leticia's eyes filled over again.

"I… I-" Leticia shook her head. "I don't want to talk about it. It hurts too much."

"It hurts too much because you haven't let it out, My Lady. Don't you remember when you was a little girl and a teenager?" smiled Washington. "I was your diary. You could tell me anything, and it was normally about Count Dracula and how trapped you felt. You can still tell me anything, My Lady. I'm still the same Washington the Diary."

Leticia smiled through her tears. "You were the best growing up."

"I still am the best, My Lady." Washington smiled at her. "Talk to me."

"Come on Mum," Jeiklee said softly. "Talking will make you feel better."

"I feel like I can trust no one. Everyone who claims to care for me hurts me," said Leticia, crying again. "Everything that happened, everything I went through- was down to my mother, Westley's parents and that evil King Harlot!"

"But what about Count Dracula, My Lady?" Washington asked gently. "Surely you're not angry with him too? He was protecting you."

"He really was, Mum," said Jeiklee, and Spirit nodded as Leticia wept "No, I'm not angry with him. I was shocked and hurt and I lashed out at him when really I was angry at King Harlot. Dracula just got caught in the cross fire and I hate myself for it! I love him! I love him so much," she sobbed, and Spirit's eyes filled up as Washington hugged Leticia.

"Then go to him, My Lady. The Monster's Ball is tonight," Washington told her, "But I doubt Count Dracula will be in the spirit of the occasion. He is missing you as much as you are missing him, I know he is. But he's scared of losing you for good if he pushes for you to see and forgive him, so he's waiting for you to come to him instead."

Leticia stared at him. "How do you know that?"

"I know," said Washington, smiling. "I was told last night by a certain green-eyed, red-haired teenager who loves you to death."

"Virginia! She was here?" said Leticia disbelievingly. "When??"

"After dark, My Lady. She snuck out," Washington told her, smiling. "She wanted me to talk to you, to tell you that she's really sorry and she hopes you aren't mad at her. And that Count Dracula has been very miserable and deeply upset and troubled for the past month. He doesn't want to come if you don't want to see him, because he thinks he will only make matters worse. So he's waiting for you," Washington added, smiling as Leticia wiped her tears away. "Miss Virginia also added that it would make his night and hers if you came to the Monster's Ball, came to Count Dracula."

Leticia opened her mouth then closed it, looking at Jeiklee and Spirit.

"What do you think I should do?"

"Go to him, Mum. It wasn't his fault," Jeiklee said gently. "Count Dracula was protecting you. I guess he must have thought you've been through enough and he didn't want you hurt anymore."

"It's a masquerade ball, Leticia," Spirit added with a smile. "I know you're going to look stunning."

Leticia smiled back, a true smile. "I love you both so much."

"We love you too Mum. Now go to him," smiled Jeiklee. "It's nine o clock. If you go in an hour, you can still spend pretty much the night at the ball."

Leticia nodded. "Washington, I need your assistance in looking my best."

"Yes My Lady."

"Spirit and Jeiklee, you may stay up until three in the morning and no later," Leticia added, and they all smiled broadly at her. "What is it?"

"You're back," Spirit said happily. "See? Talking *does* help a ton."

Leticia smiled back and walked down the corridor towards her suite, Washington behind her. Looking back as Leticia entered her suite, he smiled at Jeiklee and Spirit.

"It's going to be just fine, both of you. Don't worry about My Lady. Once she's back with Count Dracula, it will be like the latest times. Absolutely perfect."

Jeiklee relaxed big time, relieved as he looked at Spirit. "Everything's going to be ok."

* * *

Castle Dracula...

Count Dracula leant over a banister of the ballroom, watching everyone have a good time absentmindedly. He really wasn't in the mood to be at the Monster's Ball this time, wishing he was in his study instead.

"Cheer up, My Lord," a voice said softly, and he glanced at the speaker. She was gazing at him, her eyes bright blue behind her eye mask. Light brown, mousey hair tumbled around her shoulders. Dracula knew he had seen her somewhere before, but he didn't want to think about it.

"Who might you be?" he sighed, and she smiled at him.

"A vampire like yourself, sir, the daughter of Bartley."

"Oh. The same daughter he wished to become my Bride? Michelle?" Dracula asked curiously, and she nodded. "Well... hello. I'm glad you could make it."

"I wouldn't miss it for the world," Michelle replied, smiling. "It is my first time attending the Monster's Ball."

"Oh," Dracula said again. "I hope you're having a good time."

"It would be even better if you were having a good time too, My Lord."

"I just can't have a good time. Not when-"

"Not when your best friend has deserted you." Dracula gaped at her, and she stepped closer as she said "Yes, I know sir. We *all* know. All of your minions and followers know it all. The Forest of Fear has been ripe with gossip and we have all been watching the late night news."

It seemed that everyone still had no clue that Leticia and Count Dracula were a couple. That was good. But not feeling elated at all, Dracula just nodded.

"Why don't you just go to her, sir?" asked Michelle, looking at him concernedly. "I heard you are full of life at your Monster's Balls. If this friendship ending between you and Leticia of Sampson is affecting you so badly, you should go and patch things up with her."

"She doesn't want to see me," Dracula said glumly, staring down at the minions, villains and monsters partying away. "I can't force her to, Michelle. I'm not an idiot like her ex-husband Westley Inferno."

"You were never one to take things laying down either, sir."

Dracula looked at her, surprised. "I know."

"So stop moping around. Suck it up and go to her." Michelle smiled at him. "And be sure to tell her Michelle of Bartley persuaded you."

Dracula smiled back, then the hairs on the back of his neck stood. He turned and stared down at the crowd drinking and dancing, not sure who it was, but he knew someone had arrived. He stared down at his guests, and suddenly his heart started beating.

"What??" he rubbed his chest, breathing hard as Michelle stared at him.

"Sir? Are you ok?"

"I have to go down to the ballroom," Dracula said, then he shook her hand. "Thank you for our talk, Michelle."

"Anytime sir. If I cannot be your Bride, I can at least be a friend."

Dracula smiled at her. Michelle smiled back, then he quickly left the balcony.

He was sure it was her. Why else would his heart be beating so fiercely??

Ten minutes later, Dracula was panting. He had ran all the way down there, searching all over and scrutinizing pretty much everyone, but not many new faces were there.

Disappointed, he sighed. "Maybe talking about Leticia made my heart come alive."

"Or maybe she came to your Ball," a soft voice replied, and he gasped, recognising her voice. "Turn around, Count Dracula."

Dracula turned slowly, and his jaw dropped. Although she was wearing a diamond studded eye mask along with a beautiful black gown, it was her gorgeous grey eyes that he was getting lost in. So much love was in them- love for him and him only.

Dracula stepped back, unable to think straight. "Leticia…"

"Shh," she said softly, and he took a deep breath, feeling like he'd taken a blow to the gut. "I have missed you so much, Dracula. I didn't mean to take my anger out on you."

"I was trying to protect you," Dracula said quietly, and she said "I know you were. I realised that. I've been so lost without you, I…"

Leticia swallowed and shook her head, willing her tears not to fall. Seeing him was like a breath of fresh air after weeks underground.

Dracula stepped closer, and suddenly it felt like it was only them in the ballroom. Nobody else mattered as Dracula lifted a hand and caressed her cheek.

"I've been lost without you too. I'm *always* lost without you. Take your mask off, Leticia."

"I shouldn't," she whispered. "It's a masquerade ball, Dracula."

"Yes, but I want to look at you properly," he said softly, and he took in the gown she was wearing. He stepped back, eyes roaming her body. Inhaling, he murmured "You look beautiful."

"Thank you," she said softly, and he shivered before he quietly said "Take your mask off."

"Dracula, the press are here. What if-"

"Don't worry about the press. I feel it's time people knew fully about you and I anyway," Dracula said seriously. "I don't want to hide our love for each other anymore, Leticia."

Leticia slowly reached up, and she removed the mask from her face. Exhaling, Dracula drew her into his arms and brought his mouth down on hers almost desperately, making sure she knew just how much he missed, wanted, and loved her. Leticia reached up to pull him closer as he deepened the kiss, and everyone stopped talking as they realised their Lord Count Dracula was kissing a woman- *and not just any woman!!*
"It's Leticia of Sampson!" gasped excited voices, and cameras flashed, cameras rolled, and elated cheers went up.
"I don't believe it!!"
Dracula broke the kiss as the press rushed forwards with mikes, bursting with questions.
"Count Dracula, what was *that??*"
"Where did that come from?!"
"Do you love Miss Leticia of Sampson??"
"How long have you been in a relationship with Count Dracula, Leticia??"
"Will Leticia become a Bride of Dracula?!"
"Please both of you, look this way so we can take pictures!"
Smiling, Leticia and Dracula obeyed, holding hands and turning so the photographer could take pictures. Then, taking deep breaths, they answered the journalist's questions.
Watching from above, Virginia smiled broadly with Nancy.
"I want to run and give them a hug. Can I, Nancy? Please? I haven't seen Miss Leticia in ages!"
"Oh, go on then," smiled Nancy. "And come right back up! Your father only has eyes for Miss Leticia right now."
"Ok," Virginia said excitedly, rushing away. Nancy smiled, watching as everyone crowded around Count Dracula and Leticia.

* * *

"Wow. That I didn't expect," said Jeiklee happily, watching the Monster's Ball with Spirit and Washington. "That kiss was really something! Everyone is going to know about Mum and Count Dracula by tomorrow if they aren't watching right now."
"Agreed Master Inferno," smiled Washington, and Spirit said "There's Virginia!"
Cameras swivelled on screen as they saw Virginia of Dracula run across the ballroom floor in a green nightgown and slippers. Everyone turned to look at her, and Leticia opened her arms with a big smile.

* * *

Virginia fell into Leticia's arms and Leticia hugged her tightly, Virginia saying "Miss Leticia, I didn't mean to upset you! What I said- it slipped out and… I'm really sorry! I didn't mean to make you mad- make you and Father mad. I was sure you hated me!"

"It's alright, Virginia. And I could never hate you," Leticia said soothingly, stroking her red hair. "Everything is ok. You'd better go back up before your father scolds you."

"I'm sorry about everything too Father," mumbled Virginia, and Dracula smiled at his daughter.

"Like Leticia said, everything is ok Virginia. Now go back upstairs. There are werewolves here tonight."

"Yes Father."

Smiling broadly, Virginia jogged away. Some called goodnight to her, and she waved but didn't stop.

Everyone turned back to Leticia and Count Dracula amazedly.

"So you are a couple, Count Dracula sir? This is for real?"

"Yes. It's for real." Dracula put an arm around Leticia as he spoke. "I'm not going to go into too much detail and I doubt Leticia will either. Just know we are a couple and I love Leticia very much."

"Just as I love Count Dracula very much," smiled Leticia, and everyone said "Aww!"

"This is just *adorable!"*

"Were you always in love with each other, Count Dracula sir?" a journalist pressed. "You are a very powerful couple. I did notice the connection between you both the moment you had Westley Inferno brought back from the Underworld."

"Well… that would be telling," smiled Dracula. "Speculate if you must, but you won't get an answer on how long exactly Leticia and I have loved each other."

"Yes sir. Oh! King Harlot," the journalist said, and the crowd broke out in angry chatter.

"Him!"

"And Westley Inferno," the journalist added, more jotting things down as their crew filmed eagerly. "Do you think they are watching?"

"We care not," smiled Leticia, and everyone smiled back. "And I care not what the people of Severna think either. I love Count Dracula."

Cheers went up as Dracula kissed her again. When they broke apart and looked at the broad smiles on the faces of everyone there, Dracula added "Please, no more focusing on us. Enjoy the Monster's Ball!"

Applause broke out, the crowd parting happily as music blasted again. The press wanted to ask more but didn't dare disobey; after all, this was *Count Dracula,* and Leticia of Sampson. They wouldn't dare cross either of them. Dracula took Leticia's hand and kissed it. "Would you like a drink, sweetheart?"

"Yes please."

Dracula led her away, then he noticed Michelle of Bartley watching with a smile on her face. Dracula smiled back happily, then he remembered what she said.

"Leticia?"

"Mmm?"

"Michelle of Bartley was the one who persuaded me to find you."

Leticia smiled up at him. "Really?"

"In a way, yes. We spoke and earlier and Michelle was really kind and encouraging. And she's watching us," Dracula added with a smile, and Leticia looked around, then she saw Michelle of Bartley not far off.

"Michelle, come here."

Michelle obeyed nervously. "Yes Ma'am?"

"Thank you for being there for Count Dracula," Leticia said, and she gave Michelle a hug. "Even if you hadn't spoken for long."

"You're most welcome," said Michelle, hugging her back. "I would like to become a friend to you both. I am a very good listener."

"I'll definitely take that into consideration," smiled Leticia, and Dracula laughed. Leticia noticed bottles of bright green liquid in large quantities set along the tables skirting the walls. "What drink is that, Dracula?"

"Ghoul Goop. It's very strong, Leticia. We'd better get you something you can handle," Dracula replied, and Leticia pouted at him.

"I can handle Ghoul Goop."

"You've never tasted it, Leticia. I'm telling you, it will have a strong effect on you. All of the guests here know about Ghoul Goop."

"But they're still knocking it back like it's lemonade," pouted Leticia, and Dracula said "Yes, for the buzz it gives."

Leticia folded her arms. "Let me have a cup."

"No."

"Let me have a cup or I'm not going to dance with you later."

Dracula sighed. "You are so stubborn." Leticia stuck her tongue out at him, and he laughed. "Fine. You may have one cup. Just one, ok?"

"Ok."

* * *

"Oh my God," said Spirit, staring at the screen as Leticia picked up a bottle. "She's going to drink Ghoul Goop!"

"Ghoul Goop?" repeated Jeiklee. "What's that?"

"It's this very strong drink that makes most people black out and see delights, wonders, and madness," Spirit told him. "It's served only at the Monster's Ball; nobody can get a hold of it. It's a recipe that's been in Count Dracula's family since the very first Count Dracula."

"Wow. So that means it was our Count Dracula who made it then?" asked Jeiklee, and Spirit nodded. "Should he really let Mum drink it? How long do the side effects last?"

"It depends on the person," Spirit said nervously, and Jeiklee said "I bet Mum asked for some. Dracula looks a bit nervous watching her drink it."

"He does," agreed Spirit, as Leticia sipped curiously. "But I think Leticia is one woman who can take it hands down."

* * *

Dracula almost passed out in shock when Leticia finished her cup and smiled at him.

"It's not bad. I like it."

Michelle of Bartley was gaping disbelievingly. "You're completely fine!"

"Of course I am," smiled Leticia. "Like I said, I can handle it."

"Wow," said Dracula, amazed. "You really are something, Leticia."

"Thank you."

"You don't feel light headed or dizzy?" asked Dracula, and she said "No. I'm completely fine."

"Well that is definitely a first," a voice said amazedly, and they turned and saw a rugged man standing there.

"Darius. Good to see you," smiled Dracula as he clasped the man's hand, and Darius replied "Good to see you too, sir. I am glad the sky is overcast tonight. I missed the last Monster's Ball because I was in werewolf form. I savaged Bari the Tree, but he laughed the whole time."

"He was ticklish," smiled Leticia, and Darius smiled at her.

"He certainly was. I am sorry he's gone."

"As we all are," said Dracula solemnly. "Would you like a drink, Darius?"

"Yes, My Lord. I'll have a bottle of Ghoul Goop."

Dracula smiled and handed him a bottle, Darius taking it with a grin.

"I hope I can handle it as well as you, Leticia of Sampson."

Leticia smiled, Dracula putting an arm around her as Darius knocked back the glowing green contents happily.

"Easy Darius," warned Dracula, as he swayed on the spot a little. "You're supposed to drink Ghoul Goop slowly. If downed at once-"

Darius finished his drink and tossed his bottle away. He grinned stupidly at everyone for a moment, then he collapsed, unconscious.

There were shouts of laughter from the other villains and monsters.

"Ha!"

"Twelfth one down! Who's next?!"

"Twelfth one down?" Leticia repeated, staring down at Darius. "Will he be ok, Dracula?"

"He'll be fine. It's not anything to worry about," Dracula said reassuringly. "He'll wake up in ten minutes. And he'll be elated by whatever he saw in his er... dream."

Leticia was looking at Darius concernedly, and Dracula added "It's not an unusual thing, Leticia. As you heard, he is the twelfth one down. Besides, it's not a great party if no one passes out from drinking Ghoul Goop."

"Wow. I suppose I am too powerful to be affected by Ghoul Goop, just as I am too powerful to be affected by most potions," smiled Leticia, and Dracula smiled back as he replied "Indeed you are."

Michelle smiled, saying "I'll keep an eye on Darius, My Lord. Enjoy the rest of your night."

Dracula thanked her, and he and Leticia walked away.

* * *

"Are you tired?" asked Spirit, looking at Jeiklee. "It's two in the morning."

"Nah. I want to watch more of the Monster's Ball." Jeiklee was very happy. "We'd better get our hot drinks soon though. If Mum comes back at three and we're still in here-"

"She won't be cross, silly. But good point." Spirit stood. "I'll call Washington. He's just down the hall."

Jeiklee nodded, smiling. He couldn't believe how great the night was going for his mother and Count Dracula. For all of them.

He knew it would be on the news that Count Dracula was in a relationship with his mother probably as soon as possible, and his father and King Harlot would both be furious.

Jeiklee decided he didn't care. He didn't like his father right now and he despised King Harlot just like his mother did, for all that he did to her. Seeing Leticia so distressed and in tears because of the King's actions tugged at Jeiklee's heart, and he knew he would protect his mother from whatever else the silly man might throw at her.

Spirit came back in five minutes later, saying "Washington's going to bring us our hot drinks in half an hour. He said we must get ready for bed in that time."

Jeiklee sighed and stood. "Fine."

* * *

Leticia and Dracula left the ballroom, having been in the spotlight for the majority of the night.

"Nancy, will you be alright sorting everything?" Dracula asked as he saw her, and Nancy nodded.

"Yes sir. Dawn will be fully upon us by six. They all know the ball ends at five."

Dracula nodded, holding Leticia's hand. "It is four now. I will be back to thank our guests for coming to the best Monster's Ball yet."

Nancy smiled at that and so did Leticia.

"Why is it the best Monster's Ball yet, Dracula?" asked Leticia, and he kissed her forehead before softly replying "Because *you* attended."

Nancy smiled as they walked away, and she called "My Lord?"

Dracula and Leticia turned. "Yes Nancy?"

"I am very happy for you," smiled Nancy, and Dracula smiled back. "Thank you."

* * *

Leticia kicked off her heels and sat on Dracula's massive bed.

"I am so tired. When dawn arrives, I shall return home."

"I will walk you," Dracula replied as he removed his shoes also, and he walked and glanced out of his study window. "It's not getting light just yet. Would you like to sleep for a while?"

"Only if you stay with me and hold me close. Face to face."

Dracula smiled. "No problem, Leticia."

"Face to face," Leticia repeated softly. "Skin to skin… heartbeat to heartbeat."

Dracula turned to look at her, and she stood and walked towards him, pulling her hair accessories out as she did so. Her hair tumbled over her shoulders, and her gown fell to the floor seconds later, fluttering around her ankles. She stepped over it and continued towards him, her beautiful grey eyes on his gorgeous green ones. Dracula felt like he would pass out as his eyes roamed her body. She was beautiful!

Leticia threw her arms around his neck and kissed him, pulling him to her. Dracula's arms slipped around her waist, and Leticia backed towards his bed, pulling him with her.

They fell onto the pillows, Dracula taking his shirt off and removing his trousers as Leticia whispered sweet nothings, making his heart beat faster. Dracula joined Leticia in bed, pulling his duvet over their bodies. Leticia snuggled up to him, and he murmured "Skin to skin."

"Of course," she whispered, and he kissed her gently, pulling her on top of him. "We don't have time for this, Dracula... you have to go and say goodbye to... your guests..."

"Shh," he said softly. "We'll make time."

* * *

Jeiklee's mouth was hanging open as he slept, his arms around Spirit. Washington cleared his throat, but they didn't seem to hear him. "Ahem!" Still nothing.

Washington paused. He didn't want to do it, but he didn't want Lady Leticia to think he couldn't look after the children to her standards either. He conjured a megaphone and spoke loudly.

"Miss McKenzie and Master Inferno!"

Jeiklee jumped up, startled; Spirit tumbled to the floor.

"Ouch!"

"Yes Washington," gasped Jeiklee, and Washington couldn't help chuckling for a moment before he clearly said "It is almost six in the morning. Be off to bed right away."

"Ok," they both mumbled, Spirit's hair sticking up in odd places.

"The ball's over," yawned Spirit. "I didn't get to see the end."

"Well be sure to watch the news when you wake," smiled Washington. "I know Severna is going to be buzzing about Lady Leticia and Count Dracula."

* * *

"Dracula." Dracula stirred, asleep. "Dracula, wake up."

Dracula opened his green eyes to find Leticia seated on top of him. She smiled at him, saying "Good morning."

"Good morning," smiled Dracula, and she kissed him. "Mmm. What was that for?"

"Just for being you." Leticia climbed off him and stood, reaching for his robe and putting it on. "Do you mind if I wear this, Dracula?"

"No, of course not. I'll get Nancy to get you something to wear home."

"Will you come with me?" Leticia asked shyly. "I'm certain the press will be there with the public and I don't want to talk to them without you."

"Of course, sweetheart. Um..." Dracula paused. "Have you... do you feel ok about last night? Making love to each other?"

"Of course I do." Leticia smiled at him, sighing happily. "I'm sorry that you didn't bade your guests goodbye."

"Oh, Nancy passed on a message from me. It's fine," smiled Dracula. "Leticia... I was thinking. I love you so, so much."

"I love you just as much if not more," Leticia said softly, and he took a deep breath. "What's on your mind, Dracula?"

"One of the journalists asked if…" Dracula hesitated, not knowing if it was the right time. Then he decided to just do it. "If you was going to become a Bride of Dracula. And it got me thinking, while you were asleep, that there's nothing I want more."

Leticia stared at him. Dracula stared back a little nervously, and she quietly said "You… you're asking… Dracula, are you *proposing* to me? Or are we just having a conversation?"

"Both," Dracula said softly. "I want us to be together forever."

"Oh Dracula, I want the same thing." Leticia's eyes filled over. "But are you certain you want us to get married? That you want me to become a Bride of Dracula? Do you know what that will mean? I will be all powerful-even more powerful than you once I receive dark powers to add to my own!"

"Marrying me doesn't mean you have to be a Bride of Dracula, Leticia. You can be a normal bride," Dracula told her softly. "I want this so much and I want you. Will you marry me?"

Leticia's heart was racing. "You're serious?"

Dracula nodded. "I'm serious. We can be engaged for as long as you like and we don't have to tell anyone right now. But don't agree just because *I* want this," he added, looking at her. "We both have to want to be wed."

Leticia quickly wiped her eyes before she smiled at him. "I don't want anyone knowing until maybe two months after today."

Dracula's jaw dropped. "Is that a yes?"

"It's a yes," said Leticia happily, and he picked her up and swung her around as he cheered, Leticia saying "Of course I will marry you!"

Nancy burst into the room, excited. "Congratulations, My Lord!"

"You were eavesdropping?" said Dracula, amused, and he laughed. "Leticia, Nancy was eavesdropping!"

"Please don't tell anyone, Nancy," Leticia said warmly, and Nancy said "My lips are sealed, Miss Leticia. I won't even tell Virginia."

"Thank you."

"Leticia, we need to go to the jewellers to get you a ring," Dracula told her, and Leticia said "If I get a ring, everyone will have a good idea why I have one, Dracula."

"I care not. I'm getting you a ring today if it kills me."

* * *

Two months later…

"It's so obvious they're engaged," Virginia said as she ate her sandwich. "They won't confirm or deny it. That rock on Miss Leticia's finger isn't any old rock. It's an engagement ring! I wish they'd just hurry up and announce it so people can stop speculating on what the ring's for."

"It could be a promise ring," said Spirit, and Jeiklee said "Nah. Not that expensive. I'm sure Virginia's right. And have you noticed that-"

"They're engaged!" shouted a voice, and they looked up sharply. "Count Dracula and Leticia of Sampson are *really engaged!* It's on the screen, come and see!"

"They couldn't tell us before they announced it??" Virginia said disbelievingly as she tossed her sandwich away and got up, then she stopped quickly as everyone stampeded towards the cafeteria. "Gosh!"

Jeiklee and Spirit ran behind the crowd, Spirit jumping up and down, but she couldn't see the screen properly.

"Lift me up, Jeiklee!"

Jeiklee laughed as he obeyed, hoisting her up.

"Yes, we will now confirm that the ring Leticia has on her left hand is an engagement ring," Count Dracula said on screen, and everyone gasped, then cheers went up.

"AWESOME!!"

"I knew it, I bloody knew it!"

Virginia's mouth hung open in disbelief, then she cheered too, leaping up and down with everyone else. Jeiklee was smiling broadly as he put Spirit down, not as surprised by the news as he already had a feeling his mother was engaged to Count Dracula. Spirit was ecstatic like students as she leapt up and down.

"This is amazing! They're really engaged!" Spirit cried happily, and Virginia hugged her as everyone cheered and stampeded in the cafeteria.

"This is perfect!" Virginia said delightedly, when she saw even the professors were whooping and cheering like the students. "The best news ever!"

"I wish we didn't have to take our exams today," Jeiklee said musingly, then he called "Professors, can we postpone our exams?? We need to celebrate and we're not in the right frame of mind after hearing that announcement!"

"Postpone! Postpone! Postpone!" chanted the students as the Professors looked at each other, and Professor Gene sighed before she called "Quiet please! You may all go home! The exams are postponed for one week, and one week only! Now go and celebrate!"

Everyone cheered happily and bumped fists with Jeiklee, whose eyes were on the screen. He watched Dracula kiss his mother, and he felt like he would burst with happiness.

* * *

"Ridiculous," spat King Harlot, staring at the screen. "This is wrong!"
He heard a sniff and looked at Westley Inferno, whose eyes had filled over five minutes ago, and now tears were trailing down his face. "Stop crying, boy. It is time for you to move on just like Leticia has moved on. I know many fair ladies who would love to be your partner."
Westley shook his head.
"What does that mean?" King Harlot said sharply. "Leticia has moved on and she is not looking back! Stop pining silently over her and fix up!"
Westley scribbled something on a notepad and held it up.
"I won't," King Harlot read, then he snapped "Yes you will! Nothing will make Leticia of Sampson get back with you, do you understand?! Now it is time for your physiotherapy! Get some feelings back in those legs of yours and stop feeling sorry for yourself!"
They both sat in wheelchairs, in the palace of Severna. King Harlot was still paralysed from the shoulders down, but he had a lot of mouth as usual.
"I need Leticia of Sampson to remove this curse," he said angrily. "And the woman hates me for more reasons I know of. It's ridiculous! A King does not cower before a woman, no matter how powerful she is! I will summon Leticia here and demand she remove the curse!"
Westley shook his head and scribbled something else, holding it up.
"That's not the way to go about it?? Then what way is?!"
Westley sighed, then he started writing again.

* * *

When Jeiklee got home with Spirit and Virginia, they ran and hugged Leticia and Count Dracula happily.

Cameras flashed, everyone still delighted at the news revealed about Count Dracula's engagement to Leticia of Sampson.

"I knew you were engaged Miss Leticia," Virginia said happily as she let Leticia go, and Leticia smiled at her. "I totally knew, ask Spirit and Jeiklee!"

"She did Mum," said Jeiklee amusedly. "Virginia had a feeling as soon as she saw the ring the evening after the Monster's Ball."

"So you were engaged since the Monster's Ball?" Spirit said happily, and Leticia and Count Dracula nodded, smiling. "Why didn't you tell us? We wouldn't have told anyone."

"We didn't want a fuss at the time and we were still overwhelmed by it ourselves, Spirit." Count Dracula smiled at her. "Now that we've told everyone there's a matter of the wedding date."

Jeiklee was excited. "Really soon! Make it really *really* soon!"

"Well, we was thinking in maybe six months," Leticia told her son amusedly, and everyone pouted, Jeiklee saying "Too long, Mum!"

"It's perfect, Jeiklee." Leticia smiled at her son's upset face. "It gives us breathing space and time to arrange a great wedding."

"Wait," said Spirit, looking nervous now. "Will you become a Bride of Dracula, Leticia? Or will you be a normal bride?"

"Well… if I become a Bride of Dracula, Dracula will bite me at the ceremony, pouring powers into me, and I will become his Bride," Leticia told her amusedly. "I will become a Queen of Darkness with very strong powers, even stronger than I have now. I will be all powerful," she added, and everyone swallowed, then Leticia continued "To be honest I'm not sure I want that, Spirit. And Dracula vowed never to bite me. So no. I will be a normal bride. Count Dracula's bride still, just not a Bride of Dracula, or Queen of Darkness."

"Oh," said Spirit, relieved like everyone else. "I didn't know Count Dracula vowed never to bite you, Leticia."

"I vowed not to years ago," smiled Dracula. "And… my first name will be announced at the ceremony. I hope you won't mind, Leticia? It is traditional."

"Of course I won't mind," Leticia said, kissing him. "I always thought Vladimir is such a handsome name. You didn't like me calling you that."

"I still don't," smiled Dracula, and Virginia said "I like it too, Father. I always liked it. I used to ask Nancy why people never called you Vladimir when I was little. She said you preferred to be called Dracula."

"Just like the fourteen Count Dracula's before me," smiled Dracula. "Vladimir is a formality. I prefer being called Dracula and I don't want that to change. Ok everyone?"

"Yes sir," the crowd said happily, and a journalist said "So the wedding is in six months!"

"The date isn't official," Leticia replied, amused, "But yes, we think getting married in six months' time is a great idea."

* * *

Jeiklee fell back onto his bed that night with a smile. "Perfect."

Life was going great.

It was touching.

It was awesome.

His mother was finally with her true love, and that's what he wanted all along. Knowing what he did about Leticia and Count Dracula, and just how deep their love for each other was, he couldn't be happier.

"I'm glad," he said aloud happily. "I'm so glad for them. I can't wait for them to get married! We'll all be closer than ever."

* * *

Washington entered the dining room the next morning, saying "My Lady and Count Dracula?"

"Yes," Leticia said, looking at him with Dracula. "Is something wrong?"

"You have both received a summons from King Harlot," Washington told them, handing Leticia a scroll, and Leticia scowled.

"What for?"

"The soldier didn't say, My Lady. But he wants you both at the castle in an hour."

Jeiklee paused eating his breakfast as Leticia and Dracula looked at each other, and he said "I'm coming with you, Mum. If he's dumb enough to hurt you again I'll finish him off. I promise!"

"Ditto," said Virginia angrily. "I'm coming too!"

They looked at Spirit, and she swallowed her mouthful and said "Me too. I'm definitely coming. And I'm not going to wait outside while he talks to you either, Leticia. King Harlot's a cruel man."

"Fine," Leticia said, but she couldn't help smiling. "Finish your breakfast and we'll go."

* * *

King Harlot wanted to pace up and down, but he couldn't. So he wheeled himself back and forth angrily, Westley biting his knuckles in a corner.

"Stop fretting," King Harlot snapped, looking at him. "She probably won't even acknowledge you. And don't write on that magical notepad of yours either! I don't want to read it."

There was a knock on the parlour door, and King Harlot called "Yes!"

"Sir, Leticia of Sampson has arrived with Count Dracula," a voice said, and King Harlot said "Good! Send them in."

Leticia walked into the parlour with Count Dracula, already looking furious. Jeiklee, Spirit and Virginia were right behind them.

King Harlot cleared his throat nervously. "Perhaps the children could-"

"They're going nowhere," Leticia said coldly, and he flinched. "What have you summoned me here for, Your Highness?"

"I... well... stop glaring at me, Leticia! You're putting me off my speech."

"This is how I always look at you," Leticia replied flatly. "Have you forgotten?"

King Harlot swallowed. "I... I humbly request that you remove the paralysis curse and give Westley Inferno his voice back- wait," he said quickly, when she opened her mouth angrily. "Wait, Leticia. Let me finish."

Leticia sighed and motioned for him to continue.

"I realise that I have been a selfish man. An ugly man. That isn't fit to be King," King Harlot said, eyes filling over, and they stared at him.

Leticia sighed and conjured a tissue, holding it out to him. King Harlot looked at her helplessly, and she grudgingly said "You can't take it, I forgot. Apologies."

"I want to be my old self again. I know I don't deserve it, but the land needs to be ruled properly," King Harlot said, sniffing, and Leticia sighed.

"Spirit, wipe his tears please."

Spirit scowled before she obeyed, taking the tissue from Leticia and mopping King Harlot's face. She couldn't help saying "You're a big baby, King Harlot," before she placed the tissue down and stepped away.

"Please. I beg you, Leticia." King Harlot's eyes filled again as Leticia stared at him. "I apologise once more for all that I have put you through. I plead with you to forgive me. Do you feel nothing about that at all?"

Leticia was standing with her arms folded, face unmoved. It was clear that she felt nothing at all. Westley shifted in his wheelchair, but she didn't even look at him as she said "Why should I heal you? So you can cause more damage to me and my loved ones? I know if you could have, you would have had a lot to say and do about my engagement to Count Dracula."

"No, no! I wouldn't have done anything," said King Harlot desperately. "I was even telling Westley to stop crying over you and move on!"

Leticia glanced at Westley, who was gazing at her. "Is this true, Westley?" Westley tapped his throat, and Leticia snapped "You can nod or shake your head. You don't have to speak. Is what King Harlot saying true?"

"Nice try," Virginia added icily, and Dracula warningly said "Virginia."

"Sorry Father."

Westley glared at Count Dracula, then his face softened as he looked at Leticia. He nodded, and Leticia said "Thank you Westley. Fine, King Harlot. I will remove the paralysis curse in a month."

"A month!" exclaimed the King, and Leticia snapped "Yes, a month. You still get under my skin in a very ugly way and I can't help but wish you ill whenever I see you. You will be fit and healthy in a month on one condition. You leave me alone, and you leave Count Dracula alone. You do not summon me or ask me of anything ever again. You do not even mention me when asked. If Westley brings me up, you stop him and tell him you don't want to hear of it. I never want to look upon your face unless completely necessary, do you understand me *Your Majesty?"*

King Harlot and Westley were gaping at her disbelievingly, and Leticia added "Accept the offer or remain paralysed until the day of our wedding."

"And when will that be?" demanded King Harlot, and Count Dracula said "In six months."

"To hell with that," spat King Harlot, and Jeiklee couldn't help laughing. "I accept the offer to be healed in a month and afterwards leave you be,

Leticia. But what about Westley Inferno? I asked about him as well as myself."

"What about him?" Leticia said icily. "He is not my concern."

"But he has something to say," King Harlot said, pleading with her now. "Just hear him out, Leticia. Please."

Leticia sighed and walked over to Westley, placing her hands on his throat gently. Westley closed his eyes at her touch, and Dracula had a strong urge to do the same to him as Leticia was doing, but strangle him instead of being gentle.

Leticia stepped back from him. "You can talk, Westley. But briefly before I curse you again. So say what is it you have to say."

"I…" Westley took a deep breath. "I just… I want to say that I'm sorry, Leticia. For everything."

Jeiklee's jaw dropped, Spirit gaping as well. Virginia and Dracula stood side by side, unmoved. Leticia raised an eyebrow, not sure whether to buy it as she asked "You're apologising?"

"Yes."

"For everything?"

Westley nodded with a defeated smile. "Yes, Leticia. I know I was wrong and I shouldn't have gone to such lengths to keep you with me, make sure you was mine. I pushed you away when I should have been pulling you closer. I just… I want to wish you all the best, and I hope you have an amazing wedding and life afterwards. You deserve it. You deserve everything you've always wanted."

Leticia looked very touched. "Thank you, Westley. So… no more plots or plans to get me back? You'll accept me leaving you and move on?"

"I don't have much choice, Leticia. You're engaged and you'll be married in less than a year." Westley was smiling, but his eyes were very sad. "I wish you all the best and I hope we can still be friends."

Leticia opened her mouth, then she looked at Count Dracula. "What do you think, Dracula?"

"It seems legit," Dracula said grudgingly. "I can't sense deceit. I give him that. And it's up to you what you want to do, sweetheart. I can't make a decision for you."

Leticia sighed, Westley looking up at her through glassy eyes. He looked like he was going to cry as he said "I don't want you to shut me out completely, Leticia."

Leticia sighed. "Fine. It will be nice to have a friend who knows me well. But step out of line and that friendship will end, do you understand me Westley Inferno?"

"Yes. I do," Westley said, smiling now. "Thank you."

"And for Heaven's sake please start bonding with your kids again. Jeiklee really did not like the man you have become."

"Had become," Westley corrected, and he looked at his son and Spirit. "I am so sorry, both of you. I let Malinda of Brubeck put madness into my head and I pushed you away. I love you both dearly and I have missed you so much. Could you ever forgive me for my actions?"

Jeiklee and Spirit looked at each other, and Jeiklee grudgingly said "I've missed the old Dad, not the psycho one who's determined to have Mum as his."

"The psycho Dad is dead," Westley said firmly. "I just want to be a proper father to you both again."

Jeiklee smiled at his father, and Westley smiled back, relieved as Spirit said "Fine, we forgive you Westley. And you should know me and Jeiklee-"

"Are dating. Yes, I know," Westley said, rubbing his chin. "Well… you'd all better get on with your day. I'm soon due for physiotherapy."

Everyone looked at each other and smiled, Leticia saying "I will leave you with the ability to speak, Westley."

"Thank you Leticia," smiled Westley, and she smiled back before she walked and took Dracula's hand. "I will see you very soon, Spirit and Jeiklee. I promise."

"Bye Dad," smiled Jeiklee, and Spirit said bye as well. "See you later."

"King Harlot," Leticia said curtly, and King Harlot sighed "Goodbye Leticia. And thank you. For everything."

Leticia nodded and left the parlour, Dracula at her side. Jeiklee and Spirit left too, and Virginia looked back at King Harlot and said "You're a suck up and a cry baby, Your Highness."

"Virginia!" Dracula called sharply, and she quickly left before King Harlot could reply.

* * *

Six months later…

Everyone stood, turning to look at the bride.

Dracula stood with Jeiklee close to him, never taking his eyes off her as music rang through the chapel. People were smiling broadly at the bride as she walked down the isle, Spirit and Virginia behind her.

Jeiklee smiled at Virginia, and she smiled back happily. She had acted laid-back when Leticia asked her and Spirit to be her bridesmaids, but Jeiklee knew Virginia was really excited about it.

Spirit couldn't stop smiling, her eyes filling over as Leticia came to a stop next to Count Dracula.

"Please, be seated," the preacher said happily, and everyone sat down. Jeiklee noticed his father and King Harlot, at the back of the hall. He frowned at them, whispering to Count Dracula "Were my father and the King invited?"

"Leticia melted down and invited them both," Dracula whispered back. "It may be because of the pregnancy."

Jeiklee smiled and looked at his mother's growing stomach. He had two siblings on the way, and he couldn't wait to meet them.

I'm going to be the best big brother in the world, he thought happily to himself, as the preacher said "We are gathered here today, on this happy and joyous occasion, to join this man and this woman in holy matrimony." Everyone was smiling and a lot of women were dabbing their eyes.

"Marriage is a solemn institution to be held in honour by all, it is the cornerstone of the family and of the community," the preacher said, smiling at Leticia and Count Dracula for a moment, before he continued "It requires of those who undertake it a complete and unreserved giving of one's self. It is not to be entered into lightly, as marriage is a sincere and mutual commitment to love one another. This commitment symbolises the intimate sharing of two lives and still enhances the individuality of each of you."

Dracula took a deep breath. This was really happening. It had been his lifelong dream to marry Leticia of Sampson, the love of his life, and to have children with her. Now, he was loved by all, a bonus, and his dream was coming true! He hardly heard what the preacher was saying.

Leticia's heart was pounding and the babies were dancing inside of her. Sure they knew what was going on, Leticia couldn't help smiling. She loved Count Dracula more than ever, and couldn't wait to finally call him her husband.

"Please, may we have the rings," the preacher said, and Jeiklee quickly reached into his pocket for the sacred box.

"Here they are," he said quickly, and his mother smiled at him.

"The ring is the symbol of the commitment which binds these two together," the preacher said firmly but warmly, and everyone bristled excitedly. "There are two rings because there are two people, each to make a contribution to the life of the other, and to their new life together."

Leticia took a deep breath, Dracula as well as they both took the ring intended for the other.

"Count Vladimir Dracula, do you take this woman to be your wedded wife? Do you promise to love her, comfort her, honour and keep her in sickness and in health, remaining faithful to her as long as you both shall live?"

Dracula smiled at Leticia, heart pounding as he replied "I do."

He slipped the ring on her finger, and tears fell from her eyes as the preacher turned to Leticia.

"Miss Leticia of Sampson, formally known as Leticia Carmichael-"

Jeiklee's jaw dropped. "Carmichael?!"

"Shut up, Jeiklee!" Virginia said, highly amused as everyone looked at him. "Ask questions later!"

"Sorry," Jeiklee said quickly, and the preacher chuckled before turning back to Leticia.

"Leticia Carmichael, do you take this man to be your wedded husband? Do you promise to love him, comfort him, honour and keep him in sickness and in health, remaining faithful to him as long as you both shall live?"

Leticia swallowed to try and stop the tears, then she replied "I do."

She slipped the ring on Dracula's finger, and the preacher stepped back happily.

"Join hands, and repeat after me, both of you: 'wear this ring as a symbol of my trust, my respect and my love for you.'"

"Wear this ring as a symbol of my trust, my respect and my love for you," Leticia and Dracula said together warmly, looking each other deeply in the eyes, and the preacher smiled broadly.

"I am proud to pronounce you man and wife!"

Cheers went up immediately, then the preacher raised his hand, and silence fell as he smiled at Leticia and Count Dracula.

"You may now kiss the bride."

The cheers were ten times louder and Dracula kissed his wife, everyone screaming, blowing horns, stamping their feet and whooping.

Leticia smiled broadly when they broke apart, Dracula as well as he said in her ear "I love you, Countess Leticia Dracula."

"And I love you, Count Vladimir Dracula." Leticia kissed him again as music blasted, knowing this was it, this was her happy ending. She finally got it. Tears trailed down her face again like at her last wedding, but this time thank the Gods, they really were tears of joy.

Jeiklee smiled at Virginia. "Come here, sis!" He pulled her into a hug, saying "Siblings to the end. I love you, Virginia."

"I love you too," she said happily, hugging him back, and Spirit hugged her too after Jeiklee let her go. Smiling, Virginia said "We're a family now."

"Yes we are," smiled Jeiklee. "We'll protect and look out for each other always. We may have some bumpy times, but we'll always work it out because that's what most families do when they love each other."

"You're right," smiled Virginia. "This is our new beginning."

Everyone followed the new bride and groom outside to their waiting chariot, and they saw Washington run and hug Leticia delightedly, then shake Count Dracula's hand firmly.

"Now look after her on this honeymoon, do you hear me sir? She's carrying twins!"

"I will look after her. I promise Washington." Dracula smiled as he helped Leticia into the chariot, and he smiled at the Magenta Birds. "Are you ready to take us to the beginning of our new chapter in life?"

The birds screeched happily, and Dracula laughed.

"I love your birds, Leticia."

"Our birds, Dracula. They love you too," smiled Leticia. "You bonded with them amazingly. They obey you without hesitation just like they do me."

"Well off we go," smiled Dracula, and cheers went up again. "Washington, take care of the children this week. I'm a little worried about leaving them alone for a week with no supervision."

"They will be fine My Lord," smiled Washington, and he stepped back. "Now go on your honeymoon!"

"Fly!" commanded Leticia, and the Magenta Birds took flight, everyone cheering, waving and shouting goodbye.

Jeiklee released a breath, happy.

He had always wondered if he would ever fit in, growing up on Earth with fake parents. Not knowing why he never felt he belonged. Finally, all the pieces of the puzzle were put together.

He knew happiness would always be with him, no matter what.

* *

* * *

Epilogue

Three years later…

Draivon and Midnight Dracula ran around in the front garden happily, laughing.

Jeiklee and Virginia watched their little brother and sister run around, smiling as Draivon said "Got you Midnight!"

"Got me," Midnight giggled, and she beamed at Jeiklee. "Jeiklee, Draivon got me!"

Spirit entered the back garden, smiling, and Draivon yelled "Spirit!"

He and Midnight ran to Spirit happily, and Spirit knelt and hugged them both.

"How are my gorgeous baby twins?" Spirit said, cuddling Midnight and Draivon as they giggled. "How was nursery?"

"Got milk and biscuits," said Draivon, then he thought some more. Midnight beamed at Spirit as she said "And got books!"

"That's great," smiled Spirit. "Mummy and Daddy will be back soon, ok?"

"Where they go?" asked Draivon, pouting as Midnight stuck her thumb in her mouth, and Spirit replied "Just for a walk. Jeiklee, Virginia- you were keeping an eye on them, right? Remember the pool is right there."

"Of course we were keeping an eye on them," Jeiklee said indignantly. "We're twenty-one years old for Pete's sake. Besides, Mum would kill us if anything happened to the twins under our watch."

"So would Father," Virginia added. "Midnight and Draivon would be the eldest siblings after they do away with us."

Spirit burst out laughing, setting the twins down. "Just keep an eye on them."

"We are," said Jeiklee amusedly, as he saw Leticia and Dracula walk through the front gates holding hands and laughing. "Look, they're back anyway!"

"Mummy! Daddy!" squealed Midnight and Draivon happily, running towards their parents excitedly, and Leticia scooped up Draivon as Dracula swept Midnight up, and they were kissed and cuddled lovingly.

"What did you learn at nursery, Midnight and Draivon?" asked Leticia, smiling at they set her toddlers down, and Draivon said "Three piggies, Mummy!"

"Twinkle twinkle," Midnight said shyly, and Leticia kissed her first little girl and her youngest son.

"You learnt the song Twinkle Twinkle Little Star?" They nodded. "And you were told the story of the Three Little Pigs?" The twins nodded again happily, and Dracula said "Well Daddy is the big bad wolf! *Rawr!!"*
Midnight and Draivon squealed and ran away excitedly, Dracula chasing them amusedly.
"Brick house, Draivon!" Midnight yelled excitedly, and the twins joined hands, both of their bodies glowing.
Suddenly they were inside a small brick enclosure, startling Dracula and impressing Leticia.
Dracula looked at Leticia in disbelief. "They made a brick house like in the story."
"You'd better huff and puff and blow it down," laughed Leticia, and Dracula shook his head amazedly.
"I believe our twins and their bond are very special, Leticia. I'm sure Midnight and Draivon Dracula will be great beings like we are."
Leticia smiled as she joined him to inspect the little brick house, and she kissed her husband, murmuring "I believe so too."

Jeiklee   Makala Thomas

Thank you for reading Jeiklee!

Follow me on Twitter @misskelz90 and look out for posts about other available books and more!

You can also follow my Amazon Author Page if you search for me; "Makala Thomas".

I really hope you enjoyed reading this book but like any book, some will not like it and some will love it.

Be sure to leave a review!

Happy reading!

xxx Makala Thomas xxx

Makala Thomas

Other Titles by Makala Thomas

The Link: Matthew's Beginning

The Link: Colette's Beginning

The Link: Colette's Fame

The Link: Colette's Return

The Link: The Betrayal

The Link: Psycho Eruption

Integrity

The Angel (Who Knew Not Love)

Jeiklee

Count Angelo

A Witch Like No Other

Skylar Grey

Kenco: The Goddaughter

Kenco: The Return Of Her King

Krissie Taylor

Beast

Lost

Love Conquers All

The Stranger In The Woods

Unrequited Love

The Tail Of A Queen

Amaris

Gadget Girl

Contact Makala Thomas here:

Facebook Page:

The Diverse Works Of Makala Thomas

X/Twitter:

@MissKelz90

www.ingramcontent.com/pod-product-compliance
Lightning Source LLC
Chambersburg PA
CBHW051130030726
47504CB00004B/798